STAR TREK®
CORPS OF ENGINEERS

OUT OF THE COCOON

William Leisner, Kevin Killiany,
Phaedra M. Weldon, and Robert T. Jeschonek

Based upon STAR TREK
and STAR TREK: THE NEXT GENERATION®
created by Gene Roddenberry
and STAR TREK: DEEP SPACE NINE®
created by Rick Berman & Michael Piller

G

GALLERY BOOKS

New York   London   Toronto   Sydney

CONTENTS

OUT OF
THE COCOON

William Leisner

For Mom and Dad

ACKNOWLEDGMENTS

First and foremost, I must thank Melinda M. Snodgrass, for penning the *TNG* episode "Up the Long Ladder," without which this story would have been a lot shorter.

I also owe a debt of gratitude to Rosalyn Landor and Jon de Vries, for bringing to life the characters of Brenna Odell and the Ministers Granger, respectively. And while Danilo Odell may be gone, I can't forget to credit Barrie Ingham for his portrayal of the archetypal Bringloidi. A special acknowledgment as well to the episode's "atmosphere" actors who, despite being given neither dialogue, names, nor on-screen credit for their work, provided much inspiration for this story's original characters.

Thanks to fellow *Strange New Worlds* graduates Lynda Foley, Kevin Killiany, and Dayton Ward, for their advice and encouragement during the gestation of this project.

The *S.C.E.* Guide at David Henderson's Psi Phi website (www.psiphi.org) served as an invaluable reference to the series' history. (It seems like just the other day John J. Ordover first announced this new original eBook-only series, and now it's got a history.)

And of course, thanks to *S.C.E.* co-developer and editor Keith R.A. DeCandido who, in addition to letting me play in this sandbox and just generally being a cool guy, also taught me valuable lessons about the importance of patience in the writing business.

CHAPTER

1

For the forty-seventh time in the past eight days, Elizabeth Lense ran her medical tricorder up and down her abdomen and checked the scan results.

Yep. Still pregnant, all right.

She stared at the readout on the small instrument screen, head slightly shaking, still somehow unable to believe what she was seeing. She was already beginning to feel the first physical changes to her body—no nausea, though, thank God; Domenica Corsi would definitely notice her getting up to retch in their shared bathroom every morning. But even with the fatigue, the sensitivity in her breasts, all that, some part of her insisted that it was someone else in this condition. Someone else. Not her.

Which, at least figuratively speaking, was somewhat

accurate. After all, she hadn't been in a serious romantic relationship since Starfleet Medical Academy, with a man she now fondly referred to as "that jackass." Their long engagement and blink-and-you-missed-it marriage went a long way toward convincing her to focus on her medical career and forget about any hopes of finding love. Then, she found herself stranded on an unknown primitive planet in an alternate universe, with no hope of being rescued and resuming her previous life, where she found herself drawn to the handsome alien rebel leader who had taken her in, and she finally let down her emotional walls and gave in to . . .

God, it sounds like something out of a bad romance holonovel, she thought, wincing. All the more reason to consider what had naturally followed from their shared passion as being fictional as well.

Except of course it wasn't. The two subjective months she'd spent with the Jabari were real, even if they did happen in only two objective weeks. The emotional bond she had formed with Saad was real.

She looked again at the image displayed on her tricorder. At the tiny, ball-shaped life growing inside . . .

"Gold to Lense."

The doctor nearly jumped out of her skin, and immediately snapped her tricorder shut, as if the captain had just snuck up over her shoulder. After an extra couple of seconds to compose herself, and to check that there was no one else in sickbay who might have seen anything, she tapped her combadge. "Lense here, Captain."

"Captain Scott just handed us a new assignment. Staff meeting in ten minutes in the observation lounge."

An eyebrow lifted in curiosity. If this new mission had

come from the S.C.E. liaison, it probably wasn't medical in nature. But hopefully, it would still be something to keep her mind occupied. "Aye, sir," she answered.

Once the comlink was closed, she reopened her tricorder, and considered the display once more. She keyed in a sequence confirming her authority as ship's chief medical officer, and for the forty-seventh time, deleted all record of her self-examination from her medical file.

"Work, damn you," Sonya Gomez growled as she gave her computer terminal a good hard smack. None of her S.C.E. colleagues were here to witness this unauthorized technique, though most of them would probably have approved of the notion. *Stevens, certainly. Tev, not so much.*

"A valid access code is required," the computer repeated, completely unfazed by the commander's use of physical violence.

Gomez growled back. After the debacle at Hildago Station, where her personal logs and files had been hacked and her identity hijacked by a cybernetics-savvy con man, she asked Soloman and Bart Faulwell to create a new protection protocol for her. The team's computer and encryption experts had come through brilliantly, crafting for her a complex system requiring a sequence of passwords and access codes that, layered on top of standard Starfleet encryption, would make access by anyone other than her nigh impossible.

Provided, of course, that she remembered those access codes. Bart told her to find a code phrase that wasn't just a random alphanumeric string, but would not be easily connected to her—no lines from a favorite book or names of childhood pets. She'd picked a lyric from a Lurian folk song Carol Abramowitz had fallen in love with and played for her not long ago. At the time, Gomez couldn't get the insipid song out of her head. Now that she had to remember it, though, to retrieve some personal logs that related to this assignment, the exact line escaped her. *There were mountains that were as high as something, but not the sky. Or maybe it was the sky that was as high as the mountains* . . . And to add insult to injury, she now had the stupid wordless melody stuck in her head.

She heaved a sigh and, resigned to relying solely on Starfleet's official reports, headed for the briefing. Sure enough, everyone was already seated around the table, waiting on her. "Sorry," she said, as she slipped into the chair to Captain Gold's immediate right and across from Lieutenant Commander Mor glasch Tev. Tev watched her with a neutral expression, giving no outward indication of the disdain with which she knew he considered her tardiness. This she considered a sign of the Tellarite's progress.

"All right, now that we're all here . . ." Captain Gold said once she was settled. "Six hours ago, Starfleet Command received a priority-one message from a human colony in the Ficus Sector. It was sharp, short, and did not allow for the option of any response or request for elaboration."

Gold pressed a tab embedded in the tabletop in front of him, and the lounge filled with a staticky hiss, followed by the voice of a woman, with a Gaelic lilt: *"This is*

Mariposa to the Federation: We want you to come and rid us of this infernal machinery, every last bloody scrap of it!"

The initial reaction, as the message abruptly ended, was to stare around the table at one another in confusion. Tev was the first to form a response. "That's it?" He wobbled his head in disbelief. "What in Phinda's name does that mean? What 'infernal machinery'? A weapons system gone amok? An artificial intelligence gone insane?"

"And 'every bloody scrap'?" P8 Blue interjected. The low-pitched clacking sound she made as she spoke indicated she felt much the same as Tev about the amount of detail contained in the message. "Without knowing the scope of what they're asking—or any specifics at all, for that matter—how can they expect the kind of thoroughness they're apparently asking for?"

"Clearly, for whatever reason, the woman was panicked," Carol Abramowitz said. While the cultural expert was no less bewildered by the message, there was a milder undertone to her reaction. "We could sit here and pick the message apart word by word for whatever limited information we can glean, but what it's all going to boil down to is, something has gone very wrong on Mariposa."

"Though, if you're not going to pick it apart word by word, I may as well leave," Bart Faulwell said, feigning a move for the lounge door.

"Stick around, Faulwell," the captain said with a genial smile. "We'll try to find something to occupy you."

"What do we know of these Mariposans," Tev asked, "if anything?"

Gold cued the rest of the room by turning his attention

to Gomez. She nodded, took a brief glance down at her padd, then began: "In 2123, the *S.S. Mariposa*, a DY-500-class spaceship, launched from Earth bound for the Ficus Sector, carrying two parties of colonists. The main group, composed of molecular biologists, geneticists, neurologists, and other specialists, eventually settled on the planet that now bears the name of the ship. The second group were members of a 'back-to-nature' movement who disavowed all modern technology—most older technologies, too—and adopted a preindustrial, agrarian way of life. That group settled another planet in the Ficus Sector, which they called Bringloid. Unfortunately, almost all records of this expedition were lost, and the two colonies were forgotten until—"

"Lost? Forgotten? All record of hundreds of humans?" Soloman's dark deep-set eyes bulged outward. "This was only two hundred and fifty-four years ago, during Earth's Stage IV Computing Age, and well after your last world war. How would such a thing be possible?" If the Bynar didn't already have such a pale complexion, Gomez thought he would have blanched. Given his culture's heavy reliance on computerized data, he must have considered the matter-of-fact acceptance of this gap in the historical record scandalous.

It was Abramowitz who addressed the issue. "In many ways, the late twenty-first and early twenty-second centuries was one of the most unstable periods in Earth history. The reestablishment of civil society and rule of law after World War III happened in fits and starts. More than a generation after the end of the war, there were still places where local warlords were employing drug warriors and kangaroo courts to maintain control over their citizens. Even after first contact with Vulcan in 2063, when humanity realized there was a larger universe to deal with, there was significant resistance to the idea of a united human race. That's what led a lot of the early émigrés, like the Conestoga, Terra 10, and Katowa Expeditions to leave Earth in the first place; they were afraid their cultures would be subsumed by the coming 'New World Order'."

"Yes, well, as fascinating as the history lesson is," Tev grumbled, "it doesn't appear to bear any relevance to the present situation."

Gomez shot Tev a pained look. "I'm afraid I need to fascinate you some more, Tev. The Bringloidi colony was rediscovered eleven years ago, after their sun went into a period of intense electromagnetic flaring. An old emergency distress beacon the *Mariposa* had left was triggered, and the *Enterprise*—the *Enterprise-D*, I should say—was sent to investigate, and then evacuate the planet."

"Hold on," Fabian Stevens interrupted, one eyebrow raised curiously. "The *Enterprise*, eleven years ago?"

Gomez deliberately avoided Stevens's eyes as she answered, "Yes, this was during my tour aboard the *Enterprise*." Not to mention, it was also during the late Kieran Duffy's time on the *Enterprise* engineering staff as well. *Please, don't mention that, Fabe,* she thought at him. As one of Duff's closest friends, Stevens had made the connection immediately, but she didn't think anyone else in the room would. She hoped not, anyhow; the last thing she wanted was a lot of questions about her emotional state through the course of this mission.

For once, Sonya was glad to have Tev interrupt.

"Again, I must ask what these reminiscences have to do with the current situation?"

Gold fixed Tev with a steely glare. "There's someplace more important you need to be, Tev?"

Tev hesitated a split second before saying, "No, sir. I apologize for the interruption."

Gomez accepted the apology with a nod. *Maybe there's hope for him yet.* "It was the Bringloidi who sent us searching for their sister colony," she continued. "We soon found Mariposa, and . . . to make a long story short, Captain Picard convinced the Mariposans to allow the Bringloidi to resettle on Mariposa, and to integrate them into their society."

"I'm sorry?" Abramowitz leaned forward in her seat, lines of concern creasing her forehead. "You relocated a technophobic society onto a world inhabited by a scientific colony, and expected the two to integrate themselves?"

"That might explain why now they want to be rid of their machinery," Pattie mused.

The rest of the team started nodding at the logic of this conclusion—except for Lense, who seemed lost in her own thoughts, much as she had since the end of her ordeal with Dr. Bashir on the Jabari planet. Gomez shook her head adamantly, though. "Their *forebears* were technophobes. The Bringloidi themselves, once we brought them aboard the *Enterprise*, were actually quite quick to accept the wonders of modern technology, and were eager to have their children receive advanced educations."

"I suppose cowering in a cave while the sun threatens to swallow up your planet would make most people reconsider the benevolence of Mother Nature," Faulwell said.

"But then, why Mariposa?" Pattie asked. "Why not bring them back to Earth? Or better yet, an agricultural world like Gault or Sherman's Planet, where they could ease into modernity at a more comfortable pace?"

"Well, because the Mariposans needed the Bringloidi . . . for . . . they weren't able . . ." Gomez paused. She hadn't really wanted to sidetrack the briefing with the big contentious issue, but . . . "The population of Mariposa was made up entirely of clones."

Eight sets of eyes locked on Gomez for a silent moment. Then Stevens shook his head and said, "See, it's these juicy parts that get lost when you make a long story short."

"Clones?" Lense asked, suddenly fully engaged in the conversation. "An entire colony?" Gomez could see her thoughts jump to warp behind her eyes. "Huh . . ."

"What does that have to do with the Bringloidi?" Tev asked. "And why would it have bearing on the request to remove all their technology?" He seemed annoyed that Lense understood something he didn't.

Lense looked back at Tev. "If they've been cloning themselves for all these years, and then cloning from clones of clones, the point will come where the replicative fading of their DNA is going to make any further cloning impossible. Their race would die out."

"And so they were hoping the Bringloidi would help them carry on their culture," Abramowitz said, frowning thoughtfully. "I suppose there's a certain amount of sense in that."

"Oh, yes," Tev grumbled, "it makes perfect sense . . . if

Picard's primary goal was to rid himself of these refugees as quickly as possible."

Captain Gold raised a bushy eyebrow at Tev, but didn't say anything. Tev had been off ship the last time the *Enterprise* rendezvoused with the *da Vinci*, during their business with Rod Portlyn. It was possible that he was unaware that Gold and Picard had been friends since their Starfleet Academy days. Though, it was just as possible that, to his mind, it made no difference.

"And now," Tev continued, "it would seem the clash between the two cultures has effected some major, possibly deadly, crisis."

"Let's not jump to conclusions," Gold said. "We have a few facts and a lot of speculation only." He paused then to tap at his combadge. "Gold to bridge. Any luck getting a response to our hails from Mariposa, Haznedl?"

"Negative, sir," responded the operations officer.

Gold sighed. "Keep trying. Constant hails, all frequencies."

"All right," Gomez said. "Pattie, Carol, Domenica: I'll give you what we have on the Mariposans and Bringloidi. Let's get a picture of where these people stand in terms of their technological infrastructure, what sort of society is likely to have developed since their joining, and how we're going to deal with that society if it is, in fact, on the verge of falling apart."

With that, the briefing was adjourned. As everyone stood to leave, Gomez moved around the table to intercept Faulwell. "Bart, I'm sorry, you probably are going to be a little bored during this assignment."

He shrugged. "That's how it goes. I suppose you already know *mariposa* is the Spanish word for *butterfly*?"

"Yeah." Gomez smirked. "But actually, there is something you can do. Something that could mean the difference between success or failure this mission."

Faulwell gave her a slow, knowing nod. "I knew you were never going to remember that song lyric."

"Oh, shut up . . ."

CHAPTER
2

Gold tapped the disconnect tab on his desktop monitor, and Jean-Luc Picard's face disappeared, replaced by the Federation seal. He tapped his fingers on the desktop some more, staring blankly and thinking about the information his old friend had given him.

He had no idea how long he sat like that, or what had sparked in his brain that brought him back to the present and refocused his stare. He'd apparently, for however long, been watching his left hand, his fingers still beating a rhythmless beat on the desktop.

His hand. *His* fingers. He tended, whenever he thought about the biosynthetic replacement (which, many months since losing the original at Galvan VI, was less and less often, he was proud to say), to focus on the "synthetic" aspect. But it had been synthesized from biological elements—specifically, his own skin, bone, muscle, and nerve cells.

His cloned cells.

In some respect, that made him think of this appendage as being more freakish than had it been made of plastic and metal. And that was an attitude he had to put behind him before he had to deal with the Mariposans.

After Gold had asked Picard a few questions about the *Enterprise*-D's visit to the Ficus Sector over a decade ago, their conversation drifted to the topic of cloning in general. While the long war against the cloned warriors of the Dominion certainly colored their attitudes, the fact was that humanity had long been wary of the concept. Even before the discovery of DNA and genetic science, there were cautionary tales of evil twins, doppelgängers, automatons, and other soulless monsters created by those who dared to play God. Even with all the advances in human knowledge over the millennia, all the superstitious taboos shattered by science, there was still, for whatever reason, this almost instinctive aversion to this particular type of manipulation of nature.

The chime of his ready room door snapped Gold out of his musings. He sighed, dropped his hand in his lap, and called, "Come."

"Pardon me, Captain," Abramowitz said as she entered. "I hope I'm not disturbing you."

Gold shook his head and gestured to one of his guest chairs (with his right hand, hiding the left; *put it out of your mind, David*). "Not at all. Any luck in your research?"

The dark-haired woman gave a slight shrug of her shoulders. "I've been reviewing the reports from the *Tubman*, what little there is."

Gold nodded. About a year after the *Enterprise's* departure, Starfleet had sent a second ship to do a sociological follow-up. The citizens of Mariposa, having previously gone over two hundred years without outside contact, were less receptive to the visitors than they had been when they were facing extinction. The *Tubman* cut their mission to Mariposa short, and three weeks later, after the Borg massacre at Wolf 359, the isolationist world had fallen to the bottom of Starfleet's list of priorities.

Abramowitz continued, asking, "Have you spoken yet with Captain Picard?"

Of course that's what she was going to ask. "Yes, I have."

Abramowitz nodded, expecting him to expand on his answer. After several quiet seconds, she added, "I was hoping he would have offered some insight as to his decision-making process at the time."

"All the pertinent information was included in his logs and reports, as the regulations require."

The cultural specialist looked far from assured. "With all respect, sir," she said, speaking with deliberate care, "as I read those reports, I see Captain Picard making decisions based in large part on what was most convenient for him and his crew. The tone of his recordings suggest he had little tolerance for the refugees disrupting his ship, and he resettled them on the next M-class planet they found, citing 'poetic justice' as a factor."

"That is a gross simplification of the record," Gold replied, although he had to admit it was not an unreasonable interpretation. Picard's discomfort with the Bringloidi came through clearly in his reports, while the details of their interactions with the Mariposans were couched in more careful language.

"I'm sorry, sir, but . . . Picard's decision makes little sense to me. I need to have a better understanding of why this hybrid culture was created in the first place in order to formulate my own recommendations for this mission."

"I've always been most impressed by your ability to give sound advice in those cases where we know almost nothing about the cultures in question," said Gold.

The attempt at flattery did nothing to lighten the woman's countenance. "Captain, I know you and Picard are old friends, but—"

"All right, stop right there," Gold snapped, and instantly regretted the sharpness of his tone. He paused to gather himself before continuing, "Yes, Picard is a long-time friend. And as a fellow captain, who knows what it's like to sit in the center chair and make quick decisions that are guaranteed to be examined in minute detail by people who weren't there through the lens of twenty-twenty hindsight, I do hesitate to voice any criticisms I may have of his actions. That said, I strongly resent the implication that I would put my personal relationships above my responsibilities to this ship, this crew, and its mission."

"I apologize for offending—"

Gold waved her off. "The fact is, sometimes starship captains do things they don't think all the way through. They make contact with pre-warp civilizations or leave history books behind on away-team missions. Even I've made some stupid mistakes in my career," Gold added, forcing a grin. "Captain Picard recognizes that the episode with the Bringloidi was not the most admirable in his career. He could have looked for other options for dealing with the Bringloidi, and then still more options for dealing with the Mariposans. He chose the option that looked most able to help both at the same time. It could have been a mistake in judgment, sure. But making those judgment calls is what captains are expected to do. There is no more explanation than that."

"Yes, sir." Abramowitz nodded. She clearly wasn't completely appeased, but she was satisfied that there were no secrets being withheld from her. "I'll dig a little harder, and try to have some recommendations before we reach the planet."

"Thank you," Gold nodded.

Abramowitz stood and headed for the ready room door, then stopped and turned back to the captain. "You've made mistakes, sir?" she asked, flashing a tiny grin.

Gold cocked an eyebrow at her. "Let's let that be our little secret, Abramowitz."

"Ensign Gomez."

Sonya jumped like a cat, and spun around to face the superior officer who had moved up unnoticed behind her. "Commander Riker, sir."

A sliver of a smile showed through the XO's beard. He was obviously amused by her nervous reaction . . . and probably grateful she didn't have any sort of beverage in her hand at the moment. The smile didn't last long, though. "Ensign, I need to discuss something with you. We can talk in Lieutenant La Forge's office."

Sonya nodded, though the commander hadn't waited for an answer before turning and heading for the chief engineer's office. She turned back to where her current work partner still stood, gathering up her tool kit.

"Ooohhh, you're in trouuuble," Lieutenant Kieran Duffy teased, looking and sounding like a demented five-year-old.

Sonya gave him a mortified look. She woke up every morning worrying that someone would realize that they had erred, assigning her to the Federation flagship, when she didn't reach the standards required for such an honor. And here was Duffy, not only showing zero concern that they'd been caught flirting with each other while on duty (and they were clearly flirting; people didn't smile the way they were at each other while discussing datastream compression rates), but cracking jokes about it. Sonya wished she could decide whether she was shocked by Duffy's carefree demeanor, or envious of it.

She trotted around the warp core and turned the corner into La Forge's office. Riker was leaning on a corner of the desk waiting and, to Sonya's surprise, so was Dr. Pulaski, wearing a look of deep consternation. "Ensign Gomez," the doctor said. "Please, have a seat."

Sonya looked from one senior officer to the other, at a complete loss to understand why Pulaski would be down in the engineering section to talk with her. "Is something wrong?"

Neither answered immediately, hesitating for some reason. "Doctor . . . ?" she prompted, her stomach starting to flutter. "Commander . . . ?"

"Commander?"

Gomez's head jerked up, and she saw Stevens standing

on the opposite side of the mess hall table where she was seated. "Sorry, Fabe," she apologized. "I was somewhere else."

Stevens nodded, indicating the padd she held in front of her. "Old *Enterprise* logs?"

"Yep." Bart had gotten her back into her personal logs in no time at all. She almost wished he hadn't. "A real trip down memory lane."

Stevens took a seat across from her, studying her for a moment. "You okay?"

Gomez sighed. It occurred to her that forgetting her password could have been her subconscious's way to spare her both from reliving these old memories, and from having to deal with all her friends asking "are you okay?" "I'm fine," she said. And it was true; not long ago, during the *Dancing Star* recovery, she also had to review logs of a previous encounter where Kieran had been involved. At that time, she had been reduced to tears. Now . . . "I feel fine," she repeated. "Though, I'm not sure how I feel about feeling fine." Stevens gave her a sympathetic smile, and reached across the table to give her forearm a gentle squeeze.

They sat quietly like that for a moment longer before Gomez blurted, "They tried to clone us."

Stevens's eyes looked as if they might drop out of his head. "What?"

"Kieran and I were on the repair crew the Mariposans asked for when we first got there. It was one of the first times we were assigned to work together." She paused briefly at that memory, smiling in spite of herself. "I was an ensign, he was a j.g. The two of us were paired off, and we did some work on their main biosynthesizing systems. Nothing seemed suspicious; we had no idea that they had done anything at all to us. But later, after the captain had the Mariposans' cloning equipment confiscated and inspected, they found that they had stolen tissue samples from us, and almost all the human crew members who'd been down on the planet."

"My God," Stevens whispered. Then he asked, "And the stolen samples?"

"All destroyed as soon as they were identified."

Stevens pondered that silently for a second too long. Sonya could tell that he was wondering what if that hadn't been the case, and that his friend might, in some way, have been preserved.

"Good," Stevens finally said. "Destroyed. That's good."

Gomez made herself nod in concurrence.

"Now entering the Mariposa system, Captain."

"Bring us into standard orbit, Wong," Captain Gold ordered, then tapped his combadge. "Gomez and Tev, report to the bridge." He leaned forward in his seat, watching the salmon-colored world surrounded by a system of gossamer rings grow larger and larger on the forward viewscreen. "Any response to hails yet?"

"Negative, sir," said Haznedl.

"Switch from subspace to RF," Gold said, "and be sure they know we're now in orbit." From what he'd gathered about the inhabitants of this world, Gold suspected that once they knew the Federation was now on their home turf, whatever communications failures that had plagued them up until now would be magically resolved.

After a few more moments without a response, during which the engineers arrived on the bridge, Anthony Shabalala reported from tactical, "Sir, I'm detecting a dampening field of some sort being generated on the planet. It's blocking our hails and all active scans."

Or not, Gold thought.

"Why would these people so urgently call for our assistance," Tev wondered aloud as he stepped across the bridge, "only to turn a deaf ear when we arrive?"

"This is a very good question," Gold said. "Can we punch a signal through, Shabalala?"

The tactical officer frowned at his console readouts. "Sir, it's a modulated tetryon field."

"A tetryon field? To block communications?" Tev shook his head. "That's absurd! That would be akin to hunting the proverbial insect with a phaser rifle."

Gold nodded. Naturally occurring tetryon particle fields had the capability not only to disrupt a starship's warp field, but also to rend gaps in the very fabric of space. "You're right, Tev. This is for more than just blocking us."

"They're using it to disrupt their power distribution system," Gomez said. "The Klingons did this a lot during the war: they'd use their ships' deflectors to flood a planet's surface with tetryon radiation, to neutralize all directed energy weapons and force the Jem'Hadar to face them in hand-to-hand combat. This field would render any kind of energy-dependent technologies useless."

Tev grunted softly. "It seems they've found the answer to whatever problem they had on their own."

"And traded themselves a new one," Gold said. Assuming the dampening field went up sometime after their distress message was broadcast, it had been active for not quite twelve hours. In another twelve, the people inside that field would start to exhibit symptoms of tetryon radiation poisoning. "Options, people."

"There is a weak point of the field, sir," Shabalala said. "The field is being generated by a central transmission point. It's projecting its field three hundred and sixty degrees on the horizontal plane, but vertically, the highest angle of transmission is point one-four degrees off the zenith."

"Like a huge umbrella of energy covering the planet," Gomez said, "with just a very narrow cone extending straight up from its center."

Gold rubbed his chin as he visualized what Gomez described. "So, we could position ourselves directly above their transmitter?" They could then direct a signal through the "cone," like the old-style speaking tubes they'd used on ships before wire voice transmission.

"We'd still need to boost the signal enough to cut through the bleed-through radiation," Shabalala noted, "and we'd need to keep an extremely precise geosynchronous orbit."

"How precise?"

"We'd have to position the ship within a fifteen-hundred-meter diameter window, and hold it there as the planet rotates below us. It would also help if we could be inside the ionosphere."

Gold turned to the young lieutenant at conn. "Wong?"

"With one hand tied behind my back, sir."

"That won't be necessary." Gold settled back into his command chair. "Just keep us in the sweet spot."

Wong nodded, then turned his full attention to his

board. Despite his mock boasting a moment earlier, both of his hands were in constant motion across his board. Planetary orbit was normally a very automatic procedure. But then, normally it didn't require more than line-of-sight alignment with a surface station. Keeping the ship in such precise alignment with a single point rotating at a relative five hundred meters per second, while at the same time fighting the drag of the upper atmosphere, was enough to keep Wong's attention focused.

"You've got it, Songmin. Now steady . . ." Shabalala said as he adjusted his equipment. "I think we're getting through the interference now, just barely." Then, looking up with a smile, he said, "Response is coming in now, Captain."

"Good job," Gold told the young man, then ordered, "On-screen."

The image of the ringed planet on the viewscreen disappeared, replaced by the slightly staticky face of a man who looked like he hadn't slept in a month. His skin was dark, and so was his mood; his eyebrows were drawn down sharply, and the corners of his mouth curled into a frown. *"Oh, good,"* he said without enthusiasm. *"The Federation is here."*

Gold paused briefly before deciding to disregard the sarcastic nongreeting. "This is David Gold, captain of the *U.S.S. da Vinci*. We're here in response to a distress message from the leadership of the Mariposan colony."

"That message came from the former, illegitimate leadership," the man on the screen replied. *"Power has now been restored to the true, rightful leaders of Mariposa."*

Klaxons wailed inside Gold's brain. "And you would be one of those rightful leaders, Mister . . . ?"

"James Hammond, and yes, I am," he said, baring his teeth in a triumphant if weary grin. *"So, thank you for your offer, Captain, but the Mariposan people have no need of your assistance."*

No, Gold thought, with a sourness climbing up from his stomach. *But what about the Bringloidi?*

CHAPTER
3

James Hammond considered the tableau of the Federation starship bridge on his comscreen with a mixture of fascination and revulsion. Beside the elderly Starfleet captain stood some disgusting alien that might have been the result of recombinant DNA experiments with human and pig genes. Behind those two loomed a gigantic blue antennaed insect, staring at him with blank pale eyes, towering above a small and impossibly frail-looking little man with a computer circuit imbedded in the side of his hairless, oversized head. There were several other human-looking individuals scattered about, but who could guess how much actual human blood flowed in any of their veins? He felt his stomach clenching at the very thought that all the creatures in this menagerie could freely interact with one another.

But of course, he had to contain his reactions. He didn't know much about the Federation—he was just out of Incubation and had barely begun Imprinting when they first visited Mariposa—but he knew they were not a force to be trifled with. Eleven years ago, without a single shot being fired, they had bent his world to their will, destroying what his people had spent nearly three centuries creating.

Which made dealing with them now almost a greater challenge than what he had faced in the past forty-eight hours. Calling upon the interpersonal skills that the Progenitors had passed down to him through their genes and their engrams, James leaned back away from the screen and lowered his shoulders, projecting a friendlier demeanor. "You seem concerned still, Captain."

"You have to admit, this is a rather sudden change."

James couldn't help but grin at that. "From our perspective, this change has been over ten years in the making."

"And there's the small matter of the energy-dampening field . . ."

"A temporary safety measure," James said. "Once the Alliance for Mariposan Primacy has stabilized its power, we'll be able to allow normal energy usage."

"This field of yours is also blocking out our scans, and severely restricting our communication with the planet."

James had no trouble catching the unspoken meaning behind Gold's words. "You distrust us, Captain," he said, carefully masking any sign of resentment. "You think we're hiding something from you."

"The possibility did occur to me."

Well, of course it did, James realized. Earth history

was a long pattern of horrors and atrocities by charis-matic leaders, almost inevitably followed by cover-ups and historical revision. The Progenitors had struck out for the stars in order to escape the cycle of self-destruc-tion the rest of humanity had seemed caught in. Captain Gold was clearly considering him through that warped cultural filter.

"Captain, I understand your suspicion, but before you form any opinions about us, you need to take into consid-eration the nature of the Mariposan people. The Progeni-tors' ship spent months in uncharted space, searching for an inhabitable world they had no guarantee of finding. Then, once they did, they were nearly all killed by a se-ries of breaches ripped in the ship's skin upon landing. Nearly three hundred perished, while only five survived.

"Think about that. Five out of hundreds, on a strange planet light-years from anything they'd ever known in their lives. Many people in their situation would prob-ably envy the dead. But those people refused to yield to fate. They not only managed to overcome this crippling blow, but managed also to create a new society, a unique culture capable of incredible scientific breakthroughs and cultural accomplishments. Surely, you have to agree that the fact that we are here, talking to you today, verges on the miraculous."

"It is undeniably amazing," the Starfleet captain ad-mitted. James could see that Gold's appreciation was real; even the pig-man seemed to be moved by his words. James repressed another shiver of revulsion as he refo-cused his attention on the human.

"Then you must also allow that the Mariposan soci-ety that accomplished all this deserves to be preserved,"

James continued, leaning forward now to drive his argument home. "This society was created solely from the genes of these five extraordinary individuals. No mixing, no diluting, no polluting. What we've done, we did with pure genetic lines." James thumped the fingertips of his right hand on his desktop, punctuating those last three words. "That is why, Captain Gold, we had to liberate this world from the rule of outsiders, and the traitors who tolerated them, so that we could reestablish that which made us the exceptional people that we are." Then he flashed the old man his most charming, confidence-inducing smile. "I'm certain you recognize the merit of this."

Gold stared back silently, his face blank and unreadable. Then he looked to a dark-haired humanoid at a console behind him, and with a subtle hand gesture, the Starfleet ship ceased transmitting.

James Hammond allowed himself a brief moment of self-congratulation. All his life, he'd had his abilities questioned. Not only was he a 15—developed from a fifteenth-generation cell line, the furthest removed line from John Hammond's original DNA that could still develop into a viable clone—but he was also of the group of clones that, because the Federation had confiscated all their cloning equipment, was not subjected to the same rigorous screenings for hidden genetic faults.

No one could ever question him again. Not only had he orchestrated the overthrow of Wilson Granger's farcical excuse for a government, but he had also made the arrogant Federation, who had brought this Bringloidi plague on them in the first place, abandon their seemingly instinctive need to interfere in other societies.

By the time he allowed himself to consider that this sense of victory might have been premature, it was too late.

He'd dismissed the distant explosion—what he would eventually understand was the dampening field being overloaded—as just another distant skirmish between his supporters and die-hard Wilson Granger loyalists. The next three, coming in rapid succession and shaking the Security Ministry emergency control center he'd captured at the beginning of their offensive, caused the first cracks in his self-assuredness.

The ones that followed caused cracks in the walls. Despite the defensive shielding around the underground facility, the lights began to flicker wildly. He heard the distinctive whine of phase pistols firing just beyond the door to the room's single access tunnel.

Once the shock of the realization of his own vulnerability faded, James jabbed a shaking finger at the comscreen on the desk, hailing the Federation ship. Several more explosions shook the room as he jabbed at the still-darkened console, spewing a stream of curses at the filthy spawn of random sexual reproduction. When the old captain finally did appear on his screen, he didn't even bother to feign civility. "What have you done?" he screamed.

"I should think that would be obvious by now, Mr. Hammond." Gold's voice was hard and unapologetic. Had he misread the old man's reaction to his logic so badly?

The explosions were getting closer, but James did not hear them. There was little he could do, at any rate. This was in the most secure area in the Capital Complex, with only one way in, or out. If the traitors were able to fight their way through the A.M.P.'s defenses—which without the dampening field was a near certainty—he was dead. Even worse, so was Mariposa; there would be no second opportunities here. "Tell me, Captain Gold," James said, "do Earth-bred humans still believe in gods?"

James couldn't read the old troublemaker's expression through the distortions, but his voice was crystal clear. *"Some of us, yes. I do."*

"Then may they all damn you," James growled, even as he heard the blows against the door behind him, and the squeal of the locking bolts being torn from the frame. The acrid smell of scorched metal and burnt circuits followed them in from the corridor, testament to how much they had wantonly destroyed. He stood stock-still, unable to face the traitors to the Mariposan people as they burst into the room.

"Move away from the console!" a deep voice boomed. James did not move a muscle, glowering at the screen. A part of him wanted to laugh at the comic looks that had come across the *da Vinci* crew's faces as they witnessed the scene playing out for them. Then he was grabbed by the shoulder and spun around, forcing him to face the six-man assault team . . .

. . . all of whom shared with him the hard, dark face of their common Progenitor.

Knowing that the Mariposans were clones did nothing to dull the surprise of witnessing a man being attacked by an army of his exact duplicates. Gold watched in fascination as one of the counterinsurgents grabbed James

Hammond by his collar and yanked him out of his chair. He lifted the would-be revolutionary so they were nose to nose, and growled something no one on the bridge caught. He then threw the prisoner across the room, into the waiting arms of two other clones, who nearly twisted James's shoulders loose as they bound his wrists behind his back. Once James was secured and led from the room, the clone leader turned his attention to the audience watching from the comscreen. *"Do we have you to thank for destroying the dampening field generator?"*

"That was our doing, yes," Gold answered, hoping his eyes weren't bulging too far out of their sockets.

"You have our gratitude," the clone said, somewhat breathless after their paramilitary operation. He ran a sleeve across his sweat-soaked brow and said, *"I am Kevin Hammond, Security Minister of the United Ficus Colony."*

The captain nodded. "I'm David Gold, captain of the Federation starship *da Vinci*. What in blazes is going on down there?"

The Mariposan gave Gold a tired, humorless smile. *"That's the same question that's been haunting us for the past forty-eight hours."* Gold suspected the man was speaking literally; he looked ready to collapse from exhaustion at any moment. *"The prime ministers have asked that, once our situation down here is stabilized, you would come meet—"* A coughing fit suddenly seized him, his whole body shaking as if the room temperature had suddenly dropped thirty degrees. His remaining colleagues, who had been securing stations around the room's perimeter, suddenly froze and whipped their heads toward their leader. Gold thought he heard one of them mutter a profanity under his breath, and all three simultaneously bolted for the door.

The clone's coughing jag continued for close to a minute, during which Gold could only watch with growing concern. He heard Gomez quietly instructing Shabalala to pipe the interchange down to Lense in sickbay, and he gave her a nod acknowledging the move. The security minister finally stopped, and looked directly into the screen again. His eyes were watering, and a shiny layer of red-tinged phlegm coated his lower face from nose to chin. *"Well, so much for stabilizing the situation,"* he said hoarsely.

"Minister Hammond? This is Dr. Elizabeth Lense, ship's medical officer." A small box appeared in the lower corner of the viewscreen with the doctor's image; Gold assumed Hammond was seeing a similar inset on his end. *"Are you all right?"*

"I don't seem to be, do I?" he answered. *"Dammit, and I was so sure I'd licked it. Bastards."*

"What is it?" Lense pressed.

Hammond shook his head slightly, and then grabbed on to the console in front of him to keep from toppling over in dizziness. *"We don't know. It hit our hospital first. Took out two-thirds of the medical staff before they even knew what was happening. At least two hundred are already dead."* He lowered his head to take a couple of difficult breaths, then looked up again. *"At the risk of overstepping my authority, Doctor, we could really use whatever help you can give us."*

Even before he had finished his sentence, Lense was asking, *"Captain, permission to beam down immediately."*

"Lense . . ." Gold started, then hesitated. He had just

witnessed the effects of a coup, a countercoup, and some sort of highly virulent disease that he gathered had been used by Hammond's "bastards" as a biological weapon. It wasn't a situation he wanted to let any one of his people waltz into. But then, it wasn't about what he wanted. "Granted," Gold said, "but I want one of Corsi's people with you, and I want you both to take every medical precaution."

"That shouldn't be necessary, Captain," Kevin Hammond said. He was growing more and more breathless, and yet he managed an ironic grin. *"This bug is very particular about who it bites."*

"How particular?" Lense asked.

"Docs say it was designed to infect only five specific genetic profiles." Hammond coughed once, then added, *"Unfortunately, that makes it lethal to half the planet."*

CHAPTER
4

The transporter effect faded, and once again, Dr. Lense found herself in the middle of a war zone.

The Mariposan Life Science Center was a far cry from the Jabari's subterranean hideouts, of course. For one, it was quiet—the eerie calm that follows a storm. Also, the reception area where she and her security guard, Rennan Konya, found themselves was clean, bright, and commodious. The smell of disinfectant, while not quite enough to obliterate that of sickness and death—it never was—was at least the dominant scent. But still . . . the air of shock, fear, and horror was all too familiar to her. It was almost like a physical presence, wrapping itself around everything and everyone here.

Out of the corner of her eye, she saw Konya's shoulders

go tense, as if bracing himself. "Something wrong?" Lense asked.

The young Betazoid turned to her, and the doctor saw it wasn't alert concern for their security that was affecting him. "No, Doctor. Nothing," he said, trying to quickly hide the empathic pain in his eyes. Konya, she remembered, was part of the first wave of post-Dominion War enlistees. He and his family had been lucky enough to be off-world when Betazed fell, so he probably never had to face this kind of tragic emotional onslaught before.

She wondered how badly insulted the guard would be if she offered to let him return to the ship, when she saw his expression suddenly shift. Lense followed his gaze, which was suddenly and intently focused on a tall, haggard-looking man making a beeline for them. "Dr. Lense?" he asked, frowning deeply. Lense nodded in acknowledgment. "Welcome. I am Dr. Victor Granger, Minister of Health."

"Minister. This is Rennan Konya." Turning as she introduced him, she was pleased to note that Konya was now the very picture of stoic professionalism. *He's one of Corsi's, all right.*

In contrast, Granger was brimming with emotion, and not pleasure at her arrival. "I have to tell you, Doctor, I don't know what you think you can contribute here."

Lense was taken slightly aback. "I was given to understand you had lost much of your medical staff in the initial attack—"

"That's right, we did," he said, crossing his arms over his chest. "Has Federation medicine found a way to bring them back?"

Lense clenched and unclenched her jaw several times before she felt it safe to respond. "I'm here, Minister Granger, to help you in any way I can. If you're ready to turn away a willing volunteer in a crisis situation . . ."

For a moment, Lense thought he might do just that. Then he sighed, and turned to lead her back the way he had come. "If you wish to actually *help* us, Dr. Lense, that will be appreciated."

Lense wondered about Granger's tone and attitude. Some degree of xenophobic distrust was to be expected in a society that had been so long isolated, particularly in the wake of this kind of catastrophe. But Lense couldn't help but feel there was something more to Granger's instant dislike for her.

Granger led them through the hospital's busy main ward, weaving around people either rushing to get someplace else, or in need of help to rush anywhere. He stopped at a door marked AUTHORIZED PERSONNEL ONLY and pulled it open for Lense and Konya. They entered a medical supply room, not quite big enough for three people to move around in freely. The third person, a dark-haired teenaged girl, looked up from a clipboard as Granger said, "Doctor, this is Kara McClay. Kara, Dr. Elizabeth Lense."

"Hello," Kara smiled, flashing a small gap between her front teeth. Lense only stared back. This young woman clearly was in perfect health; what help Lense was being asked to give her was not medical.

She turned to Granger, blinking in disbelief. "You're asking me to do your *inventory*?"

Granger pretended to be surprised by Lense's less-than-enthusiastic reaction. "You just told me you were here to assist us in any way you could. Keeping an accurate accounting of—"

"I understand the importance of a physical inventory." Lense tried to keep her tone steady. She in fact did appreciate how vital accurate supply counts were and how the mundane task tended to fall by the wayside—a lesson she learned the hard way during a search-and-rescue mission her first year as *Lexington* CMO. "However, I would think you would want to put my talents to a better use."

"You're saying that the task I've asked you to do is beneath you?" Granger smirked at her. "That's rather an elitist attitude."

"Starfleet doctors are the elite, though, aren't they?"

Both Granger and Lense turned, more than a little surprised that the teenaged girl was speaking up in Lense's defense. "They're the ones sent off to deal with the diseases found on all the new worlds the Federation discovers," she elaborated. "Ninety-five of the last one hundred winners of the Nobel Prize for Medicine were Starfleet doctors. Ninety-seven percent of the papers published in the *Federation Journal of Medicine* are by Starfleet—"

Granger's face darkened like a summer thunderstorm. "If I had wanted your opinion, Miss McClay—"

"I was only stating facts," McClay said, showing no sign whatsoever of being intimidated by the minister. "I couldn't give an opinion of Starfleet doctors if I wanted, since I've only ever met the one. And it would be unfair to judge all of them based on my opinion of Dr. Pulaski."

Granger simply glared at his young subordinate. He was, however, spared the need to formulate any dignity-saving response by the sound of an alarm blaring through the corridors. Granger started, with a look Lense recognized as one of horrified disbelief. He spared Lense a quick glance, then turned and headed for the source of trouble at a run. Lense and Konya did not hesitate to follow.

They burst through several sets of swinging doors, down hallways lined with ashen-faced hospital staffers, frozen by fear into inactivity. All of this was new to them; they had never known the unpredictability and randomness of war or epidemic outbreak.

"Victor!"

A woman popped out of a doorway two-thirds of the way down the corridor as they turned a corner, dressed in dark gray surgical garb. She motioned to Granger to hurry, and the older man put on an extra burst of energy and threw himself into the room. Lense, running two steps behind him, nearly smacked into his back where he had stopped just inside the doorway, keeping his distance from the occupant on the far end of the room.

Lense tilted her head, and saw in the bed a woman with the same face as the doctor who had frantically directed them here. This face, however, was covered with open sores, and twisted grotesquely as she thrashed in pain. The shimmer of a sterile force field enveloped her bed, and two Bringloidi orderlies held on to her arms through the energy screen, trying to keep her from throwing herself to the floor. A cacophony of beeping and bleating and buzzing came from the bank of monitors clustered around the woman's bed.

"Sue—Dr. DiCamino—what happened?" Granger asked, not making any move to get closer to the patient.

Sue DiCamino, clearly shaken, stammered out her answer: "I . . . she . . . one minute she was fine, then she started complaining about the temperature, then all of a sudden . . ."

As Lense listened distractedly, she watched the woman's convulsions lessen in intensity, though not because her condition was improving. Without thinking, Lense wove around Granger and DiCamino, snapping the tricorder out of the pouch on her hip and flipping it open in a single fluid movement. She set her medkit at her feet as she pressed herself past the orderlies and swept the tricorder's remote scanner over the convulsing woman's chest and abdomen.

"What are you— Get away from her!" Lense heard Victor Granger bark behind her, but she wouldn't have obeyed him even without the shocking report she was getting from her tricorder. The convulsions were being triggered by a fist-sized tumor attached to the woman's pituitary gland . . . and growing at a visible rate.

"My God . . . stasizine, fifty cc's," she called out of habit, though aware she had no nurse to hand her a hypospray loaded with the drug. She set the tricorder on the edge of the bed and turned to retrieve her medkit.

She was momentarily surprised to find Kara McClay standing at her side. She held her arms outstretched, presenting Lense with her medkit, fully opened flat, with the contents arranged in their padded recesses like a standard sickbay instrument tray. Lense met her eyes for a split second, before grabbing the hypospray (set, as per standard, at the edge closest to her; either by intuition or chance, the young woman had gotten the orientation correct), adjusting its settings, and pressing the nozzle to the patient's neck. The gauges above her head, which displayed the patient's name as Lana DiCamino, fell from their extreme positions down to more moderate levels. Her convulsing muscles went slack in relief; only her chest continued to rise and fall in a normal respiration rhythm.

"Will she be okay now?" McClay asked softly.

Lense retrieved her tricorder and took a new reading. "For the moment," Lense answered, making special note that the question had not come from Granger or Sue DiCamino. "The tumor has stopped growing . . . and it looks like it may be receding a bit."

"Tumor?" said DiCamino, looking utterly stunned.

Given the rate of growth she'd just witnessed, Lense suspected there hadn't been any sign of a malignancy more than five minutes ago. But with DiCamino still frozen halfway across the room from her patient, and Granger glowering at her as if she were still nothing but a nuisance, Lense didn't feel like cutting them any slack. "Yes, a tumor. And not just in her brain; there are abnormal growths all through her endocrine system. What sort of treatment have you been giving her? Or have you even gotten close enough to treat her at all?"

"You are out of line, Doctor!" Victor Granger shouted, eyes flaring dangerously.

"So what if I am?" Lense shot back, matching

Granger's heated tone. "In case you didn't notice, I just had to save this woman's life for you!"

"And where were you two days ago when this started? Who do you suppose held these people back from the brink of death long enough for you to 'save' them now?" Granger's nostrils were flaring. "We've been fighting this thing around the clock, fighting for *our survival*. And you dare to come down here with your Starfleet arrogance and scold us for how we're dealing with a disease that you're not even susceptible to?" His lips curled back into a feral snarl. "Get out of my hospital. Get off my planet, and don't come back!" He spun toward the doorway, where Konya had been silently watching the entire drama unfold. He quickly jumped out of the way and let the health minister storm out.

As the hospital room returned to its normal ambient volume level (the patient, Lense was relieved to note, continued her sedated sleep undisturbed by the shouting match), Sue DiCamino took a step closer to Lense. "He's tired. He didn't mean that."

"Yes, he did," the Betazoid security officer muttered under his breath. Lense caught Kara McClay nodding in agreement out of the corner of her eye.

"Yes, he did," DiCamino admitted with a sigh. Then she lifted her head and looked Lense in the eye. "But for mercy's sake, please ignore what he just said. We've never faced anything like this before, not in fifteen generations. We don't know . . . none of this makes . . . she was fine, she was . . ." DiCamino was gesturing toward the woman in the bed, and Lense noticed the way her fingers were shaking. The woman was clearly exhausted—physically, mentally, and emotionally. "I've never frozen like that . . . Lana could've died, and I would have just stood here . . ."

Lense stepped directly in front of the Mariposan doctor, grasped her now shaking shoulders firmly and gave what she hoped would be a reassuring squeeze. "I'm not going to walk away from this. It's going to be all right," Lense told her in her most authoritative voice.

She only wished she could be as sure about the second part as she was determined about the first.

CHAPTER
5

For a moment, Tev wondered if they had beamed down to the wrong planet. He and the rest of the *da Vinci* team—Gomez, Abramowitz, Corsi, and two additional security officers, Krotine and Robins—found themselves at the crossroads of two wheel-rutted dirt paths cutting through a wide expanse of farmland. The air smelled of fresh green growth, and from somewhere in the near distance, hidden by wide fields of quadrotriticale, came the sounds of children laughing, running, and playing without a care in the world. One would have never suspected a war had just been waged here, particularly not one fought with anything more advanced than rocks and pointed sticks.

Gomez had her tricorder out, scanning the surrounding area. The furrowing of her brow inspired Tev to pull out his own device. "I'm picking up an incredible variety of exotic bacterial and viral microorganisms in the atmosphere."

"Trace remainders from the attacks?" Corsi asked.

Tev snuffled dismissively. While he appreciated the security chief's mindfulness of all potential threats, he found the attitude with which she approached this mission as overly paranoid. Even the most finely milled and aerosolized pathogenic agent would quickly disperse in an open rural area such as this, proving practically ineffectual. "These are just minor variants on common bacteria found in almost any M-class biosphere. Nothing we would even take note of under any other circumstances."

"But we are taking note of them now," Gomez said, completely unnecessarily; they wouldn't be having this interchange if they *weren't* taking note. "They do, by and large, seem to indicate a significant degree of gen-engineering."

Tev decided it best to humor his superior officer, and adjusted his tricorder for finer detail. "Modifications would appear designed for more efficient nitrogen fixation, chemosynthesis, and bioremediation in these crops—also not a remarkable find on any world with significantly advanced agricultural technology, Tellar and Earth included." He snapped his tricorder shut to punctuate his point. "At any rate, these readings have now been transmitted to the *da Vinci*. Should, by some infinitesimal chance, any of these organisms prove detrimental to our health, the patterns are now available and accessible to the transporter biofilters."

As soon as he had put to rest any trepidation about microscopic attackers, however, they were surprised by a slightly larger assailant.

"Aaaaah-boogala-booga-booga!!"

If the small human boy was at all disappointed he had not evoked any fearful responses with his leap out of the tall grain stalks and his fierce cry, he didn't show it. Instead, he simply stepped up right before Tev, craned his neck to meet the pair of black eyes nearly a meter and a half over his head, and said, "Hi! Are you a spaceman?"

Tev considered the youngster for a moment, with his unruly thatch of red-orange hair, and a heavily-freckled face split nearly in half by a gap-toothed grin. His snout twitched in amusement as he replied, "And what would lead you to such a conclusion, young one?"

"You look diff'rint. An' your clothes."

Tev nodded thoughtfully, and squatted down on his haunches to bring himself closer to eye level with the boy. "Keen observations, sufficient for a preliminary hypothesis. But what about them?" he asked, gesturing to the rest of the team. "They do not look as different as I, but they wear the same clothes. Do you suspect they are from space as well?"

The boy gave that a moment's serious thought before nodding an affirmative response.

"And why is that?" Tev prompted.

"My mom said spacemen are comin'," the boy answered. "I'm s'posed to bring 'em to her if I see 'em."

"Is your mother Prime Minister Odell?" Gomez interrupted, also crouching down beside him.

"Uh-huh," he answered, then added with great seriousness, "an' she gets mad if you don't come fast when she wants you to."

Tev straightened himself. "Well, then, we'd best avoid incurring her wrath." The boy nodded in complete agreement, then spun and started running up the dusty trail. Without further prompting, the away team followed after him.

Gomez fell in step at Tev's left, smiling up at him in obvious amusement. "I had no idea you were so good with kids, Tev."

"Nor would you be expected to, Commander, as you've never had opportunity to witness me in the proximity of any children. As a point of fact, I always found it most rewarding, interacting with and helping to develop young, unformed minds." After all, had things been different at Kharzh'ulla University, he would likely still be there teaching today . . . perhaps with several young ones of his own. . . .

"As opposed to the older, yet perpetually immature, minds you encounter on a day-to-day basis, right?" Gomez asked with what was apparently meant as a self-mocking grin.

"Precisely," Tev answered with a flat sigh.

The boy rounded a corner that led them into a wide yard, populated by scores of fat poultry birds scratching and pecking at the dirt, as well as a dozen pygmy-sized black goats. A narrow path, marked by rows of stones on either side, split the yard in half and led up to a plain, low-built structure of some prefabricated building material. There were more young humans here, plus a few adults, performing a variety of chores: tossing seed to the birds, hanging wet clothing over a cable that stretched from one corner of the building to a pole in a far corner of the property, working strange wooden apparatuses the purpose of which Tev couldn't even begin to guess.

As he took all this in, their young guide had run up behind one of the women hanging clothing, and tugged vigorously on her skirts to gain her attention. She turned in the direction the youngster pointed, and set her face in a scowl.

"Sweet mercy, what is this?" she demanded, loose strands of red-brown hair poking out from under her sun hat, flying behind her as she crossed the yard. "We haven't had enough troubles with swaggering egoists and their private armies; y' got t' bring one of your own?"

Tev could practically feel Corsi stiffening behind him in reaction to the woman's aggressive welcome. Gomez, though, simply opened her hands out in a placating gesture as she took an extra step forward. "Apologies, Madam Prime Minister," she said, "I assure you that we are only here to help, not to add to your difficulties."

"No, of course not," she said with a deep frown. Judging from the lines at the corners of her mouth and eyes, the frown was her default facial expression. "Heaven forfend that Starfleet visit any troubles upon me and mine, Lord, no!"

"For pity's sake, Brenna," called a voice from the farmhouse structure. Tev looked to see a gray man—plain, colorless clothing, receding white-gray hair, ashen skin, and a gray facial expression that betrayed utter weariness—standing in the doorway. "You called these people here; the least you could do is to hold your bile in check until after they've agreed to help us."

Odell answered him with a baleful glare, but said nothing. The gray man then turned to the away team, and flashed a practiced politician's smile that came nowhere close to his eyes. "Welcome to the United Ficus Colony," he said, raising his left arm in some sort of stiff ceremonial gesture. "I am Wilson Granger, Mariposan Prime Minister, and you've already met my Bringloidi counterpart and primary wife, Brenna Odell. Please, come inside."

They were ushered into the structure, which turned out to be a family residence, dominated by a large common room populated by even more children, from infancy to adolescence, along with their adult caregivers. Granger introduced them all, some as "secondary" or "tertiary" spouses of his or Odell's, the rest only by name. Tev assumed the majority had gathered here for safety and comfort in the wake of the recent hostilities, and played no role in the United Ficus government. As the series of introductions and obligatory small talk continued, he abandoned even the pretense of attention and turned to survey the rest of the structure.

Beyond the common room was a kitchen/dining area, a long faux-wood table surrounded by a dozen chairs at its center. The far wall of the room was dominated by a stone hearth, a small fire burning beneath a large black metal pot. Tev recognized the scent of Terran chicken broth, a favorite dish of the captain's. Against another wall was a tall iron pipe standing up through the floorboards and arching over the edge of a counter surface into a tin basin—a manual water pump, he determined with a glance.

And in the near corner, in contrast to these archaic items, stood a gleaming apparatus of highly polished metallic cylinders, vats and pipes, reaching all the way to the roof beams. Tev gaped, surprised by the presence of this device, whatever it was, in these surroundings.

He stepped closer, conducting an intense visual examination. A row of green lights blinked at him from a status screen, and the whole thing hummed benignly, like a well-fed *grishnar* cat.

That benign impression was damaged, though, as Corsi entered the room behind him with her still-activated tricorder. Tev had never counted how many distinct sounds a Starfleet-issue tricorder was programmed to make, but he was willing to believe Corsi's device emitted all of them at once. "My God," she said, referring to the device, "that thing is a virtual cesspool!"

Tev pulled out his own tricorder, and saw Corsi was again overreacting—there was no sign of waste material in the vessels. There was, however, an incredible plethora of microbial cultures being grown in each tank, multiplying at an accelerated rate, and excreting a variety of substances into the lower half of the cylinders. "Remarkable," he said as he studied the readouts on the device's operation. "Is this one of their biosynthesizing units you mentioned, Commander Gomez?"

Gomez stepped between Tev and Gomez to consider the device. "Yes, it is," she confirmed, an odd tone to her voice. "A smaller version of the ones I saw here eleven years ago, though."

Tev stroked the hair at his chin pensively as he continued to study the device, as did Corsi and Gomez. Though nowhere near as sophisticated or versatile as the Federation's transporter-based replicators, the Mariposans' adaptation of biotechnology to widespread practical usage was impressive nonetheless. The biosynthesizer gen-engineered a variety of simple microorganisms from a template microbe, which in turn produced such products as high-tensile plastics, medicines, and simple high-nutrient paste. Tev was surprised, as Gomez apparently also had been, to find such a complex piece of equipment in a rural residential structure.

"God help us; we're in the hands of engineers." Tev turned toward Brenna Odell, standing by the kitchen table, her large brown eyes flashing in annoyance. "Could y' tear yourselves away long enough to join the rest of us?"

Tev grunted, and moved along with Gomez and Corsi to take their seats at the opposite side of the table, along with Abramowitz and the security guards. Granger sat at the far end away from Odell, with two other colonists between them. Granger gestured to them in turn, saying, "May I present our chief of staff, Elizabeth Vallis, and our acting security minister, Reade Latta."

Vallis, a pinched-faced woman with short, jet-black hair, nodded silently, while Latta, a short, elderly man in a pea-green jacket that had seen better days (those being the days around the solstice, at a latitude where the sun never rose) grinned and tipped his round felt hat. The last introductions finally out of the way, Granger flashed his practiced smile and said, "First of all, our thanks once again to you for your quick response to our communication."

"Of course," said Gomez.

"Although, 'communication' is something of a misnomer," Tev added, "as your message did not actually communicate anything."

Granger cocked his head to one side. "What wasn't clear about our message?"

"The reference to 'infernal machines' . . . ?" Tev stared

across the table at Granger, who stared right back at him.

"Starfleet officers aren't much for subtlety," Odell said, with a hint of a smirk. "They need for things to be spelled out and pushed right in their faces."

"You must admit, your message was somewhat vague," Gomez said. "What machinery, specifically, is the problem?"

Odell tossed her head in an all-encompassing gesture. "Well, all of it."

Tev ground his teeth. "All of it," he echoed flatly.

"That sounds rather extreme," Abramowitz said. "Why would you want to do that? From what little I've seen here, it seems you've had some real success integrating Mariposan technology into the Bringloidi way of life."

"Yes, *we* have," Latta said. "We, who understand that the choice is to adapt or to die. Some others—" He looked as if he were about to spit at the mention of "others," but thankfully refrained. "—they prefer the latter option."

Granger leaned forward, arms on the table. "You have to understand . . . our predecessors left Earth because they wanted to live life by their own terms. Some of them were old enough to remember the incompetence of the New United Nations that led to the Atomic Horrors, so when the European Hegemony and the other regional confederacies started talking world government, they wanted no part of it. They were willing to cut all ties with the rest of humanity rather than go down that route again. So you see . . . we come from long lines of independent-thinking people."

Abramowitz listened to this speech as if enraptured.

"And when the two colonies were brought together, forced to make compromises and to deviate from that independent mind-set, that brought a backlash, and gave rise to extremists like the Alliance for Mariposan Primacy."

"And others, like the Dieghanists," said Vallis, with what sounded to Tev like a defensive tone.

"'Dieghanists'?"

"Malcontents," Latta said, again looking ready to expectorate. "Group of Mariposans who split off on their own about nine years ago."

"Separatists from separatists," Abramowitz muttered, apparently to herself.

"They style themselves as the last defenders of Neo-Transcendentalism," Vallis added, "but instead of preaching about life in harmony with Nature, their talk is all of how Nature will take vengeance on the rest of us— storms, floods, quakes . . ."

"Plagues." Gomez exchanged a quick, haunted look with Corsi.

Tev frowned. "But what realistic threat could an *anti*-technology extremist group pose?"

Corsi was the one who answered that question: "Never underestimate extremists, Commander, no matter their philosophy."

Tev shrugged. "But none of this explains why you would have us strip the technology from this world."

Tev had been looking at Odell, but it was the Mariposan Prime Minister who shot back, "We've just had over two hundred of our people slaughtered by this technology! That's not explanation enough?"

Tev considered the gray man silently for a long

moment. His already long face sagged even lower, and his sad eyes stared back, tired and haunted. Tev understood that it was only natural, following a catastrophic event, to automatically lash out against the most direct cause—in this case, Mariposa's biotechnology. It now fell to the S.C.E. to help these people work past their instincts, to understand the foolishness of what they were asking.

He leaned forward and looked deep into the clone's eyes. "Mr. Granger, your very existence is a product of your technology. If not for your science, you would be nothing but a few scraps of organic molecules in a centuries-old, unmarked grave."

"*Tev!*" Gomez shouted, for some unfathomable reason. But he kept eye contact with the clone, intent on making him understand the scope of what he was telling him.

"Yes, Commander Tev, that's absolutely correct," Granger said softly, his voice carrying a tone of regret. "The Mariposan people do owe our existence to our technology. But that same technology has also sealed our fate. Further cloning is no longer a viable option. In fifty or so years, we'll be gone, and all that will be left is what we are able to pass on to . . . our children." He paused, his eyes flicking to his primary wife, who pointedly did not look back. "But I will be damned if what we leave them is the tools of their destruction."

"That's a rather sweeping condemnation," said Gomez. "Look at all the positive things you've created and accomplished. And the Bringloidi, too, have benefited from Mariposa's technology in the eleven years you've shared this world."

Odell fixed the commander with a withering look.

"Commander Gomez, my people spent our last five years on Bringloid living in caves. The sun had grown so hot that our crops were literally catching fire in the fields. We slept in dirt, collected water from a trickle of an underground stream, and rationed out what little food we had so thinly that—" She stopped herself, fighting back some clearly painful memories, but offered a composed face when she was ready to speak again. "It was a hellish life, and every day I give thanks that Captain Picard found us when he did. But in all that time, with all that hardship, we were never moved to murder." She paused, looked to each of the away team members in turn, then said, "Now, you tell me how much we've truly benefited from this technology."

Gomez had no answer for that, and a thoughtful silence fell over the entire room.

It was a silence that Tev felt obligated to breach. "You have a biosynthesizer in your home! A home built of temperature-resistant plastiform, with climate control and electrical lighting! You're growing crops genetically modified to this world, and wearing clothing made of synthetic materials—"

"Creature comforts cannot compare to human lives," Odell shot back.

"And the recent deaths are tragic," Tev allowed. "But, your population has increased threefold since coming here, and your children have a much higher life expectancy. Are you truly willing to bring the kind of suffering you knew on Bringloid down on them due to your rash decisions?"

Odell's mouth drew tight. "Are you quite finished, Mr. Tev?"

"I believe I've made my point of view clear."

"And am I to take it you're not going to help us?" Odell said icily.

"We'll have to discuss the matter," Gomez said, standing and staring hard at Tev. "We'll take your request under advisement."

"Of course," Tev said, again to humor the commander. "Though I would not anticipate receiving any help in destroying yourselves from Starfleet."

"Tev . . ."

He had no idea why Gomez was acting so annoyed toward him. He was, after all, only telling these people the truth. "If you are intent on doing so, the Androssi are, perhaps, the ones you should talk to."

Gold fixed Tev with a hard glare. "Tell me that you're joking."

The lieutenant commander shifted uncomfortably in his chair. "Jokes would not be appropriate here, sir," he muttered softly.

"It's good to know you still have *some* concept of what's appropriate," Gold barked back at him. Tev had pulled more than his share of boneheaded moves over the past several months, but suggesting to the insulated, unknowing colony that they openly invite in the dangerous, mendacious, technology scavengers took the cake.

Not that he much liked anything else he'd heard in this debriefing. He moved his glare from Tev to Gomez on one side of the conference table, then to Corsi and Abramowitz on the other. "So, in summary," he sighed, "you met with these people, sat in their home, listened to their plea for help, and then told them to go to hell."

"Sir, not that this excuses the way we handled matters," Gomez said, dipping her head to indicate that by "we," she was accepting equal responsibility for the actions of the individuals under her command, "but the Ficus leaders were not very receptive to us or the concerns we raised. It seems to me they came to a very vague decision in an emergency situation, with no practical understanding of what that decision involves, and now are unwilling to step back and think through the implications of that decision."

"Commander," Corsi said as she leaned forward in her seat, "they've just been subjected to a genocidal attack. You can hardly blame them if they're not ready to step back just yet."

"No, I understand," Gomez replied, her dark eyes conveying genuine empathy. "But when they insist that we need to remove all their modern technology, how are we supposed to respond to that?"

"By doing it."

Tev looked at Carol Abramowitz, who up until now had not said a single word, with his mouth agape. "What? Are you honestly suggesting . . . That's absurd!"

"Why?" she shot back, her large dark eyes challenging him. "What reason do *you* have to overrule a decision by the legitimate leaders of this colony?"

Tev, to his credit (as well as to everyone else's surprise) had no immediate response. Gold couldn't help but let a corner of his mouth twitch upward. For all his self-aggrandizing arrogance, Mor glasch Tev was still a Starfleet officer, and as such, he recognized his obligation to respect other cultures and their right to self-determination. After a moment's reflection, he said, "I concur with Commander Gomez—these people have not thought matters through properly. We would do this colony more harm than good by simply acquiescing to Odell and Granger's request."

"And on what do you base that determination? A few decade-old reports, and a ten-minute meeting where you were dismissing Odell's position before she'd even gotten a chance to explain it?" Carol Abramowitz shook her head adamantly. "The Bringloidi managed for over two centuries without advanced technology, while the Mariposans were slowly killing themselves with theirs. Now, how can you sit there and say the Bringloidi philosophy would be more harmful?"

Tev narrowed his black eyes at the cultural specialist, getting ready to rise to her bait, before Gold put up both hands. "All right, Abramowitz, your point is well taken." Tev snorted at that, but it only took a sideways glance from Gomez to remind him of how much trouble his mouth had already gotten him into. Gold then focused on his security chief. "What's your take, Corsi?"

Corsi furrowed her brow and pressed her lips into a flat line. "These people are scared, Captain. They've just been through a catastrophic event, with hundreds killed in the span of a few hours. And scared people tend to do stupid and dangerous things. That's what we have to address."

"What do you suggest?" Gomez asked.

Corsi looked across the table, meeting the eyes of both S.C.E. officers. "These biosynthesizers they have all over the place are what concern me. I know I'd feel better if I didn't have to worry if the guy next door was brewing up a big tank of Telurian Plague."

Tev snorted derisively. "Those units are programmed to produce only a small catalogue of beneficial microorganisms, requiring only relatively minimal gene splices. It would be impossible to create such an exotic pathogen."

"Then some nonexotic pathogen." Corsi's cool blue eyes flared in irritation at Tev's dismissive tone. "Some souped-up version of dysentery or streptococcus, or something to infect their crops and bring on a famine. You can't tell me, with the wealth of gen-engineering expertise on this world, that someone couldn't find a very simple and very dangerous way to reprogram these machines and cause no small amount of chaos."

Tev hesitated before admitting, "There is that potential, yes. But," he quickly added, "there is the greater potential for harm in disrupting these people's way of life."

"Oh, and we can't have that, can we?" Abramowitz's tone dripped with sarcasm. "This society has known nothing but disruption and change for the past decade. It'll take at least another full generation of further integration and adaptation before there will be any kind of stability in need of preserving."

No one said a word, or seemingly even drew a breath for several long seconds. When Carol Abramowitz had first joined the *da Vinci*, she had been extremely soft-spoken and emotionally reserved, to the point where Gold sometimes worried she was bottling up too much inside her. There'd been a gradual change over the last few months, particularly following her brush with death on Teneb. Now perhaps, Gold considered, she had swung a bit too far to the other end of the scale.

Finally, he broke the silence. "Corsi, you'll come up with a plan for how to best deal with this situation. I suggest, too, you coordinate everything through Acting Minister Latta. And Tev . . ." He paused, forcing the Tellarite to take a good, long look into his eyes. "We'll talk later."

With that, the meeting was over. All five stood up, but as the staff turned for the door, Gold put an arm out, catching Abramowitz by the elbow. She hung back until the rest had exited and she and the captain were alone. "Is there something more on your mind, Abramowitz?"

Abramowitz pressed her dark eyes shut for a moment. "I'm sorry, Captain. It's just . . . this is very nearly a textbook case of why Starfleet should have a Prime Directive."

"I get the strange feeling we've had this conversation before," Gold cracked. It was only a few weeks ago—in this same room, in fact—that the two of them debated Starfleet's noninterference policies in advance of Abramowitz's mission on Coroticus III. "Though, this isn't a Prime Directive issue. These are humans who came here from Earth in warp-powered ships."

"With all due respect, sir, that's a ridiculous distinction. Why should human cultures be fair game when it comes to being destroyed? Especially when they left Earth specifically to avoid that very fate?"

The captain frowned. "You're exaggerating, Abramowitz." The sense of déjà vu struck him again.

Abramowitz met the captain's eyes with her own, her expression one of absolute earnestness. "No, sir, I'm afraid I'm not. Both cultures have been splintered, apparently to the point where neither a Bringloidi nor a Mariposan culture can be expected to survive. And there's no guarantee that any hybridized culture has any better chance of survival, either."

Gold didn't say anything for a long time, reflecting on how far and how long the effects of a captain's decision, no matter how well considered, could reverberate. "The situation on the planet . . . it's that grave?"

Abramowitz took a deep breath. "Like I said, it'll be at least a full generation before we can tell how things on this joint colony will take shape. And those will be the roughest couple of decades these people ever see— hopefully not as bad as what's happened here in the past two days, but it'll only take a small spark to set off this tinderbox again." She sighed and slowly shook her head. "Needless to say, this is not a job for the S.C.E."

"No," Gold agreed. "What do you suggest?"

"First, we have to understand exactly what happened down there, so we can address the root cause. Who all these political players are, who launched that biological attack, who was targeted, and why. It bothers me, too, that we have a weapon that targeted only Mariposans, which presumably would have been developed by a Mariposan scientist."

That counterintuitive fact had been bothering Gold as well. "Lense's research, I'm certain, will help point us to some of those answers. What else?"

"Well, I know Starfleet is still spread thin, and that after the way these people welcomed the *Tubman*—"

Gold held up a hand to stop her. "I will tell Captain Scott in the strongest possible terms that Mariposa has to come up on the priorities list." While much of Starfleet's resources were indeed committed to the seemingly unending postwar recovery, news of the hostilities

on Mariposa would bring in the experts of the Diplomatic Corps. He'd just have to remember to specifically
ask that Gabriel Marshall *not* be given the assignment.

"And," Abramowitz continued, "if we do nothing else
for these people . . ."

"What?" Gold asked.

"Please, do not let Tev go back down there."

CHAPTER

6

One of Elizabeth Lense's favorite pastimes as a young girl was solving hidden picture puzzles. The earliest ones were simple line drawings, usually of some natural setting, a field or a forest, and among the outlines of leaves and grass blades were incongruous objects like fish or *sehlats*. As she grew older, the puzzles grew more complex, yet she would master each new collection her father brought her in short order. Naturally, that had led her to her interest in real world puzzles, in general sciences, and then eventually in medicine.

And now here she sat, staring at the viral DNA she had isolated from the Mariposan bioattack victims, certain she was failing to see the fish for the trees. There was a pattern in these base-pair sequences, she knew, one she should have recognized. And yet, the answer eluded her.

She leaned back in her chair, rocked her head back and forth to loosen her tight neck muscles, and glanced out the open lab door into the small isolated ward beyond. Victor Granger, facing open revolt from the rest of the hospital staff led by Sue DiCamino, had grudgingly allowed her to set up down here. Ten victims of the bio-attack had been moved here and given to her care. All had had their conditions stabilized, at least temporarily, and were sleeping peacefully for the moment. This in itself was a major step forward.

Lense reached for the coffee cup at her right elbow, and was disappointed to find it empty. (Well, maybe not too disappointed; what the Mariposans called coffee was actually a "biosynthesized" liquid produced by splicing arabica bean genes into a common bacterium; it was best not to think about it.) She thought about getting a refill, about just stepping away from this lab equipment and clearing her head for a minute, maybe getting some food to soak up the bacteria juice already sitting in her stomach. After all, she did have to start taking better care of . . .

She put the cup off to the side and leaned in closer to her display screen. Her patients came first, before any concerns about herself. What would have happened at Sherman's Planet if she spent all her time getting all touchy-feely with Captain Gold? What would have happened at Pike City if she'd spent her off-duty time obsessing over what had just happened at Galvan VI? Or at Setlik if all she did was lick the wounds Commander Selden gave her at Starbase 314?

A small part of her brain tried to tell her that she couldn't simply ignore her pregnancy the same way she ignored other emotional traumas. Not that she should be keeping those bottled up and festering inside her the way she did, either, but at some point she would have to tell people, to—

"Excuse me, Doctor?"

Lense turned to see Konya standing in the lab's open doorway, with Kara McClay hovering at his elbow. *Oh God, how long has he been there? How much did he hear? Oh God, no, this is not how I want people to find out—*

"I didn't hear anything, Doctor."

All thought processes ceased. Konya gave her what must have been meant as a reassuring smile. "My telepathic skills aren't that sharp, even when I'm trying to listen. Normally, it's just so much white noise."

"But . . . you did just hear me worrying that . . ."

"Well, you were pretty much yelling at me there."

Lense allowed herself to relax and give the Betazoid guard a weak smile in return. "Was there something you needed, Rennan?"

"Commander Corsi just paged," he said. "She wants me to report back to the ship. That is, if you don't need me here anymore."

Lense cocked her head and loosed a small laugh. "No offense, but I didn't really need you in the first place."

"If only that were always the case," he answered, far from offended. He then turned to Kara and offered his hand. "It was very nice to meet you, Kara. Thank you for helping the doctor where I couldn't."

"Nice to meet you, too," she said, smiling politely. Lense found herself again impressed by the young woman's poise. When she was her age, had she been paid such a compliment by a handsome older man, she would have blushed bright red and stammered like an idiot.

"Good luck, Doctor," he said as he turned for the exit. "One of your patients is starting to come around," he called over his shoulder just before leaving.

Lense jumped out of her seat and brushed past McClay into the adjoining ward. Sure enough, one of the biobed monitors was just starting to pick up the accelerating brainwave activity Konya had already sensed. Her ten patients represented what, by Mariposan standards, was a broad cross-section of their society. She had two individuals from each of the five Progenitors' genetic lines: DiCamino, Granger, Hammond, Vallis, and Wheelock. They ranged in age from twelve to sixty (to which Lense had to mentally add eighteen years, to account for the Mariposans' inscrutable ability to bring their nascent clones to full physical maturity in the lab), and from ninth- through fifteenth-generation cell lines.

Lense moved to the side of her awakening patient, Cory Wheelock—age 18 (36), generation line 12—and ran her tricorder above his abdomen. At the same time, Kara had moved to the opposite side of the bed, using one hand to brush Wheelock's dark hair from his pale, sweat-dampened forehead. The other she wrapped around the patient's hand, giving it an encouraging squeeze. "His vital signs have fallen to the exact same level as before," she said, looking up at the display mounted above Wheelock's head.

Lense nodded as she read the same from her tricorder. Stasizine therapy had become less effective in all the infected Mariposans after an hour's time. She'd switched to an equizine-3 solution, which initially improved matters, but the virus had seemingly adapted again. "Let's see if switching back to stasizine helps any," Lense said, as she reached for her hypospray.

"Alternating therapies," Kara replied, smiling with understanding. "Kinda like keeping the virus off balance."

"In a sense," Lense smiled back as she pressed the hypo to Wheelock's neck. When Granger begrudgingly allowed her this space to do her work, he also assigned McClay as her only assistant. Lense got the impression that the health minister intended this as some sort of snub, but she could not have been more pleased with the young woman's dedicated work and professionalism.

"It's working!" Kara said, watching the monitor readings start to rise. Lense noticed Wheelock's grip around Kara's hand tighten, as if grasping at a lifeline, and then his eyelids cracked open, slowly adjusting to the light until he could see the faces of his caretakers.

"What . . . ?" he asked groggily, and then, as the sleep melted away from him, his look of confusion dissolved to something darker. "Breeders!" he snarled, causing Lense to involuntarily flinch. "Whuh've y' done t' me?"

"Mr. Wheelock, you're going to be all right," Lense said in her most soothing doctor's voice.

"Tried to kill us!" he answered, turning to look directly at Kara. "Murderers! 'Gloidi trash!" Lense cut off what would almost certainly have been an uninterrupted string of pejoratives with another touch of her hypospray, sending the Mariposan back into slumber.

"Well, that raised his vitals, all right," Kara said, giving no sign of any offense as she gave Wheelock's hand one last squeeze before laying it gently by his side.

Lense shook her head slowly. "I have to tell you, Kara . . . your bedside manner would put a lot of the doctors I've known to shame." Lense was more than a little disturbed by the pervasive human-against-human racism she'd been witness to since arriving on the surface. And though she meant what she had just said to Kara, she found her unflinching acceptance of the hatred directed at her almost equally disturbing.

Kara beamed at the compliment nonetheless. "Thank you, Dr. Elizabeth. That means a lot to me, since it was a Starfleet doctor who made me want to get into medicine in the first place."

"Kate Pulaski, right," Lense nodded, as she reloaded her hypo with stasizine and made her way around the ward administering it to the rest of her charges. "She did a couple of guest lectures at Starfleet Medical when I was there. She can be very inspirational." She could also be very acerbic when addressing a hall full of insecure med students, but Lense didn't say that to McClay. A girl needed her role models, after all. "But you didn't pick all this up in a couple days on the *Enterprise*."

"Well, no. I do a lot of reading on my own off the subspace link to the Federation infonet, and Dr. Sandra was always very good to me."

Lense thought she heard something in her tone. " 'Was'?"

Kara lowered her eyes to the biobed in front of her, but looking through it. "She was one of the ones who didn't make it."

Lense hesitated, knowing that it would be little help to say she was sorry. Then, her chance to say anything was gone, as an alarm sounded from Cory Wheelock's monitor.

Lense was across the room in an instant, checking both the overhead readouts and her own tricorder. "Dammit," she muttered, as she watched the virus continue its rampage through his body. "It's built up a resistance already!"

"Dr. Elizabeth," Kara called from behind her. Lense turned to see her studying all the rest of the monitors, in the order in which she had dispensed the latest round of injections. "They're all slipping back."

Lense cursed the tenacious little bug as she reloaded her hypo once again, this time with equizine-1. She had hesitated in employing this therapy up until now, because if the damned bug was to develop a resistance to this, there weren't any other options. She injected Wheelock once more, and once more the treatment seemed to work. Lense couldn't muster up much optimism, though.

"How did the virus build a resistance so fast?" Kara asked.

Lense shook her head. "It couldn't have. Or, it did the first time we used the therapy." She ran her fingers through her short curly hair, as if trying to stimulate the brain cells through her scalp. "The immunity was there, and this tenacious little bastard just . . . faked remission." Lense realized how ridiculous that sounded the moment the words were out of her mouth, but she couldn't help but see this damned virus as some kind of fighter, playing with his opponent, lulling her into a false sense of confidence, then suddenly switching his sword to his stronger hand and launching a more powerful offensive . . .

"Oh, my God."

Kara shot Lense a wide-eyed, worried look. "What?"

Lense beamed at Kara, and slapped the hypospray into the young woman's palm, first ramping down the dosage. "Administer this to all the rest of the patients, and then get the message over to Sue DiCamino: ten cc's of equizine-1, no more than that per hour. If I'm right, the war shouldn't last any longer than that."

Kara looked at the hypo in her hand, and then up into Lense's eyes as if overwhelmed. The doctor would have added a few words of confidence, but she was just too excited, and instead turned directly into the lab and pulled the genetic map of the virus back up.

This time, she saw the fish plain as day.

CHAPTER
7

After the way the meeting at the Prime Ministers' residence had ended, Reade Latta feared Starfleet would be abandoning them for another decade, if not longer. So when he learned that a Starfleet team was to come calling to discuss security matters, he resolved to show them how much he welcomed their presence.

"Ten-year-old whiskey," he announced, holding up the bottle and beaming at his guests. "Distilled from the finest Bringloidi-raised quadrotriticale; none of that biosynthesized swill for you good folk." The Starfleeters—Corsi, the tall blond security chief he'd met earlier, and Soloman, whose large skull clearly identified him as some manner of technological genius—were clearly overwhelmed by his graciousness, and they could only smile silently as he filled their glasses. "To fallen comrades," he said as he lifted his glass, "and absent friends."

Corsi nodded solemnly, raised her glass in kind, and added, "And to new friends."

The Starfleeters both brought the drink to their lips, but Latta hesitated. He stared into the amber liquid for a long guilty moment, as if only then remembering his promises and his responsibilities. *But you only promised Brenna you would stay sober for the duration of the crisis*, the demon in the back of his head reminded him. *Well, now Starfleet is here to put things right, aren't they? Besides, you were the one who proposed that toast; it would be an insult to Kevin Hammond and all the rest not to—*

Latta slammed the untouched drink down on the desk, sloshing a good share of it onto his hand. *Stupid weak old man*, he cursed himself. Pulling out a handkerchief to wipe his hand, he put on a smile to meet the questioning gazes from across the desk. "Well then, friends, shall we get to business?"

Corsi set her still half-full glass aside. "The *da Vinci* stands ready to offer our assistance in securing the safety of this colony. Soloman and I are here to determine how to best organize those efforts."

"Ah, yes, yes. Very wise, very forward thinking."

"Thank you," Soloman said. His glass was also sitting forgotten in front of him, the level barely a centimeter lower than what he had poured. "To this end, we hoped you would grant us access to your computer systems."

"Oh, well, certainly," said Latta, gesturing to the fancy chrome and glass panels set into the wall to his right.

The Starfleeters looked at the device, and then back to Latta, as if they had expected something else. After a moment of awkward silence, Mr. Soloman spoke. "Minister, we would require an authorization code in order to fully access your systems."

"Um . . ." Latta replied. "Yes. An authorization code. Of course." Kevin Hammond had mentioned something to him about codes, maybe, when he set off on his counterstrike against those A.M.P. madmen. But all power was out then, so Latta hadn't bothered remembering any of it. Hell, in his younger days, back on the Old World with Danilo Odell (God rest his sweet soul), you didn't need computers or any of the rest of this machinery to keep order. Danilo lay down the law, and Reade needed nothing but his own two fists to enforce it. Now, *that* was how you maintained security. . . .

Soloman and Corsi were still staring at him expectantly. "Well, the thing is, you see . . . these contraptions are very temperamental. They have to be dealt with in just such a way—"

"Minister," Corsi interrupted, frowning at him suspiciously, "I understand that you would be hesitant to give outsiders access to restricted data at any level—"

"Oh, no, it's not that," Latta insisted. He still needed help from these people—over half the Public Safety Force was dead, another quarter were gravely ill, at least eight of those remaining had revealed themselves as A.M.P. sympathizers. But to admit his ignorance, to appear weak to them . . .

"Perhaps I could attempt to circumvent the encryption protocols myself," Mr. Soloman suggested. "With your permission, of course, Minister."

"Yes, of course, permission granted," Latta said magnanimously. Soloman rose from his chair and went straight to work on the machine. In the back of his mind, he wondered, what with all this to-do about access authorization and restricted files, whether he was too readily giving away the store.

That worry was shoved aside when Corsi said, "I'd also like to hear from you a narrative of what, exactly, happened here. What was the trigger event, the chain of events that followed, the parties involved?"

"Ah, that I can tell you," Latta said. "Twas an explosion and fire, dead center of the Life Science Center, in the cloning labs."

Corsi's entire body snapped taut at that. "Cloning labs? But I thought—"

"Oh, they're not used for cloning anymore, of course. They're just regular science labs now. One woman working down there was killed in the blast—Sandra Vallis, a fine lass, deserved much better. Then when the emergency responders answered the call, they started dropping dead on the floor. Just the clones, of course. By the time anyone realized what was happening, it was all up in the air ducts, and everything went straight to hell."

"Any way of tracking who'd been in and out of there?" Corsi asked. "Any security restrictions? Visual recordings?"

"No, not that I know of. And like I said, it's the middle of medical center; everyone goes through or around there. Would have been too simple." His hand went to his whiskey glass again, and he had to fight the urge to wrap his fingers around and pick it up. "It would have taken less solution than this to do the damage, I'm told. Could've been snuck in in a small pocket flask, and no one'd be the wiser."

"You would think there would be more protection

OUT OF THE COCOON   83

around what used to be their clone labs," Corsi said. "So
you have no idea who could've done this."

Latta sighed and shrugged. "The A.M.P., the Dieghanists,
the Wilmut Party, the Sons of Bringloid . . . any group of
bloody splitters who think they can run this world better
than it is now."

Corsi showed deep concern hearing that. "Is there really that much discord in this colony, that any of these
groups is as likely a suspect as the next?"

Latta shook his head. "As you said yerself, miss, we
cannot discount anyone."

Corsi looked ready to say something more, but then
Soloman announced, "I've gained access."

"Good. Let's start by pulling together all the professional and educational information on the colony inhabitants we can, ranked by level of expertise."

"What are you looking for?" Latta asked.

"We need to find individuals who would have the
knowledge and ability to have created this bioweapon—
not just the actual work of gene splicing, but the design
of complex new genomes."

After several seconds, the chrome contraption beeped.
"I have the list of geneticists' names," Soloman said.

Corsi rose from her seat, and went to look over Soloman's shoulder at the display. Latta joined her to look at
the fifty-one names, all with the surnames of the Mariposan Progenitors, listed on the screen. Poor Sandra Vallis's name immediately jumped out at him from the list.
"You should know, Commander Corsi," he said in a somber voice, "if you're looking for a guilty party to charge,
that a goodly number of these people have already gone
on to their Final Judgment in recent days."

He saw a twinge of sadness pass behind Corsi's eyes as she said, "Cross-check this list against hospital records over the past three days."

With another beep from the wall panel, the list of fifty-one shrank to fourteen. Both Latta and Corsi drew in a short hiss.

"Transmit this list and the associated files up to Hawkins," Corsi told Soloman. "Let him know these are our 'A' level investigative targets." She then looked to Latta. "Do any of the rest of these names stand out for you, Mr. Latta?"

Latta squinted at the list, though he didn't expect to see anything. He'd only noticed Sandra Vallis because he'd just been talking about her; the rest of the names all blurred together just like the clones themselves. Di-Camino, Angela. DiCamino, Frances. DiCamino, Martha. How was he supposed to—

"Wait a tic," Latta said, his eyes flicking back up the column of names, then stabbing one with a forefinger. "Frances DiCamino? Why is she still on yer list?"

"She holds advanced degrees in microbiology, with secondary degrees in—"

"No, no," Latta said, beginning to wonder whether it was the contraption or the Starfleeter making such an outrageous mistake. "That's not the problem."

"What is the problem?" Corsi asked.

"Frances DiCamino is more'n ten years dead," he said. "That's the problem."

★ ★ ★

The Bringloidi prime minister crouched on her hands and knees in the dirt, digging the weeds out from around her beets. It was almost as if they understood she had greater matters to deal with, and decided to take full advantage of her absence. With a soft grunt and a tug, she pulled another long invading weed out by its roots. She smiled in small satisfaction as she tossed it on the pile behind her with its mates.

If only everything could be so simple, she thought as she attacked the next offending stalk with a small hand trowel. Leave the good plants, get rid of the bad ones. Her mother had taught her how to tell the difference between the two when she was barely out of nappies. The Bringloidi lived an idyllic life then. Oh, it was a hard one, certainly, working dawn to dusk, helping Mother and the other womenfolk cook and clean and a hundred more chores, then practicing her letters and numbers by oil lamp until bedtime. But by the time the family did turn in, there was a great sense of pride in all that had been accomplished.

Then one morning, Mother didn't wake up, and the whole world seemed to fall apart. Now that she was suddenly the woman of the Odell household, she was entrusted with the knowledge that the sun had been growing measurably hotter for years. When her da was a boy, he would tell her, the entire valley had been lush green, not just the narrow strips along the riverbanks. But of late, the droughts had been worsening, and the adults—including Mother—had been letting themselves go hungry most nights to keep the young ones fed, and to save enough for the truly bad times to come.

And they did come.

It fell to young Brenna to take up all the responsibilities that were inherent to the wife of the colony's leader, from organizing the work groups, to caring for and teaching the younger children, to making sure the men's thirst for *poteen* was kept under some semblance of control.

Once the *Enterprise* had found them, and Starfleet and the Mariposans introduced them to the technical advances of their worlds, she thought life might possibly become simple again. But she only traded one set of hardships for another: her "courtship" (if one could call it that without laughing) with Wilson, the Dieghanist emigration, and of course, poor Danielle. . . .

"Madam Prime Minister?"

Suddenly jerked back to the present, Brenna spun inelegantly on her knees to face the white-haired man in the Starfleet uniform who had appeared behind her. "Sweet mercy, what do you mean, sneaking up on a person like that?" she snapped, hoping that her broad-brimmed sun hat kept the tears that had been welling in her eyes in shadow.

"Sorry. I didn't mean to startle you, Minister Odell. I'm David Gold, captain of the *da Vinci*."

"Oh, ho. So you're the man who gives that gasbag Tev his orders."

Gold gave her a pained smile. "In theory, I suppose. Actually, I came to offer my personal apology to you for Lieutenant Commander Tev's impolitic behavior, and for any offense he may have given you and yours."

Brenna studied Gold's kindly eyes and grandfatherly face, and found she couldn't doubt his sincerity. "Thank you, Captain. Although my delicate sensibilities are hardly the issue."

Gold lowered himself on his haunches, matching their eye levels. "No, obviously, you have greater concerns— the future of your world, and your people."

Brenna nodded. "Yes. And whether we will even have a future."

"Let me ask you, Minister," Gold said, taking a stalk from her pile of weeds and absently twirling it between his fingers. "As I understand it, this world has actually been quite peaceful in the years since the Bringloidi and Mariposans were reunited. Despite the vast differences, you have made considerable progress integrating yourselves. You've raised a generation of children together." He paused, and looked her in the eye. "After more than a decade of this, how is it the two cultures are now incompatible?"

Gold had such a mild manner that she almost missed the criticism beneath his words. But Brenna resolved to maintain the civil tone of their conversation as she answered. "Our cultures were never compatible, Captain. Good heavens, they're complete opposites! All that we've ever had was our mutual dependence on each other for survival. And as recent events show, survival isn't a concern for some."

"Some. A small minority."

"A small minority who can kill hundreds of innocents at a single blow, because of this clone technology!"

"Yes. And it's terrible," Gold said with a grimace. "But don't you need to look first at why those few would want to do such things—"

"'Why?' When has 'why' ever mattered? Since Cain and Abel, killing is just what men do."

Gold said nothing in response to that, but just stared at her, trying to read her. Brenna set her face as she stared back, willing herself not to betray any emotion, any deeper thoughts or insecurities.

"You do understand the scope of what you are suggesting here," he said. "The logistics of dismantling so much technology, so integrated with the existing infrastructure, are daunting to say the least. The *da Vinci* is a small ship; our engineers wouldn't be able to do it all on their own."

"Well, there're more ships in the Starfleet, aren't there?"

"Of course . . . and there are also a lot of places across Federation space for those ships to be. It would probably be weeks before a ship suitable to the task could be dispatched, if not months, or years." Brenna waited for Gold to drop the other shoe. "However, it would only be a matter of a day to bring in a negotiator from the Federation's Diplomatic Corps."

"To talk me out of it. Ho, I should have known better than to think your grand Federation would willingly lift a finger to help us!"

Gold took a long breath before saying, with not a little heat in his tone, "My people are right now looking for whatever gen-engineering equipment and bioweapon stocks are out there. My chief medical officer is in your hospital taking care of your sick. And I am here right now to try to help you understand how a rash, ill-considered decision impacts—"

"Oh, you're one to talk about rash, ill-considered decisions, Mr. Starfleet Captain! For over ten years I've been trying to make the best of an ill-considered decision one of yours made for us. But the decisions on how we live our lives are now ours to make. And if you're not willing to respect that, then you can go straight to the devil."

Gold said nothing for the longest time, but simply stared at her. She couldn't quite read his expression, but there seemed to be more sadness in his eyes than anything else. He pushed himself off the ground, back onto his feet. "You remind me of my oldest daughter, Eden," he told her as he brushed the dirt from his knees. "Being in Starfleet, I missed a lot of her childhood, and that caused a lot of tension and animosity between us, all the way through her adulthood. I can't go back now and be the father she wanted me to be. The best I can do is say I'm sorry for my mistakes, and let her know that even though I realize she's an adult—a grandmother, no less!—I still care, and I only want what's best for her."

"That paternalistic attitude is a bit arrogant, isn't it?" Brenna asked, surprised to hear how mild her voice sounded as she posed that question.

He shrugged. "So be it." With that, he turned and walked off toward the road to the Capital Complex. Brenna watched him until he disappeared behind a row of quadrotriticale stalks. Then with a loud sigh, she turned back to the simplicity of her weeding.

CHAPTER

8

Sonya Gomez sat in the captain's chair at the center of the *da Vinci* bridge, her crew around her, standing ready to fill any orders she might issue . . . and silently felt sorry for herself.

Rarely was she given command of the ship—despite her position as first officer, the separate structures of the ship and S.C.E. crews dictated that one of the bridge officers take the conn when the captain was off duty, leaving her and her engineers free to concentrate on their specialized duties.

Right now, though, David Gold's skills as a veteran starship captain were in greater demand than any engineering contributions. And, as she had so spectacularly demonstrated earlier, her own diplomatic and people skills didn't amount to jack.

You can't blame yourself for Tev's inability to carry himself like a proper Starfleet officer, she tried to tell herself. That was Tev being Tev. He had shown some improvement of late, though it had taken one of the harshest ass-chewings Sonya had ever had to give to get him there. She really had believed they had turned a corner, and now this . . .

Gomez stopped, and reexamined the last thought that had just flashed through her mind: *believed* they *had turned a corner*. Maybe she was putting too much on Tev, when she should've been examining her own shortcomings. After all, Tev had been in Starfleet for close to twenty years. He'd earned his promotions from ensign up to lieutenant commander, and while his record did include more than a few marks, there was nothing that indicated the kind of regular interpersonal conflicts that had marked his tour on the *da Vinci*. Maybe it was her command style, or her lack of understanding of Tellarite psychology, or something she said when they first met that pissed him off.

Her reverie was interrupted by the arrival of Domenica Corsi on the bridge. "Commander," she said, frowning. "The captain hasn't beamed back yet?"

"He's only been down there half an hour or so," Gomez said, standing up from the center seat.

"Only half an hour," the security chief grumbled. "Like nothing can go wrong in so short a time as thirty minutes." She and the captain had a nice, loud shouting match when he announced that he was going down to meet with the prime ministers, that he was going alone, so as not to create the same negative first impression they had earlier, and that Corsi was not going to stop him.

"He is a grown man, Domenica," Gomez reminded her. She understood that there were regulations about when a captain should or shouldn't leave his ship, and that Corsi took those regulations seriously, but there was such a thing as overkill.

Corsi shut her eyes and took a short deep breath. When she opened her eyes again, she looked significantly more composed. "Could I talk to you in the captain's ready room, then?"

Gomez nodded, and the two stepped off the bridge into the small office. They both took seats in front of Gold's desk. "Soloman and I met with Minister Latta, and together we compiled a list of fourteen members of the Mariposan scientific community who we determined could pose a future risk to this colony by advanced biological attack. Of those fourteen potential risks, five are dead."

Gomez dipped her head. "In the bioattack."

"No," Corsi said, causing Gomez's head to snap back up. "That list of fourteen *excluded* anyone confirmed dead in recent days. These other five deaths all happened nine or more years ago."

"And their deaths were never officially recorded?"

Corsi shook her head. "They were also, all five, still on file as still being on their jobs. Now, a death certificate doesn't get filed, that's an oversight. Five don't get filed, that's incompetence. All other official records pointing to them still being alive? That's a cover-up."

Gomez's jaw fell slack. "How could they cover it up for ten years?"

"There was a huge influx of people here eleven years ago. They start up these rural settlements, and the population starts spreading out from the enclosed complex the Mariposans have concentrated themselves in for two hundred and some years. Not to mention," Corsi added, with a half grin that conveyed no amusement, "there are dozens of duplicates of these dead women walking around all over the place; how hard is it going to be to miss any specific one?"

Gomez furrowed her brow. "All five were women? That can't be random chance."

"No," Corsi agreed. "It couldn't be."

Gomez studied the security chief's expression. "You have a theory."

Corsi nodded slowly. "We managed to track down the families of two of the women. We're looking for the other three. I don't want to jump to conclusions before I have more facts . . ."

"But?"

"But . . . I'm afraid this colony's problems could run far deeper than any of us imagined."

The first thing Gold noticed entering the special ward in the Life Science Center was its peacefulness. The ten patients slept steadily, their faces marred by scabbed-over sores, but nonetheless serene. He'd been in enough sickbays and infirmaries in crisis situations, and he was comfortable saying that the crisis here was passed.

Lense approached from the opposite end of the long room, a young woman he guessed for a medtech tagging along beside her. "It looks like congratulations are in order here, Doctor."

Allowing herself only a slight smile as she rubbed a finger at the corner of her tired-looking eyes, Lense said, "The battle has been won."

Gold cocked his head to one side. "But the war?"

Lense took a deep breath, then turned to the Bringloidi woman at her elbow. "Kara, would you run a series 'A' blood test from all the patients, and a series 'B' from the thirteens, fourteens, and fifteens." Kara nodded and went to carry out her orders, as Lense turned and led Gold into the small office.

Once they'd both been seated, Lense said, "I've isolated and identified the viral agent used against the Mariposans, Captain. It's *rop'ngor*."

Gold's eyes widened slightly. He recognized the language, of course, but was surprised to hear it spoken in this context. "This is a Klingon bug, you're telling me?"

"Yes. Or it was. It's been significantly altered, to the point where it was almost unidentifiable."

"How would these people get their hands on such an exotic . . ." The answer dawned on him before he had even finished asking the question. "Ambassador Worf. Of course; he was a lieutenant on the *Enterprise* at the time."

But Lense shook her head. "*Rop'ngor* is a childhood disease; it would've been quickly diagnosed and treated in an adult Klingon. But humans can be carriers, and never know. I believe that's the reason for the violent relapses I've been seeing here."

"I don't follow."

"*Rop'ngor* got its name—it roughly translates as 'the cheating disease'—because it will attack the body, and then go into a dormant state before antibody production can get up to full strength. That 'tricks' the immune system into thinking it's beaten the thing back. Then, when the white blood cells start dying off, the virus comes out of dormancy, and hits hard, fast, and often."

"A disease that fights with no honor," Gold noted. Little wonder the Klingons had given it such a pejorative name.

Lense nodded. "Now, in humans, when they're first infected, there's the same trigger for antibody production, just like with any foreign microorganism. But when the virus launches its secondary attack, there are no Klingon proteins for it to feed on. That gives the human autoimmune system plenty of time to counterattack. Except for a mild fever, you'd never even know you were sick."

"So how does that account for the relapses?" Gold asked.

"Those people who had previously contracted *rop'ngor*, in its unaltered form, had already built up a resistance to the disease. That let them 'recover' from the initial infection by the modified virus."

"Which was in fact just the virus's dormant phase," Gold nodded in understanding. "But now that you know what it is, you have it under control?"

"Not quite," Lense said through gritted teeth. "I can trigger its dormant stage, but its taking more time to kill it off. The thing is, it's not *rop'ngor* anymore. It's been gen-engineered to target different cell types, mutate their DNA, tie the entire endocrine system in knots. . . ." She sighed and pressed the heels of her hands against her eyelids. "Whoever created this damned thing was one sadistic *petaQ*."

Gold considered the top of the doctor's head in silence for a long moment. "Why don't you take a break, Lense, now that things are under control?"

The doctor's head snapped back up immediately. "No. There's too much more. Too much I don't know yet."

Gold sighed softly. "You're not doing yourself any favors by—"

"Captain," she cut him off sharply. "I can do this. I have to."

Since her rescue from the Jabari's homeworld, Gold had sensed that the doctor had been affected by the ordeal in ways that went beyond what she reported in her debriefing. But she had refused to take any recovery time, and now Gold was worried she was pushing herself too hard, too soon. Yet, he knew from past experience that nothing, short of the ship's tractor beams at full power, was going to pull this woman away from a medical puzzle she had set her mind to solving.

"All right," he said, standing up from his side of the desk. "Good work, Doctor." Maybe once they wrapped things up here, he would "suggest" they resume their informal weekly counseling sessions. He could only pray she didn't push herself past the breaking point before then.

Wilson Granger stood in the middle of the small one-room structure that had, long ago, been the first shelter built on Mariposa. His hands were solemnly folded in front of him as he read the names etched on the two hundred and eighty-nine individual gold-plate plaques bolted to the four walls, honoring the men and women who had not survived the landing of the *S.S. Mariposa*. He'd visited this memorial many times before, but his eyes had always just skimmed over the names. The reality of such a mass tragedy had been inconceivable to him. Until now.

What kind of hell must Walter Granger have gone through, he wondered. On what should have been the triumphant end of a months-long journey, he was faced with the task of burying all but four of his ship's complement, including his own wife and their son. Wilson Granger felt a twinge, the genetic memory, perhaps, of his Progenitor's anguish. He wondered if the courage Walter had found in the face of tragedy had also been carried down in his genes.

"Mr. Prime Minister?"

Granger turned toward the man standing in the entryway that connected the memorial to the rest of the Capital Complex. "Captain Gold, I presume," he said, extending his hand.

Gold took it with a firm, dry grasp. "Thank you for agreeing to talk with me."

"Not at all," said Granger. "I'm glad for the opportunity to discuss matters in a more . . . tranquil setting."

"Meaning, without your Bringloidi counterpart."

Granger smiled in appreciation of the Starfleet captain's directness. "Brenna is . . . well, she's a force of nature. Sometimes, everything and everyone around her just ends up getting swept up and away."

Gold nodded in understanding. "Well, given the nature of your situation, we absolutely want to make sure all voices are clearly heard and considered."

"I'm glad to hear you say that, Captain," said Granger. "Because I want you to hear me say this, without any other voices coloring your understanding: as Mariposan

Prime Minister, and on behalf of the Mariposan citizens of the United Ficus Colony, I request that the Federation help eliminate all advanced technologies from this world."

Gold tried to hold his expression, and failed. "I have to say, I'm more than a little surprised to hear you say that."

"I don't doubt it. Honestly, it surprises me as well." Granger started to pace slowly around the perimeter of the small memorial. "When our scientists discovered our DNA had degraded to the point where our future was threatened, we became obsessed with the need to preserve our society. We were willing to forget everything, even our most basic sense of morality, in order to survive."

"You wouldn't be the first people to do so," said Gold, not without some sympathy. "The survival instinct is a powerful—"

"That's not my point, Captain," said Granger, shaking his head. "My point is, before the Bringloidi came, we never paused to consider what, exactly, we were trying to preserve. When I was confronted a decade ago with the idea of taking a wife . . . *several* wives . . . and of having conjugal relations with them, my first reaction was not a positive one. Nor, for that matter, were my second or third reactions.

"However, I had to adapt to our new reality, for my own self and as an example to the rest. So, like some medieval warlord forging a political alliance, I agreed to be married to the Bringloidi leader's daughter. In the years since we've been together, however, sharing our lives, working in tandem toward our common goals, I've come to discover something."

A tiny grin cracked Gold's lips. "That you loved her."

Granger shook his head slightly, even as he smiled back. "That I am even *capable* of love. That I can hold another person in that kind of regard. That had been leached out of us, along with our individuality, and our need to live life rather than just propagate it." Granger swept his arm in a circle around him, indicating the names on the walls. "These people left Earth centuries ago because they wanted to better humanity. But with all their genetic expertise, they forgot the part of being human that isn't in our DNA."

Granger sighed, and turned to look Gold in the eye again. "Cloning saved Mariposa two hundred and fifty years ago, but it became a crutch. When Captain Picard forced us to put an end to it, we were saved again. All we're asking you now is to continue what Captain Picard began."

Gold's expression was unreadable. "This decision, for you, isn't about the attacks then, is it?"

"No," said Granger, "I've given this considerable thought for several years now."

"And it took these hostilities for the *Bringloidi* prime minister to come around to this way of thinking."

Granger smiled. "Ironic, isn't it?"

Before Gold could agree, he was interrupted by a chiming sound, and then a woman's voice. *"Lense to Gold."*

He tapped the badge on his chest and replied, "Gold here."

"Are you still with Prime Minister Granger?"

"Yes, he's right here."

"Good. I need to speak with him, and Ms. Odell, too."

"What is it?" Gold asked. "You've discovered something

about this bioweapon?" Gold frowned when his question was answered with silence. "Lense?"

"Yes and no," the woman responded.

Gold exchanged a confused look with Granger. "What does that mean?"

"Yes, I've discovered something about the virus," Lense's voice answered. *"And no, it's not a weapon."*

CHAPTER

9

"Viruses are, by their nature, highly lethal agents, and have been used militarily for centuries." Lense sat on one long side of the observation lounge table, with Captain Gold at his spot at the head, and the two prime ministers, along with their health minister, sitting opposite her. Lense made eye contact with each of them as she spoke, except Odell. "Genetic engineering can make viruses that propagate faster, that spread more easily or are more resistant to treatment. . . . but the reason there are biological weapons in the first place is because these start out as dangerous biological organisms."

"Except this Klingon bug, you said, would only cause a slight fever," said Gold. "That's why all the gen-engineering you saw, no?"

"That was what I assumed. The thing is, someone with

a mind to do so would only need to splice one short gene sequence from, say, a common rhinovirus into the *rop'ngor* genome to translate its effects from Klingons to humans. The virus that was loosed in the Life Science Center has over three hundred such splices, and still counting."

That seemed to surprise the Mariposans, but they were content to listen and allow Gold to continue asking the questions. "Would that be so it only affected Mariposans, and left Bringloidi immune?"

Lense shook her head. "Even though the alterations are designed to target and mutate specific DNA patterns, it still would be a case of overthinking the issue. The Mariposans and Bringloidi lived in two completely different ecosystems for close to three hundred years. There are physiological differences between the two—trace elements in the blood, mineral buildups and deficiencies— relatively minor distinctions, but pronounced enough on a physiochemical level that, again, a fraction of the gen-engineering done here would have sufficed. No, the person who reprogrammed this bug had a purpose other than killing this certain group of people."

"Begging your pardon, Doctor, but it *does* kill!" Odell said, her eyes flashing with exasperation. "By the hundreds, it kills! How do any of these discoveries say that it *wasn't* a weapon?"

It took some effort for Lense to meet Brenna Odell's eyes. "I haven't yet catalogued all the recombinant sequences in the virus, let alone figured out why those specific alterations were made. But they were less directed at *who* the virus can infect than *how* it affects them." Lense took a deep breath before continuing. "While *rop'ngor*, in its natural state, spreads itself indiscriminately throughout the host's endocrine system, this altered virus appears designed to target its mutagenic effects on the hosts' reproductive glands and organs."

Wilson Granger's entire face seemed to fall in slow motion. "Oh my God . . ." he whispered, as Odell's hand went to her mouth and her eyes went wide, and Victor Granger frowned with great consternation.

Gold displayed a different kind of shock. "Their reproductive systems? So someone wanted to cause fertility problems in the Mariposans?"

"No, Captain," Granger said quietly. "They wanted to solve those problems."

A long uncomfortable silence settled over the room. Both Wilson Granger and Brenna Odell made pointed efforts not to look at each other.

"It was Corsi who discovered the discrepancies in the colony records. Deaths had been covered up, all Mariposan women, all pregnant at the time of death."

"It was during the first years after reunion," Wilson Granger said, not defensively, but simply matter-of-fact. "It was already a challenge to convince my people to perform the procreative act. We tried to contain those stories that would have discouraged them." Odell said nothing, her eyes downcast, trying to hide the pain in them.

"Based on Corsi's tip, I did my own investigating," Lense continued, now directing her report to Gold. "The record of miscarriages, stillbirths, and other genetic birth defects . . ." Lense trailed off, fighting with all her willpower from betraying the fears and emotions that had been pressing on her chest in recent days.

"But, there are children all over the place down there," Gold said, his tone one of disbelief.

Victor Granger stepped in when Lense couldn't bring herself to answer immediately. "All products of Bring-loidi-Bringloidi pairing. Mariposan-Bringloidi couples . . ." he said, giving a brief sideways glance to his duplicate and his partner. "Well. It seems that, where cloning technology was able to compensate for some degree of genetic degradation, the natural procreation process is infinitely more particular about how much damage it will tolerate."

"Can't have kids." Mara glared at her, pitiless eyes set in a grotesquely deformed face. "Kornaks, us. Oh, we get a couple. But usually something's wrong with them. Most of them die."

Lense clenched her jaw and willed the memory of the Jabari woman's words back down. She had to stay in the here and now, concentrate on the many instead of the one.

"However," the shift in Victor Granger's tone helped to pull Lense back, "nobody in my hospital was working on any such research, not that *I* know of. And, regardless of whatever discoveries Dr. Lense has come up with, the fact remains that it was released in an explosion in the middle of the Life Sciences Center, and that it killed two hundred people."

Lense bit back her annoyance at Dr. Granger's arrogance, and as calmly as she could, told him, "Commander Corsi learned that Dr. Sandra Vallis, one of the experts she identified as capable of designing and engineering this mutagen, was also in the former cloning labs at the time of the initial explosion. I think it's reasonable to believe she was using those facilities to carry out this research surreptitiously."

"And why would she do that behind my back?" Granger demanded.

"To avoid raising hopes prematurely," the other Granger answered, "among other reasons. From the first, Sandra was one of the strongest supporters for a united colony and a united people." He gave the health minister a pointed look, and got a scowl back in return. "How tragic that her work would've ended this way."

"So then . . . this whole horrible business came of some . . . *accident?*" Brenna Odell looked at the others around the table for someone to dispute that conclusion. She closed her eyes briefly, and muttered something incomprehensible just under her breath. Opening her eyes again, she then turned to Gold with an accusatory glare. "Now? Now do you understand why we need to be rid of these blasted machines?"

The captain gaped back at her, stunned. "Minister Odell, your argument before was that your technology was being misused for destructive means. Now that we've learned that there was no intention of doing harm . . ."

"There's an old, old saying about good intentions, Captain. Over two hundred people were killed. How am I supposed to feel better about that, knowing those deaths were accidental?"

"Madam Prime Minister," Lense interrupted. "Before you make this decision, you should know that Dr. Vallis, I believe, was getting close to a working treatment."

That stopped her short. "Say that again?"

Actually, Lense reflected, *I shouldn't have said it the once.* The most she could honestly say for Sandra

Vallis's mutagen, based on the limited amount of time she'd spent studying the altered virus—most of that trying to determine what it was and how to kill it—was that it was slightly closer to a working treatment than natural *rop'ngor* would be. But, if it meant an end to the tragedies that had been haunting these people all these years . . . "Sandra Vallis's work shows great promise, and I believe it should be pursued further. If it were possible to recover anything from the damaged lab—notes, samples, equipment—I could re-create—"

"Re-create?!" Odell blurted. "Are you mad? After the hell we've been through, you want to start this all over?"

Lense assured her, "It would be under the most stringent safeties and controls, of course."

"Oh, of course." Odell sneered. "More grand promises from the bloody Federation!"

"Brenna!" Her husband put a hand on her shoulder and turned her in her swivel chair to face him. "Are you even listening to what the woman is saying? She thinks she can cure us!"

"That's not what she said, Wilson; that's what you *wanted* to hear. 'Technology will save us again!' It's like the Sirens' song for you!"

"Madam Prime Minister, with all respect," Lense interrupted, "this really is your best hope for saving this colony. Unless you want to subject more women like Frances DiCamino to their fates, or more children like Danielle to theirs."

"What? How . . . ?" Brenna Odell's eyes turned as hard and cold as winter's frozen ground, and Lense found it impossible to look away from them. She had found, in the course of her investigation into Corsi's tip, the birth record for Danielle Willa Odell-Granger, dated some forty weeks after the *Enterprise*'s departure from Mariposa. The infant's death certificate had been issued the following day. "How dare you try to play my emotions like that?" the Bringloidi woman demanded, the heat of her outrage still not melting the cold of her glare. "You have no right! You have no idea, with your lofty position on your grand spaceship, what I carry in my heart every day!"

Lense felt as if she were pinned to the back of her chair, the air squeezed out of her. No, she didn't know; she didn't *want* to know, couldn't even bring herself to imagine . . . to even *think* . . .

"All right," Gold said, the sound of his voice pulling Lense back into the moment. "You want us to relieve you of the technology that set off this tragedy. Fine. I assume, then, that what we decide to do with it once we have it, you have no objections?" The captain gave Lense a look, making sure she understood and accepted this proposal. She somehow managed a slight nod for him.

"There was extensive damage to that lab," Victor Granger told them, frowning. "I wouldn't count on there being anything of worth left to recover."

"That sounds like just the sort of impossible challenge the rest of this ship's complement has been waiting for," Gold told him, flashing a broad grin. "So, if there's nothing else . . ." he said as he rose, effectively preempting whatever "else" might have been brought up.

They all rose and started to file out of the observation lounge. The new security guard, Tomo Kim, stood just outside the door to escort the colony officials back to the transporter room. Victor Granger, however, fell back beside Lense. "Doctor, may I have a word, please?" he asked in what Lense considered an uncharacteristically civil tone. She hesitated for a moment, then nodded to Kim, who took the cue and moved off with the two other colonists in tow.

Once alone, the health minister said, "Dr. Lense, I want to formally thank you for the work you did to bring our epidemic under control. I also want to apologize for my prejudiced and distrustful initial attitude."

Lense understood this was more of a political nicety than a genuine admission of fault. But the fact that he had said the words at all, whatever the motive, was more than she would have expected. "Thank you, Doctor. I appreciate your saying so."

"I see you now as a dedicated physician concerned for the well-being of others," he continued, perhaps a bit more sincerely now, "which is why I ask you now . . . please, just walk away from this."

Lense blinked as she took a second to register that request. "Excuse me?"

"The last time the Federation 'helped' us with problems related to the propagation of the Mariposan people, they stripped us of our most highly advanced technologies, and placed the burden of four hundred backward bumpkins upon us. This time, we prefer to take care of our problems by ourselves."

Lense clenched her teeth to hold back a few choice words about Granger's "backward bumpkins" comment. "It is going to be a long, hard time before your medical community recovers from this incident," she said when she finally trusted herself to open her mouth, "and I've already spent more time studying this gen-eng virus than anyone else alive. What possible reason could you have for cavalierly dismissing my help?"

"Because it comes under Brenna Odell's technophobic terms," Victor Granger sighed. "And that's too high a price to pay. If I stand back and allow you to take this over, in a nonemergency situation, then I am tacitly agreeing with her that we cannot be trusted with our own technology."

Lense shook her head. "No, that wouldn't be the case at all. These are singular circumstances."

"Dr. Lense, do not patronize me," Granger snapped. "I've been dealing with the woman since she and her people arrived here. She was an arrogant, pigheaded authoritarian when she was operating from out of her father's shadow, and she's only gotten worse since he died. Believe me, she won't rest until she has things her way."

Lense fumed. "I will concede that you grasp the finer details of the local political situation better than I do. However, I really don't give a good hot damn; all I'm concerned about is the continued health of this colony."

"I am talking about the continued health of this colony, dammit!" Veins were now pulsing visibly at Granger's temples. "Odell will use this as precedent to have everything else taken away. Before long, we'll be reduced to treating patients with leeches and prayers. If this were your sickbay, and your captain was asking the Romulans to take charge of your work, you would be just as adamant in defending it as I am."

Lense glowered at Granger. "I don't quite see the parallel between Starfleet and the Romulans," she said hotly. "Although, if they had any expertise in the health concerns of cloned humans, I wouldn't refuse their help."

"This isn't help you're offering! This is enfeeblement!"

Lense sighed, and tapped her combadge. "Lense to Kim. Please return to the observation lounge. Dr. Granger is ready to leave."

"So, that's your answer?" Granger asked, the contempt not so much dripping from his voice as it was overflowing.

Lense met his haughty expression with a hard-eyed stare of her own. "Doctor, I'm very sorry you feel this way. But I am not going to simply walk away from a major health-care crisis, particularly not when said crisis would then be overseen by such a shortsighted, self-important ass as yourself. Now if you'll excuse me," she said, as the lounge doors slid open and Kim reappeared, "I have work to do." She turned her back on both men and stormed out of the room.

CHAPTER
10

Domenica Corsi's hands glided easily over her console, guiding the shuttle *Shirley* planetward through the dark of a thick cloud cover. Her jaw was hard-set, though not out of any concerns about flying blind on instruments only; the fact that she was on a shuttle in the first place was reason enough for concern. "Why can't we just beam into the cloning lab, grab what we need to, and beam right back out?" she had asked, not unreasonably, during the pre-mission briefing.

"If there are any identifiable traces of viral DNA that survived the explosion and fire," Lense had explained, "they're going to be extremely damaged and fragile. The risk of damaging them further by subjecting them to the matter-energy conversion process of the transporter is too great."

And of course, risks to random molecules trump the risks to people, Corsi thought ruefully. To make matters worse, they would need to put down at a large, highly trafficked gateway into the Capital Complex in order to get in and out of the cloning labs. Even on the friendliest of worlds, drawing the attention of spontaneous crowds was more risk than was wise to take.

The shuttle broke through the cloud ceiling into only slightly less darkness. It was about an hour before sunrise, and the overcast skies dulled the light beyond the eastern horizon. Yet there were already a number of people milling around the circular brick courtyard that was the convergence point of several rural roads leading into the complex. Vendors were setting up kiosks and carts with merchandise and food, anticipating the early morning influx of foot traffic. Also from their altitude, Corsi could see local farmers out and about taking care of their early morning chores . . . now distracted by the descending spacecraft, and starting to drift in the direction of their landing site. "Aw, crap," she muttered.

Gomez reached over from her spot in the copilot's seat to give her forearm a quick squeeze. She gave the commander a quick sideways glance, and saw her reassuring smile. After the fiasco at the prime ministers' residence, the commander had just been glad that she and her people were getting a second chance to prove themselves, no matter how odious the engineer in her found their mission. *Well, if she can grin and bear it*, Corsi thought, *so can I*.

"All right, people," Gomez swiveled in her seat to face the rest of the mission team seated astern. "We've already started attracting attention, so the faster we get in and out, the better. Are we all clear on our objectives?"

"Crystal," Makk Vinx answered, while Soloman and Andrew Angelopoulos simply nodded.

The fourth team member, though, seemed lost in thought. "Doctor?"

"Identify and recover forensic biological samples, while you assess the state of the equipment, Soloman searches for research files, and Corsi's team investigates the cause of the initial explosion."

A quiet warning bell went off in the back of Corsi's mind as she listened to the doctor's dull recitation. Something, she knew, had been bothering Lense since her return to the *da Vinci*, something that happened on that transdimensional planet she'd been stranded on. She refused to talk about it, though. Lense had always, as long as they'd served together, been a very private person, slow to open up to others, holding everything close to the chest. *Probably why we manage to deal with each other in close quarters so well . . .*

She put it out of her mind when Gomez seemed satisfied with the doctor's response, and concentrated instead on landing. She switched from thrusters to antigravs, and guided the *Shirley* down onto the brick surface of the courtyard with only the quietest of thumps. "Okay," she said, standing out of her seat and moving to the shuttle hatch. "Let's get this done."

A group of thirty or so onlookers had gathered around the edge of the courtyard, ignoring the merchants and the scent of cooking breakfast foods from one of the vendor carts. "Good morning," Corsi greeted them as she led the rest of the team toward the complex entrance.

"Please, just go about your business. We have a few matters inside that—"

"What are you doing, landing that thing there?" A
bearded Bringloidi man moved to intercept Corsi, causing her and the rest of the team to stop short. "You can't
just park that thing in the middle of the plaza!"

"I'm sorry for the inconvenience. We won't be long, I
promise."

"What sort of business do you have here?" shouted another man, stepping out ahead of the rest of the crowd.
This one was a Mariposan of the Hammond line, with
the same dark skin and muscular build they'd seen on
Kevin Hammond and his security force. "You here to
steal more of our machines?"

Corsi did not care for the tone behind that challenge,
nor for the supportive murmur that arose from the
crowd in response. "We're not here to steal anything,"
she answered, as she brought her right hand behind her
back and made a subtle gesture. Vinx and Angelopoulos
shifted position so that they and Corsi formed a loose
semicircle around the rest of the team.

"Oh, no?" Another Mariposan, a woman with shoulder-
length auburn hair, stepped forward now, approaching
Vinx. "This one was at my house yesterday, practically
accusing me of being behind the attack two days ago,
saying my name was on some list and threatening to take
my biosynthesizer away."

Vinx's eyes narrowed, but he held himself motionless.
"Hey, I was just doin' my job. We got no beef with you no
more, so why don'cha just step back, sister?"

"Who do you think you are, pushing us around like

this?" she demanded, taking another step forward, chin thrust out.

"I axed you nice already, lady. Now petrify, or I'll—"

"Vinx," Corsi barked, though she kept her eyes on the crowd, which seemed to have grown quite a bit in just the past few seconds. "People, we are here to do a job, at the request of Prime Ministers Granger and Odell. Now, please—"

"Now, don't you be lying to these good people, Miss Corsi."

The crowd rippled before her, people stepping aside for Reade Latta to make his way up to the front of the group. The acting security minister tipped his hat cordially to his Starfleet counterpart. "Word travels quickly, lass: Dr. Victor has already told us what really transpired up on that ship of yours."

"And what did he tell you?" Corsi asked, even though it didn't really matter; whatever it was had inflamed the populace, turning whatever degree of goodwill they may have had up until now against them.

"That you think we're some child race. That we can't be trusted to take care of ourselves."

"That son of a bitch," Lense said from behind her, in a louder voice than she probably intended.

"No, he's not that," said the bearded Bringloidi man. "He may be a navelless freak, but he ain't nobody's son."

Most of the crowd laughed, with the exception of the several Mariposans. "Watch your mouth, 'Gloidi . . ."

"Why don't y' make me, y' overgrown Lysserian larva?"

"Put it aside, both of you," Latta snapped, and to Corsi's mild surprise, they obeyed him. Obviously, she realized darkly, Starfleet was considered enough a common enemy that whatever other civil conflicts existed here paled in comparison.

This is not *a good thing*.

"Dr. Lense?" Corsi said out of the corner of her mouth, and took a couple small steps backward. Her eyes stayed on the crowd before them, just as their defiant eyes stayed warily on her.

She heard a pair of familiar footsteps move close behind her. "Commander?" Lense's voice asked.

"I'm not liking the way this situation is shaping up." She spoke in a low, neutral tone, and kept her face, still turned to the mob, an unreadable mask.

"Could have been better," Lense agreed.

Corsi allowed herself a slight nod. "They really don't have navels?"

"Why would a clone need one?"

"None of them look like they're armed. We pull our phasers, they're likely to disperse."

Lense frowned. "Are you asking my opinion on tactics?"

"I'm asking if this is important enough that we go down that road," said Corsi. She understood Lense's determination to follow through on what she had started, and to do what she could to save the future of these people. However, even the threat of using weapons against a nonviolent, unarmed gathering was a drastic act, one that Corsi was not eager to take. "If this clone doctor is this dead-set against us getting access, it might not be a bad idea to rethink our strategy."

Lense sighed behind her. Corsi understood how she felt. The idea of backing down from bullies, even as a strategic retreat, stuck in her craw as well.

Then it occurred to Corsi that what she had heard from the doctor wasn't a sigh, but a deep bracing breath. This did not occur to her, however, until after she saw what Lense was bracing herself to do. She stepped right up past Corsi, up directly in front of Reade Latta. "Sir, I'm Elizabeth Lense, chief medical officer of the *da Vinci*."

Latta nodded. "I've heard of you."

"Yes, I'm sure Victor Granger had plenty to say about me," said Lense with a sardonic smile. "But, sir, you have some firsthand experience with Starfleet officers, don't you? While you were aboard the *Enterprise?*"

Latta didn't answer, but Corsi could see that Lense had struck a chord. "You've seen for yourself the kind of people we are," the doctor continued, also sounding confident that she was reaching the man. "The kind of people who would take you in, feed you, take care of your sick. We've helped you in the past; all we're asking now is that you let us h—"

"*Incoming!*"

Instinctively, Corsi grabbed Lense by the shoulder and pulled her back, even as she spun in Vinx's direction, then toward a low grassy knoll to the north of the plaza where he was looking. The Iotian guard had likewise grabbed Commander Gomez and forced her to the ground, just a second before an arc of orange flame flew over their heads and struck the hull of the shuttle. There was the sound of shattering glass, then the whoosh of an expanding sphere of fire.

"*Down! Get down!*" Corsi shouted as her phaser came out and she swept their surroundings with her eyes. Sounds of screams and general panic and fleeing erupted at Corsi's back as the entire starboard side of the shuttle lit up ablaze from the Molotov cocktail that had exploded on impact with the hull. The shuttle itself, designed to withstand the heat of atmospheric descent, would not be damaged by such a low-tech weapon.

Its level of sophistication, though, meant nothing to the team of six trapped out in the open, now easy targets.

Well, guess all that worry about biosynthesizers was for nothing, Corsi thought ruefully.

"Another one!" shouted Angelopoulos, this time looking in the opposite direction from which the first missile had come. He fired his phaser at the incoming firebomb, scoring a direct hit in midair. The blast obliterated the container and most of its contents, but resulted in enough of a fireball to set off another wave of frightened screams from the civilians. Meanwhile, Corsi motioned for her guards to tighten their formation around the rest of the away team, and went to help Lense up and into the cluster.

But the doctor was gone.

She spat out an Italian obscenity that was a favorite of her uncle's, then called out, "Lense!" She spared a second of watching for additional firebombs to scan the now largely abandoned courtyard. She almost missed it, but Corsi caught a brief glance of a blue-trimmed Starfleet jumpsuit. Its wearer was apparently being led by another dark-haired figure, down the southeast road and out of sight around a thick copse of trees.

She uttered another colorful metaphor as a full volley of firebombs came arcing toward them.

★ ★ ★

The rough bricks of the courtyard scraped away the skin of Lense's palms, as well as ripping through the knees of her uniform. She looked up from where Corsi had forced her onto the ground, and then blinked at the bright explosion that erupted against the shuttle hull. She winced as blossoms of color floated before her eyes, and almost failed to notice Corsi's feet, as the security chief paced in a tight arc while scanning the near horizon. Lense scrabbled out of the way just quickly enough to avoid being tripped over.

"Another one!" Lense looked up in time to see the second firebomb explode in midair, raining debris and sparks on the people below. Without thinking, Lense pushed herself onto her feet, and ran against the scattering crowd to check on any potentially injured parties. A few scorched shards of glass littered the ground when she reached the spot, but no bodies or blood, thank God.

She stopped to take in the courtyard as a whole. Vendor carts had been tipped over, fruits and other goods spilled across the ground. One of the hot food carts was now ablaze and billowing dark smoke. The majority of the former crowd had pushed their way into the safety of the Capital Complex, guided by Reade Latta and his makeshift security team in between breaking up minor scuffles between individual Bringloidi and Mariposans. Witnessing this scene, Lense almost wondered whether this wasn't all for the best, to just walk away, wash her hands of these people . . .

"Dr. Elizabeth!"

Lense turned to see Kara McClay rushing toward her from behind one of the abandoned merchant stands.

Lense started toward her, meeting her halfway. "Kara, are you all right? Are you hurt?"

The young woman didn't answer, but instead took the doctor's left hand and, gesturing with the free hand to follow, led Lense away from the courtyard, following one of the unpaved roads leading from the complex. Lense went without hesitation, trusting the urgency of McClay's demeanor, and so was confused when they veered off the path and into the shade of a small grove of trees and stopped. She looked around for an injured colonist or something else to explain why she'd been led here, and noticed that they were out of sight of the courtyard and Complex. "Kara? What is this about?"

"I needed to talk to you, before you left," she said. "You came back to try and find Dr. Sandra's research?"

Lense nodded, wondering what all this drama was leading up to. That question was answered when, after casting a quick look around them for other prying eyes, Kara reached into a large pocket in the front of her skirt and pulled out an antique wooden box. Smiling, she held it up for Lense and removed the lid.

"Oh . . ." The doctor's breath caught as she saw inside the box a collection of plastic disks, six centimeters in diameter and strawberry red in color—Yoshimitsu Systems data disks.

After weighing her options, Corsi turned, aimed her phaser, and fired on the shuttle.

The alcohol residue from the Molotov cocktail disintegrated in the low-power energy beam, the sudden molecular phase change robbing the flame of its fuel while leaving the hull unmarred. "All right, go! Go!" she shouted at the S.C.E. team members, then to Vinx and Angelopoulos, without a pause for breath, "Keep them covered!"

She couldn't help but catch the insolent look Angelopoulos shot her way before turning his focus on Soloman. Only a couple of weeks earlier, she had given him a harsh dressing-down for failing to stick with Tev during the mission to Artemis IX. Now, she had essentially repeated the same mistake. She couldn't worry about that now, though. They needed to get out of the fire zone, then find Lense, which was going to be easier from the air than on foot.

Soloman ran the ten meters to the cover of the shuttle, bent over double to present as low a profile as possible. Gomez adopted the same posture, placing her hands at the small of the Bynar's back as she brought up the rear. The two guards kept pace beside them, while the commander took up the rear position, visually scanning for further assaults. The plaza had been almost completely deserted by this point, the frightened screams replaced now with chants of "Our Mariposa! Our Mariposa!" from the surrounding hillocks.

"And you're welcome to it," Corsi muttered through clenched teeth. Her eyes flicked briefly to the spot where she saw Lense disappear. *There better be an injured colonist out there you just saved*, she thought. *If not, dear roommate, you're going to have hell to pay.*

Her thoughts were interrupted then by the far-off sound of a throaty battle cry. This was soon blended with what sounded like a hundred more such cries echoing in a long tunnel, followed by the rapidly approaching pounding of stampeding feet. "Get them inside, now!" Corsi shouted as her eyes fixed on the Capital Complex entryway, watching a small army charge for the outside.

Vinx all but threw the diminutive Soloman in as he reached the hatch, and Gomez leapt in after, moving quickly for the cockpit. The engines came to life just as Corsi saw the leading edge of the mob clear the arch of the portal, with Reade Latta leading the charge.

Both Vinx and Angelopoulos hesitated before following the others into the shuttle, neither wanting to be the first to leave their colleagues to face the approaching mob. Corsi was about to bark at them for holding up . . . but stopped when she saw that the approaching mob was not, in fact, approaching them.

Instead, they had split into two groups, each moving for either side of the plaza, where the bomb throwers were hidden. Corsi watched as a squad of Bringloidi rushed the hillock to the north, weapons blazing, while another squad of cloned gunmen climbed the grassy knoll at the other end of the plaza. The chants were replaced by screams, and an orange glow blossomed from behind the rise, apparently from a lit firebomb either dropped or shot apart while still in the assailant's hand.

Meanwhile, Reade Latta marched up to Corsi, a swaggering spring to his step. Clearly, this entire episode had invigorated him. "Are you and yours all right?"

Corsi nodded, watching as flames and smoke lifted above the hill to the south. The Mariposan crew roughly dragged a pair of teenage Bringloidi boys up over the rise back toward the plaza, one crying out and holding his burnt and bloody hands out in front of him. "Who are they? Dieghanists?"

Latta snapped his head around, eyes blazing. "You haven't caused enough trouble, you gotta be looking to stir up s'more?" he practically growled at her.

"What?"

"You want to know who they are? They're nobody. They're a bunch of hoodlums you got all riled up with yer pokin' and yer proddin'—"

"That *we* got riled up?"

"Well, who were they attackin', now?"

Corsi caught herself before she could be dragged any further into this purposeless conversation. She took a deep breath, turned, and ushered Vinx and Angelopoulos into the shuttle ahead of her. She climbed up front as Vinx shut the hatch, and folded herself into the pilot's seat beside Gomez. "Let's find Lense and get the hell away from this damned planet."

Lense looked up from the box to the young woman's face, and knew these disks held Sandra Vallis's research notes. "Kara . . . how did you . . . ?"

"She always wanted to be sure she had backup copies of her work in a safe place. She trusted me . . ."

Lense was overwhelmed by the sudden transition from hopelessness to wide-eyed optimism. *My God*, she thought. *This is too good to be—*

And, as if in karmic punishment for that thought, Kara snapped the lid back on the box and pulled it to her chest, clutching her long fingers tightly around the edges. She looked up into Lense's eyes, her expression showing a graveness that seemed beyond her years.

"Take me with you."

Lense's eyebrows arched. "What?"

"I need to get away from here," she said plainly. "I know I haven't had a lot of formal education, but I'm always reading stuff off the subspace, and I'm a hard worker, and if I were only given a chance to do more—"

"Kara. . . ." Lense said, searching for the softest way of dissuading her, one that would not lose her the disks. "If it were up to me . . . this isn't the kind of thing where you can just make a snap decision."

"Dr. Elizabeth, please," she said, in a tone that sounded not so much like a plea as simple, weary despair. "I can't stay here. I can't. You've seen how Dr. Victor treats me. Like being Bringloidi makes me less of a person. Even Dr. Sandra, when she was mentoring me—she wasn't so bad, but she still . . ." She stopped herself, uneasy speaking ill of the dead. "I'll never be anything more than what I am if I stay here."

Lense bit her lower lip as she considered the young woman. As she did, her combadge came to life. *"Corsi to Lense."*

She tapped her badge. "Lense here."

"We're airborne and headed for your location, Doctor." Even as Corsi related this news, Lense could already hear the humming engines of the small craft growing close. *"What's your situation? Everything okay?"*

"Yeah, fine," she frowned, then looked back to Kara, wearing a hope-against-hope look on her face. Lense sighed and her shoulders dropped. There was no guarantee, even with Sandra Vallis's files, that she would be able to save the Mariposan gene pool. But if she could save just one person . . .

"We are going to be taking on a passenger, though, Commander," she said, which drew a wide grin as a response.

CHAPTER
11

David Gold tabbed open the door to the guest cabin. He saw the young woman who'd been sitting on the single bunk, staring at the stars out the portal, immediately jump to her feet at the soft hydraulic hiss and turn to face him. "Kara McClay. I'm David Gold, captain of the *da Vinci*."

"Yes, sir," she replied, putting her hand out for him to take. "I saw you earlier in the lab with Dr. Elizabeth." Her palm was dry and she made strong eye contact, but Gold could clearly tell that she was as nervous as hell having to talk with him.

Gold resisted his natural urge to put her at ease. He folded his hands behind his back instead, and slowly paced the cabin. It had the same layout as his own captain's quarters—a single bunk, desk and chair, set of shelves, computer, replicator, and small 'fresher. Otherwise, it was completely Spartan, with none of the homey touches his or any of the other crew quarters had. Perhaps that would make a subconscious impression on the girl.

After about a minute of silence, Gold turned to face McClay again. "Have a seat." She settled back onto the edge of the bunk, while Gold leaned on the edge of the desk. "Ms. McClay, I want to tell you that I appreciate your help in recovering Dr. Vallis's research."

"You're welcome, Captain," she said with a shy smile.

Gold did not return the smile. "What I don't particularly appreciate, however, is the fact that you used this material, which Prime Ministers Granger and Odell had already granted us unconditionally, to extort a commitment from one of my officers."

It took a moment for McClay to find her tongue and respond. "I know that what I did wasn't very fair to Dr. Elizabeth . . . or to you, sir. If you wanted to, you could put me into your transporter and send me right back and I couldn't do anything about it. All I can do is . . . ask for your mercy."

Gold couldn't help but snort at that. "I'm sorry, I wasn't laughing at you. It's just that, even as a captain, I'm not used to quite *that* degree of deference, not on this ship, anyhow." He paused, turning more serious. "I want to make sure you understand exactly what it is you're getting yourself into here, Ms. McClay. You've lived a very isolated life here, and on Bringloid before. It's a very different universe out there. Reading about it is a very different thing from living it. And, you're going to be living it largely on your own, with no one to rely on but yourself. Are you ready for that?"

McClay lifted her chin and looked the captain straight in the eye, all hint of her earlier nervousness dissolved away. "Yes," she answered. "More than I can tell you."

Lense was waiting in the corridor when Gold emerged from the ship's guest quarters. "Well?" she asked expectantly.

Gold gave her a crooked smile. "This is something they teach at Starfleet Medical? How to identify smart, promising young people on backwater planets?"

Lense looked nonplussed. "I'm sorry, sir?"

"Private joke. Forget it," he replied as he started toward the turbolift, the doctor falling in step beside him. He had been quite surprised by Kara McClay. He'd seen her at work in Lense's ward earlier, and had listened in bemusement as the doctor, en route back to the ship on the *Shirley*, rambled enthusiastically about the potential she saw in the young Bringloidi. But when he'd gone into his chat with McClay, it was not with a good feeling about her.

"As you said," the captain told Lense as they entered the lift, "given all the circumstances, she is quite an impressive young woman."

Seconds later they entered sickbay, and headed for the diagnostic lab. Gomez and Soloman were already absorbed in their work. The Bynar was hunched over a bulky piece of auxiliary equipment sitting on top of the table console, with a long coil of opticable running between it and the panel interface. Gomez, meanwhile, was studying readouts on the large wall-sized monitors, tracking the progress of their download. And curiously, the EMH had been activated, and was standing immobile in the corner, a strangely pensive look on its face. Gomez looked up as they entered, pushing a lock of dark hair away from her face. "Captain."

Gold nodded back. "Gomez. How are we doing?"

Gomez simply sighed, while Soloman turned from his console and said, "We've so far downloaded the data from fifteen of sixty-seven disks." The machine in front of him beeped, and a small door popped open. Soloman extracted a red disk and replaced it with another from a small wooden box sitting at his left elbow. "Unfortunately, we are restrained by the physical limitations of this technology, in regard to the speed of data retrieval."

"How long until we have all the data in?" Gold asked.

"Approximately one hour, thirty-eight minutes."

"Which is why we brought the EMH on line," Gomez said.

"Yes, I was wondering," said Lense, looking over to the holographic doctor.

Noting the shift of focus toward him, the hologram straightened to attention. "Dr. Vallis's notes on her *rop'ngor* research and experimentation are being loaded directly into my program matrix, where I am able to organize each new file into a more dynamic systematization. This will allow for more immediate analysis of the work as a whole, and quicker identification of the most promising avenues for further research."

Gold nodded, impressed. Though the EMH program had lost the equivalent of several years of practical experience due to the damage done at Galvan VI, the refurbished version seemed somewhat more capable of adapting and learning than "Emmett" had been.

No matter how impressive everyone's efforts, however, Gold knew they were likely to fall short.

"Good work, people. Carry on." He then turned to Lense and, with a tilt of his head, indicated her office. Once the door slid shut behind them, he said, "Lense, assuming Vallis had been working on this problem for the last ten or so years with . . . let's say mixed results, how likely do you think that, even with all this, the cure is going to immediately reveal itself to you?"

"Honestly? Not great, Captain. But that's not reason—"

"—not reason not to try, no, of course not," Gold said. "Here's the thing, Lense. Mariposa has been handed off from the S.C.E. to the Diplomatic Corps. They have a ship, the *Hammarskjold*, en route right now."

"I thought the prime ministers were still dead-set against any negotiation; they want what they want, period."

Gold frowned. "Yes, but that's for Captain Conley and Ambassador Crane to deal with now. We get to deal, instead, with a failing seawater desalinization plant on Drovoer II. Once you've briefed the *Hammarskjold*'s CMO on whatever you find in these files—"

"No."

Gold stopped, and simply stared at Lense with both eyebrows raised.

"Sir, I have an obligation—"

Gold cut her off. "Your first obligation is to this ship and her crew. I know that you want to see this thing through, but as long as there is no immediate medical threat, I can't justify delaying—"

"Then I request a transfer."

Again, Lense stunned him into silence. "Say that again?"

"I will not walk away from this, Captain. You will not make me walk away from this."

Gold studied her, searching for whatever it was she wasn't saying. "What is this all about, Lense?"

"What is this about?" she echoed, sounding incredulous.

"That's what I said."

Lense blinked at him, her head shaking like a miscalibrated warp coil. "It's about . . . about miscarriages, and stillbirths, and . . . and . . . fatal birth defects and women . . . women dying . . ."

"No, Lense. What is this *really* about?"

Lense lowered her brow and all but sneered at him. "I don't know, Captain, why don't you tell me? If you don't believe me, *you* tell me what it's about!"

"All right. It has something to do with what happened on the Jabari world."

Her face turned to stone. "Oh, really?"

"Really. Because whatever it is, it's been eating at you since well before we got to Mariposa."

Lense snorted in disdain. "Excuse me, Captain. I have work to do."

She tried to slip around him to the door, but Gold grabbed on to her upper arm and restrained her. "You painted a hellish picture of life on that planet, Lense. War, death, filth, disease, hopelessness. But you didn't tell everything in your debriefing, did you?"

Lense stood stock-still, saying nothing and keeping her eyes forward, avoiding Gold's.

"You're doing yourself no good keeping this bottled up, Elizabeth. You know that."

She turned to the captain, her eyes deep and filled with barely contained emotion . . .

. . . and with a hard yank, pulled her arm free from his grasp. She glared at him with unreadable eyes for a long extra moment, then without a word walked out of her office. Gold remained where he stood, replaying the entire exchange in his mind and hoping to convince himself he had not, by reaching out to her, pushed her away past the point of retrieval.

Carol Abramowitz watched as Kara McClay poked unenthusiastically at the plate of *gespar* in front of her. The young woman had purposely selected an alien, exotic-sounding dish from the replicator menu, and appeared now to regret it. "Vulcan food is something of an acquired taste," Abramowitz said, as she scraped the last bits of icoberry torte off her plate. "If you want something else, go ahead. It's no problem."

"No," McClay answered, laying down her fork and picking up a teacup. "Just not as hungry as I thought I was."

The two of them had the mess hall to themselves, after having completed the grand tour of the ship. The cultural specialist was usually not the first crewperson chosen to show visitors around a starship, especially not on a ship full of tech-heads who could actually tell you why access tunnels were called "Jefferies tubes." But Captain Gold had asked Abramowitz to do the honors, in part, she suspected, so she could see that the joined Mariposan-Bringloidi colony had managed to produce at least one nice, bright, well-adjusted young person.

She might have been more encouraged if this same young woman wasn't now leaving said colony.

"Nerves?" Abramowitz asked, grabbing both their dishes and returning them to the replicator for recycling.

"You could say that," she said. "It's like seeing all the different futures that might happen, and knowing you have almost no control over which one."

"All you can do is make the best decision you can, and hope everything else pans out."

McClay nodded. "Dr. Elizabeth, she's a good doctor, isn't she?"

"One of the best," Abramowitz said as she sat back down across from the Bringloidi woman. "Top of her class at Starfleet Medical. Completely dedicated to her patients. I'm sure, if there's any way to help your people, she'll find it."

Something odd flickered across McClay's face then, in reaction, Abramowitz thought, to the term "your people." She had overheard Lense making the case for taking McClay aboard to the captain, describing the animosity of some of her Mariposan patients toward McClay, and the young woman's poise in its face. As well adjusted as she may have seemed on the surface, she had probably accumulated her share of emotional scars over the last decade of childhood.

Whatever unpleasant thought had passed through McClay's mind just then, it was gone now, and she simply nodded. "But you think they need more than just medical help, don't you?"

Abramowitz sighed. "It's a difficult process. People have to adjust—"

"Why?" McClay interrupted.

Abramowitz cocked her head. "Why?"

"Why do people have to adjust to the new culture? Why doesn't the culture adjust to the people?"

"Well, it does. Living cultures are affected by all kinds of different influences, external and internal . . ."

"But people still . . . I mean, you don't choose your culture. I was born on Bringloid, so I'm Bringloidi. Then we were brought to Mariposa, where everyone was Mariposan. And we were told, 'now you must all live this new United Ficus culture.' But why do I have to be any of them? Why are these cultures more important than the people in them?"

It was a good question, and one Abramowitz would have enjoyed discussing. Just then, though, they were interrupted. *"Lense to Abramowitz."*

"Yes, Doctor?"

"Is Kara McClay still with you?"

"Yes, right here."

"I need to see her in the diagnostics lab."

There was something in Lense's tone that Abramowitz felt did not bode well. "It's not good news, is it?" Abramowitz asked.

"I need to speak with her here, now."

Taken aback by the vehemence of the doctor's directive, Abramowitz turned her head back to consider McClay's reaction. The nervousness in her eyes was now, to her surprise, replaced by a kind of calm resignation. "On my way," she said to the comm, and then to her tour guide as she stood up, "Thank you, Dr. Carol."

"Kara?" Abramowitz called as the young woman turned toward the mess hall doors. She didn't stop or turn back; whatever she thought Lense had to tell her, she was clearly set to face it.

Abramowitz remained seated in the empty hall, trying to sort through the new impressions of the United Ficus colony she'd picked up in the past hour. Somehow, her view of the matter was more muddied than ever.

Lense stared at the long tableau of computer readouts displayed across one wall of the lab, and pressed her hands to either side of her skull, as if trying to squeeze the inevitable conclusion out of her brain. The original text of Sandra Vallis's meticulously detailed notes appeared in tandem with the *da Vinci* computer's representation of the corresponding genomes, as well as the genome of the actual pathogen that had gotten loose in the Capital Complex. Presented this way, there was no question: the *rop'ngor* strain that had infected the Mariposans was not one Sandra Vallis had created.

"Are you unwell, Doctor?" the EMH asked, standing just off to the side behind her. "Shall I bring you an analgesic?"

"No, thanks," Lense growled. "You've done plenty already." The EMH had caught the contradictory data as soon as the file hit its matrix. Lense only wished she could feel better about the breakthrough.

"Are you certain?" the EMH persisted.

Lense whipped her head around to glower at the EMH as it ran its empathy subroutine. Like all the later-generation medical holograms, this one had been programmed to simulate actual concern for its patients. Seeing it offering her its faux-friendly sympathy was almost enough to make her miss the arrogant Mark I version that had originally been in use on the *Lexington.* "Yes, I am certain, dammit."

"Then is there anything else I can do?"

"Yeah. You can go and . . . deactivate yourself."

The EMH nodded and did just that. Once it disappeared, Lense saw Kara through the transparency of the lab walls, waiting in sickbay. Lense got to her feet and waved the young woman in. Kara obeyed wordlessly, and stood just inside the door as Lense slid it shut. The two just stared silently at each other, Lense calling on every bit of strength within her to keep herself composed. After a long moment, Lense finally asked, in a low, pained voice, "What did you do, Kara?"

"What do you—"

Lense slammed the palm of her hand down on the console before she could get any further than that. *"Don't!* You were Sandra Vallis's assistant. You were one of the only people who knew about her secret work. You were the one she trusted with her backup files. She trusted you!"

And she wasn't the only one.

Kara did her best to hold herself steady, although her eyes started to blur behind a layer of incipient tears. "I didn't mean—"

"Didn't mean what?" Lense demanded. "The virus that got loose? It was a mutated strain, Kara. A cross-mutation between two different strains." She jabbed her right index finger toward the displays on the wall. "Strain number 543, and strain number 467. Four-sixty-seven was the last from what Vallis called 'a dead-end line of experimentation.' It propagated too quickly and too uncontrollably, so she wrote it off, and confined the strain to cold storage." Lense fixed Kara with a hard glare. "This was *three years* ago! How could those two strains have come in contact with each other?"

"I didn't mean for anyone to be hurt," Kara said, through slow, controlled breaths. "I only wanted to stop her work."

Lense put a hand over her mouth and said nothing. Even though she already knew, she'd hoped she would have denied it, that she would have pointed the finger at some other unknown confidant of Vallis's. Hearing her admit to the act so plainly, with more emotional restraint than Lense felt herself capable of at the moment, was more than she was ready for.

She turned away from the young woman, tabbing the comm on the lab table behind her. "Lense to Gold. Please come to the diagnostic lab right away."

"Acknowledged," came the captain's response.

Lense tabbed the line closed, and remained with her back to Kara, hands on the edge of the console supporting her entire weight. "Did you think I wasn't going to be able to figure it out?" she asked.

"I figured you would," Kara answered. "Better you than Dr. Victor."

"Why?" Lense turned back around to challenge her. "Did you think Starfleet would go easier on you? Or that you could run away without having to face the consequences from the people who were affected by what you did?"

Kara's only reply was to look down at the deck and hitch her shoulders a couple of centimeters. Before she knew what she was doing, Lense's hands were on those shoulders, her long fingers pressing into the flesh under the thin yellow sundress. "Did you?!" she demanded. "Over two hundred people dead! Half the population sterile! And here you are, ready to run off into the big universe, with dreams of being a doctor yourself?"

"I swear, if I knew what would've happened—"

"But you knew what you wanted to happen! You didn't know you were killing Sandra Vallis, but you knew you were killing her chance to ever . . . and for all the Mariposans!"

Kara wrenched herself out of Lense's grasp, and backed away toward the opposite side of the lab. "But that's why I had to stop her!" Kara shouted, tears now rolling down her cheeks. "They already see me as a lesser person. If their infertility was cured, what would I be to them then? The only reason they let the Bringloidi come was because they needed someone to have their babies. All I would be to them is a uterus—"

"And what about the women who want to have babies? What right do you have to make that decision for them?" Lense was full-out shouting now, feeling the restraints of her well-honed emotional self-control snapping loose. "That's their choice, isn't it? To bring a new life into the universe, to commit to raising a child—that's a personal choice, one that we have to make for ourselves! How dare you . . ."

Suddenly, she felt like a balloon with all its air let out. She panted and blinked at the Bringloidi woman standing in front of her, almost in a state of disorientation. As she mentally flailed about, trying to find her center, she felt a hand fall on her back, between her shoulder blades. "Doctor?" a gentle voice close to her ear said.

Lense straightened, instantly finding herself before

turning to face David Gold. "Captain." She had absolutely
no clue he had been in the room, or for how long. The lab
door had closed behind him, which was some small comfort. "Captain, in the course of my analysis of—"

"Yes, yes," he said, his hand still on her back. "Good
work, Lense. Ms. McClay," he then said, the gentle voice
gone, "step out into sickbay, and wait for me."

Kara did as ordered, leaving Lense and Gold alone in
sad silence.

"She sabotaged Vallis's work?"

Lense stared out through the transparency, where she
stood with her back to the lab. "Yeah."

"Positive?"

"She admitted it."

Gold sighed. "All right. I'll see how we have to play this
out. Again, good work, Lense."

"Thank you, sir."

"And," he added in a whisper, *"mazel tov."*

Lense turned to face the captain, eyes wide, perfectly
aware that he was not congratulating her on any of what
had just transpired. "Excuse me?"

"Six times a father, nineteen times a grandfather,
you'd think I'd have recognized the signs by now." He
shrugged, and walked out into sickbay to join Kara.
Lense watched them walk out into the corridor. Once
she was sure she was alone, she collapsed into a chair,
completely limp, feeling for the first time in months the
sweet release from tension.

CHAPTER
12

*B*reeding stock.

Gold cringed as those words echoed in his mind. They had been there in the *Enterprise*'s mission recordings all along, but being familiar as he was with Kate Pulaski and her blunt, plainspoken personality, he'd let the phrase roll right over him. But taken by itself, and disregarding the rationalizations and justifications that had surrounded it, the ugliness of the phrase struck hard.

"Are you telling me that you think this girl's actions were justified?" Wilson Granger asked, his jaw slack in disbelief. Brenna Odell, sitting to his left on one side of their kitchen table, made a valiant attempt to shoot phasers out her eyes at both Gold and Abramowitz.

"I absolutely am not arguing that her actions were justified, and she will, of course, have to face justice for her actions." How such justice could be carried out, Gold wished he knew. "But, I am telling you that the fears that drove her to her actions are real."

"Captain, I may not be a young girl anymore," said Brenna Odell, "but I daresay I'm more familiar with their feelings than you. I wasn't all that keen back then on the idea of taking three husbands and bearing them all children. But that was what we needed to do."

"Actually, it really wasn't," Abramowitz said, frowning. As unhappy as she was about the *Enterprise*'s interference here before, now her disdain for the legacy Picard had left on this world was completely undisguised. "The establishment of the three-spouse arrangement served only one purpose: to allow for the proliferation of Mariposan genes in this new society. The Bringloidi genome was—and is—broad and healthy; there was no reason they couldn't continue monogamous relationships. But a united colony requires a uniform set of rules, morals, and mores, so polygamy was demanded across the board. With the inability of Mariposan genes to propagate, however, there is no justification for this social arrangement."

"But," said Granger, "you can give us that ability. You said Sandra's research could still hold promise."

"That's right, I did," Gold said. That was one of the few questions he'd bothered Lense with before beaming down here. "The question is, should we?"

"What?" Granger slammed his hands on the table and launched himself up out of his chair. "You can't be serious! You would bring us right back to where we were eleven years ago? You would let us all just die?"

Gold stayed seated, and in a calm voice said, "You

told me earlier that you regretted what you'd done to the *Enterprise* officers in the name of preserving yourselves. That with your wife and her children, you'd found an aspect of your humanity more important than what was encoded in your DNA."

Brenna Odell raised an eyebrow at that, while her husband answered, "Yes, Captain, but—"

"Then think about what you're passing on here, Mr. Granger," Gold said. "You'd be passing on the idea that Mariposan genes are superior to Bringloidi genes. That a Bringloidi woman's most important function is to help propagate the Mariposan race, no matter her wants, talents, or abilities."

As Granger mulled that over, Abramowitz leaned in, eyes on Odell. "And you—"

"What, me?"

"The one thing the Mariposans have been able to pass on to your children is their knowledge. You strip that from this world, what have these young people left? The gang that attacked our people did so because they were afraid of what they were going to lose." Odell looked unmoved, though she did give her husband a quick glance out of the corner of her eye. "You'd be putting the same kind of limits on these young people's potential, where the best they can hope to do is scratch out the same hard simple life your people were so eager to put behind you over a decade ago. Do you really want to leave them with that kind of hopelessness?"

And in Odell's eyes, Gold saw the first cracks in the hard shell of her resolve. It was a look he was all too familiar with—the look of realization that everything you thought or believed up until that moment was mistaken.

She found herself with nothing to say, her eyes moving around the room as if searching for her fading certitude.

Gold relaxed his facial expression, and waited for Odell to glance back his way. "I know you only want to do what's best for your people," he said, addressing Odell and Granger both. "That's what we all want. Let us help you figure out how to do that. The Federation owes you at least that much, after getting you to this point."

"How did Da make this look so easy?" Odell whispered to herself, just barely audible. Then she lifted her head, and looked from Granger to Gold. "What if they say we should split the two colonies up again?" she asked.

Gold reacted to that with surprise, but not quite as much as Granger did.

"They couldn't force you to be isolated from each other, not if you didn't want to be," Abramowitz answered, registering no small amount of surprise herself.

Odell looked to Granger again. "I suppose it wouldn't hurt to hear these diplomats out?" she said, then offered him a wisp of a smile.

Granger returned her smile. "I can't see how it would," he said, placing his left hand on her right.

For the first time since their arrival at Mariposa, Gold felt hope that the union would be preserved.

"Captain, this has been an emotionally trying day for me; maybe we could put this off another day or two?" Lense laughed at herself, the sound echoing off the narrow walls of the extendable gangway tunnel linking the *da Vinci* to Starbase 73. "Yeah, that'll work."

The airlock hissed, and she reboarded the *da Vinci*. She took the left corridor, heading for the captain's quarters, even though she felt she would have been perfectly justified in begging off their appointment, given the task she'd just performed.

Between Gold and the prime ministers, it was decided any kind of trial or criminal proceedings against Kara McClay would only incite more ethnic conflict. So the decision was that she would be exiled, forbidden to return to Mariposa for at least twenty years, such travel restriction to be enforced by the Federation.

It was really the best Kara could have possibly hoped for—and Lense, too. Despite all that had happened, despite all her conflicting emotions, Lense genuinely did hope the young woman would be able to fulfill her potential, and somehow find a way to atone for what she had done.

Kara had been quick to accept all the terms of her exile, but the reality of her sentence didn't truly dawn on her until they'd reached the heart of the starbase. Suddenly finding herself in the middle of a surging ocean of aliens and other strangers, Kara realized how totally alone she now was, and that there was no going backward. Lense sympathized.

She reached the captain's door, and hesitated before pressing the door chime. A second later, the door slid open, and she entered Gold's quarters. "Good afternoon, Captain."

"Good afternoon, Lense. Come, sit." Lense took a seat as the captain stepped to the replicator. "Get you anything?"

"Tangerine juice?"

He keyed his requests into the pad, and a moment later handed her a chilled glass while he held a steaming mug of green tea. Sitting, he raised the mug in a toast. "To the mother-to-be."

Lense hesitated, then touched her glass to the captain's mug. "You know, Captain, I *was* planning to tell you . . ."

"Sometime before the *kinder*'s high school graduation, I'm certain. The question I have: Who have you told? Your mother, at least, I hope."

Lense shook her head, and the captain "tsked." "So far it's just you, and Julian Bashir."

"Well, you didn't tell me so much as I found out in spite of you."

"Yeah, that's actually pretty much how Julian found out, too," she said with a small laugh. "I just . . . first there was just this shock, and disbelief. Then reality slowly seeps in and you realize you have to face it—"

"And you do all you can to avoid thinking about it. Rachel, she would cook. You never saw such meals." Gold smiled as he revealed this memory, but then shifted to a more serious mien. "With you, though, Elizabeth, you do the same to avoid *any* personal grief. It took a direct order for you to open up, after two years, about Commander Selden. To this day, I don't know what happened with you right after Galvan VI. And I find it disconcerting that, after all the time you put in on that Shmoam-ag ship, you've talked so little about the boy."

"Sir? I did an entire paper on Dobrah and the Pocheeny virus," she reminded him. It was that paper that earned her the nomination for the Bentman Prize, and set this whole thing in motion.

"Yes, a paper," Gold said. "A cold, professional paper

with big, impressive, award-worthy doctor words. But you don't talk about the boy."

He was right, of course. The time she spent with that lonely little boy (two hundred years old, yes, but still very much a child) had touched her like nothing in her life ever had. Her third day there, she'd had to wake him to run some tests, and in his half-sleep, he'd looked up at her and said "Mama?" That had hit her right in the heart.

Now reflecting on Gold's words, reflecting on an entire lifetime of pushing her own emotions away and doing everything she could not to deal with them, she felt a new pain growing there.

As if he were reading her thoughts, Gold reached over and put a hand on her forearm. "Elizabeth . . . I know it's your nature to be concerned about everyone except yourself. That's what makes you a good doctor, and part of what is going to make you a wonderful mother." He leaned back into his chair and picked up his tea again. "That's also what will make you *meshuggeh ahf toit*. You're not alone. You're part of a family here. You just have to decide not to be alone, hiding in that shell of yours."

Lense smiled a tiny smile, even though she'd always taken a bit of a jaundiced view of calling any group of non-related people a "family." Friends, maybe. People she'd put her life on the line for, definitely. But the *da Vinci* was not a *Galaxy*-class ship or a starbase. It was not designed for families. When the time came, she knew, Starfleet would have her somewhere else, and this "family" . . .

"So," the captain said, switching to a lighter tone, "when do you plan on sharing the good news with every-one?"

"I don't know," she sighed. "I haven't even thought . . ."

She trailed off, and Gold shrugged slightly. "This hasn't been a very happy mission for anyone. The engineers stuck most of the time sitting on their hands, Abramowitz all bent out of shape, and now having to turn the whole *megillah* over to another ship without having resolved any of the big issues . . . we could all use something to get together and celebrate."

Lense couldn't help but laugh at the captain's transparent psychological ploy. *If Lense won't come out of her shell for her own sake, maybe she will for the crew.*

Then she laughed again, this time a little more genuinely, because—well, hell, the old *momzer* was dead right. "Yeah, sure, why not?" she said with a grin. Besides, if she did in fact only have a limited time before having to leave the *da Vinci*, then she should make the very most of the time she had left with these people. "Let's celebrate."

HONOR

Kevin Killiany

To my wife, Valerie, light of my life and treasure of my heart, whose irrational stubbornness in sticking with me no matter what has made all that I have possible. And to our children, Alethea, Anson, and Daya, who make all that I do worthwhile.

ACKNOWLEDGMENTS

There are so many people who have made my developing life as a writer possible and have helped—and continue to help—me along the way, I'm not even going to
pretend I'm trying to list everyone. But a few deserve
special mention: My family, of course, who look people
straight in the eye and tell them I'm a writer (and understand that staring blankly into space is work). The whole
Trek writing and publishing community, which has been
is unbelievably helpful, welcoming, and supportive. I will
be forever indebted to Dean Wesley Smith, the editor
who bought my first story and became my teacher; Keith
R.A. DeCandido, who trusted me enough to let me play
with the Corps of Engineers; Kristine Kathryn Rusch,
whose unflinchingly brutal and delightful guidance has
brought me so far; Loren L. Coleman, who opened doors
beyond *Star Trek* to me; and Sharon Mulvihill, editor ex-
traordinaire, who shepherded me through my first novel
experience. These people have become my friends.

CHAPTER

1

Domenica Corsi decided she wasn't dead.

Determining whether she was dying or not took a little longer.

The pain was certainly sufficient for fatal injuries. And she couldn't move. When she pushed past the pain enough to try, nothing happened. More disturbing than either the pain or the immobility was the floating in darkness, along a dark tunnel toward a light. She'd heard about that. Generally speaking, in terms of being alive, that was a bad sign.

The light went out for a while and when it came back she decided it meant she'd fallen asleep. Or passed out.

There was a sound, like leather against wood, and another like clicking or ticking, but they faded and were gone. They'd sounded alive, not like machines. There was a smell, too—peppermint and cedar. That stayed.

Pain still gripped her, but it was not as intense. More an ache than agony. And it was universal, as though someone had methodically pummeled every square centimeter of her body with a loving attention to detail.

She still could not move. But now, more aware, she realized a tightly wound blanket, not paralysis, held her in its grip.

The light she had been floating toward resolved itself into a softly glowing . . . She wasn't sure. It was irregular, but vaguely spheroid, and seemed to be overflowing out of a basket of woven vines. The basket was on a shelf, maybe two meters away. The shelf looked as though it had been carved out of a wall of living wood.

She let her eyes drift shut and considered the possibility she was delirious. As far as she could remember, no Federation starships were carved of wood.

Corsi forced her eyes open.

She was not delirious. She was wrapped in a blanket on a bed of something soft, the source of the peppermint and cedar scent, she decided. Her bed was low to the floor of a dimly lit room or cabin that seemed to be carved from a single block of heavily grained wood.

Turning her head the few degrees the wrappings allowed, Corsi could see the one shelf with the odd lantern, a wooden bucket or trough that was not carved from the floor, and a dark wall covering that may or may not have concealed an entrance. She had no idea where she was or how she'd gotten there, but she was reasonably certain it had not been of her own free will.

There was a padding sound again, something soft—

leather?—sliding over wood. And again the series of clicks and ticks. Movement and voices, she decided, beyond the wall hanging-covered door.

Corsi let her eyes droop shut to slits, no tension to her face as she feigned sleep. Through the haze of her lashes, she saw the wall covering bow inward, then aside.

A head appeared, long and broad, just over a meter above the floor. At first she though it was an animal, but then she realized it was carrying a tray with folded cloths of some sort. She couldn't make out its color through her lashes in the dim light, but it was dark. What she could discern of the face looked remarkably like that of a Terran chipmunk, minus the split upper lip. The tiny rounded ears that projected above and wide, lemurlike eyes compounded the effect.

It turned to one side, chittering in a series of clicks and ticks, and Corsi realized the creature was longer than it was tall. The body that extended back from the upright torso had at least two pairs of legs. The blend of disparate features struck her as being like nothing so much as a cross between a chipmunk and a centaur.

A second chiptaur entered the room, and then a third. With that many eyes on her, she couldn't risk her surreptitious observation and let her eyes drift fully shut.

Corsi willed her body to remain limp as the creatures unwrapped her from the blanket. They were as gentle as they could be; at least they seemed to be taking care, chittering softly to one another as though mindful of disturbing her. But it was hard not to tense against the pain that shot through her at every turn and pull. She thought she heard the rustle of the doorway hanging beneath the sounds of their voices and thought perhaps one had exited into the outer room or hall or whatever lay beyond her small chamber.

As they lifted her legs Corsi caught the sharp scent of urine and realized they were changing her diaper. She couldn't stop the hot flush she felt spreading up from her throat.

A sharp chirp stopped the gentle flow of clicking conversation. A pad, feeling like warm suede, pressed against the side of her face. They'd noticed her change in hue.

Corsi felt the sharp prickle of coarse fur as one of the creatures laid its broad head against her chest, evidently listening for her heartbeat. No way to hide her racing heart.

There was a startled *whuff* of warm breath against her chin.

This wasn't the best tactical situation for making a move, but Corsi realized she wasn't going to get to choose her moment. She followed the broad head up as it pulled away from her chest.

She hadn't been able to tell much about their physiology from her cursory observation, but she did know they breathed air through noses in front of their heads. Assuming their lungs weren't in their skulls, that meant their windpipes passed through their throats. That was the only point of attack she could be sure of.

But a blow to the throat could be fatal. She wasn't about to kill anyone unless she was sure it was the only way out. So she rolled toward the being, gasping through the pain as she came up on one knee. Grabbing a furred shoulder at the base of the neck, she threw her offside leg over its back.

The chiptaur gave a startled *clack* and tried to shy

away, but before it had taken a step, Corsi was astride. Guessing similar plumbing and ventilation, she leaned her shoulder into the back of its skull, preventing it from throwing its head back, and snaked her left arm around the being's throat in a classic "sleeper" hold, gripping her left fist in her right hand for leverage.

Of course, given the alien's short stature, this meant Corsi was bent almost double. Which was just as well. Now that she was on her feet, or at least crouching, she could see the wooden room—the wooden walls curving seamlessly into the wooden floor—was barely tall enough for her to have stood erect. She'd have to crawl to get through the door.

There was only one other chiptaur in the room; she'd been right about one leaving. It froze by the bucket beneath the shelf, regarding her with its lemur eyes.

With her eyes wide open, Corsi could see the beings had four arms. Two small ones, about the size of a ten-year-old human's, were mounted on narrow shoulders just below the neck. A second pair about twice as large jutted from broader shoulders a half-dozen centimeters below. The arrangement made the chiptaur's upper torso vaguely reminiscent of a ziggurat.

Because all four hands were extended toward her, spread wide in an evident warding gesture, Corsi could see the upper hands had four radiating fingers. The lower hands had a central pad with two opposable thumbs like a pair of surreal mittens.

From what she could see of the horizontal lower torso, the chiptaur's four legs were arranged like a cat's.

Her captive had frozen the moment her arm had slipped around its neck. Now it seemed to settle, forcing her to one knee to maintain her grip as it apparently made itself comfortable on the floor.

The second chiptaur, evidently over its shock at her sudden attack, followed suit. Tucking its legs under its body, it braced its upper torso on the elbows of its heavier arms. Without a sound, it regarded her solemnly, almost sadly, over two pairs of folded hands.

The chittering clicks and ticks continued from the other side of the wall covering. The third chiptaur was evidently continuing its side of whatever conversation Corsi had interrupted. When it paused she knew from the give and take of the earlier exchanges that whoever was out there expected a reply from either her captive or the being looking on with an unnervingly level gaze.

She prodded the back of her captive's skull with her shoulder, the only thing she could think of to urge it to respond. She was certain it understood, but it remained silent, as motionless as a statue in her grip.

"Speak," she murmured in the round ear next to her cheek. Probably a useless sound without her combadge and its universal translator. "Answer him."

The round ear flicked at the feel of her breath, but that was all.

After a moment there was a short series of ticks from beyond the doorway. A query, Corsi suspected, though there was no rising inflection.

Still the creature beneath her remained unmoving. But for its breathing she would have thought it was carved from the same wood as the room.

The behavior of the second chiptaur was even stranger. Unencumbered by a clinging human, it showed no inclination to either answer its companion on the other side of the curtain or leave on its own. It simply sat, or lounged, and regarded her with an expression of what looked to Corsi like unflinching resolution.

At last the third chiptaur evidently decided to investigate the silence and thrust its head around the edge of the curtain. It blinked once, its already wide eyes going wider in an almost comical expression of surprise at the sight of Corsi evidently strangling its companion.

Then, with an almost human—and clearly heartfelt— sigh, the tension left its body. With the same unhurried resignation as the others, it tucked its legs up under its body and settled down, blocking the doorway in its repose.

Corsi considered her tactical options.

A tug on her captive's head confirmed it had no intention of moving. It was clear if she wanted it to come with her, she was going to have to drag it. Now that she had a feel for how densely muscled it was, she estimated its mass at about one hundred kilograms. Not an easy burden, particularly given its awkward shape. Not to mention the problem of keeping her hostage hostage while shifting its equally massive and inert companion out of the only exit.

With a heartfelt sigh of her own, Corsi released her captive's neck. She wasn't going anywhere.

CHAPTER
2

P8 Blue sat in darkness, looking toward a patch of grayish light her sensors told her was the mouth the hundred-meter tunnel Waldo Egg had made.

Egg without the Waldo, Pattie corrected herself. *The arms came off while we were still in the stratosphere.*

The good news was the soft peat was firm enough to hold its shape. At least the tunnel showed no signs of collapsing in the immediate future.

The bad news was the peat was firm enough to hold its shape. Which meant it was dry enough to ignite if she fired her attitude thrusters. Not that the heat of burning peat would present a threat to the EVA pod; it had recently withstood the temperatures of atmospheric entry, after all. But if the peat burned, it may close off her only escape route.

At least, she thought the material was peat. Her field was structural engineering, not organic chemistry. And Waldo Egg, as Faulwell had dubbed the EVA pod, was designed to operate in space. Which meant the sensors could accurately assess the molecular makeup of the densely packed, fibrous, organic material in which she was suspended, but the computer was not programmed with the vocabulary to give it a name.

Whatever it was, it filled a basin over a kilometer in diameter with a mean depth of two hundred and thirty meters. Which meant if the peat beneath her caught fire she could conceivably sink another one hundred and ninety meters.

Pattie had thought the peat basin was a dry lake bed coming in. Not that she'd had a good look at it. She'd just had a momentary impression of a clearing in the forest that looked softer than the volcanic mountains she was streaking toward.

Whatever it was had looked like her best chance for survival. She'd rotated the pod, retrofiring thrusters never meant to combat a gravity well, in a desperate attempt to bring herself down before mashing into the rock face.

She'd succeeded, plowing stern first into what she expected to be—comparatively—soft ground. Only instead of gouging a trench along its surface, the EVA pod had plunged underground at a shallow angle. The shuddering stop had been nothing like the savage bounce and tumble she'd been braced for, but it was still the roughest landing she had ever walked away from.

Or would walk away from if she could figure out a way to get out of here.

The escape hatch was on the side, pressed firmly against a solid wall of presumed peat. If the hatch had opened inward instead of out, she might conceivably have dug her way through the fibrous vegetable matter to the tunnel proper. Though it would be tough going with nothing approximating a shovel available.

Actually, she had no tools available. There had been several attached to the outside of the EVA pod. Though they were designed for satellite repair, several of them could be adapted for digging. If they were still out there after her rough descent. And if Waldo Egg still had its arms.

At the moment her escape depended on either rotating the pod so its hatch faced the tunnel or making a hole in the transparent aluminum viewport big enough for her to crawl through.

Pattie opened the emergency repair locker, extracting all of its contents and arraying them as best she could on the deck of the pod. There were a half-dozen spare isolinear chips, opti-cables of various refractions and lengths, a universal spanner, a first-aid kit appropriate for a variety of soft-bodied races, and a selection of hull patches. After a moment she removed her combadge and Klingon engineering dagger and added them to the collection.

At first glance the collection of mismatched items did not look to Pattie like the tools she needed to break out of the buried EVA pod. However, being part of the S.C.E. meant learning to think outside the box, to see solutions that weren't obvious at first glance.

Pattie rearranged the materials, grouping them by function, and considered how she could combine their applications. In several minutes of intense thought, she brought all of her structural engineering knowledge, along with a few tricks from the other disciplines she'd picked up along the way, to bear on the problem. At last she realized she was right.

These were not the tools she needed to break out of a buried EVA pod.

She looked again at the frame of the viewport. Perhaps. . . .

The tunnel was collapsing.

Not rapidly, and not by much, but there was a definite sway to the roofline. As she watched, a clump of material fell.

"So the choices are sit in the dark for a week until the *da Vinci* comes looking for us or try rotating with the attitude thrusters," she said. "Which might ignite the peat and maybe burn a hole down another hundred and ninety meters. Then I could sit *there* in the dark for a week."

There was no water or food aboard the pod; she'd only intended a three-hour duty tour, but surviving a week without either was possible. Barely. And the *da Vinci* would have no trouble finding the pod. Even if its beacon had been fried on the way down, her combadge would guide them in with little trouble.

Reattaching her combadge, she keyed it on for the first time in half an hour.

"Blue to Corsi. Commander? This is Pattie. Do you read me?"

Nothing. Just like last time. And the time before.

Pattie shut out the image of Corsi falling—in an EVA suit, not a pod—toward the planet below.

I might survive a week at the bottom of a hole, but Corsi could be injured.

Strapping herself back into the Nasat-supporting acceleration couch, Pattie reviewed the status boards. Main thrusters and all the attitude thrusters she could angle to point directly back had been burned out in her braking maneuver. That left her with four, which should be enough, and a choice.

Her inclination was to make several spaced micro burns, allowing the surrounding peat to cool away from combustion temperatures between gentle thrusts. However, the rate at which the tunnel was collapsing suggested she didn't have the time to spare on caution.

Pattie unhooked her safety straps. If she was going to do this, she was going to need to move fast. She'd worry about the hundred and ninety meter drop if and when she felt herself falling. First priority was reaching the hatch.

With that in mind, she triggered the hatch release. Hopefully, when it faced the empty tunnel it would pop open of its own accord, saving her precious seconds.

It was possible all of this was unnecessary, that the EVA pod would simply turn in place and she'd be able to exit at her leisure. But one thing she had learned was to never count on things going well.

A section of the tunnel sagged.

Pattie couldn't preprogram the attitude thrusters—there was no formula for plowing through peat. She adjusted their angles and triggered the all-fire, holding the contact down as the pod shuddered and began to turn.

Thirty, forty degrees, then it seemed to hang up. Something more solid than the rest of the peat had snagged one of the pod's few projections. Or perhaps the material had started to collapse, holding it more firmly.

Pattie was already giving the thrusters full burn. There

was nothing she could do but keep them firing, the chance of conflagration increasing with every second.

With an abrupt lurch that almost threw Pattie from the couch, the pod came loose. The viewport became a mirror as it turned away from the tunnel.

Pattie released the thruster control as the hatch popped open. A cloud of smoke and a rotting vegetable stench filled the tiny cabin as she dropped to all eights and scurried through the opening.

The pod shifted beneath her as she leapt from the metal sill. There was a sucking, crackling sound and another billow of smoke and stench washed over her as she scrambled up the crumbling tunnel.

The peat was not completely dry, she realized, then as quickly realized her pod wouldn't have dug a tunnel if it had been. Perhaps in moist peat the danger of fire wasn't as great as she'd supposed.

She almost slackened her pace at the thought. Then a section of ceiling twice as broad as she dropped, nearly blocking her way.

"I'm arboreal, not burrowing," she reminded no one in particular as she frantically dug her way over the obstacle.

Past the mound of fallen ceiling was another and a third. But beyond that the last thirty meters looked clear. The ceiling bowed but had not yet broken loose.

She was going to make it.

Then from behind her came a sullen *fwump* as though someone were dumping a massive load of pillows. Or dirt. A cold gust of escaping air washed up from behind. The tunnel was collapsing.

She wasn't going to make it.

CHAPTER
3

"I should have gone with her," Fabian Stevens said for perhaps the hundredth time.

"What?" Bart Faulwell asked, pulling his attention back from the vista of aqueducts and canals stretching to the horizon and focusing on his friend at the other end of the narrow oval table. "And given up the chance to be Tev's personal adjunct on Bundinal?"

Stevens growled at the linguist with what was evidently his best impression of an angry Klingon.

"You have the inflection wrong," Bart pointed out mildly. "Unless, of course, you didn't mean to call me a muffin, in which case you have the wrong word entirely."

Stevens sighed heavily and scowled at the view.

The two friends had met for lunch at an open-air bistro perched on the brow of a hill overlooking the township of Brohtz. Though its cheerfully faux rustic decor was clearly aimed at the tourist trade, the Bundinalli librarian Bart was working with had assured him the food was excellent, faithfully representing the regional cuisine.

From this vantage point they could see no less than four canals and three aqueducts. A major hub was a few hundred kilometers west of Brohtz. There was a haze from the water vapor above the elevated aqueducts; as Bart understood it, the humidifying effects of evaporation were nearly as important as irrigation to the ecology. With the sun over their shoulders, they could see hundreds of tiny rainbows hanging in the mist.

Even if the food didn't live up to expectations, Bart reflected, the view was worth the trek up the hill.

Actually, he'd enjoyed the uphill walk past antiquated homes that exactly mirrored one another across cobbled streets. He'd spent hours combing through centuries-old civic records in the dusty bowels of the town archive. Library research, especially when it involved sifting through folios penned when the Romans were invading Britain, was always enthralling—the first few weeks. After that, it became a chore.

Bart knew his search through the local archives of the Bundinalli was right on the cusp of transmogrifying from adventure to drudgery. Frequent breaks, like this native lunch with Stevens, were helping him stave off the inevitable.

It was equally clear his friend and cabinmate Fabian had needed a break as well.

The task of coordinating the various specialists trying to figure out the Bundinalli aqueduct system had fallen to Lieutenant Commander Mor glasch Tev, second in command of the *da Vinci's* own S.C.E. team. Though the job Bart had heard described at the planning session had been that of facilitator, the Tellarite had—in typically Tellarite fashion—understood his role to be micromanager of all aspects of the endeavor.

Realizing this would be a big job, even for him, Tev's first official act had been to co-opt Stevens, who would otherwise have been idle, as his personal assistant. For the last dozen days the tactical systems specialist had been bouncing from one Bundinalli township to the next, personally following up on instructions Tev had already broadcast in meticulous detail.

Tev's specificity was in direct contrast to the vagaries of Bundinalli. The language, and the way the natives seemed to organize thought, guaranteed Bart stretched his intuitive translation skills as he tried to decipher—or even find—the original routing instructions for Bundinal's ancient aqueduct system.

Eons ago, generations of ecological mismanagement had turned seventy percent of Bundinal's arable land into a dust bowl. The Bundinalli were facing planetwide famine. Extinction was a real possibility.

However, it wasn't a possibility they were willing to accept. At about the time humans first began experimenting with bronze, the Bundinalli were constructing a network of interdependent aqueducts and canals to irrigate their planet. Their job was made simpler—just—by the fact they inhabited only two continents, both on the same side of the globe and both extending from the poles almost to the equator. Still, it was a prodigious task.

What fascinated Bart was the fact there had never been a centralized plan, no unifying vision. Instead, the network's form had been governed by the Bundinalli's absolute insistence on symmetry. Everything in their architecture balanced. Whether it was the airy stucco and tile arches of Brohtz or the stolid timbers of Prshdt, every culture on the globe was built with symmetry.

Sometimes this led to amusing quirks, like houses with faux front doors to balance the real ones. But on a global scale it had enabled the Bundinalli to create an incredibly intricate system that had grown almost organically as they'd diverted runoff from their melting polar ice caps and desalinated great volumes of seawater to irrigate their planet.

That last had seemed particularly suspect to Bart. He didn't understand planetary ecology in any great detail, but he'd always thought worlds depended on their oceans to renew their atmospheres.

Case in point was a pair of what the locals called birds flitting about the edge of the open-air bistro. They had serpentine bodies with two sets of wings arranged in tandem. As nearly as Bart could tell, the wings never flapped in unison, or in any pattern he could discern. The entire arrangement looked aerodynamically impossible. But there they were, dashing after crumbs the tourists tossed their way, blissfully oblivious to their evolutionary improbability.

His reverie was interrupted by a trencher of hearty stew, thick with meat but steaming with the scent of walnuts and cinnamon, appearing at his elbow.

"I thought this was supposed to be a soufflé," Stevens said from his symmetrical position at the other end of the oval table.

There was an elongated mass on the platter that had

been set before him. It looked to Bart as though an in-different artist working from a verbal description had molded a fish out of pudding.

"Either it fell or it's an omelet," Bart agreed. "Though it's possible the UT just used soufflé as the closet approxi-mation of the name."

Stevens sighed.

Calling the server back, Bart inquired into the dish's preparation. This involved a particularly Bundinalli ex-planation of growing seasons and traditions, but before his stew had cooled he had the gist of it.

"It's a half-dozen eggs from our friends over there," he explained, indicating the snake-birds he'd been watch-ing earlier. "The whites—that's the green part—and the yolks—that's the gray part, are separated and whipped into a froth. Two froths, I guess. The bits of purple, bur-gundy, and blue are a mix of fruit, finely diced, which is called *rastentha*. The fruits involved change with the seasons. Alternating layers of whites, fruit, and yolks are then poured into a mold—fish-shaped for reasons I didn't follow—and baked. Technically, I suppose soufflé comes closer than omelet, but it's somewhere between the two."

Stevens sighed again and eyed Bart's stew with obvi-ous envy.

"At least give it a try," Bart urged.

Choosing a forklike utensil, Stevens carefully pared off a sliver of the mass and popped it into his mouth.

"Whoa."

"What?" Bart asked.

"This," Stevens swallowed and scooped a large forkful from the soufflé, "is marvelous. We have got to figure out how to replicate this stuff. We could make a fortune."

Bart grinned at his friend's change of mood and attacked his own stew. Not the rousing sensation Stevens's soufflé evidently was, but it was still pleasant. Chicken, mostly, he decided, with walnuts and celery. That he tasted no cinnamon despite the aroma confused his palate, but not unpleasantly so.

The Bundinalli network of canals and aqueducts had worked well for centuries until the Breen swept through the system. Intent on more significant targets deeper in Federation space, the Breen had simply bombarded Bundinal in passing, a side jaunt to upset a bit of Federation infrastructure rather than a campaign of invasion. One of the Federation historians had called it a drive-by shooting. Abramowitz had appreciated the cultural allusion, though its significance escaped Bart.

Whatever the Breen's purpose, the effect of their raid had been to throw Bundinal into agricultural chaos. Flooding and drought had cost them years of growing seasons in both hemispheres.

Repair of the irrigation network had been a priority.

A straightforward retro-engineering of existing foundations and structures, it had been repaired by the S.C.E. within months of the war's end. But even though everything was in place, the system hadn't worked. The aqueduct network was so large and complex it had been subject to coriolis effects and lunar tides—a complex consideration on a world with two moons.

Generations ago the Bundinalli had installed tens of thousands of locks, but never a centralized control. Village lock masters had known that when the sun was *here* and the first moon *there* and the second moon *there* they should open the lock. Or, in different positions, close it.

Thus thousands of individuals, faithfully attending their singular duties without communication with any others, had kept the waters flowing.

It was a balance almost impossible to regain once lost. But finding that rhythm again was why the *da Vinci* was here now.

"I should have gone with her," he said again once his soufflé had disappeared.

"What would you have done?" Bart asked. "Useful to the mission, I mean."

"Anthropological survey satellites are tactical systems," Stevens said. "There was a lot I could have done."

"The satellite transponder reported structural damage," Bart pointed out. "That's Pattie's specialty. And you don't have the training—or the security clearance—in stealth technology Corsi has. There was nothing for you to do."

Stevens shook his head, unconvinced, and frowned at the cavorting birds.

Bart glanced at his chronometer and made a side bet with himself on how many minutes would pass before Stevens said he should have gone with Corsi to the Zhatyra system. Bart hoped she was having a better time than the one she'd left behind.

CHAPTER
4

"What I need," Corsi repeated, "are my clothes and all the equipment you took from me."

The chiptaurs continued to ignore her, chittering to one another as they worked.

Two were changing her bandages, slick membranes that looked like veinless leaves. Peeling them away revealed drying poultices of what appeared to be chewed leaves and several deep cuts to go with bruises and scrapes that covered the rest of her body. The third, which had disappeared with the feltlike blanket she'd been wrapped in, returned with a fresh blanket folded over its upper arms and its lower pair wrapped around a bundle of fresh greenery for her bed.

Of course, it could have been a complete stranger bringing the new bedding. However, the mottled brown on brown pattern, distinctly darker along the left side of its face and upper torso, was familiar enough for Corsi to be reasonably sure this was the same one that had blocked her exit earlier.

Corsi stood, remembering to keep bent to prevent bumping her head on the ceiling, and sidestepped out of the way. One of the nurse chiptaurs moved with her, continuing to wind a fresh leaf bandage around her shin. The other helped the newcomer put down the fresh bedding neatly.

"In fact, keep the clothes," she told the top of the head even with her knees as the nurse focused on tying off the bandage. "Just give me back my equipment. Can't let you keep it anyway. Prime Directive and all that."

The chiptaur—the one she'd held hostage—stepped back and surveyed its handiwork. Apparently satisfied, it chirped and chittered at her for several seconds, ending its speech with what looked like a gesture for her to stay where she was. Corsi decided this one, slightly larger than the others, was the head nurse. It certainly seemed to give most of the orders. With a brief aside to the pair working on the bed, the head nurse flowed out the door.

Deciding "stay where you are" did not include holding the same head-stooped position, Corsi eased down into a crouch, balanced on the balls of her feet.

She watched the two chiptaurs removing the greenery from the low bed frame, trying to determine if there was any social order or pattern to their behavior. She decided the one with the darker left side was older, if only because the other, with a distinctive patch of lighter hair on the back of its upper torso at the base of its neck, seemed to make an extra effort to assist it.

She mentally dubbed the pair Lefty and Spot.

Corsi couldn't help but notice she was between the open door and the two chiptaurs bundling up the old bedding. From what she'd seen, she was willing to bet they'd do nothing to interfere if she tried to leave.

On the other hand, she wasn't sure how much she'd accomplish crawling naked through an uncharted labyrinth of wooden tunnels. Probably not much before the rest of the population, however many that might be, immobilized her with another example of applied nonviolence.

Corsi rocked her weight back, taking a load off her aching muscles, and leaned against the curving wooden wall. The wood had a cool feel, slightly moist, and Corsi realized the room was carved from a living tree. A pretty big one.

For a moment she had an image, a memory, of a clouded sky arching above and a sea of branches—the canopy of a rain forest—stretching out in all directions around her. But what rain forest? What planet?

The image was gone as quickly as it had come, leaving no answers behind.

Corsi pulled her mind away from worrying at the problem. The best way to work through trauma-induced amnesia was to not work through it. Left alone, the mind would heal itself. Would if it could.

Distracting herself, Corsi considered the basket of light on the shelf across the room. The glow was too steady to be flame and she doubted her hosts—or captors—had the technology for even electric lights. Looking directly at the light was not painful, but the luminescence was bright enough to fog details. As nearly as she could tell the light source was dozens of balls of knotted yarn packed to overflowing in the rounded basket. There was no discernible radiant heat, and no apparent convection currents, which suggested air was not warming on contact. Bioluminescence? Probably.

Of course she could have just gotten up and made a closer examination to be sure. But then again, the object of the exercise was to occupy her mind, not parse alien home decor.

With what sounded like a triumphant chitter, her former hostage returned, a bundle of black and gold in its upper arms. Corsi's moment of hope faded as she unfolded it and found only her uniform.

"My combadge?" she asked, tapping her own body to indicate where the equipment would have hung. "My phaser?"

The chiptaur chittered and tilted its head, making a gesture that could have indicated no, or that it didn't understand, or that an unseen insect was annoying its left ear.

"Okay then, how about underwear?" Corsi tried. "Or boots?"

Similar chitter, same gesture. Could be the beginning of communication. Or a persistent insect.

Examining her uniform, Corsi realized it had been cut open and repaired. After a fashion. All of the seams had been ripped out and carefully resewn, obviously by hand, using a vegetable fiber almost like twine, though it may have been a sort of vine. Hundreds of tiny knots, along the outside, thankfully, held the seams together.

Considering the pounded feltlike material of the blankets and the leaf-skin bandages, Corsi suspected they'd never seen woven fabric before. Certainly they'd never had need of clothes given their thick coats of coarse— well, it wasn't exactly fur. More like two-centimeter-long flexible scales or fused feathers. She was sure there was an official Starfleet exobiological classification for their body covering, but for the short term she was going with hair.

At any rate, it was likely the thinner elastic materials of her underwear would have thwarted the experimental resewing process. The chiptaurs probably lacked the technology to repair her synthetic boots once they'd cut them off as well.

Her socks were undamaged; the chiptaurs evidently had no trouble figuring out how to get them off. However, bare feet offered better traction than stocking feet. She resolved to keep them handy in case the nights turned cold.

Though now that she thought of it, she had no way of knowing if it were day or night outside her little room. It was possible the current temperature, which she estimated at twenty degrees, represented the dead of their winter.

Filing that speculation under "find out later," Corsi spent a few moments demonstrating how the clothes fastened and unfastened to the chiptaurs. This seemed to release a swarm of ear-annoying bugs. She decided the gesture meant something besides "no." She let them practice a bit with the fasteners, ensuring the next human they encountered would escape with his or her wardrobe intact, if nothing else.

Watching the intelligence with which they examined the new technology and the way they evidently discussed it among themselves, Corsi decided the chiptaurs weren't barbarians. She'd already suspected that—nonviolence was a pretty sophisticated cultural concept—but there was a civility to their behavior that reassured her.

Evidence was tipping the scales in favor of her hosts being rescuers rather than captors.

Now if she could only remember how she got here.

CHAPTER
5

Pattie woke to the stench of rotting bog plants and an unpleasant sensation of moistness. The clatter and caw of what sounded like a dozen disparate animals in close proximity echoed flatly as though they were in an enclosed space.

She knew the situation wasn't good before she opened her eyes.

A cage. About twice her body length square, standard low-tech metal frame and floored with peat and mud. There was a rectangular box, evidently an overturned packing case of some sort, just big enough to hold her with an opening cut in the near side. Several varieties of what she assumed were local wetland plants were arranged in neat piles along one side of the cage, no doubt a selection of potential foodstuffs.

"Let me guess," she said, addressing the humanoid shape beyond the bars. "You found me sticking out of a hole in the mud and assumed I'm a large burrowing insect."

The animal keeper, if that's what he was, started at the sound of her voice and moved closer.

He—Pattie based her assumption of gender on the fact that the alien appeared to be both mammal and flat-chested—had charcoal gray skin and a thick helmet of copper-red hair. If he had external ears they were hidden by the hair, but the thin nose, generous mouth, and widely spaced yellow eyes were all classic humanoid pheno-types. Another descendant of the ancient progenitors who'd spread their DNA over so much of the galaxy.

The keeper made cooing and clucking sounds. Not language, Pattie realized, but nonsense noises meant to soothe a possibly hurt and probably frightened animal. Reaching through the mesh of her cage he picked a sprig of a plant from one of the piles and offered it to her.

"There is no way a collapsing tunnel of peat moss knocked my combadge off." Pattie tapped her thorax to indicate where the device had been. "That means you have it."

The keeper froze, his eyes locked on the bare spot on Pattie's chest.

"Struck a nerve, did I?" she asked. "Why don't you give it back so we can have a real conversation?"

The keeper's eyes shifted from Pattie's chest to her face. She could not believe he mistook the reasoned tones of her bell-like language for animal noises. Whatever he thought they were, however, scared him. He dropped the sprig of greenery and backed away from the cage.

"Don't overreact," she said. "I'm really quite harmless."

This did not seem to reassure the humanoid. Turning quickly, he disappeared behind a rack of smaller cages. A few moments later Pattie heard what sounded like an exterior door slamming shut.

"That went well."

The animals in the nearest cages—and given the zoo-keeper's mistake, she studied them for several minutes before deciding those in her immediate area *were* animals—regarded her silently. They knew she didn't belong there, but there was nothing they could do about it. Counting, she saw they all had eight legs. A few of the smaller ones even had exoskeletons. So the zookeeper wasn't a complete idiot; she did bear a passing resemblance to the local fauna. Or at least what a humanoid might mistake for a resemblance.

Except there weren't supposed to be any humanoids—zookeeper or otherwise—on Zhatyra II.

But that was a question for another time. Right now her priority was escape.

Thirty minutes of thorough study later, she decided to reassess her priority hierarchy. At least in the short term. The cage was solidly built and the lock unreachable from the inside. And neither any of the bog plants nor the packing box were sturdy enough to pry the mesh work open far enough for her to squeeze through.

Evidently the most recent addition to the zoo, her cage faced an open expanse of floor and the rest of what was apparently a warehouse of some sort. The walls she could see were log, though the roof looked like metal. She thought the floor was made of half logs fitted tightly together, their sawn faces sanded smooth but unfinished.

If her theory was correct, floor polish was likely a low priority.

Directly in front of her cage was an assembly and repair area, judging by the organized tool racks and various stains on the wood floor, with storage of parts or materials beyond. There was also an office area of sorts, with desks and cabinets along the nearest wall.

There were a dozen things she could see that would have made short work of her prison. The closest was three meters out of reach.

"Since I can't get myself out," Pattie explained to a neighbor with reddish fur or feathers, she wasn't sure which, "I'll have to convince our host that I don't belong here."

The neighbor seemed to agree. At least it bobbed up and down several times, which seemed to indicate assent.

Thus encouraged, Pattie began cleaning out her cage. The neat piles of vegetation were transferred, still neatly arranged, outside her cage. She then improvised a shovel from a panel torn from the packing crate and scooped as much of the dirt as she could from the enclosure. It wasn't as neat, shoving the dirt through the mesh, but she did her best to ensure it was clearly an organized effort and not the random behavior of an animal. What she couldn't get out she swept into a neat pile in one corner of the cage.

By the time she was done the room full of cages had become almost dark. Though she could see no windows from where she was, Pattie suspected the illumination was natural. Either a storm was coming or night was falling. The gradual dimming and the lack of wind noises convinced her it was nightfall.

So did the falling temperature. It had been over twenty when she had awakened. Now it felt closer to ten. Not cold, but cooler than she liked.

Particularly in her exhausted state. Whatever her injuries from the tunnel's collapse, not to mention the stress of events leading up to it, the toll on her system had been high. Pattie felt the stiffness in her joints and the ache in her muscles. She knew she had very little left in the way of reserves.

Though she hated to do anything that might be mistaken for animal behavior, Pattie decided to take advantage of the insulation the packing box offered. Curling up in her makeshift shelter, Pattie settled down for the night.

CHAPTER

6

Apparently having decided she was well enough to forgo being tightly bound in blankets, her three nurses let Corsi sleep unencumbered through the night. At least she assumed it was night. In a windowless room lit by a basket of glowing yarn, it was hard to tell. Sticking her head out the low doorway proved her nurses doubled as guards; all three of them were asleep across the only other exit from the next chamber.

In the morning Lefty presented her with a wooden bowl of water and a pack of survival rations. Predictably, the seal of the pack had been ignored and the foil sliced open.

"That had to be sharp," Corsi said. "How many of these did you mangle before you figured out what it was?"

There were only four in the emergency jump harness's

survival kit. Two thousand calories of essential nutrients and vitamins each, along with a half-dozen water purification pills, good for a liter each.

The bowl was a bit more than half a liter, but she wasn't going to try and split one of the tiny tablets. She dropped it in, accepting the metallic taste as fair trade for the knowledge she wasn't ingesting any unwelcome microbes.

As she ate, she demonstrated the pouch's unseal and reseal feature to the chiptaurs. This led to another round of left ear brushing. Corsi tentatively decided the gesture meant either *wow!* or *arrgh!*

After brunch, Head Nurse, Lefty, and Spot led Corsi through a series of small chambers that opened abruptly into a large indoor amphitheater. At least that was her first impression. Her second was that she was in the root system of a giant banyan tree.

Apparently realizing she needed time to take it all in, her nurses paused and made gestures that seemed to invite her to look around. Corsi did, turning in place as she surveyed her new surroundings.

Around three-quarters of the edges of a roughly oval clearing about two hundred meters across its long axis, columns of wood several meters thick rose from the ground to meet what appeared to be a network of even wider branches some thirty meters overhead. There was no sky, though the foliage above glowed with a diffuse green light that suggested daylight somewhere beyond.

Broad roots, like the one from which she and her companions had emerged, diverged horizontally from the base of each column, while smaller trunks arched between columns at apparently random intervals farther up.

The air was pungent with a dozen odors she couldn't identify. Or almost could. A smoke, very like incense; the peppermint and cedar scent of her bedding; a sharp, sweet tang like a mixture of apples and oranges; and a musky, nutmeg odor she suspected was her hosts en masse.

And they were en masse. There were dozens of chiptaurs moving across the open area, heading in and out of tunnels carved into the wooden pillars, or angled shallowly into the ground, or disappearing into the rock face that broke into the circle of roots along about a quarter of its arc.

Corsi realized it was a city, made up of carved spaces in both rock and wood built within the root system of a giant forest, or a single tree. Though superficially the image of the chiptaurs with their mostly horizontal bodies moving about plants that dwarfed them resembled a nest of carpenter ants, there was nothing insectoid in their movements. No one seemed to be in a hurry and knots of conversation seemed to form and break up again with companionable informality.

She noticed the chiptaurs came in two sizes. Some, like her nurses, were broad and rounded, usually with a softly mottled brown on brown pattern to their hair. Others, with a more distinctive dark brown on reddish brown pattern, were narrower and seemed to have a leaner build. If chiptaurs followed the pattern of most mammalian species Corsi knew of, the broader ones were females.

Having the consideration of female nurses to a convalescing female stranger was another mark in their favor. Not enough for Corsi to drop her guard completely—female nurses might have been a cultural norm that had nothing to do with her gender. But her attendants shifted in her mind from being *its* to *hers* and their threat status went down another notch.

Corsi expected her three nurses to lead her to some sort of central authority. Instead they took her on a wandering tour of what seemed to be a vital community.

Wide corridors with curving walls and ceilings carved from living wood or earth and lit by myriad baskets of bioluminescent spaghetti connected the first clearing to others. Most of the tunnels were tall enough for her to walk comfortably erect, but the chiptaurs were apparent minimalists when it came to doorways. Some were a tight fit for Head Nurse, largest of her nurses.

Corsi had noticed that Head Nurse had spent the most time dealing directly with her and seemed to be in charge of the others. She'd wondered if the chiptaur's broader frame had indicated a higher status, but seeing her ease her way through a couple of doorways she realized that Head Nurse was simply overweight.

Nearly half of one clearing into which they led her was enclosed by an endless expanse of solid wood. Corsi surmised it was the central trunk of the "banyan" tree. Several wider corridors, arranged in apparent randomness, disappeared into its depths.

Everywhere there were chiptaurs. Some followed along for a while, strolling comfortably behind, beside, or even ahead of her little group. Others acknowledged them in passing, nodding their broad heads at Corsi as though she were a familiar acquaintance. Many at a distance waved or made gestures that appeared friendly.

Dozens of times, also apparently at random, her

escorts stopped to introduce her to an individual or small group. These impromptu confabs seemed to involve a good deal of explanation or perhaps storytelling on the part of her nurses. Corsi suspected she and the details of her convalescence were being discussed, but she could not tell to what purpose nor what the hearers thought of the tale.

In every instance, at the end of her nurses' recitation, the chiptaur or chiptaurs to which Corsi had been presented addressed her directly with two distinct phrases of clicks and ticks. She assumed it was the chiptaur equivalent of *pleased to meet you* or *glad you're here*. In any case, it seemed friendly, if a bit formal.

Corsi did her bit for interspecies goodwill by smiling, stating her name in pleasant tones, and assuring them she was delighted to be there and to meet them whenever it seemed she was expected to contribute to the conversation. In fact, she was enjoying herself a bit. The constant motion was working the kinks and aches out of her joints and muscles while the unfamiliar sights and sounds kept her conscious mind busy. That last was doing more to help her subconscious sort out where it had misfiled her memories than lying alone in a wooden room would have done.

Extrapolating from the numbers of chiptaurs she could see in the amphitheater clearings and the flow of traffic in and out of tunnels, she estimated the population of the community was somewhere between eighteen and twenty-four thousand. Not a city, but certainly larger than a village.

At the far end of one amphitheater they entered was a raised stage on which several chiptaurs moved about in an organized fashion while a sizable crowd lounged on the ground and watched. She had no way of knowing if it was a theatrical performance or a religious ceremony. In any case, her nurses had no interest in attending and led her out another way.

They were well down another corridor when she realized there hadn't been any music to accompany the organized movement. Whether it was a ballet, a play, or a mass, she would have expected some sort of music.

Now that she thought of it, there was no music anywhere. At least, she thought there wasn't. Some of the chittering clicks and ticks that made up the background murmur of the chiptaur city could have been local opera for all she could tell. What were definitely missing were musical instruments.

There were niches or hollows lining the walls of some of the broader corridors and carved into the bases of many of the root columns. These appeared to be shops offering wares she could only glimpse in passing. Apparent fruits or vegetables, baskets of every description, a wood carver, and what might have been a physician.

She wasn't sure, but Corsi thought she remembered Abramowitz once explaining that an active economy in nonessentials and decorative arts indicated something significant about a culture's development. Of course, she couldn't remember exactly what that significant thing was.

What she could do, with a tactician's eye, was evaluate the technology around her.

No metal, of that she was sure. Cutting and carving tools appeared to be made of volcanic glass, similar to obsidian but in a variety of colors. She saw levers, pulleys, and inclined planes in use everywhere, but evidently the chiptaurs hadn't thought to attach their pulleys to the bottom of a platform to make wheels. Every burden she saw was carried; no carts or even sleds were in evidence.

Nor were any weapons. She couldn't be sure if it was planetwide or just the rules of this particular community, but there was nothing remotely resembling a spear, club, or bow anywhere to be seen. There were edge tools in abundance, from wooden shovels to chisels and vegetable choppers apparently shaped from volcanic glass. But none were shaped and balanced as weapons.

Corsi began to suspect the assertive nonviolence practiced by her nurses reflected the cultural norm here. Wherever here was.

There were cultivated areas beyond the columns of roots bordering some of the amphitheaters. This didn't seem right to Corsi, particularly since the spaces received less indirect sunlight than the clearings. Perhaps the pinkish-yellow growths were more akin to mushrooms than true plants.

Lining each mushroom garden were rows of simple lean-tos with pounded felt blankets draped over their open ends. Corsi's companions led her to one of these and made several ambiguous gestures that communicated nothing, then stood by expectantly.

"Uh-huh," Corsi said. "It's a lovely lean-to. Are these the guest quarters?"

Evidently realizing she hadn't understood what they'd meant to communicate, the chiptaurs repeated their pantomime, which seemed to involve several uncomfortable postures.

Looking past their performance, Corsi saw individual chiptaurs entering other lean-tos in the row, then emerging a few moments later. She laughed, the sudden sound startling her nurses.

"Got it," she said. "Public toilets fertilize mushroom garden. Thanks for the thought. Not now, maybe later."

At length the nurses decided she'd understood their message and declined the offer. Corsi waited with the head nurse while Lefty and Spot availed themselves of lean-tos, then followed them back toward the cliff face that bordered the other side of the clearing.

Corsi realized they were back in the first amphitheater. Orienting herself to the cliff, she headed back toward the tunnel from which they'd emerged hours before.

Her nurses headed her off and led her again toward the cliff. As they got closer she realized a stream of water ran along a stone trough at the base of the wall.

Several chiptaurs were kneeling on their front pair of legs as their back pair remained standing, dipping all four arms into the flow of water.

"Hand washing?" Corsi asked, pantomiming scrubbing.

Her nurses seemed to approve, mimicking her gestures.

"Hygiene is good," Corsi agreed and knelt beside them to wash her own hands in the water.

It was hot.

She snatched back her hands, expecting them to be partially cooked by the brief contact with the boiling water.

Leaning back on her heels, Corsi looked up at the cliff face. Now that she was looking directly at it, she realized it was strangely uniform, rising at a constant slope.

"This is a volcanic cinder cone, isn't it?"

The image was back. She was on the roof of a rain forest canopy, beneath a white sun and hazy sky. In the near distance was a ring of volcanoes, cinder cones as symmetrical as a child's sand castles barely protruding above the giant trees. Smoke or steam rising . . .

The head nurse chittered at her, getting her up and moving toward a tunnel leading into the face of the cinder cone.

"If the only reason you guys patched me up was you needed a virgin to sacrifice to the volcano, I'm afraid we're both going to be disappointed."

Great. Trapped and alone on a strange planet and the first time I think of Fabe is when I make one of his lame jokes. Sentimental fool, that's what I am.

As soon as they crossed the threshold, Corsi saw this tunnel was different from the others she'd seen. It was paneled, for one thing. Or wainscoted. Great broad planks laid horizontally covered the rough pumice walls to just above chiptaur height. Which was to say about even with Corsi's elbows. For another, the walls slanted in, disappearing in the darkness above the glow baskets without ever coming together. This was a natural fissure, perhaps an ancient steam vent from the volcano's early days, not a passageway the chiptaurs had carved by hand.

Corsi could sense a difference in her escorts as well. They seemed subdued, but excited as well. Their chirps and chitters took on a hushed quality, but their eyes were bright and active. Anticipation? Reverence? Something like that. Corsi couldn't put her finger on it.

The temperature within the tunnel rose, to at least

thirty-five degrees she estimated, feeling the sweat trickle down her back. A sharp, sulfurous tang watered her eyes and scratched at the back of her throat. From the deep breaths the chiptaurs were taking she guessed this was a good thing.

The tunnel abruptly opened into an irregular chamber, roughly thirty meters across, well lit by hundreds of glowing baskets. Corsi fought gagging against the stench of chemicals as she looked around. This was obviously something special to the chiptaurs and her collapsing in a spasming heap would probably spoil the moment.

Two streams, each staining the gray rocks around it with orange and red chemicals, poured from the walls, their flows caught in a series of troughs. The troughs in turn carried the water to a series of pools. Something about the interconnected waterways snagged a corner of Corsi's mind, but it was gone before she could catch it. Vents in the floor of the chamber released pungent steam; she estimated the temperature to be somewhere above forty now. From the bubbling of the pools, she guessed there were also vents under the water.

Most of the pools had a chiptaur occupying a low couch of carved wood. Other chiptaurs moved about, apparently providing their seated relatives with food and water or just companionship.

Her guides presented Corsi to each of the reclining chiptaurs in turn. She repeated her self-identification and expression of joy at being there when she thought it was indicated, wondering if she was being at last introduced to royalty of some sort. For their part the seated chiptaurs repeated the two clicky-tick phrases she'd heard so often.

As part of each interview she was directed to regard the bubbling pool of water. Some contained dozens of what appeared to be glass spheres, similar to ancient fishing net floats, others had various numbers of what looked to Corsi like koi, only mottled copper and black instead of white and gold. One pool seemed to contain a pair of large tadpoles, with two sets of legs and arms in addition to their stubby tails.

Corsi parsed that there was some connection between the contents of the pool and the status or office of the chiptaur presiding over it. Or at least she thought there was. With the complete lack of language it was hard to be sure.

They came at last to a pool with no one beside it. The attendant chiptaurs, smaller than any Corsi had yet seen but with the brown on brown color scheme she associated with females, were just finishing arranging pounded felt blankets over the couch and arranging shallow bowls of what looked like berries nearby.

Head Nurse turned to her and took both her hands into her upper pair. Sensing this was a solemn moment, Corsi dropped to one knee, drawing a sharp breath at her back's protest, to bring herself at eye level with the chiptaur.

The nurse chiptaur spoke at some length. While there was nothing in the tones of her chitters, clicks, and ticks that corresponded to human speech, Corsi had the impression it was something along the lines of a benediction.

"Amen," she said when the speech was finally over. "And same to you. Really."

Apparently satisfied, the head nurse dropped Corsi's hands and settled herself on the reclining couch the attendants had prepared. Corsi decided her earlier guess had been right. Head Nurse was a member of some sort of ruling class. Whether she ruled because of her size or had put on weight due to the extra calories being waited on entailed wasn't clear.

Corsi's two remaining nurse guides made it plain she was to leave with them. As she followed Lefty and Spot down the tunnel toward the outside world she wondered what having a personal nurse on the ruling council said about her status as a guest—or prisoner—of the chiptaurs.

CHAPTER

7

Pattie awoke to discover the dirt and piles of plants had been cleared from around her cage. Looking about she spied what she thought were the zookeeper's legs extending beneath a counter that held a variety of small cages a half-dozen meters away.

She decided it was best not to startle someone who might be handling a dangerous animal and waited for him to finish whatever he was doing. When he stepped into view, Pattie rose to her hind legs to bring her eye level as close to his as possible. It took her a moment to decide it was indeed the same fellow she'd met the day before.

"Good morning," she said.

A sibilant mutter responded from a pocket in the

zookeeper's trousers. The man tried to jump away from his own pants.

"Still have my combadge, I see," Pattie said conversationally.

The zookeeper stopped dancing and swatting at his pocket. He stared at her wide-eyed, his mouth agape.

Humanoid dumbstruck amazement, Pattie observed. *That one's definitely universal.*

"In my culture, when we discover we've mistaken a sentient being for an animal, common courtesy dictates we release her from captivity and return her belongings," she said. "Do your people have a similar custom?"

The zookeeper pulled her combadge from his pocket and held it in the flat of his palm. Eyes fixed on Pattie, he stepped closer to the cage. For a moment she dared hope he was actually going to give it back and let her out of the cage, but he stopped a meter beyond her reach.

Why is it never the easy way?

"Who are you?" the zookeeper asked, bending toward her. "What is this thing?"

Not wearing the combadge, Pattie could hear both the zookeeper's words and the translation. She was surprised by the liquid sibilance of the language. Given his gray skin and dark clothing, Pattie had expected her captor's speech to sound like Cardassian. A silly bit of prejudice, she realized.

"My name is P8 Blue, though I'm known informally as Pattie," she answered the literal question. "The device you took from me is my combadge."

"How does it work?"

"As you can hear, it's a translator," Pattie said, keeping her tone pleasant. She wasn't going to lie; lies were too hard to keep straight. But she wasn't going to volunteer any information, either.

For a moment the zookeeper seemed to accept that noninformation as an answer.

"Where are you from?" he asked.

"Pretty far away," Pattie said. "The vehicle I was traveling in sank in the bog. Were you the one who rescued me?"

"Yes," the zookeeper seemed surprised to be asked a question. "My name is Solal. I am a [student animal husbandry authority]."

Pattie recognized the awkward phrasing of a term the universal translator couldn't render exactly.

"Either you've lost some arms and legs," Pattie said, diverting the conversation, "or you're not from around here."

In fact, Pattie had a pretty good idea where Solal was from. If she was right, the Prime Directive was in full effect; do or say nothing to indicate civilizations on other planets nor interfere with civilization on this one. Aided by the eight-extremitied physiology of the local fauna, she was going to play Zhatyra II native.

If possible, she was going to get her combadge and disappear into the forest until the *da Vinci* arrived. Failing that, she was going to focus on avoiding vivisection until Captain Gold rescued her.

And Commander Corsi.

"I come from beyond the sky," Solal was saying.

"Really?" Pattie asked, packing the word with amazed interest. "Literally? Not metaphorically? Fascinating. Pull up a chair and tell me about it."

Whatever Solal would have said died with the sound

of a distant door opening and closing. Suddenly tense, he leaned close to the cage.

"Do not speak," he hissed. "Animals that speak are killed."

Pattie nodded, shocked.

Solal stood, then as quickly stooped again.

"What do you eat?" he asked. "Do you need anything?"

Student animal husbandry authority, Pattie thought. *Keep the livestock healthy.*

"Just distilled water," she said aloud. "Local food doesn't agree with me."

Solal nodded and rose again. Wrapping Pattie's combadge in a rag, he shoved it deep into the back of a drawer in a nearby cabinet just as another of his kind arrived.

Pattie held perfectly still, making no move that might attract the newcomer's attention.

She guessed from his build that the new arrival was also male and, from the texture of his skin, older. His hair was a darker red than Solal's, almost a brown, and he seemed to have about twenty percent more mass, most of it girth. Perhaps Solal was an adolescent.

The newcomer, folio of some sort in hand, seemed to be reviewing information it contained with Solal. If Solal was a student, the newcomer's attitude indicated he was a teacher animal husbandry authority. Senior zookeeper at any rate. Apparently satisfied with whatever Solal had to report, the elder zookeeper then issued what sounded like a series of instructions or list of tasks.

He turned his back to Pattie, evidently pointing in the direction of something beyond the walls of the menagerie.

Taking advantage of his distraction, Pattie lowered herself to all eights, making no sudden moves that might attract his attention. Carefully, as silently as possible, she backed into the packing case shelter Solal had provided. Easing herself as far into its shadow as she could, she settled down to wait.

Animals that speak are killed.

CHAPTER

8

"Another week." Fabian Stevens glared into the fire.

Bart Faulwell, seated across the table from his friend, shook his head sympathetically. The two had met for lunch at a tavern in a ski resort in Pludnt. Their table was comfortably near a massive fireplace, the exact mirror of its twin at the other end of the long room paneled in dark and highly figured woods.

A few thousand kilometers to the south hundreds of solar mirrors focused their light on the face of the southern polar ice floe, starting the water on its journey north to irrigate the temperate zone. Here, however, the snow-clad slopes of long extinct volcanoes provided the best skiing in the southern hemisphere.

It was dark outside, Stevens and Bart's personal lunchtime coinciding with local dinner, and the tavern was filled with what Bart assumed were tourists. They had the festive air of people far from home and responsibilities.

It was remarkable to him that on a world close to global famine, populated by a people who across a dozen regional cultures were emphatically uninterested in events beyond their horizons, tourism was a universal passion. He'd discussed it with Carol Abramowitz. The cultural specialist had explained global tourism was a recent phenomenon, something that had developed in the last two centuries.

When the Bundinalli had developed warp drive and discovered space around them was crowded with dozens of alien species and civilizations, their definitions of "local" and "familiar" had undergone a radical change. Now they routinely took vacations to places their great-grandparents hadn't even imagined. But fundamental natures didn't change that quickly. Tourism off-planet was essentially nonexistent. For all their newfound mobility, their destinations were still local.

His thoughts were interrupted by the arrival of their meal. The local specialty was a game animal that tasted very much like lamb roasted with dried fruit put up in the traditional manner—dried in front of the very hearth they were enjoying now—from the previous summer's growing season. They both had identical platters; local rules of symmetry did not allow different meals to be served at the same table, and the aroma was enticing.

Bart carved a forkful of meat and skewered a slice of fruit. Good. Every bit as good as the aroma. If he were stationed here another week he'd probably put on a kilo.

He said as much to Stevens.

"It's good," his friend said. "Almost in a league with *rastentha* soufflé."

Bart snorted. Stevens had been singing the praises of the Brohtz specialty to anyone who would listen.

"Any luck finding someone willing to program it into the replicators?" he asked.

"Not yet." Stevens shrugged. "Soloman said he'd look into it once the present mission was over, but . . ."

He let his voice trail off.

"What did Corsi say when you told her about the delay?" Bart asked.

"Nothing," Stevens said, slicing a thick chunk of meat from his portion. "Just the automated response from the shuttle."

"Isn't that unusual?"

"Not really," Stevens gestured with his laden fork. "Like Tev said, the Zhatyra observational array was due for its ten-year download when the war broke out. They've got one cloaked satellite they know is down and eleven more that need their recordings downloaded, memories purged, and other routine maintenance. Even with the extra week Dom and Pattie will probably still be at it when we get there."

Bart said nothing. The additional week was only an estimate. They both knew that if the S.C.E. couldn't get a handle on stabilizing the Bundinalli water system in that time they would be here even longer.

Reaching into his shoulder bag propped against the leg of the table, Bart pulled out a leather folio and placed it on the table.

"Here."

Stevens looked at the folio, then at Bart. "What? Your letters to Anthony?"

"No. I replicated a folio for you," Bart explained. "It's just like the one I use for writing to Anthony. I figured you might like writing to Commander Corsi."

"Writing to— I'll be seeing her in a week or so."

"I know that," Bart said. "I also know that when I write letters to Anthony they don't actually go anywhere until I see him again and can put them in his hand. But when I'm thinking about him, writing *to* him is the best way I know to feel as though he's there with me."

"Oh." Stevens picked up the folio and hefted it. "Thanks. I'll have to try that."

Lacking a shoulder bag, he set the folio on the edge of the table at his elbow.

Bart reached into the bag again and drew out his own folio. Eyeing the location of Stevens's, he placed his carefully on the edge of the table at his own elbow.

Catching his friend's questioning look, he waved his hand, indicating their precisely symmetrical surroundings.

"Just in case," he explained.

CHAPTER
9

The next day, instead of bringing her the usual survival rations and water, Spot and Lefty led Corsi through a number of tunnels, all of which looked familiar. At last they entered a large room, completely open along one wall. Corsi realized a wooden room so wide and deep could only be in the main trunk of the tree. She wondered how much of this carving out it could take.

There were several raised surfaces coming directly out of the floor, like truncated pillars that reminded Corsi of mesas rising out of the desert. As the number of chiptaurs lounging about them registered, she realized she'd been literally correct. The truncated pillars were tables.

"A restaurant?" she guessed.

Her two companions, evidently agreeing with whatever they thought she'd said, led the way to a table near the open wall. They were no more than a dozen meters from the ground, Corsi saw, overlooking a clearing she didn't recognize.

"Lovely," Corsi said, "And I'm starving. But without my tricorder, I'm not sure what foods of yours I can eat."

This seemed to please Spot and Lefty. They settled in. Tucking their four legs beneath them, they each leaned their upper torso forward to rest the elbows of their lower arms on the table. They both indicated with their free hands that Corsi should also sit.

Corsi looked around the restaurant and saw they were being politely ignored by the other diners. The few whose eye she caught nodded politely before turning their attention back to their own tables.

More significantly, a row of chiptaurs was approaching from a different entrance, laden with bowls of food and wooden plates.

"You called ahead for reservations, didn't you?" she asked Lefty.

The chiptaur chirped, making what Corsi was fairly sure was an encouraging gesture.

She sat, tailor fashion, ignoring the scream of protest from her left knee and thigh. The tabletop was a little too high for comfort and a bit too far away for convenience. However, with the table being a solid pillar, there was no way to slide any closer and the chiptaurs had evidently not developed booster-seat technology.

Come to think of it, how come I haven't seen any children?

Her thought was interrupted by the arrival of the waitstaff with bowls of fruit and vegetables, some raw and some steaming, and cauldrons of soup and water. These they placed in the center of the table. Wooden platters, two sorts of wooden bowls, wooden utensils that looked remarkably like human forks and spoons, were set in front of each diner.

Glancing around, Corsi saw similar communal arrangements on the other tables. The chiptaurs were continuing their practice of behaving as though she were just like everyone else. Fair enough, provided their food didn't kill her.

Bobbing politely, the servers withdrew.

For their part, her two companions continued to make their encouraging chirps and clicks, indicating various bowls as they did.

Hoping local microbes didn't like humans, Corsi indicated she would like some water. Spot poured half a liter into the smaller of her two bowls, then poured some in her own and Lefty's. It was cold, with the mineral tang of an artesian well.

Despite her thirst, Corsi was careful to sip. She couldn't help trying to taste for microbes.

From that point she was committed. She tried a tiny sample from each bowl, waiting several moments between bites to check for adverse reactions. The fruit was so bitter the tiniest nip had made her scalp contract, but the steamed greens with what looked like walnuts were delicious.

Corsi was just deciding the flavor of starchy tubers was a constant throughout the galaxy, when a scuttle of brown movement at the edge of the table caught the corner of her eye. *Scorpion!*

She swung without thinking. But fast as her battle-trained reflexes were, Lefty was faster. The chiptaur's heavy lower arm flashed across the table, taking the full force of Corsi's backhand before it connected with its target.

For a heartbeat no one in the restaurant moved. Then Spot rose and came around the table with an empty platter and sprig of green from a salad and began trying to coax the intruder onto the plate.

Now that she had a chance to study it, Corsi was sure she would have swung even if she'd seen the creature clearly. About twelve centimeters long, the pseudoscorpion was heavily scaled and armed with a pair of lobsterlike claws. Otherwise its general layout was similar to her hosts', with four legs for locomotion, the heavy pair of claws, and two smaller manipulative arms near its mandibles.

However, Lefty's intervention and the care Spot was taking to rescue the creature told her swatting at the thing had been a bad choice. Hadn't she just wondered where the chiptaur children were? For all she knew, this was a chiptaur toddler going through some sort of larval stage. Or it could be a pet. Or a deity, for all she knew.

From the surreptitious glances she could see their table was getting from the other diners, Corsi suspected she'd just undone a lot of the goodwill she'd spent so much time trying to build up.

Corsi watched as Spot traded the plate with the passenger for a clean one provided by a server, trying to make her concern apparent. She was sure it was the violence of her instinctive reaction, more than the potential harm to the animal, that had upset the chiptaurs.

She just hoped a show of remorse would repair some of the damage.

The rest of the meal passed without incident. By the time she and her companions rose, the other diners had regained their relaxed and convivial air. Though, as she returned the waves of several on the way out, Corsi realized chiptaurs had been coming and going. Most of those now eating may not have witnessed her moment of savagery.

They had not traveled far along the broad corridor before a commotion broke out behind them. Or as close to a commotion as anything Corsi had seen among the chiptaurs. Several voices were raised above the general buzz of clicks and chitters, all of them apparently calling out similar phrases.

Spot and Lefty wheeled in place to face the way they'd come. Corsi turned as well, noting there was no interruption in the flow of traffic and general conversations around them. Her companions weren't looking back because they were curious; the calls were directed at them.

A party of chiptaurs was approaching, as close to a mob as anything Corsi had seen, clearly excited and in a hurry. Even in their haste, however, they did not push past anyone. Most in the corridor saw them coming and moved out of the way. However, if a chiptaur seemed unaware of them, the group paused in its rush, speaking with what looked to be courtesy and waiting until the way was again clear.

How do these people get anything done?

At last they were upon her and her entourage, but rather than crowd around her as humans would have done, the mob compressed itself along one wall of the corridor. Though Corsi's height and the curving ceiling kept her near the center of the corridor, the chiptaurs

were doing their best to leave the right-of-way unobstructed.

There were four chiptaurs to the core group, Corsi deduced from the loose formation of the small crowd. But
just as individuals had joined her tour of the town earlier,
another dozen chiptaurs had apparently attached themselves to the central four as they passed. She still had no
idea whether this was a show of support or curiosity.

The leader of the core group, a male whose reddish
hair was almost copper in the light of the glow baskets,
was holding something concealed in his clasped fore-
hands.

Taking a small step forward from the others, he extended his clasped hands 'slightly and he chittered at
Corsi.

"What is this?" asked a voice from his hands.

Corsi almost whooped.

"My combadge," she answered, keeping her voice level
as chitters and ticks emitted from the chiptaur's hands.
"It enables me to talk to others."

Without ceremony the chiptaur opened his hands and
extended the combadge to Corsi.

Trying not to snatch, but not giving him time to rethink the gesture, Corsi took her combadge from the
chiptaur's palm and affixed it to her uniform. Pretending
to adjust its position, she pressed a contact, broadcasting
a nonverbal signal. There was no response. Either there
were no other Starfleet personnel in range, or something
had happened to them. Neither thought triggered any
memory.

"It was silent for many meals," the leader observed,
bringing her mind back to her surroundings.

Many meals? How long was I unconscious?

"The universal translator needed time to learn your language," she explained.

The chiptaurs regarded her blankly for a moment. Given the level of their technology, she wondered if they thought she'd told them the combadge was a living thing.

"My name is Domenica Corsi," she said, moving on. "How are you called?"

"We are the K'k'tict," the copper-colored male answered. "My name is—"

The universal translator rendered a series of clicks and ticks Corsi couldn't follow. The other three in his group apparently introduced themselves as well, oblivious to the UT's inability to render K'k'tict proper names in a form she could track. She wondered how her name had sounded to them.

Corsi looked to Lefty and Spot, expecting them to tell her their names as well, but they remained silent. She deduced there was a social order at work and that they were not far enough up the ladder to take part in the conversation.

"I thank you for the return of my combadge," Corsi tapped the badge and smiled her most diplomatic smile. "Will you be able to return any more of my tools?"

"No," the lead K'k'tict replied simply. "We fear one or more of them may be instruments of harm."

No arguing with that.

"I have no memory of how I came to be here," she said, trying another tactic.

"You fell from the leaves," one of the females flanking Copper answered. "Perhaps from the sky above."

The image returned, clear and isolated, without

context. The roof of the rain forest, the volcanic cones with streamers of steam, an objective . . . what? She was moving, reaching from branch to branch; a white sun with thin, high clouds overhead and a sense of great depth below. She tested a mossy branch, then trusted her full weight to it as she reached for the next. But the branch was an arm or a leg of some giant tree dweller. Like the sloths of Earth, it allowed moss to grow over its fur as protective camouflage. The creature twitched and twisted, trying to escape. She hurtled downward through branches toward darkness.

With a start Corsi came back to herself in the middle of the crowded corridor. She realized she'd missed the last thing Copper had said to her.

"I'm sorry?" she said. "I didn't understand."

Better than "I wasn't paying attention."

"We want to know," Copper said patiently, "why are you killing the K'k'tict?"

CHAPTER
10

It was by Pattie's estimation midday when Solal returned. He apparently took her earlier invitation to heart, pulling a chair from a nearby desk along with him. He had what was evidently his own lunch, biscuits with small slabs of a cheese-like substance, and a variety of local greenery in a bag.

"I'm trying to get you to eat," he explained, the combadge in his breast pocket chorusing its translation.

Pattie nodded, understanding the cover story. If she couldn't convince him to give her the combadge, she was going to have to teach him how to turn it off. If it started speaking Nasat when one of Solal's supervisors was around . . .

She had remained in the packing crate all morning, venturing out only to retrieve the bowl of distilled water

Solal had left on his way out to do whatever chores had been assigned.

Three others of his species had worked in the menagerie for brief periods or simply walked through, apparently on rounds of some sort. Two of the strangers had been clearly female, their body shapes confirming Pattie's theory the invaders were mammals.

And they were invaders. Perhaps it was just her response to the knowledge they killed what they considered talking animals, but just as she knew Solal's people were not native to Zhatyra II, she knew their purpose here was not good.

While hiding in her packing crate, Pattie had given some thought on how best to go about pumping Solal for information. She'd decided her initial tactic of friendly interest had been wise. That he classified her as an animal worked to her advantage in that he evidently did not regard her as a threat—which did not bode well for any "talking animals" his people had encountered—and that he seemed genuinely fond of all animals.

From what she had seen of the others, she thought her estimate of his youth was also valid. If their social hierarchy mirrored most humanoids'—and if their operation on Zhatyra II was far enough along for secondary support personnel to be on site—he might not be the brightest example of his species as well—though she didn't want to make the mistake of counting too heavily on that.

"How do beings from beyond the sky come to be on the ground?" she asked, taking control of the conversation as quickly as possible.

"We come from Smau, a world like this one, only

prettier," Solal explained. "Not so green. We fly into the sky with sleds. We travel for many days and then glide down to land here, on New Smau."

Electromagnetic rail sleds to launch their vehicles and gliders to land. Both fit her theory. Both also meant all of the Smau-folk on Zhatyra II had made a one-way journey.

Significant was Solal's matter-of-fact presentation. He expected an "animal" native to this world to understand interplanetary travel, agree that a world "less green" than this would be preferable, and accept the idea its home was now "New Smau." Absolutely no evidence of the concept of native rights, or even native people, entered into his reasoning at all.

Chance may have placed her at the mercy of the kindest of the invading monsters, but he was a monster nonetheless.

She was interested in Smau technology, but could think of no way to inquire without revealing a higher level of understanding than a talking animal should have. Also questions about the Smau-folks' purpose on "New Smau" might overemphasize their keeper/keepee relationship. She focused instead on playing the role of eager student—or inquisitive pet—and asked open-ended questions about Solal himself and his aspirations, topics near and dear to any young male's heart.

Over the next half hour Pattie learned quite a bit about adolescent social life on Smau. Unremarkably, there was a great deal of competing with members of his own gender for the attentions of the other, but also involved struggling to attain what the universal translator rendered as "right of [responsibility/self-determination]" without which he would never attain honor. Solal's winning that right through some series of achievements he clearly regarded as exceptional had enabled him to request emigrating to New Smau.

His personal hero was Sonandal, the leader of the expedition to New Smau.

Sonandal had been the first of the Smaunif—Pattie deduced that was what the Smau-folk called themselves—to land on New Smau even before the scientists had been sure the world could support life. Going first was the leader's responsibility, Solal explained proudly. His honor depended on his taking his responsibility seriously.

Solal explained there was no higher moral principle than being responsible for your own actions. Pattie agreed it was a better ideal than many she'd heard.

Her Smaunif zookeeper was not surprised she did not instantly recognize that it was not just "better" but was in fact the only moral code of any worth. What separated people from animals was self-determination. With that came responsibility and through that, honor.

Interested in more useful information, Pattie didn't dispute the issue. But once started young Solal seemed determined to make his point.

"Our scientists have proven that we are the pinnacle of evolution," he explained. "We are the only ones who have developed the capacity to understand that we are making choices. Thus we are the only ones with the spirit to take responsibility for those choices."

"On Smau, yes," Pattie said, unable to let that bit of elitism pass despite herself. "But could not the evolution of other worlds lead to the development of other people?"

Solal shrugged.

"We have found no other people on New Smau," he said, as though that closed the issue.

Yet you're comfortable conversing with a "talking animal," Pattie thought. *Undisturbed that it's "animal" technology that makes that possible.*

Much as she wanted to confront the massive conceit underlying Solal's assumptions, Pattie forced herself to let the issue go. No ally was ever won over through religious debate. Not to mention the potential danger of reminding him the "talking animals" of New Smau were perceived as threat enough to warrant slaughter.

"So Sonandal leads in all things?" she asked.

"Any task which must be done, he must do first. The greater the responsibility, the greater the need for the leader to be first partaker."

Pattie could see how this philosophy could lead to a sort of meritocracy. Leaders who did not dare take risks led no one anywhere and leaders who took foolish risks eventually removed themselves from the picture entirely.

Sonandal's risk in leading the first one-way expedition to a world that might not have been inhabitable had been a big one. A potentially very foolish one, in fact. But one that had paid off with him becoming the planetary ruler. Or at least ruler of this growing colony.

Solal had been too young to be first among those who followed Sonandal. But he had been the first student of his university or trade school (the universal translator was not sure which) to meet the challenges and qualify to come.

Pattie revised her estimation of Solal's intelligence. Apparently it was wisdom he lacked.

She did not follow all of his explanations of how he

saw his personal career on New Smau leading to his becoming leader of his own colony or research facility; again Smau semantics confused the universal translator. However, she did pick up on the fact he thought being the first to study her species would be a major stepping-stone in his advancement.

That Solal was keeping her existence secret out of self-interest reassured Pattie. Altruism was far too amorphous and fickle a motive for her to trust. Her survival would have depended on his moment-to-moment perceptions of whether the greater good was protecting her or serving the mission. Solal would go to greater lengths to safeguard her if he believed this served his own ambitions.

However, if his subterfuge were discovered, it might put her in a worse position. What would he do to avoid discovery or punishment if found out? If she was in danger of being given up, or killed, she wanted some way to know what to expect.

She missed a good deal of his explanation of social life as she puzzled out how to bring up the subjects of crime and punishment. Preoccupied, she almost missed the opening when he offered it.

"A challenge of authority?" she asked, infusing her voice with several gigajoules of interest. "I've never heard of such a thing. How does it work?"

"If I have a better way of doing something than I have been told to do it, I can refuse to follow orders and do things my own way." Solal struck a pose that Pattie thought suggested self-importance. "My supervisor can either acknowledge the superiority of my method or he can order me to conform. If he orders me to conform, I can challenge."

"In my culture, such disputes are settled by presenting both sides of the issue to a mediator," Pattie said. "Would that be a challenge?"

"Anyone who must rely on a mediator is failing to take responsibility for their own judgment," Solal said tersely. "A challenge can be a comparison of data. Or a duel. Important challenges, challenges to honor or to leadership of the community, can be battles to the death."

Apparently excited by his topic, Solal leapt to his feet, leaving the debris of his lunch where it fell. Pulling a cleaning cart, a lamp, and another chair into the clear area near Pattie's cage, he marked out a rectangle about five meters by three.

"Actually, it's a square," he said, adjusting the position of his lunch chair, "but then I'd have to move the racks— of poles this high." He indicated something just above his head—about two meters, Pattie estimated. "The one issuing the challenge stands here, in the center, and points to the one he challenges, then to the ground in front of him." Solal pointed at an imaginary adversary somewhere to Pattie's right, then to his feet. "The one being challenged selects the weapons, if any, and they fight."

Solal leapt about the rectangle, evidently miming some form of martial art. The awkwardness of his movements caused Pattie to suspect he wasn't very good at it.

"To the death?" she asked.

"Rarely," Solal said, ending his bout in an apparent draw. "Sometimes points, sometimes first blood, usually when one admits defeat."

"So, Solal," came a woman's voice from among the racks and shelves at the far side of the warehouse. "Who have you defeated?"

Pattie dropped to all eights, resisting the temptation to roll into a defensive ball.

"Uh, no one, Slilila," Solal stammered, clumsy in confusion. "I was just—"

"Imagining great victories," the woman finished for him as she stepped into the open area. "We all do it. Just most of us take more care not to be overheard. Or do you plan on challenging Sonandal over the eradication?"

"No!" Solal uttered his protest emphatically, apparently missing the teasing tone that even Pattie could discern. "The tree dog infestation is a danger that must be addressed thoroughly and directly."

"You quote well." Slilila chuckled. "Which is as directly and thoroughly as a youth exempted use of weapons can take responsibility for the solution."

When the Smaunif spoke, Nasat tinkled from Pattie's combadge, lying with its rag among Solal's lunch trash. Fortunately, it was close enough to the cage that the sounds could seem to be coming from Pattie. She tried to help the illusion by waving her antennae every time the combadge repeated the Smaunifs' words.

Solal belatedly realized what was happening. He hurriedly scooped up the combadge, bundling it tightly in the trash and rag, then stuffed the lot into the waste can on the cleaning cart. He had the wit to park the cart next to Pattie in case any further sounds emerged.

Solal left with Slilila, apparently already late for some shared chore, leaving Pattie with her combadge less than a meter away but completely inaccessible.

CHAPTER
11

The devastation covered several thousand acres.

A dense carpet of what looked like saplings, though Corsi realized they were trees built along a more normal scale, washed up around the base of the giant banyans. The abrupt demarcation between rain forest and what looked like conifers must have indicated something about the soil, but Corsi didn't know what.

From her vantage point beside Copper on a low branch of one of the giant banyans, Corsi could see a giant rectangle of the conifers about a kilometer distant had been clear-cut. There were several low buildings of wood and metal near the center of the cleared area. Just beyond them was what looked like a broad straight road to nowhere. A landing strip, she decided, for something very large or something that needed as much margin of error as they could give it. To the right of the buildings a shallow basin, perhaps a hundred meters across, had been dug in the soil and lined with metal. The thin metal tower at its center confirmed her suspicion it was an antenna. Corsi was not an expert on agronomy, but much of the cleared land seemed to be in various stages of cultivation. Not so much a working farm, she decided, as an experiment to see what would grow.

Whoever these people were, they were here to stay.

More immediately significant was a broad road, a dozen or so meters wide, that was being carved through the trees directly toward the rain forest. Progress appeared to have been slow, trees felled near the edge of the cleared area had had time to turn brown. But the leading edge of the incursion was close enough for Corsi to hear the thud of hand axes.

"How long have they been here?" Corsi asked.

Copper batted at his left ear. "Long enough to do what you see."

"Many meals?" Corsi guessed. It was plain the K'k'tict didn't measure time. "I've been meaning to ask: What does that left-ear gesture mean?"

"Surprise, embarrassment, confusion."

"Ah. We do this for the same thing," Corsi slapped her forehead.

"Yours is a violent people," Copper said.

"Many would agree with you. But we have learned to moderate our violent nature through reason and compassion." She indicated the clear-cut forest below. "That is not the work of my people."

Copper batted at his left ear again.

"However, my people are not the only ones of this

general design," Corsi added, spreading her arms to indicate her two-arm, two-leg construction. "If we could get closer, I may be able to tell you who these rude guests of yours are."

Copper began descending, which Corsi took as expressing a willingness to take her closer to the strangers.

The forest floor beneath the giant banyans was covered with a variety of fernlike plants, most only about knee-high; chest-high on K'k'tict. There was no real underbrush, and the areas between banyan root systems were like broad boulevards. It was Corsi's impression the trees and ferns got larger closer to the volcanoes.

As soon as the invaders hacked their way to the edge of the banyan forest, it would be an easy march to the K'k'tict tree town.

"[unintelligible noise] and [unintelligible noise] will go with us," Copper announced, indicating Spot and Lefty from among the several K'k'tict waiting at the base of the tree. "The experience will aid their [maturity/education]."

Corsi revised her earlier theory that Spot and Lefty had not spoken in the presence of the leaders because they were of a lower caste. Apparently they were youngsters.

The three immediately headed in the direction of the strangers. Some of the remainder settled down to await the expedition's return, while a few headed back toward the tree town.

"Do your names mean anything?" Corsi asked after they had gone a short distance. If she was going to communicate, she'd have to address individuals as something besides *hey, you*. "Corsi is a shortened form of the name for an island my family came from."

"Our names are our names," Copper said, stopping. "We are who we are, not where we are."

"I understand." Corsi decided to set aside explaining that *Domenica* meant *Sunday* to a species that did not measure time. It was tempting to leave the name issue alone, but she had no idea how long she would be among the K'k'tict and clear communication was essential.

"My combadge does not comprehend, and renders your names as sounds I cannot emulate," she explained. "Do you have simplified names?"

Blank stares all around.

"Would it be offensive if I gave you nicknames so that I might indicate individuals?"

"What names?" Copper asked.

"Well, your coloration is the feature most apparent to my eyes," Corsi said cautiously, aware external coloration was the galaxy's most common source of prejudice. Seeing only expectation in her listeners, she went on. "I think of you as Copper, you as Lefty, and you as Spot."

Lefty bowed her head low to the ground and began shaking it back and forth. Spot began batting her left ear furiously. For his part Copper seemed content to watch the other two.

"What did I say?" Corsi asked, concerned. "Did I give offense?"

"Spot has been her [tease her name] since she emerged," Lefty said. "She *hates* it."

"Ah," said Corsi, making a note that violent head-shaking near the ground indicated laughter. "Sorry about that."

Though the smaller trees of the forest looked like pines, they were of much denser wood. Corsi found it impossible to bend any but the smallest saplings and branches could not be casually brushed aside. If the hand axes she had heard were the invaders' only tools, she was impressed with their tenacity.

For their part, the K'k'tict moved silently through the thick and thorny underbrush. Corsi noted they did not travel in straight lines and they varied their pace, frequently pausing to listen. Remembering Copper's question about why she was killing K'k'tict, Corsi wondered if this stealth was instinctive or a survival skill recently mastered.

She noticed they kept their large, lemur eyes squinted almost shut long after they'd left the twilight of the banyan forest. Apparently adaptation to life beneath a few hundred meters of shade tree meant even the dappled sunlight they were moving through was painfully bright.

Copper had led them in a curving route that brought the recon party to the edge of the cleared roadway several dozen meters behind the workers. They were indeed clearing the land with only hand tools, watched over by guards armed with what looked like stylized crossbows. At first Corsi thought she was looking at slave labor, then realized the guards were watching the underbrush, not the workers. They were protection.

The beings themselves were humanoid, with skin as gray as Cardassians', but not scaled. They also seemed to share the Cardassian fondness for wearing black, but their hair color ranged from blonder than hers through orange and red to a maroon that was almost brown. When the closest guard glanced her way, she saw his eyes were a metallic yellow that looked almost artificial.

Zaire? Zoysia? Something. Corsi knew she'd seen a

data file on these people, but they were advanced way beyond hand axes and crossbows. And they should not be here. Something was not right. She rocked back on her heels, unfocusing her eyes, and waited for the memory to fully develop. Nothing.

Giving up, she signaled Copper she had seen enough. The elder K'k'tict led them away from the strangers.

"I know of this species," Corsi said as they regrouped in a small clearing, "though I have never seen them."

She received understandably blank looks from the other three. However, she was not about to explain data files and life on other worlds to them.

"These are not my people," she repeated, holding up one hand back toward them. "Coloration."

The K'k'tict bobbed, acknowledging the point.

"Could we get closer to their camp?" Corsi asked. "Perhaps we can learn more about them."

With a typically K'k'tict lack of comment, Copper turned and began moving silently through the underbrush in a new direction. Corsi followed, bent low to stay under the stiff branches of the trees, with Lefty and Spot behind her.

The clear-cut area was not as flat as it had appeared from the banyan tree. There were piles of logs apparently curing in the sun, the acidic tang of their resin threatening to trigger a sneeze with every breath. Conical mounds of smaller branches waited to be dry enough to burn. About two hundred meters from the buildings, however, near the edge of the shallow basin lined with metal, the cover ran out. Corsi wished for a set of binoculars, but made do with squinting.

By the long runway was what appeared to be the

frame of a glider being carefully dismantled. Though it was large—she estimated it could have carried perhaps two dozen of the newcomers—it was not huge. Which meant the runway's expanse was indeed to give the landers a wide margin of error.

Gliders arriving without power and cannibalized for parts and metal meant the—*what* is *their name?*—were making a one-way trip to get here. It also explained the hand tools and crossbows. Keeping mass to a minimum meant no heavy machinery and weapons that used locally available ammunition.

But while the details made sense, the overall picture was wrong. What were these people doing here?

As if in answer, a column of blinding light descended from the sky.

CHAPTER

12

"It looks like weapons damage," Corsi said, eyeing the warped access panel beneath her gloves.

"*I would love to disagree with you,*" Pattie's musical notes sounded in the helmet of her EVA suit. "*The thought of someone shooting a cloaked anthropological satellite is disturbing. Especially one orbiting a preindustrial world. But armor damage is consistent with a barrage by several very large lasers.*"

Corsi nodded to herself as she keyed the release sequence on the access panel. She could have done this from the Shuttlecraft *Shirley* hanging a few dozen meters away, its rear hatch gaping toward them, but where was the fun in that? She enjoyed the EVA work.

Not as much as Pattie seemed to be enjoying Waldo

Egg. The Nasat was delighted with what she called her demi-Work Bee.

Resembling an upright egg with four manipulative arms, the Nasat-specific design had been the brain-child—and personal project—of Louisa Weldon, an engineer with the S.C.E. team on the *Khwarizmi*. Her special interest was adaptive technologies to enable nonhumanoids to interact effectively aboard admittedly humanoid-centric Federation vessels. She'd known Pattie for years, Corsi had learned, and had designed Pattie's special chairs aboard the *da Vinci*.

Her latest invention was allowing Pattie to be the main muscle as they uncased the anthropological satellite. An unaccustomed role she was clearly enjoying as she easily manipulated the massive sections of shielding.

For her part, Corsi was finding it a little tougher going than she would have liked.

When working this close to an atmosphere, Starfleet SOP required her to wear an emergency jump harness over the standard EVA suit. Little more than an ablative heat sheath that gloved over the suit proper with a rear-mounted chute harness, it was designed to get a space-walker safely to the surface in an emergency.

She had jumped in an emergency rig before, of course, in training. Though it was nowhere near as maneuverable or versatile as an orbital jumpsuit, it got the job done. She also understood the logic behind using safety equipment, especially in such a hostile environment. What she hated about it was the fact that it was piggybacked on her regular EVA suit, adding stiffness and bulk she did not enjoy working against.

And this was the first of twelve satellites, though—if things went according to mission specs—it was the only one they were going to have to field strip.

The Zhatyra system was unusual in that it had two class-M planets, both of which had developed sentient life. Corsi wasn't up on the details, but knew Zhatyra II, floating directly behind her, had a preindustrial culture while the most advanced nations on Zhatyra III were analogous to mid-twentieth-century Europe. The orbits of the two worlds were such that twice a year they were close enough to affect each other's tides.

The effect was small, only detectable with sophisticated seismic scans. And it was twice during one of the planet's years, but not the other's.

Corsi shook her head, clearing the cobwebs.

"What have you got there, Pattie?" she asked, realizing her partner had been silent for several minutes.

"I'm changing my assessment from one heavy laser barrage to several individual laser hits," the structural specialist said. *"The damage indicates remarkably consistent and massive bolts, but metal fatigue and decay around the hits varies from two years to a few weeks."*

"So whoever's been shooting our satellite has been coming by every few weeks, firing one shot and then going away again over the last couple of years? That makes no sense."

"Even more interesting to me is how they were able to detect one, and apparently only one out of a dozen, cloaked anthropological satellites to shoot at in the first place."

"Might be a—"

The satellite exploded.

After the fact, Corsi's mind had replayed the vision of a massive column of coherent light coming from deep space somewhere beyond Pattie's work bee. But that hadn't registered in the first heartbeat.

With the exterior shielding removed, the laser beam had struck the fragile interior of the satellite. The exposed sensor arrays, data storage cores, and isolinear networks had exploded in an expanding cloud of gas, shrapnel, and droplets of molten polymer. An armor panel, propelled by the expanding cloud, slammed into Corsi before she could react. Its speed had not been great, but its mass was sufficient to swat her out of orbit like a fly.

"Pattie!"

"Here, Commander," Pattie answered promptly over the comlink. *"Waldo Egg lost two and—I think—a half arms, but the pod is tight. Louisa evidently anticipated explosions."*

Corsi nodded inside her helmet. Zhatyra II rose and fell as she tumbled. It wasn't getting appreciably larger, but she knew she was falling. She applied thrusters minimally, conserving fuel as she oriented herself for atmospheric entry.

"What's your status?"

"It appears the blast gave me a retrograde boost. Waldo's thrusters aren't up to regaining orbit, so it looks like I'm taking a long spiral to Zhatyra II. You?"

"Taking a direct route," Corsi said.

She was glad neither would be drifting alone in space. Intellectually she knew it was no more dangerous, perhaps even less dangerous, than waiting for rescue on the planet's surface, but the idea of hanging alone in the emptiness in nothing but an EVA suit . . .

Bringing her left forearm up, she tapped the shuttle interface. Time to send an emergency signal.

Nothing.

"Pattie," she said, retapping the command sequence, "I can't get a response from the *Shirley*."

"The stern bay was wide open and facing the satellite," Pattie pointed out. "It's possible the internal systems were damaged."

Corsi cursed. "Nailed all four targets with one shot. What are the odds on that?"

"I don't believe it was a weapon. I was scanning when it struck the satellite. I believe it was an interplanetary communications laser."

"With our geosynchronous satellite directly over its target?"

"Apparently. Close, at any rate. Projecting along its path, I'd say the intended destination was somewhere near that ring of volcanoes."

Corsi squinted at the globe below. Nothing but mottled grays and greens.

"You've got better visuals than I do."

"Sending you coordinates."

"Got 'em."

The numbers were very close to where Corsi's fall was taking her. She fired her thrusters, bringing her trajectory more in line.

"You going to make a complete orbit coming down?" Corsi asked.

"Two at least. Though I have enough thrust to slow for atmospheric insertion, I may go a bit farther. Hard to say.

Louisa never mentioned how Waldo was coming down on a planet."

"I'm going to try for that ring of volcanoes," Corsi said. "If you can get close, maybe we can meet up. Otherwise, just button down and hang on till the cavalry gets here."

"Will do." Pattie's voice began to break up as her pod arced over the horizon. *"Good luck."*

CHAPTER

13

"Are you okay?" Corsi asked for the dozenth time.

The three K'k'tict had been completely blinded by the planetary communications laser striking its dish a hundred meters in front of them. Each was now tightly clutching the one ahead with a lower hand as Corsi led them through the underbrush. With their upper hands pressed over their damaged eyes, they were nowhere near as silent as they'd been. Corsi exaggerated the arc of their path, putting as much distance as possible between her charges and the wood chopping party while still keeping their objective in sight.

When they reached the others, the waiting K'k'tict teamed up in pairs, one on each side of a stricken comrade, and rushed them through the ferns toward home.

Corsi kept pace for a few dozen meters, but her

injuries and common sense made her slow to a walk. She waved on the few K'k'tict who'd stayed with her, assuring them she would catch up.

"Corsi to Blue," she said as soon as she was alone. "Come in, Pattie."

She had not been alone since recovering her combadge and had kept the verbal transmitter disabled. Wouldn't do to have strange voices pop unexpectedly out of the air. But there had been no response to her nonverbal signals and she thought it was time for a more direct approach.

Nothing.

Tabling any worry about her companion, Corsi considered their tactical situation.

She now remembered she was on Zhatyra II. Which meant the invaders were from Zhatyra III. Neither race had warp capability and the Prime Directive was in full effect. Actually, the people of Zhatyra III should not have had space flight. Their presence was as improbable as mid-twentieth-century Europe colonizing Mars.

No, that wasn't true, strictly speaking. Zhatyra II and III passed very close to each other every . . . She couldn't remember the interval. At least once a year for the outer world, she recalled. Close. Zhatyra II would be a tempting target dominating their night sky for months at a time—quite a motivator.

The communications laser wasn't a mystery. Many cultures, whether because of the spectral behavior of their primary or their planet's magnetic field or any of a dozen other factors including they just never thought of it, managed a high level of technology without developing radio. For a visually oriented culture laser communication was the logical extension of the semaphore.

The size of the laser and the violence of the beam were impressive. It indicated tremendous power being used very inefficiently. They couldn't be firing something like that from inside their atmosphere. Did Zhatyra III have a moon? Probably.

Two things, maybe three, were clear. First, the invaders were here to stay; they didn't have a choice. Second, their method of colonization was to reshape the world they'd found to fit their own image. And third, for whatever reason, they were coming after the K'k'tict. Given what she estimated was the invaders' rate of progress chopping their road through the forest, they'd be to the edge of the world, and an easy walk from the tree town, in a couple of days.

Her rescuers were going to have to make a choice, and soon, between fighting and getting out of the way. Moving twenty thousand plus individuals would not be easy, but from what she'd seen, the K'k'tict weren't likely to fight.

These last two suppositions, the impending genocide and the K'k'ticts' refusal to fight, were confirmed by Copper when she found him reclining in the shade of a notch cut into the base of one of the roots. His eyes were bandaged, covered with leaves that no doubt held in place a poultice of some sort.

"We befriended the first of the Tznauk't when they arrived," he said. "They were beyond the edge of the world, but foragers had seen their silver leaf fall."

World was banyan forest and *silver leaf* was glider, Corsi deduced. The first landing without a runway must have been rough.

"We met as many as we could so that we could know

one another, but they did not understand," Copper said. "They have a [consensus of one], which we do not fully understand. He is named Tzuntatalc."

"Their leader," Corsi supplied.

"[Consensus of one]." Copper nodded. "A difficult concept."

The K'k'tict made decisions by consensus, Corsi realized. They didn't have leaders. That certainly fit with her wandering tour. Every K'k'tict in the tree town had been given a chance to observe her so that each could make up his or her mind about their guest.

But what did that mean about the ruling class being pampered in the cave? Something else to find out after the current crisis was over.

"When you say they did not understand you," Corsi said, trying to find a handle on the situation, "do you mean they didn't understand your speech or did not understand your intent?"

"Both." Copper sighed, remembering. "In the beginning I believe the Tznauk't did not recognize our speech as speech. We tried speaking to them in their own language, but they use many sounds we cannot make. Our first efforts were clumsy. They were amused until we became more successful."

Copper stopped speaking and simply sat, the weight of his upper torso on the elbows of his folded lower arms, and rocked. After a while Corsi realized he'd finished.

"What happened after you were successful?"

"They became afraid." Copper sighed again, a heavy sound.

"That's when the Tznauk't began killing K'k'tict," Corsi said.

Copper said nothing, rocking.

"Do you know why the Tznauk't are coming here, toward your tree town?"

"Yes."

Corsi watched him rock for a long ten-count.

"Could you—" She stopped herself, recognizing she'd almost invited another dead-end *yes*. "Would you explain to me why?"

Copper stopped rocking, turning his bandaged face toward her as though regarding her through the poultice. "They know of our birthing caves," he said at last, his voice heavy. "Of the place of emergence. They know we can live nowhere else."

Corsi gaped.

Spot's "tease her name" since her *emergence*.

She'd wondered why she'd never seen any K'k'tict young, never realizing she'd been taken on a tour of their nursery. They gave birth or laid eggs or whatever the process was called in the mineral spring cave. Dozens of spheres that looked like glass globes, which became something like fish, then something like tadpoles and then "emerged" as chiptaurs. The ones she had taken to be attendants were what? In day care?

Head Nurse hadn't been fat; she'd been pregnant.

On the heels of that thought came the realization that the K'k'tict metamorphic process, whatever it was, must be violent. At each stage of development, the larger the inhabitants of the pools, the fewer there had been.

She set that speculation aside and focused on the situation at hand.

"Are there other caves?" she asked. "Other birthing places?"

"We know of no other."

Corsi realized moving the K'k'tict away from the Tznauk't's landing site was out of the question. They could not abandon their young and they had no place else to go.

"Do the Tznauk't know the location of the birthing caves?" Corsi held on to one last hope of misleading the invaders, gaining the K'k'tict some time. Time for what she wasn't sure. Negotiations?

"Yes," Copper said simply. Then, anticipating Corsi's follow-up question: "They asked. We told them."

Corsi scrambled to her feet and stalked away. It was that or call Copper a suicidal idiot to his face. When death had landed on their doorstep, they had gone out and invited their own destruction.

If the K'k'tict would give back her phaser she'd solve their problem—decisively.

No, she wouldn't, she admitted a few steps later. The Prime Directive was clear. Events on this world must be allowed to follow their natural path. She could not interfere. She could not . . .

Could not reveal the existence of advanced technology or life on other worlds . . .

"Cortzi?"

Corsi spun, startled.

Spot was seated, eyes bandaged, in a patch of darker shade at the base of a root column. As with Copper, others were sitting in attendance, but moved off as Corsi approached.

"How did you know it was me?"

Spot swung her head close to the ground. "You are the only one who walks on two legs," she said. "Nothing thumps about like you."

"Why will your people not fight?" Corsi asked when she was settled beside her former nurse. "If you do not, the Tznauk't will destroy your birthing cave. The K'k'tict will be no more."

"Then the K'k'tict will be no more," Spot said. "We share life. We are one spirit. How can we harm our own spirit?"

"This isn't a time for philosophy," Corsi couldn't keep the edge of frustration from her voice. "This is a time for action, for survival."

"If we harm others, we do not survive," Spot answered. "We share life—"

"You won't share life for very long," Corsi cut her off angrily, "if you don't do something to stop the slaughter!"

"But we shall do something to stop the . . . hurting."

"You will? How?" Corsi snapped. "Because unless you're disguised Organians, I don't think you stand a chance."

Spot batted at her left ear.

"I do not know what that is." She sounded hurt. "But we are preparing, those of us who will meet the Tznauk't."

"Meet the Tznauk't?" Corsi tried to soften her voice. "What are you talking about?"

"We know where they will enter the world," Spot said as though speaking to a child. "We will meet them there and tell them the truth. When they understand, the hurting will stop."

"The truth?" Corsi demanded, as annoyed by the tone as the fact that her friend was talking nonsense. "What truth?"

"We share life," Spot repeated. "We are one spirit."

"Wait a minute. Say that again."

Corsi turned off her combadge and heard Spot recite the same two phrases of clicks and ticks intoned by everyone she'd been introduced to on her first tour of the tree town. They had meant nothing then and they had no power now.

"The Tznauk't have no universal translators," she said when hers was back on. "They will not understand you."

"We have been practicing their language," Spot explained. "They taught it to many when they thought we were animals that mimicked sound."

The young K'k'tict uttered two phrases of slurred sound. The universal translator could make nothing of them. Corsi could not tell if Spot had indeed spoken in the language of the invaders. Or, remembering the natives substituted *tz* for the *s* in her name, whether what she'd said would be intelligible to the Tznauk't.

"That is what you are preparing for?" she asked. "To recite words in a foreign language to those who would kill you?"

"Oh, no," Spot said. "We are preparing to die."

CHAPTER

14

Bart Faulwell grinned as he listened to Fabian Stevens try to sway Carol Abramowitz and Soloman to his choice of lunch spots.

Actually, it would be lunch for Bart and Stevens. For Soloman it was breakfast time and Abramowitz was looking for a late dinner. While transporters made it possible for members of a globe-spanning effort to meet for a meal, they did nothing to simplify the choice of restaurants.

At the moment the four of them were strolling under a noonday sun in Trizist, a pleasant enough town though its only claim to fame was a single aqueduct junction just visible over the rooftops to the south. Plus a library stocked with reliable copies of scrolls from several neighboring towns lost to the Breen bombardment.

The local architecture had a square and stolid look, though the blocklike buildings were topped with upswept gables—perfectly balanced, of course—and incongruous bits of gingerbread. The absolute symmetry dulled the spontaneity a bit, but Bart still found the effect pleasantly whimsical.

He noticed he was the only one enjoying it. Stevens and Abramowitz were deep in their debate over restaurants and Soloman had his nose to a padd, evidently counting on his companions to keep him from banging into things.

Pleasant as the architecture and climate were, however, lunchtime fare in Trizist tended toward raw vegetables, jerked meat very similar to venison, and a stew thick with barley and simmered until it was almost solid. Having sampled it yesterday, Bart came away fairly certain he would choose it over survival rations, but it would be a near thing.

"There's plenty of reasons for having lunch in Brohtz," Stevens insisted, focusing his argument on the cultural specialist as the harder sell.

"There are?"

"*Rastentha* soufflé!"

"Again?" Bart shook his head at Stevens's enthusiasm. "I think it's time we gave rustic Brohtz a rest. The cuisine of Franthc is, I'm told, very like Earth Asian barbecue."

"Sounds good," Abramowitz said. "I'm in the mood for spicy. And we need to take another look at the southern hemisphere's concept of lunar cycles anyway. I'm thinking there's a fundamental disconnect between how they timed their lock cycles and the schedule employed in the north."

Soloman's head snapped up, his large eyes locked on the cultural specialist.

"That's it."

"What's it?"

"A fundamental disconnect," the Bynar said.

"I know," Abramowitz said patiently. "We have to figure out how to resolve it."

"You misunderstand." Soloman turned his padd to show his companions, then realized the screen was too small for them to see clearly. He glanced about, but there were no display panels in the tourist area with which to interface. "If I could draw . . ." he murmured.

Bart offered him his folio, but the Bynar waved off the fine parchment. Stooping low, he snatched up a twig and began sketching in the dust. He drew a circle, remarkably precise, about half a meter in diameter.

"Bundinal."

The humans nodded.

Soloman drew two parallel lines a hand's width apart, bisecting the circle.

"Northern aqueduct system," he said, indicating the hemisphere above the double line. "Southern aqueduct system."

Then he drew a series of short lines connecting the two parallels.

"Forty-eight aqueducts, evenly spaced around the equator," he said. "Connecting the two networks."

"Yes," Abramowitz said, "one for each week of the Bundinalli calendar. The length, twelve *zrht*, corresponding to the number of days."

"They should not be there."

"But they were always there."

"They were never there."

"Wait a minute, Soloman," Bart spoke up. "The foundations were there. The measurements are Bundinalli tradition to the core and their placement corresponds to Bundinalli records. The reconstruction team simply restored the superstructures destroyed in the bombardment."

"Where are the locks?" Soloman asked. "Nowhere in the Bundinalli water systems do canals or aqueducts meet without lock gates to control the flow of water. Yet there are no locks at either end of any of these forty-eight spans."

Bart frowned at the drawing in the dust, then up toward an aqueduct junction in the middle distance. Even at a couple of kilometers, the boxy structure of the lock mechanism was clear. And he knew, from studying hundreds of drawings and verbal accounts, that every single juncture had been constructed to exactly the same specifications.

Except the forty-eight, the calendar aqueducts that had joined north and south. Those had simply connected the two hemisphere-spanning networks with plain right angles.

The houses between where they stood and the arch of the aqueduct caught his eye. Each was laid out in perfect bilateral symmetry, with windows, gingerbread, gables, and gardens all exactly matching. Including a faux front door to balance the real.

"Symbolism," Abramowitz said, a half second quicker than he on the uptake. "The forty-eight aqueducts weren't real, they didn't actually connect. The Bundinalli just needed their symmetry to keep the world in balance."

"Would the Bundinalli actually forget to tell us something like that?" Stevens asked.

"Most Bundinalli would have assumed it was so obvious they wouldn't have thought to mention it," Abramowitz said. "Do you remind everyone you meet not to stick their hand in a fire?"

"But if they knew what we were doing—"

"Fabe, in all your traveling has even a single Bundinalli asked you about what we were doing beyond his or her own village?" Bart asked. "Curiosity about the big picture is not in their nature."

"If we restore the aqueducts properly," Soloman said, focusing on the problem at hand, "and close off both ends of the connecting spans, the two systems should attain equilibrium."

"Immediately?"

"No, they are much too massive for that. The parameters and variables are too complex for me to evaluate without computer models." He shrugged. "Four local years, maybe six. But once started, the process will be inevitable."

"Fabe," Bart said with a grin, "why don't you give Tev a call?"

CHAPTER
15

A dozen Smaunif were working on small electric motors, taking them apart and checking each circuit individually. From what Pattie could see, they were finding different things wrong with each one. A broken connection, dirt or moisture inside a sealed casing, a fouled or broken gear. Little things, any one of which could be attributed to normal wear and tear or misadventure.

That all of these minor breakdowns had happened at once indicated something other than chance was responsible. Pattie could not tell from the technician's body language if they were simply frustrated or they suspected someone was responsible for their difficulties. For her part, she took it as evidence Corsi was somewhere close at hand.

Over the last couple of days she and Solal had

talked—or he had talked and she had listened—about the problem of the tree dogs. She had only to explain she was from far away and was eager to learn more about them to trigger an exhaustive and wide-ranging lecture on local fauna, religion, and responsibility.

The tree dogs, who looked very much like her red-haired neighbor but about three times the mass, had appeared shortly after the first landing. They were clever mimics who had amused the first explorers by approximating Smaunif gestures and performing various antics.

Their most annoying trait had sprung from their playfulness. Whenever a Smaunif hunter had been about to gather game, the tree dogs had run about making loud noises, frightening the animals away. They apparently thought the point of hunting was to surprise animals.

The tree dogs had gone from amusing near-pets to threat sometime just before the third wave of gliders had arrived. (From context Pattie deduced the third landing had been a few months ago and that Solal had arrived aboard one of those gliders.) It was then that the tree dogs had started imitating speech.

The imitative speech was a natural outgrowth of their mimicry, of course. There was no intelligence behind it. But it was disconcerting, particularly when they began putting individual words together in new orders. And it raised a possible problem for the colony.

Because, although those who had been around the tree dogs from the beginning understood they were simply animals, a newcomer might mistake their mimicry for intelligent speech. And if they were tricked into believing the tree dogs were intelligent, the question of whether the tree dogs were—and here the universal translator could not decide if the phrase meant *self-aware, responsible for their actions*, or even *possessed of a soul*—would arise. That would throw the entire validity of the colonization of New Smau into question. Valuable years would be lost in foolish debate over the behavior of animal mimics.

Fortunately the tree dogs were limited to the forest of huge trees not far from the landing site. There were no others in all of New Smau.

Pattie wondered how he had come by that information, particularly since he'd proudly explained earlier that the colonists here were the only Smaunif to ever visit New Smau. But that was only one inconsistency in a myriad and she had not wanted to interrupt the stream of information, no matter how skewed it was.

Sonandal, leader that he was, had decided how to avoid wasting those years that should be spent establishing the colony and developing the planet. Having heard this sort of logic before in the histories of dozens of worlds that made up the Federation, Pattie was braced for the leader's solution. Still, it had been a shock to actually hear it.

"Sonandal will lead us to the forest," Solal had explained, then amended: "Those of us authorized to use weapons. We will eradicate the infestation of mimicking tree dogs. Once the animals contaminated by interacting with people are removed, there will be no cause for confusion. In the future, colonists will be careful to avoid tree dogs to prevent similar problems."

That had been yesterday.

Solal had left before Pattie could rebut any of the horror he'd spewed, apparently unaware of his madness. Pattie had come closer to wanting to commit violence then than she could ever remember. She'd wanted to shake him until his brain rattled, force him to see the stupidity of his racism.

Today from first light she'd been treated to the sight of disgruntled technicians repairing equipment. Evidence, she was sure, of Corsi taking a hand on behalf of the tree dogs, or whatever the indigenous people of Zhatyra II called themselves.

But she knew sabotaging equipment—while it might distract the colonists from their goal for a while—was not going to be enough. She hoped the techs would take their noon meals elsewhere and that Solal would come for their usual lunchtime discussion.

Technically the letter of the Prime Directive dictated that she do nothing. But she could not sit by and not try to help. She could not reveal who or what she was, of course. That would do far more harm than good. But she had to try and reach Solal, loyal follower that he was, and try to make him see the crime that was about to be committed.

She might do nothing more than get herself killed as another tree dog, but she had to try.

At last the technicians left. And Solal, carrying his usual lunch, came in, exchanging greetings with the others in passing.

Pattie remained silent as he retrieved her combadge from its hiding place and dragged his chair over. After three days of her refusing anything but distilled water he had stopped offering food.

"Solal," she asked when he was comfortable. "What am I?"

Solal smiled with what Pattie recognized from years

among humanoids as a condescending smile. She knew his answer before he opened his mouth.

"You are a talking animal," he answered. "A very clever and charming one."

"And why are you studying me?"

Gesturing with his cheese, Solal said, "Because if I can learn how and why you imitate people, we can avoid problems like we are having with the tree dogs."

"Solal," Pattie repeated firmly, making sure his eyes were on her, "how do I imitate people?"

"You talk," he began—and stopped, looking down at her combadge.

"Yes, I talk," she said. "Expressing ideas that did not come from you, speaking a language you do not understand but which is made plain to you by a technology you have never seen before."

Solal did not look up from the combadge.

"Solal, how do I imitate people?"

The young Smaunif looked up at last and met her gaze. His eyes were full of something too confused and subtle for Pattie to read. She wished the lad had antennae so she could better judge his mood. She couldn't tell if he was on the verge of a breakthrough or racial violence.

"Your gliders landed in a very primitive region of the world you call New Smau," she said, making sure he tied the unknown technology in his hand to this world and no other. "The people here do not use tools as we do. They do not believe animals should be hunted for food." That was a guess based on his description of their reaction to hunters. "But the native people you call tree dogs are not animals. They are people. They have a right to live their lives the way they want to live."

"Like the Smaunif?" Solal asked.

"If you mean a culture on your world that chooses to live simply," Pattie said. "Then, yes. Like the Smaunif."

Solal's eyes focused elsewhere. Some point of infinity between his chair and Pattie's cage.

"Solal," she said, trying to find the right balance between gentle and firm, "Sonandal is about to make a terrible mistake. Many innocent and harmless people will die because he does not have all the information he needs to make a responsible choice."

At least she hoped that was true. It was quite possible the Smaunif leader knew exactly what he was doing in slaughtering the locals. But she didn't want to confuse Solal further by raising the possibility his personal hero was evil.

"Solal, please give me my combadge and let me out of this cage. We need to help Sonandal. If we do not, he may become responsible for a tragedy. And we will carry the responsibility of not having done what we could have to prevent it."

The Smaunif's face suddenly contorted and Pattie started in sudden fear, fighting the reflex to ball. Solal's body heaved, shuddering with silent sobs.

"What?" Pattie asked, belatedly recognizing grief, feeling the first stab of dread. "What is it?"

"This morning," Solal gasped between spasms. "They left to kill the tree dogs this morning."

CHAPTER
16

Corsi could not move.

The K'k'tict had not appreciated her act of sabotage the night before. Though conceding she had harmed no one, Copper—his eyes now unbandaged and clear—had condemned the hurtful intent of her actions. And the general consensus concurred. Now, aware of her violent nature and knowing she wanted to help, K'k'tict hemmed her in on every side. Held gently immobile, she could see all that was happening but could do nothing about it.

The Tznauk't had chopped their way through the last meters of woods and underbrush under the watchful eyes of the K'k'tict. A hundred meters away, concealed among the root columns, it was impossible for Corsi to gauge what they were thinking.

What she could see, above the heads of the assembled K'k'tict, was the woodsmen clearing the last of the underbrush with a curious thoroughness, scraping the ground to create an unobstructed path a dozen meters wide. As they dragged the last of the vegetation away, back toward their base camp, a hundred or more Tznauk't parted to let them pass.

These were different from the woodsmen. They carried crossbows, with loaded quivers over their shoulders and heavy swords at their belts. When the last of the deforesters were through, the armsmen had closed ranks and advanced, all deadly business as they approached.

Looking in from the bright sunlight, they could not clearly see what awaited them. That changed when they stepped across the shadow line.

They stopped abruptly.

A thousand K'k'tict stood in neat ranks, filling the fern-carpeted boulevard between the giant banyan trees from side to side.

Whatever the invaders had expected, this was not it. They hesitated visibly, unnerved by the sheer number of K'k'tict. Or perhaps by the calm with which the natives stood, not a weapon or closed fist among them.

The Tznauk't in the center of the first rank, larger than most with a thick helmet of bright red hair, stepped forward into the open space between the two groups. Corsi could not read his expression, but his body language had nothing of bravado or victory about it. He seemed businesslike, weary but resolved, facing a job, not a battle.

He turned his back on the K'k'tict and addressed his

own men. Nothing rousing. Flat instructions. The troops decocked their crossbows and slung them.

Corsi's moment of hope died as they drew their swords. The leader, sword in hand, turned again to the K'k'tict.

But before he could speak or act, a lone K'k'tict stepped forward to greet him. Even at this distance, Corsi could see the distinctive circle of bright golden hair high between her shoulders. Spot.

Hefting his sword, the Tznauk't leader raised it over his head, then paused as Spot began to speak. Corsi could not hear her words, but could see her arms spread wide, open palms up as she addressed the invader.

"Blue to Corsi, come in, Commander!" said Corsi's combadge.

The K'k'tict around her shifted in surprise, but did not move away.

"Go."

"There's an extermination force headed for the natives!"

"They're here, Pattie."

"I know how to stop them," Pattie said.

The heavy sword of the Tznauk't came down. Slashing through bone and flesh, it split the circle of bright gold in two.

Corsi was drowned in a sea of nutmeg and musk as loving arms surrounded her, stopping her and pulling her gently, irresistibly, to the ground.

Pattie's voice, muffled by the earth and press of K'k'tict, barely reached her.

"It's honor. You can challenge their leader to a duel."

Corsi stopped struggling.

"Primitive racism," Pattie was saying, *"they think the*

natives are animals." Corsi had never imagined the tinkle of Pattie's bell-like laughter could sound bitter. *"They think I'm an animal. But you're humanoid. They'll see you as a person."*

Sensing she was no longer trying to get up, the K'k'tict eased away from Corsi. She knew they could understand the words coming from her combadge. She wondered if they understood she was talking to someone far away or thought the golden piece of metal had come to life.

In the distance she could hear a sound, repeated, of wet rags slapping wood. Or melons being split. Around her the K'k'tict moaned as Corsi kept her eyes focused on the ground, keeping her emotions in check as she listened to her friend explain the Smaunif code of responsibility and the challenge to authority.

Corsi's first thought was to get to Copper. But he wasn't a leader. The K'k'tict made decisions by consensus; each of them had an equal say. She'd have to reach them all. Or maybe just enough.

She started with her guards, explaining as quickly as she could a plan that involved concepts alien to them and behavior they could not understand. Corsi felt her first hope when her guards turned away from her without comment and began addressing their own knots of K'k'tict. Her plan was helped, perhaps, by the sounds of death reaching them from the front of the crowd. It was clear that what the K'k'tict were doing was not working.

The slaughter, when she steeled herself to look at it, was continuing. A rank of K'k'tict would step forward. Some would have a chance to speak, some would not before the heavy swords of the Tznauk't, the Smaunif, rose and fell. Then the next rank stepped forward.

Not wanting the Smaunif to see her before her challenge, Corsi crawled from group to group, explaining her plan. Some moved on to tell others. Some stood, looking straight ahead at their brothers and sisters dying beneath the invaders' swords. Waiting their turn.

Every so often the carnage stopped for a few minutes. The front rank of the Smaunif would drop back, exhausted, and make way for the next to take their place. Now that she was close enough to see their faces, Corsi was heartened to see weariness, even revulsion. These were not warriors being carried to excess in the heat of battle. If they even imagined the beasts they were slaughtering were people . . .

The red-haired leader—Sonandal, Pattie had called him—stood to one side, the point of his bloody sword to the ground. Corsi pointed him out to the K'k'tict, tried to explain the concept of leader, of consensus of one. He had struck the first blow—Corsi fought to keep the anger out of her voice at the memory—and now stood witness, taking responsibility for his actions.

And supporting Corsi's argument to the K'k'tict.

Against the bizarre background of death and those waiting to die, Corsi crawled and politicked. How many K'k'tict were killed while she struggled to make her case?

Copper made his way to a group Corsi was addressing. Her heart leapt at the sight of him. He might not be a leader, but his opinion carried weight. Many K'k'tict would go along with any plan he endorsed without question.

"You cannot fight for us," he said before she could

open her mouth. "We share life. It is better we die than we take another life. Or let a life be taken for us. We are one spirit."

"I will take no life for you," Corsi said. "If I can, I will do no harm at all. But to stop this madness I must challenge their leader to a duel."

"But they hear us," Copper said. "They hear our words of life. If we do not waver they will see the truth of our words."

"There are no words," Corsi said. "They cannot comprehend what you say."

"We speak their language."

Corsi bit back her hot retort.

"I'm going to turn off my combadge," she said to Copper and the knot of K'k'tict around them. "I want you to repeat the words I say and listen—listen—to the differences."

With her communicator switched off, Corsi pointed to the row of invaders, then to their leader.

"Smaunif."

"Tznauk't," the K'k'tict chorused.

"Sonandal."

"Tzuntatalc."

Corsi looked Copper in the eye and challenged: "Fickle Fizzy fancies sausage and rice."

Copper managed a stuttered series of ticks and clicks before he fell silent. None of the others made the effort.

"Their understanding is stunted," Corsi said, turning her combadge back on. "Because you do not look like them they do not recognize you are people. And because you cannot make the sounds they do, they do not recognize your words."

"But I spoke with them," Copper said.

"Let me guess," Corsi said. "You understood their questions and they understood only your yes or no."

Copper hung his head and Corsi realized she had won.

"I am a chief of security," she said. "I protect those who might be harmed from those who would harm them. Please let me save your people."

CHAPTER
17

Corsi crouched low, her face centimeters from the crushed ferns, waiting her chance. It had to be done right, according to honor, if it were to work.

At last the horrible sound of chopping ceased. How many dead? A hundred? Two? She forced the thought from her mind, making sure the eyes she turned toward Copper carried no rage.

"Now."

"Now," the K'k'tict around her murmured and pulled back.

Lefty, Copper, and two of her recent guards delayed for a moment, standing up stripped saplings and jamming them firmly into the loamy earth. Then they withdrew without haste.

Corsi uncoiled, coming to her full height in the center of the challenge square.

The Smaunif froze. Some with their swords half drawn, some stooped to drag bodies from the way, one with his hand halfway to his crossbow. For a long moment there was no sound.

She knew she was a sight, bruised and wounded in her hand-tied uniform. But she was a humanoid, the first non-Smaunif humanoid the invaders had ever seen. And where she stood right now spoke to their very core.

"Sonandal!"

The Smaunif leader snapped from his daze at the sound of his name.

"Your lack of honor and failure to take responsibility for your mistakes has cost innocent lives." Corsi based her challenge on forms Pattie—and someone named Solal—had explained, trusting the language file transferred from Pattie's combadge to choose the most stinging phrases. "The lives of my friends require recompense. I challenge you, now, here, to defend what honor you hope to possess."

Sonandal looked at his troops. The troops looked at Sonandal. If he hoped to ever lead again, he had no choice.

He gestured to a young male close to him. The trooper pulled his sword from its sheath.

Clean, Corsi saw. Perhaps the slaughter had not been going on as long as she'd imagined. The K'k'tict bodies stacked like cordwood said otherwise.

She had hoped Sonandal, seeing her unarmed, would choose to fight hand to hand. It would be harder to keep her promise to the K'k'tict with swords.

Holding it by the blade, Sonandal tossed the clean sword to Corsi as he stepped into the ring.

She caught the hilt, twirling quickly to parry his charging lunge. When he spun back around, she was ready, guiding his scything blade up and over with the broad of her sword.

The Smaunif sword was more a cutlass that anything else. Nowhere near as subtle and balanced as the saber she had trained on at the Academy. Almost a chopping tool.

In fact, she realized as she wove it in front of her, parrying Sonandal's attacks, it probably was just that, more machete than sword. These blades had probably traveled to Zhatyra II as part of a wing assembly or a bulkhead.

And Sonandal was not a swordsman. With each flurry of chops and thrusts he came at her as though she were a tangle of vines.

Which was a very good thing, Corsi realized as she almost missed a step. She was not fully recovered from her fall; her left side was beginning to betray her. Against a master swordsman she'd have been hard pressed to keep her feet, much less keep her opponent at bay.

She had to end this before her body gave out. But not with swords.

Ignoring the tremor in her left thigh, she lunged forward, slapping at Sonandal's blade with the flat of her own sword. Startled, he staggered back, barely able to keep his blade up as she drove him across the square with rapid fire slaps; loud, frightening, and harmless if he'd had his wits about him enough to realize what she was doing.

Corsi stopped abruptly, letting the Smaunif stumble a few steps clear of her. She fought to breathe steadily, not let her chest heave. The stamina wasn't there. Flourishing her sword, she leaned right and drove its point into the ground just outside the square.

Hoping she wasn't making a mistake, she held both hands toward him, palm up, then beckoned with her fingers. *Come get me.*

Sonandal reversed his own sword, thrusting it into the ground. Technically it was still inside the ring, but Corsi suspected stopping proceedings now on a point of order would be counterproductive.

The Smaunif surprised her.

Leaping forward like a frog, he planted his hands on the ground two meters in front of her and spun. It was an awkward-looking round-off, but before she realized his target he drove his heels into her left thigh.

Pain spiked from her knee to her scalp. She barely managed to pivot away without breaking the joint.

Clinging to balance, she turned to take his next attack.

Rolling out of his frog kick, Sonandal came up from the ground with all of his weight behind a smashing roundhouse.

Corsi almost thanked him.

The edge of her hand met the back of his fist, deflecting the force of the blow away and down as she rolled her hand to grip his wrist. Her other hand came up, catching Sonandal below the shoulder blade. Turning at the waist, she let herself fall away, pivoting, and leveraged her weight into his momentum.

The redirected energy of his lunge tumbled the Smaunif leader through the air. He landed with a hollow thud, the breath forced from his body.

Corsi danced lightly to her right, hoping her bounce did not reveal the electric shot of pain stabbing up from her left knee with every step. A duller ache radiated from the center of her back and a ghost of numbness flowing down from her elbow warned her not to depend on her left hand's strength.

She wasn't going to last much longer. If she was going to win, she had to win quickly.

Taking advantage of Sonandal's slow roll to his feet, she turned to Copper, standing closest to the violence of all the K'k'tict.

"If I am to prevail, I must attack."

"Then do not prevail."

Sonandal's bear hug caught her from behind, crushing the breath from her. The Smaunif arched his back, raising her in the air, then slammed her to the ground.

Her senses reeling, Corsi rolled away, scrambling to gain distance. Roaring in triumph, Sonandal came at her, his arms wide for another grab.

Coming up on her hands and damaged left knee, Corsi lashed out with her right leg; the from-the-hip kick connecting solidly with Sonandal's knee. He shrieked, stopping himself before his forward drive snapped the joint backward. Getting her right foot back under her, Corsi pushed off from the ground. The right move, the power move, was to come up in a left mule kick to the Smaunif's gut followed by the heel of her right hand to his nose, driving the shattered sinus bones back into his brain. But she knew her left knee couldn't take the impact.

The patched fabric of her trousers popped in the wind as she snapped her left leg up and around in a roundhouse.

Pain flamed up her leg as the top of her bare foot slammed into his cheek, spinning him bonelessly away.

Corsi's back muscles spasmed, turning her pivoting recovery into a crablike stumble.

Sonandal hung, his arms limp, slowly swaying forward, away from her. If he fell, he'd be outside the ring. The fight would be over, she would have won, but not the way she wanted. Not the way that mattered.

Lunging forward, she caught a fistful of the Smaunif's uniform just as he fell. Hauling back with all her strength, she pulled him into the ring; tripping him over her right ankle so he sprawled in the bloody mud.

Her left arm would not respond, still bent against her ribs by her spasmed back. Corsi had to turn her back on Sonandal, even as she saw him gathering himself, to reach his sword. Grabbing its hilt, she yanked it from the earth, backstepping with the same motion and slashing it backward.

Her back screamed as she halted the swing.

On his knees, Sonandal met her eyes along the length of the bloody blade.

Corsi deliberately dropped her game face. She let her professionalism drop from her like a cloak and let her horror and disgust at the slaughter show through. Digging deeper, she focused on Spot, her life blood spilling as the Smaunif blade—the blade she held in her hand—split her body, willing the butcher to see her hate and rage.

He saw it. She could see in Sonandal's eyes he saw her hate and knew he was dead.

There was a moan from the K'k'tict, low and despairing.

From the Smaunif, stony silence.

Her left arm would not move. She needed her left arm

for what she had to do. But it was still trapped uselessly by her traitorous body's leftward crouch. She was going to have to improvise.

With a curse she flourished the sword, the blade flashing dully as it spun. Reversing her grip, she drove the point of the blade into the ground. Keeping a firm grip on the hilt, she risked switching her weight to her left leg. She took a moment to gather her focus, then she lifted her right foot and kicked down to the side, against the flat of the sword.

Her luck held. The blade snapped first try. And she stayed on her feet.

Corsi brought the broken blade up, almost in a salute, then flung it away.

"We share life," she said quietly. Then again loudly so the nearer crowd could hear. "We share life!"

"We share life!" the K'k'tict chorused. Her combadge— and another, she was sure, now somewhere close behind them—carried the words clearly to the Smaunif.

She felt tears streaming down her face, but she didn't care. She swung her right arm wide, indicating the K'k'tict, the Smaunif, and the bloody corpses strewn about the killing field.

"We are one spirit!"

"We are one spirit!" the K'k'tict repeated.

Corsi leaned close to the kneeling Sonandal. She'd had a speech prepared, what she would tell these invaders when she had the chance. But as she looked into the bewildered eyes centimeters from her own she realized none of those things were right.

None of those things were K'k'tict.

"We all share life," she said quietly. "We are all one."

CHAPTER
18

Corsi stood across from Captain Gold's desk in his ready room. He hadn't invited her to sit. He was reading her report, rereading it, she knew. He didn't look happy.

"What would you recommend for the Zhatyra system, Corsi?" he asked at last. "What would you like to see happen next?"

"I'd like to see the Smaunif sent packing," she answered promptly, keeping it formal. "Failing that, relocate their colony to the southern continent."

Though Copper and his tree town had not known of other volcanic birthing caves, the anthropological satellites had documented dozens more, all in the northern hemisphere and around the equator. The southern continent, with its placid plate tectonics and lack of volcanoes, was the only uninhabited region on Zhatyra II.

Gold sighed. "How would you characterize your compliance with the Prime Directive?" he asked.

"Under the circumstances, fair," Corsi replied. "Particularly given both Pattie and I were injured and unconscious when contact was made. Except for our combadges, the natives saw no advanced technology function."

All of their personal equipment, the Waldo Egg, even Pattie's Klingon dagger, had been recovered by transporter without witnesses. Just as Corsi and Pattie had been.

"Starfleet may determine your actions on Zhatyra II warrant an inquiry."

"Sir?"

"You're a Starfleet officer," Gold said. "Blue isn't held to the same standard you are because she hasn't had your Academy training. You're expected to know, and to uphold, the Prime Directive."

"Neither Pattie nor I ever did or said anything to indicate we weren't native to Zhatyra II," Corsi said, careful to keep her voice in report mode. "Nor did we at any time mention the possibility of life on other worlds."

Gold rubbed the back of his left hand. A sure tell he was worried. "Of course protecting developing cultures from the disruption of advanced technology or life on other worlds is part of the Prime Directive," Gold said. "But those considerations are not the key, not the fundamental reason behind the directive." He sighed, leaning back from his desk. "The purpose of the Prime Directive is to remind us we do not have the right to impose our moral view, our cultural values, on another people simply because we have better weapons. It's there to keep us from playing God."

Corsi blinked.

"You mean I shouldn't have done anything?" she asked. "And we aren't going to do anything?"

Leaning back in his chair, Gold again sighed. "The answer to your first question is no—absolutely, you had to act. And, in fact, what you did may not have been to the letter of the Prime Directive, but it was definitely in the spirit. By letting the Smaunif know what the K'k'tict really are, you made it more likely that they'll stop damaging the K'k'tict's culture. But it also means the answer to your second question is yes. We can hope the Smaunif remain bound by their own honor and allow the K'k'tict to flourish. But the Federation can't interfere with events on Zhatyra II without being as arrogant as the Smaunif invaders; certain of their place as the crown of creation."

"But when we see something wrong and don't fix it . . ." Corsi let her voice trail off, gathering her thought. "Doesn't the Prime Directive let the Federation avoid its responsibility to the rest of the universe?"

"On the contrary, Corsi. The Prime Directive, by its very strictness, requires and enables the Federation to honor its greatest responsibility: To respect the right of all peoples to find their own way."

BLACKOUT

Phaedra M. Weldon

For my father, Leonard C. Weldon, who always wanted to travel to the stars. And to Dean Wesley Smith, who was willing to give a hick from Georgia a chance to play in Roddenberry's sandbox.

CHAPTER

1

*P*ressure.

The morning sun burst through the small cavern's recently excavated stained-glass window, casting reds, greens, blues, purples, and yellows against the carved back wall. Dust glinted as it moved lazily through beams of light, sparkling now and then. The room smelled of old books and forgotten knowledge.

Water moved nearby in an underground stream no wider than a meter, discovered half a kilometer from the first chamber.

Pressure, pressure, pressure. Jewlan Omi thrust her lower lip out in a small gesture of frustration as she stared at the beige pages of her notes. Every letter of every word placed together to form every sentence was perfectly drawn, painstakingly positioned in her grandmother's own style, which had been commended by the Board of Linguistic Anachronisms as being the finest in historic realism.

And how is any of this supposed to help me?

"*Pffft*," the sound came out as a pressing of air between her lower lip and the teeth of her upper jaw. There was no word on the page that closely resembled the sound— it was just something that Jewlan had done since childhood. A noise that irritated her father, whether he were in Beta or Alpha States. "This has to prove there are more than four laws, right?"

Her voice echoed against the walls, as no one answered her.

Not that Jewlan expected anyone to really hear, or care.

She sat alone in the First Chamber. The others in her group had returned to the city, forty kilometers west of this latest archaeological find on a planet her people claimed more than a century ago. Two artisans, two news tellers, the team's former expert in mechanical investigations, and the site's financial backer. Everyone used the mechanic's shift to Beta State as their reasoning for departure, proclaiming a new mechanic should be found, interviewed, and approved for work.

And no one in their right mind had declined an opportunity to return to the city to partake of the modern conveniences there.

No one except Jewlan, that is.

The painful truth was Jewlan failed to crack the symbols leading out of the Fourth Chamber. After six weeks, people were tired, dejected, and very grumpy.

The First Chamber had been an accidental find. Digging in the area had revealed a door covered in unfamiliar markings. There had been four distinct symbols, each framed in an equal-sided box. Jewlan, an instructor and professional in cryptography and linguistics, had been brought in from the local university to translate the symbols. Working with Doren Hazar, one of the capital city's brightest experts in cultural mechanics, had been easy. The two combined their skills in engineering and linguistics to decipher the first combination of symbols to open the first door.

It'd been simple once the base root letters had been identified. Jewlan found the key within the Four Laws of Life, discovered decades ago on tablets carved in the Temple of a site south of where they were now.

The First Laws were of Light, which she'd corresponded with the universal element of fire, or a common beginning of all things.

She took up the pages and moved through the bits of floating dust to the Second Chamber door. Inside, artificial lights illuminated a trickling fountain, fed by the underground stream and decorated with carved symbols representing the Second Laws of Water.

In the Third Chamber they'd found tables, chairs, beds—all manner of archaeological treasures to give Jewlan's people a better understanding of the race that had perhaps lived on the world of Asario before her people colonized it.

Jewlan had liked the books best—especially the ones written by hand—and had made formal requests to be involved in studying them once her task at opening all the doors had been complete.

That task had now come to an abrupt halt for two reasons.

Finding a fifth door was the first.

The second was Doren's Beta-shift to Loran Hazar. Loran was a regional representative in the Primary Conclave, and refused to go against their strict laws of gender-based occupations.

Archaeological Mechanics was not Loran's profession. She insisted on returning to the city and once again take up her role as a lawmaker.

Which left Jewlan alone with the problem. No one knew of a Fifth Law. A team had been sent to the Temple to look for any clues to this new site. They had found nothing helpful.

What if it were going to take science to open the door and not the magic of words? Everything had to work off a trigger mechanism. Simply pressing the right combination of plates triggered the door to open. Mechanics.

Jewlan neared the door and looked closely at the seams. She imagined looking *through* the walls to either side. If they had some way to look through the rock into whatever mechanism these people had used, it could be possible to find the—

She stopped her thoughts from traveling any further. They were wrong thoughts. They were mechanical thoughts.

They were Jolen thoughts.

She looked around the room, almost expecting to find someone watching her, reading her mind. Ready to point a finger at her.

But that was impossible. No one could read minds. Especially not the Conclave.

She blinked. *Could they? They sure as hell knew it was*

me that set off the sprinkler system at the party two months ago. Accidents happen, right?

Focusing on the four panels in the door, Jewlan listened to the hum of a nearby lamp. The heat felt good against her exposed skin. The sun had set some time ago, and the temperature had dropped. It would be two days before anyone returned to the site—that is, if they found a mechanic to replace Doren.

I only hope I don't Beta-shift, or I'll be removed from the entire expedition. There would be no need for a computer specialist. Not in the middle of ancient ruins.

And that would just suck.

There was no one around. No one in the caves. The two guards left behind to protect Jewlan were outside in one of the temporary shelters, warming up to a good game of Bathces. The project supervisor was no doubt sleeping off her latest cup of Polin tea. She'd be unconscious for hours.

Jewlan tapped her lower lip with the index finger of her right hand. The papers remained half folded, clutched in her left hand.

Had anyone considered the consequence of simply pushing random buttons? She couldn't remember ever suggesting the idea to Doren, mainly because the two of them had had such a good time solving the puzzle that neither had thought of it. There hadn't been a reason for guessing.

Well, why not?

Dr. Sesar had told her to continue working on deciphering the Fifth Law while he headed back to the city for a hot bath, but he hadn't said anything about not touching the door.

Right?

Jewlan set the papers on a nearby table and rubbed her hands together. With a deep breath, she stepped forward and pressed each of the symbols she recognized in the order she'd identified them, leaving the final two symbols for last.

Nothing happened.

But then, she hadn't really expected anything.

Until *all* of the artificial lights went out.

"Oops," Jewlan muttered in the darkness. "At least we hadn't installed sprinklers."

CHAPTER
2

The airy, lithe plucks of eighteenth-century harp music inside the small cabin onboard the *U.S.S. da Vinci* did little to ease the nervous anxiety of Bartholomew Faulwell. The linguist felt tension in his hand as it rested upon a long-grain sheet of paper. Between his first three fingers he held his favorite pen, its nib sonically cleaned after every use.

On the paper he'd written "Just a brief note," as he'd always started his letters to his lover, Anthony Mark. He stared at the words. Crisp, blue-black ink. Flawless curves and extenders above and below each word.

Everything was perfect.

Everything except the words. There were none. And for a linguist to have no words—this was something indeed.

I—I don't know how to begin. What should I say to him first? Should I apologize for my behavior at the wedding, or do I start by describing my experience with releasing the Koas pyramid? Do I tell him about Caitano and Deverick? I've not even told him of Elizabeth's pregnancy.

Where were those words he'd so carefully stored in his memory for the past month, waiting for this opportunity to write them down?

And yet—that wasn't all he'd noticed was missing. There had been no stain on the tip of the finger of his right hand for several weeks. After Anthony's less than subtle suggestion the two of them marry, Bart had all but stopped writing letters.

No—that wasn't completely true. He'd tried to write them. Began the ritual he so loved—of pulling the crisp, off-white sheet of paper from its box and smoothing it against his desk, selecting the perfect pen and filling the reservoir with the exact shade of ink. All of these tiny steps had brought him uncommon pleasure and peace.

Because they'd always brought him closer to Anthony.

Bart sighed aloud, the sound little more than a whisper amid the harp's chords. He set the pen down and leaned back, his arms crossed over his chest. Staring at the simple phrase did nothing to help the words come any faster.

While in space, floating above the wonder of creation as the Koas's world was restored and her people once again safe, Bart had believed there was nothing more pure, more fulfilling in life than companionship, and he was richer because of his relationship with Anthony.

And he'd wanted to write him and tell him what he'd

seen. Anthony would understand. Words had jumbled themselves into Bart's mind since then and he had planned for this down time to finally put into words his experience at that moment.

Looked forward to it.

Needed it.

And yet nothing came to him.

He compared the feeling to revving an engine, pressing simultaneously against the fuel pedal and the brake, only to slam into an unforeseen wall the moment the brake was released.

Splat.

I'm avoiding the larger issue. Bart rubbed absently at his salt-and-pepper beard with his right hand. *All those pretty words in my head mean nothing if I can't even talk with Anthony about serious commitment or the reasons why I just . . . can't.* He groaned as he rubbed his forehead. *It'd been easier to write that article for the Sato Linguistics Institute.*

A familiar sound interrupted his thoughts as his cabin's intercom whistled. *"Faulwell,"* came Captain Gold's gruff but pleasant tone, *"please report to observation."*

Saved once again by the call to adventure.

As Bart removed the pen's reservoir a bit of ink splashed onto the tip of the third finger of his right hand, in precisely the spot where it usually stained. After setting the nib into the sonic cleaner and replacing the paper to its box, Bart grabbed up a towel and rubbed at the ink, knowing it would have to wear away.

He stood and tossed the towel onto the desk as he looked at his finger. Bart had always thought of the stain as a badge of honor, a symbol of his dedication to

Anthony, a dedication he carried through in his writing of letters.

But no letter had been written. This stain was little more than a red herring—a false clue. He rubbed at it harder with the palm of his left hand as he turned to the door. "Out, out damned spot," he muttered as he stepped into the corridor.

Perhaps after whatever it was the captain wanted was finished, he could return and finish the letter, and then the stain would mean something. Maybe the words would come to him with what lay ahead. Buoyed by that completely false hope, and with a final glance at his stained finger, he departed the cabin he shared with Fabian Stevens.

Bart couldn't remember looking up even once during his walk to the observation lounge, yet somehow he'd managed not to run anyone over. When the doors opened for him he stopped just inside.

Everyone was seated around the table and the combined looks from all his colleagues nearly bowled him over. Were they all looking at him for some reason other than he'd been the only one to just enter the room? Likely.

"Faulwell, please be seated," Gold said from his seat at the head of the table.

Carol Abramowitz, the ship's cultural specialist, stood just behind Gold beside the viewscreen. Displayed was a planet of greens, blues, and whites. It looked very much like Earth.

Commander Sonya Gomez sat to Gold's left. Seated to Gold's right was the Tellarite, Mor glasch Tev, the *da Vinci*'s second in command. Beside Tev was the single

Bynar, Soloman, the ship's computer specialist. Beside Gomez sat Domenica Corsi, chief of security, and the one that would protect the S.C.E. team's rear ends in case of any emergency. Standing just behind her was Makk Vinx, the *da Vinci*'s Iotian security guard.

This looks interesting, Bart thought as he took up the chair opposite the captain's. He made note of P8 Blue and Fabian Stevens's absence. And where was Elizabeth? Not quite a month had passed since she and Dr. Julian Bashir had been rescued from an alternate universe. Elizabeth had been quiet and subdued since her return. The news of her pregnancy had spread throughout the ship, and Bart had been one of the first to congratulate her.

What he hadn't expected was the haunting sadness he saw in her eyes. Not even a forced smile could hide it. Bart recognized it. He sometimes saw it reflected in the mirror.

Something was bothering Dr. Lense, harsh and very personal. And when it came time to talk, Bart was sure he'd be the first one she came to.

They always did.

Captain Gold interlaced his fingers as he rested them on the conference table before him. Bart wondered briefly if the captain's artificial hand actually felt the pressure of the knuckles of the other hand. "Asario is one of the Federation's newest members, its technology on an independent level very close to our own. Unfortunately, as of seventy-two hours ago, Asario experienced a planet-wide power blackout."

"Planetwide?" Gomez frowned. "How did we receive any calls for assistance from the Asarions if they have no power?"

"Captain Scott received the message via subspace." Gold glanced at Tev.

The Tellarite nodded to the captain and took over the discussion, his snout thrust high. "Apparently two of the government's ships were staffed and in orbit when the blackout occurred. They immediately sent out distress calls that reached Federation ships. One of the ships, the *Mercury*, was able to establish a small communication with the government's leader. A female by the name of Corlis."

"Do their scientists know what caused the blackout?" Soloman asked. "Electromagnetic pulse?"

"That was Stevens and Blue's first guess as well," Gold said. "I briefed them as soon as I received the message from Captain Scott. Our primary concern at the moment is to get power restored on a larger scale. Primarily to hospitals."

"I take it they're having trouble turning the power back on?" Gomez said.

Tev nodded. "Nothing with an amp output of more than sixty-five megawatts will work. We suspect a higher output with portable fusion reactors might be more efficient."

"What type of power source do they use?" Gomez asked.

"The Asarions are a sparse race, their population only numbering half a million or so, refugees from a Borg invasion of their homeworld over a century ago. They occupy only a small part of the larger continent. Their main source of power is a single fusion reactor located in the center of the city."

"And something knocked it out," Gomez said.

"And is keeping it out," Gold finished. "Apparently whatever caused the initial burst that shut systems down is also preventing them from restarting power."

Tev nodded. "Small fields are unaffected by this dampening effect."

Gold's bushy white eyebrows furrowed as he looked at the team. "At present, they've been able to make do in keeping the more critical patients alive and comfortable. The worst of the situation is the heat. Asario is in its summer months on the larger continent and the heat index during the day can reach zeniths near those of Death Valley on Earth. They've started gathering the elderly and children into common areas where some generators can still power cooling units. Either way, it's our job to get these people's power back up. They're working on small reactors now, but there aren't enough of them to power the entire city."

Bart had kept quiet during the exchanges, listening intently. He was also aware of the stain on his finger and kept tucking the hand under the table. After a few seconds, the linguist finally cleared his throat and asked a question that had started rolling around in his thoughts. "Captain Gold—why was I called in?"

Gold smiled. "Corlis has expressed interest in any help we could give her people in linguistic science—her words exactly. She believes the initial reason for the blackout has something to do with ruins found several kilometers outside the main city."

"The blackout," Bart glanced at Carol, who had remained quiet since he sat down, "was caused by ruins?"

Gold nodded. "That's what the leader said."

"Fabian, Pattie, and Soloman will work with Tev and

me on the power problem," Gomez said. "Vinx will be our security. Bart, you'll go with Carol and Domenica to take a look at the excavation."

Bart nodded, as did everyone else. He was excited about the prospect of looking at an alien culture, of studying their letters and their words, the syntax and their language. But not even that excitement could quell the nagging guilt he felt at not writing to Anthony.

"Now," Gold said and turned toward the patiently waiting cultural specialist. "I'm going to turn this over to Abramowitz, who is going to brief you all on the cultural and the unique physiological nature of the Asarions. So please, everyone, listen carefully." Gold shook his head. "You're all going to need to know this."

Carol gave her commanding officer an arched eyebrow. "Thank you, Captain." She looked at everyone. "Asarion culture isn't much different than our own when looked at in generalizations. They developed their technology much the same way we did. They used fossil fuels and even had their own dark age of a sort. What does set them apart are their severe physical differences."

Bart narrowed his eyes as the screen changed. He expected to see some sort of bipedal, scale-covered insectoid from the way Carol was building it up. Instead he saw an attractive, almost human-looking woman. Broad shouldered and lean body-type. The only noticeable difference between a human female and this one was the eyes.

As he leaned forward to see the image better, Bart couldn't put his finger on what made the eyes different, only that he knew he would recognize an Asarion among the crew of the *da Vinci* by just looking into their eyes.

Bart couldn't see what other physical differences Carol was talking about.

"Asarions have two states of being. They possess an Alpha State, the sex in which they're born into, and a Beta State, the sex into which they shift. These states are not always the same, meaning female isn't always the Alpha or vice versa. Their Alpha is determined by their birth state. Or their home state."

"Whoa." Makk Vinx abruptly spoke up. "Beggin' your pardon there, Doc, but are you saying these people—" He winced. "—they shift sex? A broad could be a fella, just like that? All—" He glanced around the room, his gaze apologetic to the women in the room. "I mean," Vinx made a nodding gesture to the lower part of his torso, "even . . . ?"

Carol nodded. "Yes, very much so." Bart could see the excitement evident in her expression.

He took a step back. "Unbelievable."

"Vinx," Corsi said in a low voice, "be seen, not heard."

"Yes, ma'am."

Carol continued, a slight smile on her lips. "You can only imagine the sort of culture that would grow out of this physical change. Puberty brings about an Asarion's first shift, where the body changes to the opposite sex into what will be their Beta State. Shift states can last from one year to three years, and there is a record of a Beta-Shift lasting up to six years."

"You mean they're male until puberty, then wake up one morning and now he's a she?" Corsi asked. "They're not Hermats? Because I've met a few Hermats. They even have their own set of pronouns."

Bart glanced at the security chief. She looked as puzzled and awed as he felt.

"No, they're not Hermats. They don't possess the genitals of both male and female simultaneously. Their bodies actually become a single-species sex other than the one of their birth state. There's also no change of identity of the individual's likes and dislikes, their personality, or their knowledge. Some Asarions shift in even amounts. Two years Alpha, two years Beta, without fail. Others shift 'off-clock,' or randomly. An Alpha State may last three years and a Beta only one."

"Interesting," Tev said, turning his face from Abramowitz to the screen, where the Asarion pictured abruptly mutated into a male version of the female.

Carol smiled. "Once an Asarion female gives birth, she loses the ability to shift. This life choice is considered an honor. Because of this the balance of female Alphas to male Alphas has increased. And that imbalance long ago triggered the Asarions' present governmental structure to relegate their society's skills to gender-particular trades."

"Now that's just crazy," Gomez rubbed at her forehead. "Gender-dictated life paths?"

"In a way. The males are the defenders, the builders, and the craftsmen of the society, while the women are the scientists, the business leaders, and the political officers."

Tev made a rude noise. "There is their greatest flaw—no men in government. Vastly debilitating philosophy."

Ooh, Bart winced inwardly. *I think the commander needs to juice up the dosage on Tev's sensitivity classes.*

To his credit, Tev noticed the looks his comment was earning him, and he said, "I would say the same if there were no women in it. If a government is to be properly representational to the needs of its people, it should include both male *and* female."

"Even so," Carol said while glaring at Tev, "everyone should be aware that you could possibly be working with one person one day, and then they're abruptly replaced by someone else."

Gomez lowered her head, but looked up at Carol under her eyebrows. "So, if I were an Asarion female, and suddenly became a man, I could no longer work with woman things. I'd have to do man things now."

Carol nodded. "Yep. Any questions?"

Corsi nodded. "I have one. Will my being a security officer offend anyone? I am, after all, a female, and a defender."

Bart nodded, pursed his lips. Good question.

"No, the Asarions aren't a proselytizing race. There are no records of any of Starfleet's emissaries being forced to adhere to their societal rules. So we should be okay."

Bart sat in silence with the team. He could only imagine what was going through their minds. His own thoughts were a jumble of questions, ranging from what would happen if your lover or husband's sex suddenly became unsuitable to one's tastes?

He was sure the society had compensated for this small glitch, just as his own had. But still . . . the thought of Anthony abruptly becoming Antoinette was more than a bit . . . unnerving.

"Thank you, Abramowitz," Gold took charge of the briefing once again. "We'll be arriving in the Asarion system in four hours. I suggest we all make the best of that time. Dismissed."

CHAPTER
3

"Bart," Carol touched Bart's arm on the way out of the conference room.

The linguist stopped in the hallway just outside as Carol stepped through the door. He really wanted to return to his quarters and prepare himself for their arrival. But, as usual, someone needed to talk. "What's up, Carol?"

Carol Abramowitz had a slight build, with large eyes and a full mouth. Her close-cropped dark hair shone under the lights as did the twinkle in her eye. "Congratulations—you're writing again?"

Bart frowned. He'd made the mistake of sharing his recent tardiness in writing to Anthony with Carol over dinner. But how did the woman know he'd actually attempted a letter?

Catching the look of confusion in Bart's expression, Carol reached down and grabbed Bart's hand, the one with the stain. She held it up for both of them to see. "It's nice to see that little mark again."

With a little more force than intended, Bart pulled his hand out of Carol's grip. Guilt pressed down harder against his shoulders. "It's nothing. It's not what you think. I didn't . . . couldn't . . ."

Carol leaned toward Bart. "You didn't write Anthony a letter?"

He opened his mouth to respond and then closed it. A loud sigh escaped him as he leaned against the nearest bulkhead. They were alone in the corridor. "I started to. But then I wasn't sure what to say. I wanted to tell him about the Koas and what I saw. And about Caitano and Deverick and about Elizabeth's baby. And then a small voice told me I was only avoiding the larger issue. But something kept staying the words."

"You mean Anthony's mention of marriage." Carol put her hands on her hips and leaned her head to one side. "Bart . . . why would someone like you, who enjoys a stable, long-term, long-distance even, relationship with a wonderful man, be afraid of commitment?"

Though his own inner voice had asked the same question over and over, Bart hadn't heard it verbalized. It immediately put him on the defensive. "I am not afraid, I'm just . . ." he paused.

I'm just what? Cautious? How often had he used that excuse on himself, sabotaging relationships before? Cautious because of his own job? Since joining Starfleet over eighteen years ago, his life had been full of adventure as well as danger. He knew he'd overrationalized the higher road—knowing casual relationships were best as he never knew if one mission would lead to his death.

All that changed when he met Anthony Mark on Starbase 92 over a year ago.

Or so he'd believed.

In space, on a ship, how would anyone know what next step would spell the end? *It seemed so easy while I'd been out there, watching the Koas pyramid unfold, watching a miracle take place. Knowing then I'd wanted Anthony in my life always, to share such experiences with me. So what happened? Why can't I even verbalize my own anxiety at the thought of marriage?*

"Bart? You're doing it. You're overthinking."

He blinked at her. "I am not. I'm just trying to figure out what's wrong with me."

"Well then, talk to me."

He frowned. "About what?"

"Whatever is bothering you. People always go to you when they're confused or need an ear. Why won't you talk to me? Or to Fabian? Or Pattie? Or hell, even Tev— you seem to get along with him better than anyone."

That much was true. Bart didn't feel the same animosity toward the Tellarite that the rest of the crew did. "Look, you're right. Maybe I need to talk. And maybe I will . . . one day. I have to figure out what's wrong with me, and I have to figure it out on my own."

"Nothing's *wrong* with you. You're just a man with cold feet."

"I do *not* have cold feet."

"Iceberg."

"Eh," Bart turned and pressed his forehead against the nearest bulkhead, a little harder than he intended, making a nice *thunking* noise. He closed his eyes as he spoke. "I don't have cold feet. I'm only considering Anthony, that's all. My life—our lives here—are in constant danger. Something tragic could happen at any moment."

"To him or you?"

"Both."

"And this is something no other Starfleet officer has faced before?" Carol frowned.

Bart opened his eyes and straightened up. "I'm not an officer."

"No, but Anthony is. And he accepts those risks every day. I don't think you're being fair to him. I think you're being selfish. I think this is all about you and something you haven't faced."

Selfish. Me?

Bart rubbed at his forehead before running thin fingers through his thick, salt-and-pepper hair. "When I think about a permanent commitment, something inside . . ." He searched for the perfect word and plucked it from his stressed mind. "Twists."

"You're repulsed at the notion of marriage? Bart, you and Anthony are in love. I saw the way you two were at the wedding. That man adores you." She shook her head. "I think you don't know why marriage gives you cold feet."

"No, no, no. Argh . . . I'm not saying this right." *Me. A linguist, and I can't even put into words the reasons why I can't—*

"*Hey, Bart,*" came Fabian Stevens's voice from Bart's combadge. "*You there?*"

Bart touched his badge with a sigh. "I'm here. What's up?"

"We just got another subspace message from Asario. Apparently they've picked up some sort of low-level emission from the excavation site."

"Emission? Like a radiation emission?"

"No." Fabian paused. *"More like a repeated message. It's sort of riding piggyback on whatever's dampening the planet's magnetic fields. I'm going to pipe it to the communications station on the bridge. Can you check it out?"*

"On my way," Bart turned in the direction of the bridge and Carol followed. "Do we have anything on the planet's history?"

"I'm afraid not. Or not much more than what the Asarion people have found since their colonization of it."

"Upload what you can to the communications station." Bart preceded Carol onto the bridge and turned immediately to the station.

Captain Gold sat in his chair and gave a half turn to watch Bart seat himself. "You received Stevens's message?"

"Yes, sir." Bart grabbed a receiver and slipped it into his left ear as he sat down. He tapped a sequence of pads on the console and found Fabian's upload. Making sure the receiver was snuggly in place, Bart cued the message, adjusted the volume, and played it.

At first he thought something was wrong with his receiver, as the message was little more than a series of static whistles and clicks. He adjusted the resonance and compensated for distance and stream.

Abruptly the whistles and clicks became a voice—but not any voice Bart had heard before, or in any immediately recognizable language. He glanced at the captain, who was watching him patiently. Frowning, the linguist quickly analyzed sounds, looked for repeating patterns, pinpointed consonants and vowels.

"Anything?" Gold prompted.

Bart pursed his lips as he fed what he heard into the computer. The universal translator was busy doing high-speed comparisons. But the linguist didn't really need the computer's aid to understand the meaning of the message. Tonal inflection as well as basic language syntax was all Bart Faulwell required. He had deciphered thousands of codes, languages, and symbols.

"Captain," the linguist said. "It's a warning."

"A warning?"

"A warning?" came Fabian's voice from the speakers. Obviously the tactical specialist had been monitoring bridge communications. *"From whom to whom? And what?"*

"Dunno," Bart said. "I can tell it's a warning, and it's being repeated in precise intervals. I'd say it's automated."

"But no idea on who and what?" Gold said.

"Not yet. But I'll have it."

"I know you will. Keep at it." Gold lifted his chin. "Stevens, you and Blue come up with any more power scenarios?"

"Not on the whys, sir. We've scraped together a little over fifty or so portable fusion generators. They'll help get the city's basics back online for us to work with. I think we'll do better once we can actually take a look at the situation. Get a hands-on reading."

Bart allowed himself to become immersed in the message. He closed his eyes, allowing his fingers to move over the station's controls on their own as he listened to each word, broke it down, and reinvented it.

Words. He loved words. He loved sounds, their shape and form in his mind. Communication was a subjective science and one that depended on as well as interwove with a culture's beliefs. Their spiritual doctrines.

And their military might.

This message had the sound of being military-based. Sparse. Staccato. Powerful.

This was a people who were confident in their control of the situation. Whatever that may have been.

Bart checked the information Carol had given him. The newest site, the one where Corlis believed the blackout originated, was the oldest of the discoveries. He displayed images of symbols, the language written, on several of his monitors, quickly identifying sounds with representations.

Speaking a language and seeing its symbols written were two different experiences, and Bart could only have imagined what linguists who worked on the ancient pyramids at Giza had thought after so many years of seeing the language of the ancient Egyptians when it was actually spoken.

The translator beeped at him, and Bart scanned the computer's interpretation of the message. He did a double take as he checked the computer's findings. "What the—"

"Found something?" Gold rotated his command chair to face the linguist.

Bart glanced up at Gold. "I've got a tentative translation. And I mean tentative. I'd have to check the computer's findings against my own knowledge, but . . ." He paused. "The tone of the message—the way the language is spoken—it doesn't make any sense when considering what I think the words mean."

312 Phaedra M. Weldon

"Oh? What does it say?"

Bart had the whole of the bridge crew's attention; though many remained focused on their stations, everyone was listening.

He took a deep breath. "'Do not to your neighbor what is hateful to yourself.'"

No one spoke.

Then Gold sat forward, his expression as incredulous as Bart's own. "Faulwell-that's impossible. That's a famous maxim by *Hillel*."

Bart nodded his head slowly. "I know, Captain."

"And that's all it says?"

"Yes, sir."

"What about the rest?" Gold asked.

"Rest?" Carol said. "There's more?"

"The quote goes on to say, 'the rest is commentary; go learn it.'"

Bart knew the famous maxim. Knew that finding the exact same passage on a world thousands of light-years from Earth was implausible. But here it was.

"Wong," Gold said to the helm. "Let's see if we can get this ship to Asario a little faster."

The flummoxed linguist looked down at the computer's translation. *Go learn it, indeed. Apparently, we're on our way to do just that.*

CHAPTER
4

The Asarion system nearly paralleled the Terran system in its size and structure. Eight planets orbited a single sun. Asario was the fifth planet. Rich blues and fluffy whites decorated the shimmering sphere.

From orbit, Pattie scanned the surface and found several more city ruins, evidence of the planet's former inhabitants. These sites were all aboveground, where Corlis said the present active excavation was being carried out.

The *U.S.S. da Vinci* passed the terminator into night, less than twenty hours since the Asarion distress call.

No lights glittered from the surface, evidence of the planet's troubles.

After a brief communication with the orbiting *Mercury*, Gold gathered the away team and established an unstable link with Corlis. The image wavered and blurred at regular intervals, but Bart was sure he saw red hair and bright, bright green eyes.

Chief Engineer Nancy Conlon and Transporter Chief Poynter assured Gold and Gomez that the transporters weren't affected by whatever it was that was now keeping the planet on low-level power. With a final reassurance, Poynter beamed down Gomez, Tev, Pattie, Soloman, Corsi, Carol, Fabian, Vinx, and Bart.

The room they found themselves in was circular and shadowed from small octagonal lanterns placed along the floor and on tables against the wall. Couches of muted dark colors lined the walls. It looked like a reception area.

Bart wished he could see the colors and textures of the walls around him, but the light wasn't bright enough.

Corlis met the group first, flanked by two other females. She was of medium height and slightly built. Her fiery red hair was back in what Bart would call a severe bun. The way it pulled at her face reminded him of Ms. Hutchins in primary school. Bart had always assumed the woman had pulled her hair tight just to smooth away the wrinkles.

It hadn't helped.

Gomez took care of the introductions, referring to herself only as the leader of the away team and not as an engineer in her own right. However, Bart noted only a slight hesitation in Corlis's demeanor at the mention of Bart's position as linguist and Corsi's as security chief. He could almost see the woman readjusting her own paradigm to fit the situation.

Good. Adaptable. But I guess they have to be, seeing as how half of her life was spent as a man.

"It's wonderful to have you here, Dr. Faulwell. We're in

desperate need of your expertise." She shifted her attention to Gomez. "We've been able to move shuttles on low power at extremely slow speeds. I've arranged for one of these to take you immediately to the excavation site."

"We'll do our best, ma'am," Gomez said. "Maybe it would be better if we transported them there."

"We've already tried. It's impossible to get a lock on the site perimeter from here." Corlis sighed before continuing. "I'll apologize for the duration of the trip in advance. Our own cryptographer is still at the site. Jewlan Omi. I'd like for you to meet with her and learn her exact movements in the last two days. Find out exactly what it was she did."

Something in Corlis's tone alarmed Bart. "Ma'am— Corlis—we're here to lend a hand with deciphering text and symbols at the site. You want us to investigate her actions? You believe your cryptographer was the one that triggered the blackout?"

The Asarion leader gave Bart a half smirk. "Who else."

It wasn't a question. Bart wasn't sure how to respond to it either. Apparently there was a sardonic side to the Asarion leader. And obviously Jewlan Omi brought it out of her.

Corlis waved her hand in front of her. "Never mind. Please forgive me. I'm afraid my Alpha State is near and I'm usually cranky the week prior. Just be cautious. Jewlan's accident ratio is higher than most. I've made sure to leave a supervisor there to monitor her work."

She turned to one of the other females and retrieved two palm devices much like Bart's padd. She handed one to Bart and one to Carol. "This contains all the information we have on the site, as well as anything we've noticed or monitored since the blackout."

"You're still sure the reason for the power decrease originates at the site?" Soloman said as he turned to Gomez. "Perhaps we should accompany them to the site. It is always better to solve the problem, not treat the symptom."

But Gomez shook her head. "Right now, getting partial power up and running in key areas is primary. Let's get that done and diagnose what kind of effect this is having on the fusion reactor itself. It might give us clues as to what to look for at the site."

Soloman nodded.

"You are a Bynar, are you not? Is it true your species matches up in gender-opposite pairs?" Corlis's eyes had widened and she reminded Bart of a small child investigating a bug.

"And you are an Asarion. Is it also true that you will soon inhabit a male body?"

Bart smiled. Soloman had been developing quite a dry wit lately.

Corlis narrowed her eyes at Soloman. "I like you." With a sigh she looked at Pattie. "Now you're something I've never met before."

"And you'll never meet a better one," the Nasat piped up. She leaned forward on her many legs and offered her two front pincers in the Asarion greeting. To Corlis's credit, the leader didn't miss a beat and returned the gesture in kind.

"We should really get started," Bart said, somehow sensing a long, witty banter was about to commence. "Could we get to the site?"

The Asarion leader smiled. "Of course. Please, follow Myaa," and she nodded to the smaller of the two women.

Myaa had yellow hair and wore a look of curiosity as she stepped forward. "Please, follow me."

The shuttle was comfortable with soft couches, side desks, and footrests. Carol found an Asarion counterpart to a Starfleet replicator when she commented about wanting water. A purple light appeared in a small alcove to her right and a clear glass of water materialized. Bart wanted something a little stronger and found a button that projected a holographic menu. He checked several of the selections against his sparse knowledge of the Asarion language and ordered what he thought was coffee and sat down to read.

There wasn't much more in the notes than he'd already seen, save for sidebars on the four discovered chambers. There had also been a fifth chamber, which had puzzled the author, a Doren Hazar, in its differences in comparison to the first four chambers.

After half an hour, Bart finally remembered the coffee sitting on the shelf beside him and tasted it. The flavor was interesting—somewhere between licorice and peppermint. It numbed the back of his tongue but he took several more sips before setting the cup down.

The numbness spread to the back of his neck and down his throat as the coffee settled into his stomach. Abruptly the numbness became a smoldering heat. He felt flushed and set the Asarion device on the seat beside him. He closed his eyes and pinched the bridge of his nose with the index finger and thumb of his right hand.

Uh . . . oh. I'm not feeling so good anymore. He leaned back in his seat and closed his eyes.

"Bart?"

Keeping his eyes closed, he answered Carol. "Headache. I think maybe I'm . . . dehydrated."

He heard her moving over the cushions, and felt her

cool hand on his forehead. "Dehydrated? You're very warm. Can you . . . Bart . . . Bart? Can you hear me . . . ?"

". . . advisable to give him that sort of thing? We may resemble each other on the outside, but human and Asarion physiologies are very different."

"I agree. I've studied some human biology. Which is why I believe the stimulant was worth the risk. He could have been unconscious much longer."

"I think we should have called for Dr. Lense."

Bart winced at the bright light behind his eyelids. *Why was Carol arguing about stimulants? And who was she arguing with?*

And why does my head hurt so bad?

"He's waking."

That was a new voice. Bart cautiously opened his right eye—to test the waters. Something moved in front of him, blocking out the light; he could make out shoulders, and a vaguely outlined face.

"C-Carol?" his voice was thick, and his enunciation slurred. *Damn . . . I sound drunk.*

"She's over there," said the new voice and Bart realized the person leaning over him and pulling his eyelids open wasn't Carol. The light around the silhouette was still too bright and he batted at this person's hands, commanding with his feeble whacking for them to cease and desist.

"Bart, can you hear me?"

Okay, now that was Carol.

"Yeah . . ." Bart said in a low voice. "Just stop yelling."

"I'm not yelling. Can you sit up?"

I wasn't aware that I wasn't.

He felt hands grab at his arms and shoulders and gently pull him into a seated position. As soon as he was perpendicular, he wished he wasn't. The pounding in his head only increased in volume and intensity and he pressed both palms of his hands into his eyes. "Did anyone . . . get the name of the shuttle driver that hit me?"

"No shuttle, Bart," Corsi's less than sympathetic voice broke in. In fact, she actually sounded amused. Ah, the new and improved Domenica Corsi. "It was something you drank."

Drank. Bart tried to remember what he'd drunk in the past forty-eight hours. He managed to open both eyes and found four women staring at him. He focused on the smaller of the unfamiliar women, as her face was in the middle. "I drank coffee."

"No," Carol shook her head. She was to his right, beside the smaller woman. "You drank," she held up her hands and wiggled the index finger and middle finger of both hands in quotation marks, "spirit water."

"Spirit?" Bart tried to look at Carol, but his attention continually moved back to the bright eyes in front of him. This woman was an Asarion. "As in disembodied ghost?"

"No." Corsi sighed. "As in firewater. As in cocktail, brew, hooch."

Bart squinted at the tall, statuesque security chief. "You mean as in alcohol?"

"More like the equivalent of pure grain alcohol," Carol said. "You went down like a house of cards."

The Asarion woman turned a curious expression to Carol. "What an interesting analogy. May I borrow it?"

Carol smiled. Shaking her head she said, "Jewlan, it's not mine. I don't own the phrase. It's just a common metaphor where I come from."

Jewlan Omi. Ah. Bart nodded inwardly—doing so outwardly could cause great pain. He offered the young woman his hand. "Bartholomew Faulwell, cryptographer and linguist." He managed a lopsided grin. "And sometime drunk, obviously."

Jewlan took his hand in hers, then took his other one and molded them into the same greeting Corlis had used with Vinx. "Greetings and well met, Bartholomew Faulwell."

"Bart." *Ouch*. "Just call me Bart." He looked at their surroundings. "I take it we're here." He winced.

"You'll be fine until the stimulant wears off," the other woman said. She wasn't as young or as attractive as Jewlan. In fact, she had a pinched look over her nose, as if she smelled something bad. All the time. "My name is Riz Shedd. I'm the supervisor of this excavation."

Jewlan rose and moved away. Bart was a bit taken by her sometimes fluid, then jerky movements, as if her body were very much two different types. She appeared to be his height (that is, if he dared to stand at the moment), and her hair was dark, cut much shorter than Carol's, and stuck out and up at the crown. Her face was delicate with high cheekbones framing those bright Asarion eyes. Her skin was as smooth and nearly poreless as carved marble, which was something he noticed about Corlis as well. Another Asarion difference.

Riz looked just like her name sounded. Rigid.

Jewlan caught Bart's expression and smiled. He tried

to return the gesture, thinking somehow she knew what he'd been thinking about her coworker.

Ow. Even moving facial muscles hurt a little. Now he remembered all the reasons he'd stuck to synthehol. Carol was also being oddly nice.

Bart waved at Carol. "How long?"

"How long what?"

"Have I been unconscious?"

"You were passed out," Corsi said, a slight pull at the corner of her mouth.

Oh, great. She's enjoying this, and once Fabian gets wind of it, there'll be no end to the drunk jokes.

"You snore."

Bart pointed at Corsi. "That's enough. According to Fabe, you're not exactly a peaceful sleeper."

Corsi's smirk vanished. Bart knew he'd hit a nerve, and with "Core-Breach," that wasn't exactly a smart thing to do. The security chief was also several centimeters taller than he, and perhaps antagonizing her wasn't such a bold move. And it certainly wasn't something he'd have done normally.

Must be the effects of that coffee. Or whatever the hell it was I drank.

"Is the stimulant working?" Carol said, moving to stand beside Riz.

"Yeah. I'm awake." He looked around. "And we're still in the shuttle."

Jewlan nodded. "We thought it was better you stay here. You're going to be a bit off balance for a day or so."

"You mean I'm going to fall down a lot?"

"Noooo . . ." She frowned. "You're not going to be yourself. Riz gave you a stimulant to combat the effects of Poplin. It's really more of an aphrodisiac to my people than a beverage consumed to get drunk."

"Aphrodisiac?" Corsi let a snicker escape her. "Bart took an aphrodisiac? Of all the things you could order on that replicator menu, you chose a sexual stimulant?"

"I'm sure Jewlan means they drink it much like we drink wine or beer in order to loosen up, so to speak." Carol glared at Corsi before looking back to Jewlan. "To get in the mood. I wonder . . ." She looked at Bart. "You think I should take some of that stuff back with me so Vance and I can try it? Maybe lose ourselves in our lack of inhibitions?"

"No." Bart shook his head. "If you remember, the only thing I lost was consciousness." And though Bart really wasn't interested in what went on behind closed doors between Carol and Vance Hawkins, he was sure the two would not want to share the ultimate hangover banging about in his head.

Though taking a bit of the drink home to Fabian for those nights the tactical specialist decided to practice Tellarite might give Bart an easier night's sleep. Slip a little into his *raktajino?*

"Good point." Carol put her hands together.

"To be honest, Dr. Faulwell," Riz said, clasping her hands in front of her, "if you'd ingested the real Poplin, and not the synthesized version, it would have stopped your heart."

Carol blinked. "Well. That's nice." She looked down at Bart. "Are you ready to get started? Jewlan and Riz are ready to give us a tour of what's been found and where the problem is."

Bart nodded and stood.

And sat right back down.

Jewlan leaned in close to him and gently laced a thin but strong arm under his left shoulder. He caught the whiff of what he thought was jasmine as she leaned into him.

"That smell—what perfume is it?"

"No perfume," Jewlan said as she tugged at him to stand up. "Wow . . . you're a tall man."

"I smell something," Bart insisted. "Like flowers."

"Oh, that." Jewlan gave a light, if not pleasant laugh. "I've been writing. That always happens when I write. Okay, here we go."

Bart wanted to ask more questions about the scent, but his concentration was shaken when he was practically lifted off his feet. The Asarion was indeed a lot stronger than she looked. The two stood together, Jewlan cautioning him to take it slowly. "See? You're just going to have to depend on me for the day. Remember, just take it slow and you should be fine."

The linguist nodded, though he kept a firm hold on the Asarion's shoulder. The smell of jasmine was fading. But the memories the perfume brought back to him of the garden he'd had on Earth, before the Dominion War, lingered.

He hadn't thought of that house or that garden in years. *Why? Why was I remembering my life before before the S.C.E.?*

Before Anthony.

"Ready?" Riz was watching Jewlan and Bart. "Now, let's see if we can straighten out this mess Jewlan's made."

CHAPTER
5

Communication with the other S.C.E. team was sketchy when it worked at all. Whatever was preventing full power restoration appeared to be stronger during the day. Jewlan had a niggling suspicion that by entering the wrong combination she'd inadvertently triggered some sort of protective dampening field.

Jewlan didn't believe she'd entered anything really wrong; it was right for activating the defense of—something. Only it was wrong because it wasn't the key to open the door. Doren's notes were specific; she'd tried several combinations on the other doors in private, and hadn't triggered anything like this. *So—either I lucked onto the "on" combination, or this door opens into something that needed protecting.*

Something dangerous, perhaps?

All these things ran amok in her head. Theories, ideas, suppositions—but she kept silent. As a linguist Jewlan wasn't allowed to speculate as to the mechanism's purpose. That would be for her Beta State, when and if it arrived.

Just not yet. Not yet. With Riz present, if she shifted, there was a chance her Beta job of mechanic wouldn't be allowed by the supervisor. And Jewlan was sure both Riz and Corlis wanted any excuse to bring her back.

Riz had already let her know several times how upset the Primary Conclave was at her actions. In fact, Jewlan was sure she'd counted the supervisor's account of the meeting seven times. And, how it had been she—Riz Shedd—who had protected Jewlan's position and prevented her from being recalled immediately.

That much was pure fiction. Jewlan knew the only reason Riz had stood up for anyone was because she liked being out at the site so she could drink more tea.

The thought of tea made her look at the linguist again. He seemed different than the two women. Forget the fact he was a man studying language and symbolism. Jewlan had encountered other species before that were gender-locked. There was something else about him—something deeper. He seemed almost lost, distracted.

But about what?

It still worried her that Bart had completely lost consciousness. He seemed okay now, if not a bit off balance from the stimulant. He'd been very pale, and very still when she'd stepped into the shuttle and found the small brunette female kneeling over him.

The fusion generators brought by the S.C.E. team brought light back into the excavated chambers. There wasn't enough power to run any cooling units, and the heat index during the day would be uncomfortable.

Riz pointed this out during their walk to the site entrance. And as the sun rose, so did the temperature in the first two chambers, making work inside the site uncomfortable, but not impossible.

Carol, Bart, and Corsi used their handheld lights to focus their combined illumination on the path ahead. Jewlan stayed close to Bart, watching him as well as the Starfleet team's reaction to their discovery. Her attention was split between making sure the linguist didn't fall down, and her own enjoyment at their excitement.

The first thing Carol noticed about the chambers, other than their impressive size and artistic nuance, was their ascending levels in technological development. The First Chamber was built to resemble a cave, carved from bare rock, though preliminary tests showed it wasn't the same rock indigenous to the geological area surrounding the front door.

Pictographic images decorated the walls, none of which resembled any other paintings found in other sites. Neither Bart nor Carol could make out any discernible informational value to them. The other furnishings were sparse. Chairs carved from stone. Pots and urns were arranged on either side of the door as if they had, at one time, given offering to some deity.

"That was our first thought," Jewlan said, conferring with Carol. "Only what culture cements the decorations in place?"

"Cements them?" Carol knelt beside them and attempted to pick up one of the colorfully painted bowls. It wouldn't budge. She straightened. "Now that *is* odd."

The Second Chamber was much smoother, the walls more even and less jagged. Instead of pictures painted directly onto the walls, tapestries of strange creatures hung from modern hooks, each depicting a woodland scene. High-backed chairs flanked this chamber door.

Bart looked at Jewlan. "Is that running water?"

But it was Riz who answered. "Behind the left chair is a small running stream. Very small. The water is artesian. We analyzed it."

Jewlan smiled at Bart. He winked, and she knew at that moment he was as bored with Riz as she was.

Bart took several careful steps closer and ran his right hand over the armrest of the chair on the right. Jewlan noticed his fingers were long and thin. An artist's hands. She also noticed a dark smudge on the tip of the middle finger of that hand. Jewlan glanced down at a dark smudge on her left hand and gave a slight smile.

Soft, fine-woven fabric covered each of the seats. Bart looked over at Carol. "Thrones? King and Queen? Renaissance?"

"That was my first thought. It's like Earth history—but it isn't. This just keeps getting weirder."

Bart nodded. "It's like each chamber is some throwback to a time period. Very much like Earth's. If the first chamber were prehistoric humanity, and this chamber is more Renaissance or Middle Ages . . ." He let the sentence trail as Jewlan opened the door to the Third Chamber.

"Then I'd say this one is more along early twentieth century," Carol said as they stepped through. "Earth's pre-outer-exploration age. Before Zefram Cochrane created warp drive."

The walls of the Third Chamber were also smooth, polished wood. There were no seats in front of this door or cemented bowls. The pathway was clear with only a wood podium to one side.

Carol stood in front of it with her tricorder and shook her head. "Pulpit?"

Bart shrugged. "I have no idea. I'm just along for the ride at this point."

"Oh, it gets even better." Jewlan went to the door beside the podium and pressed the symbols in sequence.

Light spilled from the opening door. Jewlan muttered a slight curse when Bart stepped unsteadily back, wincing at the light. She reached out and grabbed his left shoulder to steady him. She knew his present condition was an aftereffect of the stimulant. She'd seen the same behavior in Riz when she used the stimulants. It was making him light-sensitive and she could only imagine how it affected his headache.

He reached out and took her arm as well and squinted at her. "Well, I guess whatever's causing the blackout hadn't had any effect in here."

"None," Jewlan said. She waited for his eyes to adjust to the light before leading them into the Fourth Chamber.

"This is the only chamber that came with its own lighting," Riz commented as she moved to stand at Bart's opposite side. He was now flanked by Jewlan and Riz.

Carol made a long, drawn-out whistling sound. The light emanated from the walls themselves. The floor was polished smooth, and there was a subtle hum surrounding them. Every time Jewlan stepped into this chamber she felt as if she were going to be transported to a distant world at any moment.

There were no other furnishings in the room. No pictures. It was completely sterile. The light was almost *deafening*.

"Lovely," Bart muttered and moved to the next door, his boot heels clicking on the floor.

Jewlan stood beside him, watching him in a sideways glance. He was an attractive man. Slight of build, but tall. And he carried himself with a grace and elegance very common to her own people. "Each combination to enter the next chamber is made up of four of these symbols. But they have to be pressed in the right order."

"How did you figure out the order?"

"Luck, I thought. I figured out the first one—having seen these symbols at a site miles from here. There's a temple there, or what we assume is a temple. We found scrolls of this language in a room behind the main altar."

"And you discovered the Rosetta Stone in there as well?"

She frowned at him even though the left side of her mouth pulled up in a half smile. His eyes lit with an inner fire when he spoke, and she wondered offhandedly what he looked like without the beard. "The what?"

"Sorry—an old Earth term. You found the key. The dictionary, so to speak, of how to read the language."

"Oh—the basis text. Yes. There are five base symbols, each corresponding to fundamental elements."

"You mean like water, fire, earth, and air?"

Jewlan's grin broadened. It was so refreshing to talk to someone who understood the basics of communication. "Yes, but not limited to just those universals. They refer to a great number of elements and their combinations."

"Periodic table," Carol chimed in.

Jewlan belatedly smiled at the small brunette. She'd almost forgotten the two S.C.E. women were there.

Bart nodded and touched Jewlan's arm. The cryptographer felt a light chill ripple up her arm. "Jewlan, in the notes I read on these keys, you used a set of rules to open each chamber."

"Well, not so much as rules as laws to live by. They're called the Laws of Life, and there are four. The first one is light, which corresponded to fire, then motion, which corresponded to water; the third was stillness, which referred to earth, and this one," she held her arms out at her sides, palms up, the "Law of Unity."

"Unity?" Bart looked around at the room behind them. "Well, maybe. If a society based its belief on unity being nonindividuality, I could see it. Wouldn't want to live in it."

She nodded in agreement. "Then maybe you can definitely be of assistance in this next chamber." Jewlan pressed the symbols in their order of Unity. Air.

The Fifth Chamber—and the bane of Jewlan's present predicament—spread out before them.

"This room's twice the size of the first four." Carol moved past Jewlan and Bart as did the tall, quiet blonde. "It's also as well lit as the Fourth Chamber."

The room was filled with *things*, unlike the sparseness of the previous chambers. Furniture, pots, trunks of both wood and stone, rusted, mechanical items that even Jewlan's people were at a loss to discover their functions.

"This place looks like a junkroom," Carol said as she held up her tricorder. "I've got one of these in my house back on Earth."

"Does your junk room have pieces from every era on

Earth?" Bart asked. "Because that's what I'm seeing in here. It's like someone cleaned out the first four rooms and stuffed it all in here to make way for guests."

"We were getting ready to catalog and clear this room out when Doren went into Beta State," Jewlan said, though she kept an eye on Bart, who'd moved several steps away to one of the less cluttered walls. The walls in this chamber were also self-illuminating.

"What makes this door different?" Bart said.

Jewlan moved forward into the ceiling-high stacks of objects to a barely visible pathway. "We've been stalled in this room for weeks," she called back to them.

The light was dimmer through the path. A place had been cleared around the door where Jewlan had set up her worktable to the right. Her papers, both synthetic and pulp, were scattered about, along with scrolls from the temple site and several containers of pens.

She wasn't surprised when Bart stepped past her to the table. He tentatively touched one of the scrolls. Riz started to move toward him, but Jewlan put a hand out. *Trust him*, she hoped her gesture said.

The chamber door to the table's left caught his attention before he lifted any of the scrolls. He moved his hand and took several steps toward it.

Carol moved up beside him, the hum of her analyzing device the only other sound in the chamber. Corsi came to stand beside Jewlan.

"This is the door that won't open?" the blonde asked.

Jewlan nodded, but kept her attention on the other two. Her gaze tracked the way the female touched Bart's elbow to get his attention. The way her fingers lingered on his as he took the device from her hands and looked at the information displayed as the female pointed it out.

She hadn't noticed it before, and scolded herself for being less observant than she should have been, but there appeared to be a close bond between the two. Jewlan should have realized this when Bart had been ill—the way the female had worried and tried to contact their people.

Obviously the two were mates.

Jewlan wasn't prepared for the blow to her gut that came with this realization. How was it possible that she could develop such a liking for a gender-bound humanoid such as Bart?

Unless it was that very uniqueness about him that had spurred the attraction.

"Jewlan?" Carol called out to her. "Can you come here?"

Masking any emotion that might be apparent on her face, the Asarion linguist moved toward them, and out of respect for their bond, stood beside Carol, even though Bart held the device.

Her heart skipped a beat as he moved closer to her. His shoulder pressed against hers as he held the device where she could see the screen. He smelled of musk and ink. "Jewlan, we picked up a piggybacked message along a subspace pulse that we believe is the reason for your planet's blackout. When we translated it, this was the message."

Jewlan read the sentence. "That sounds like one of our own lay texts."

Bart's eyebrows arched. "Lay texts?"

"My people have their own love of history—preserving

it, mostly—since our flight from the Borg a century ago. So many of our scholars have dedicated their lives to preserving the doctrine and rituals of as many of my people's religious and social beliefs as possible." She shook her head. "Not all of us practice Layism, though I personally think it's a fascinating doctrine, but we know the basics because we used them to build our society here."

"Sort of like having the Ten Commandments," Carol said as she looked at Bart. "Some humans still follow the teachings espoused in that ancient religion, but nearly all of us follow those commandments, with basics set such as 'thou shall not kill,' 'thou shall not steal' . . ."

Jewlan nodded. "Very much the same principle. Here." She stepped to the table and picked up a small, flat pad.

"What is that?" Bart asked. "What do you call it? I looked at one on the shuttle ride here."

"The manufacturer has some long, drawn-out name for it. We call it a palm-pad. It's basically a minicomputer, complete with its own language database and input speaker. Bart, you already found the base alphabet?"

"A good sixty percent. Haven't indexed vowels as clearly—it's like the language didn't use many."

Jewlan nodded. "That was our assessment as well. Transmit your alphabet and I'll add it to my own."

Almost immediately the palm-pad came to life when it sensed the signal. It began running through the database to find the closest word translation. "I was right. It translated into: 'A cut upon another's arm infects the heart of the one who wields the weapon.'"

Carol grinned. "Bart, I'd say this proves the translator simply looked through the database on the *da Vinci* and chose the most appropriate translation, same as Jewlan's just did."

"I'm afraid the captain's going to be disappointed. No long-lost Jewish settlers here. Though I am curious why it didn't just pick out standard metaphors like 'Do unto others as you'd have them do unto you?'"

That was the moment the floor moved in a really big way.

CHAPTER

6

The lights went out.

When the dust had settled and the floor no longer moved Bart took a quick inventory of all moving parts. Everything appeared to be working—except his nerves, which seemed to be on permanent edge.

"Everyone okay?" Carol called from the darkness.

"I . . . I think so," came Jewlan's voice. She was near Bart and he reached out in the direction of her voice. He brushed against something soft. Bart found her hand and clasped it. "Bart, are you all right?"

"I'm okay. Was it something I said?"

"Shhh . . ." Carol said. "Do you hear that?"

"All I hear is a hum—sort of like on a ship."

"Exactly. That sound wasn't there before the quake."

The lighted walls abruptly flickered back on. Jewlan stood to his left, his left hand in her right.

"What the hell was that?" Corsi asked, her phaser drawn and ready. She looked at Jewlan. "You didn't say anything about this place being unstable."

"Because it wasn't until yesterday," Riz said. She glanced at the table to make sure nothing had fallen. "Those quakes started up about twenty hours after the blackout. That was the third, and the strongest."

"Gold to Abramowitz."

Carol tapped her combadge. "Abramowitz here. We read you very clear, Captain. I couldn't reach you earlier."

"Oh? Was something wrong?"

Carol glanced at Bart. He shook his head and gave her his meanest frown, which of course turned into a wince. His head still rang. "Not anymore. We handled it."

"Conlon was able to punch through whatever's holding full power hostage. Apparently its range doesn't extend into space. It's easier to establish a link from space to you, instead of the other way around. You people all right? We registered a significant quake with your position as the epicenter."

They looked at one another. Carol spoke, "We're okay. Has the other team been able to establish what it is that's causing the problem?"

"Gomez and Tev are disagreeing. One believes it's something within the planet's core."

"That would be Tev."

"And Gomez thinks it's artificial. Stevens is having a harder time discovering the source, which he believes will shed some light on things. Whatever it is, it's apparently working as a blanket over the entire planet."

Jewlan frowned. "For something to work like your captain is saying, it'd either have to generate an enormous amount of power, or it's working through relay points—" Her eyes widened abruptly and she yanked her hand from Bart's and stepped back.

Riz took a step toward Jewlan, her eyes narrowed.

Bart looked from Riz to Jewlan. Was Ms. Grumpy Jewlan's watchdog? What was wrong?

"Whoever that was just echoed Stevens's assessment. He lost twelve of the fusion reactors after that last quake. Those particular ones were working at a higher field rate than the others." Gold paused. *"Apparently whatever's zapping power detected the increased power output and successfully eliminated them. We don't have any more generators to spare and the increase of demand on those in use is going to reach a critical mass."*

Carol ran her right hand through her close-cropped hair. "Captain, is there any way we can evacuate the sick and injured to the *da Vinci*? In case we can't find the source and shut it off?"

"Lense is heading up that contingency plan. One of the wrenches that got thrown into it is the da Vinci *isn't big enough to hold the number of people L'Olan quoted us, but the* Mercury *might be able to clear room. She's only a small cargo ship."*

Corsi spoke up. "L'Olan, sir?"

"Corlis's replacement. She Beta-shifted about an hour ago."

"Which means she's now a he, right?"

"Right. And no longer able to help us." Gold sounded irritated. *"She—he—wouldn't even update L'Olan on what's happened so far. So we had to waste a good half hour doing a recap. Oy, this is insane."*

Bart noticed Jewlan retreat another step. She held her hands out in front of her, studying them. *Is this it? Was she about to shift herself? I hope not—I need her knowledge here with me. And is there a way to get rid of the ol' life of the party over there?*

"*Faulwell, have you made any progress down there?*"

"Not yet, sir. We're at the final chamber where we believe the problems started. I'll give you an update as soon as we find something."

"*Good. Any more Jewish maxims?*"

"None, sir. I'm afraid that first one was only a fluke."

"*Well, Rachel will be disappointed. Is there anything else we can do from our end?*"

"Captain," Carol said as she held up her device. "Have Ensign Haznedl do a geothermal scan of this area as well. I want her to dig as deep as the ship's sensors can go."

"*You have that scary tone in your voice, Abramowitz. Does it have something to do with your cultural findings?*"

"No," she looked around and up at the high ceiling. "But it has everything to do with what I'm hearing right now. Abramowitz out."

Bart narrowed his eyes at Carol. "Care to let us in on your scary tone?"

"Not yet. I'm going to take Corsi and do a bit more looking about at the artifacts here. I think you and Jewlan should continue with trying to open that door."

"I'll go with you," Riz said.

With a glare in Jewlan's direction, the older Asarion followed Carol and Corsi from the chamber.

Bart shook his head, a slight smile on his lips, and turned to look at Jewlan. She'd moved into the shadows. "Nice lady. She the talk at parties?"

She shook her head and smiled. "Riz is okay. She's just doing her job keeping me straight. But I'm afraid I might not have much time left."

He raised an eyebrow. "Are you in Alpha State right now?"

Jewlan nodded again. "I'm—I'm a random shifter. Most people know when they're going to shift, down to the minute. They don't always prepare, which drives me nuts. I mean, to have that luxury and not use it." She stopped talking as if she were afraid she'd said too much. "My shifts come suddenly, and I'm overdue for one. I've been in Alpha State for over three years."

"What do you do for a living in Beta State?"

"Mechanic."

"Mechanic—like an engineer?"

She nodded.

If he understood Carol's briefing earlier, it meant that Jewlan also had the skill of an engineer.

There was just one problem. "It's my understanding that once you shift, you're no longer allowed to use the skills held by the other state?"

Jewlan nodded.

Bart wasn't going to profess to understand this cultural limit, but he would abide by it. For now. He hoped her Beta State didn't impose too quickly, though he was curious what she would look like in male form. He liked Jewlan's easygoing attitude. She was fun to talk to—and she listened. Very much like Anthony.

He gave her a smile both to ease her obvious worry and to wipe away any evidence on his face of the surprise he'd just given himself at such thoughts. Why had he compared her to Anthony? "What you said is true—about the power output needed. That either there is an incredible storage of power being used or there are relays all over this world. And our people will find out which it is. For now, let's look at this door, okay?"

Bart turned and gave the door a narrow look as well as the symbols. They followed the same straight-line pattern as the other doors, but there were six of them instead of four. He absently rubbed at his beard. "How far in the translation have you gotten with these?"

Jewlan stepped forward. She pointed to the four left-side symbols without touching them. "I haven't seen these other two before, and they're not on any of the scrolls we brought from the temple site."

"Did you try to press a combination and that's when the blackout occurred?" Bart said.

Jewlan chewed on her lower lip. "You've been talking to Corlis."

"Then it's true," Bart said. "You triggered it. What did you do?"

"I was upset. I was frustrated. I know it was stupid. But I wanted so much to prove to them I could do this— that I didn't have to wait for a new partner to be brought from the city."

Bart reached out with his right hand and gripped her shoulder. There was something disarming about Jewlan that touched him. Something very innocent and yet intelligent. He'd also noticed the smudge on the middle finger of her left hand.

Same as his own. Opposite hands.

Opposite sex.

For now.

He continued to give her shoulder a slight squeeze,

locking his gaze with her own in the dim light. Her eyes were the colors of the Mediterranean Sea. A deep, blue green. "Jewlan, I understand frustration. Lately I seem to be drowning in it to the point of impotency. Okay—that was oversharing. You have that effect on me. But just tell me what you did so we don't make the same mistake again. I'm not here to judge you, but I am here to help."

She expected him to be angry. He read that in her expression. Everyone else had been angry with her. Bart made sure he didn't look angry; he probably looked pretty damned awful if he judged that on how he felt—but he wouldn't look angry.

"I pressed the symbols in order of their relevance to the other chambers." She nodded to the door. "And then I pressed the two remaining ones in order."

"And that set off the blackout."

She nodded. "I think that's when I triggered some sort of defense protocol, which I'm sure is being powered by something behind that door."

He stared at her. "A what?"

Jewlan chewed on her lower lip. "Defense protocol. You've never encountered one? If this building, structure, whatever, was something of value to the indigenous race, then what better way to ensure no attacks than to simply put up a nullifying field? At least with powered weapons—but to throw up a planetwide dampening field?"

He stared at her as he reached out and touched a hand to each shoulder. "Jewlan, that's it. Of course that's it! It's so obvious—I mean, even Starfleet Academy has dampening fields on campus, for the students' protection. Why haven't you said something before now?"

"Because Riz was watching me," she said, putting her

hands over Bart's. "Bart, I'm a random shifter. We're different. We're loose cannons, for lack of a better term. I share my Beta State's knowledge sometimes. Most of my people don't."

"You don't? Our information says you retain your Alpha or Beta State memories."

"No." Jewlan smiled. "Not as much anymore. Before the Borg, we were mostly randoms, like me. But we adapt and change, and one started to forget the life of the other. But what I said about the dampening field—Bart, that's Jolen's field of expertise, not mine."

"That doesn't matter." He smiled at her. "Not to me."

Jewlan slid her fingers between his. "I like that. I like that a great deal. I can be . . . me, and it doesn't matter if I'm a man or a woman." She moved closer. The aroma of jasmine filled his senses and his head swam. "I like you, Bartholomew Faulwell—a great deal."

Okay, that last statement made him uncomfortable, but not too terribly so. It was becoming obvious to him that Jewlan had developed a crush—and he could see where it was an easy thing to do. He found himself attracted to her as well, on a more intellectual level. They shared the same love of words, of language; she obviously wrote in longhand, evidenced by the smudge on her finger. He'd found himself occasionally attracted to the opposite sex during his long life—mostly on superficial levels.

And those attractions had ended up as good friends. Which he hoped Jewlan would be.

So maybe now was the best time to bring her back to reality and possibly quell any more possible romantic thoughts. They needed to get to work. "Jewlan . . . I'm not really in the habit of sharing my personal life with other people, but I think you should know that I have a partner."

To his surprise, she nodded, though her expression remained peaceful. Jewlan removed her hands from his and stepped back. "I know."

"You do? Who told you?"

"No one. It is very obvious the way you and Carol Abramowitz work together. You are very close. And you are very lucky that your professions complement each other."

He could hear Fabian's laughter ringing on the wind even now. Bart could also see the jovial laughter coming from Vance Hawkins as well upon hearing his lover was having an affair with the linguist.

"Jewlan . . ." he shook his head. "Ah, Carol and I are just good friends. You're right in that we do work together a lot because of our professions, but she's only a friend." *A very talkative friend, but a friend nonetheless.*

The look of relief that opened up Jewlan's face made Bart take a step back. "Then you are not taken?

"No, I mean yes, I am taken. I have a lover. He works on a starbase."

Jewlan's expression fell. "You have a lover . . . someone locked to your soul and heart—but you are not together?"

"No. Anthony's job takes him to a different place."

She reached out to touch his arm and her expression as well as her tone were full of concern. "I do apologize. I didn't know you were married."

"I'm not married." His teeth ached as he tried not to clench them.

"Do you not have marriages in your culture?"

"Yes." Bart stopped himself from snapping at Jewlan. It did no good to be angry with her. She had no idea of what had been plaguing him the past few weeks. "But Anthony and I aren't."

"Do you not love one another?"

"Yes . . . we do. Look, Jewlan . . . it's a lot more complicated than just loving one another."

She frowned. "Do you risk social taboos?"

"No."

"Are there cultural differences that prevent marriage?"

"No. Look, Jewlan—"

"Ah, perhaps Anthony isn't ready for marriage." She smiled at this.

Bart put his hands over his face. *Is screaming okay? 'Cause I could use a really good primordial wail right about now.*

"Bart?" Her touch was light on his left wrist. "What is wrong? Do you miss him so very much?"

He moved his hands down, aware of the headache he still wore from his brush with the Poplin. Or was it the stimulant? "Jewlan, let's say *I'm* not ready for marriage and leave it at that, okay? We've got a lot of work to do even though this subject is just rousingly stimulating." He blanched at his own words. "If you have a state-shift coming, we're racing a clock."

He didn't know what he expected from Jewlan. Maybe another round of questions about his and Anthony's relationship. What he didn't expect was for her to step forward and kiss his forehead. That's when he noticed she was slightly taller than he was.

No, that's not right. Jewlan had been shorter before. Carol's height. This comparison made him curious if a state-shift happened instantaneously, or slowly.

"Let's get to work on that door." Jewlan turned and walked to the table full of scrolls.

CHAPTER

7

"How is it possible that Bartholomew came up with a defense theory? Was it something they found in the ruins?" Tev stood just inside the front glass doors of the reactor plant. The sky overhead had muted from brilliant blue to shades of lavender and yellow as the sun set over the horizon. The temperature had cooled considerably since mid-afternoon.

Stevens had wanted to use one of the portable reactors to power at least one of the building's cooling units, but Tev had been against such an action. It would have been a useless expenditure of power.

Gold's voice filtered through the combadge on Tev's uniform. *"He said Jewlan had suspected it ever since the blackout. I can't believe we never found it before this."*

Tev blanched. It wasn't that he hadn't thought of a

planetwide dampening field that irked him. It was that with all his wasted brilliance they hadn't seen the answer from the start. They had been looking at the situation from the standpoint of coincidence. Tev suspected the dampening field keeping things running at a minimum had to be because of a fault in the Asarion's system and not that of an exterior caustic anomaly.

"The dampening field—if that is what it truly is, though I highly doubt the word of a linguist—isn't operating on a normal modulation," Tev said. "Most dampening fields work on a continual, low-emission power output. Single modulation. The ones running on the grounds at Starfleet Academy put out enough power to nullify phaser weapons."

Stevens emerged from the reactor's inner doors at that moment, wiping his brow across his forehead. Vinx stepped out just behind him, yawning. Sweat darkened the collars on both men's uniforms. Stevens whistled at the setting sun. "Beautiful."

"Is that Stevens?" Gold asked.

Stevens tapped his combadge. "Here, Captain. Did Tev tell you this dampening field, or whatever it is, runs in pulses, very much like small EMP bursts?"

"I was getting to that point," the Tellarite said.

The captain said, *"But it's not a continual output?"*

Stevens shook his head. "No, and the pulses aren't evenly spaced. It's more like the thing waits till something rebuilds power and then it zaps it again."

"So it has a sophisticated sensor array somewhere."

Tev spoke up. "Yes, sir. But I've been unable to pinpoint where these sensors are. If I—we—can't find the source of the field, perhaps we can damage a sensor or rewrite its prime directive to shut down the dampening field instead of empower it."

"Or maybe we'll stumble on a booby-trap and blow the whole thing up." Stevens sighed. "It's annoying to get the reactor back online only to have it zapped again. What's even more disturbing is what Soloman just discovered; the pulses are gaining in strength."

"Gaining strength? The EMPs?"

"Yes. Another fifteen hours or so and these small fusion generators won't even work."

"Is there any threat to the da Vinci*?"*

"Not sure at this point. The range isn't extending, only the strength of the pulses sent to keep the planet in a lingering blackout. What's got me stumped is the purpose." Stevens knelt in the increasing shade of the building. "Why build a defense system that keeps everybody neutral? No one benefits from it."

"Well," Vinx said hesitantly as he glanced at Tev, "beggin' your pardon, boss, but I was thinkin' this here thing ain't built as no defense system. Seems to me this kinda situation is made for one reason—invasion."

Tev shook his head. "Preposterous."

But Stevens shook his head. "I'm not so sure Makk's not on to something. The only question remaining is, invasion from outside, or invasion from inside."

"My guts tell me it's outside." Vinx shrugged and gave a palms'-up gesture. "Black out the entire planet, knock out its defenses, ba-dah-boom, ba-da-bing, you can slip in and take over."

Stevens nodded. "What about the invading force's weapons? Wouldn't any weapon with a power signature be shut off?"

"Heaters, yeah. But not your old-timey weapons."

"'Old-timey'?" Tev said with a sniff.

"Y'know, swords, clubs, sticks, stones, daggers." The Iotian winked. "Works for them Klingon mooks. Hell, a good rifle'd work fine, too."

Stevens smiled. "Yeah, yeah—I get the point. Not sure about the Klingon analogy, though—seems like a cowardly way to press in."

"Aw, no. Less muss. No fuss. And," he held up the index finger of his right hand, "not so many bodies for the coppers to clean up."

"*Interesting theory, Vinx.*" Gold spoke over the combadges.

"Sir?" came a familiar voice behind them. They turned to see Gomez and Soloman standing at the inner door to the reactor controls. "We've pinpointed the dampener's point of origin."

Stevens said, "I'll lay ten-to-one odds it's the excavation site."

The Bynar tilted his head to his thin right shoulder. "Then you would win."

"Why am I not surprised? You copy that, Captain?"

"*Yes, I did. I'll contact Corsi, see if they've found anything.*"

Gomez said, "Sir, I'd like to go help them out, try to find the power source and shut it down. That would solve most of our problems."

"*Good idea. Later on, we can worry about the whys and what-fors. Gold out.*"

Tev nodded to Gomez. "I'll contact L'Olan and request a shuttle." He looked at Stevens and Soloman. "Specialists, I suggest we get back to solving this world's power problems."

Stevens frowned. "What for? We've already proven no matter what we do to get the fusion reactor going that dampening field is going to just zap it back out."

Tev straightened his posture. Because Stevens remained on his knees, his back against the building's wall, he towered over the noncom. Otherwise he would have had to strain his neck to look the officer in the eye. "Our assignment is to help these people get their systems back online. We will not give up on them, even if the odds are difficult. Is that understood?"

Stevens stood and smiled. "Yes, sir." He, Soloman, and Vinx headed to the reactor room.

Gomez smiled at Tev. "Nicely done." She headed off toward the administration building.

Tev gave the setting sun a final glance. The crew was finally starting to adjust to his leadership. He was pleased.

Bart tossed the pen onto the table and rubbed at his face. Fatigue pressed down on his shoulders—that and hunger. His stomach wouldn't accept much of anything to eat, thanks to the remaining effects of the stimulant. His hands shook and his vision blurred every now and then.

I need a nap. Jewlan and I've been working for six hours straight on this. He looked up at the small corridor made of stacked obstacles and wondered if the sun had set. He'd assumed so because of the drop in temperature. Earlier he'd removed his outer jacket and draped it over Jewlan's chair. Now he thought maybe he was going to need to put it back on to avoid the night chill.

He also wondered where Jewlan had wandered off to.

He'd not seen her or Carol or Corsi in nearly three hours. Together they'd deciphered the fifth symbol as a representation of spirit, or life.

As for the sixth, they still stumbled in the dark.

He heard a footstep behind him. Bart started to rise, to turn and look at who had entered. Hands pushed down with gentle firmness on his shoulders, then squeezed with just the right amount of pressure. Massaging away tension he didn't know he had.

Carol sometimes rubbed his shoulders, though she tended to use the motion as a way to think out loud. Bart enjoyed it from time to time, only not when she got excited as she conveyed to him her idea, whatever it might be at the time. That was usually when he cried "uncle" from the floor.

Bart sighed. "Oh, that feels nice . . . a little lower."

His masseur pressed harder, lower on his back. The grip was strong and warm.

"How does this feel?"

That wasn't Carol's voice. Nor was it Corsi's. Or Jewlan's . . .

Bart moved to his right and turned, twisting out from beneath the nice hands. His hip bumped the table and several scrolls moved to the side.

A tall, dark-haired male Asarion moved quickly, preventing the precious parchments from dropping to the floor.

Bart froze as he watched the man set the scrolls back on the table. The movements—even the slight hesitation when he smiled—they all belonged to Jewlan.

But this wasn't Jewlan.

The male dipped his head and smiled. "Hi, Bart." He

then offered the linguist his arms, bent at the elbow, his hands palms up. "Please, I know this is going to be a shock for you, so I figure an introduction is right."

Bart could only stare at the outstretched hands. He looked up into the face. Everything was different, but similar. This could be Jewlan's brother—not a twin—but a close match. His hair was close-cropped as Jewlan's had been. High cheekbones sloped down to a strong, firm, squared chin.

And his eyes.

Those were Jewlan's. Bright, and very blue.

"Bart?"

"Uh . . ." The linguist stepped forward and hesitantly placed his hands over his. "Sorry. I'm just a bit floored."

"As you should be. In this form, I'm called Jolen."

"Nice to meet you, Jolen."

"I'm afraid we don't really have as much in common like this," he said, and then held up his left hand. Bart noticed the smudge was still there. "I can still write, and I do every day."

"Well, nothing inside has really changed," Bart said, and realized his left arm and Jolen's right were still interlocked. He pulled his hand back and rubbed at his beard. "I mean, you're still Jewlan. Inside. Just not on the outside."

"Bart!"

He jerked at the sound of his name. Frustration flared for a brief second. It felt as if he'd been interrupted at a first contact moment. "Yeah, back here."

Carol and Corsi appeared around the corner. Carol nodded to Jolen before speaking. "I see you two have re-met?"

"You already knew this had happened?" He frowned at Carol, and then at Corsi.

"You were busy. We watched." A slight quiver pulled at the security chief's full mouth. "Fascinating."

"Where's Riz?" Bart looked about the room.

"She's sleeping off her latest stimulant," Jolen said. When Bart and Carol looked wide-eyed at him, he put up a hand. "I'll explain later about Riz's little Poplin addiction."

"Which is what has me worried about you," Carol interrupted, fixing Bart with a concerned stare. "Evidently when the stimulant ends there is a crash point. So—maybe you'd better go lay down in the shuttle."

Bart waved at her. "I'm fine."

Carol nodded slowly. "Okay . . . but don't say I didn't warn you."

"I'll keep an eye on him," Jolen said.

She raised an eyebrow at the Asarion. "Uh-huh. Anyway, Gold called. Gomez is coming out to help us shut down the dampening field."

"Then I was right?" Jolen's eyes lit up. Brighter than usual.

"Apparently so," Carol said. "The dampening effect is originating here and pulsing out using a very well-hidden array of sensors all over the planet. The only thing I'm afraid of is that the control panel for such a device is probably through that door." She pointed to the chamber door.

Jolen shook his head. "Actually, I think I know exactly where it is. I found it when I was exploring the day before the blackout."

"You knew?" Bart said. The other two looked at the tall

Asarion with the same expression of incredulity. "And you didn't say anything?"

"I couldn't." Jolen raised his shoulders and gave a palms'-up. "I wasn't Jolen. Riz was watching me."

"Oh, this is nuts," Corsi muttered. "Well, Jolen, can you show us where this panel is located?"

"Yes, I'd love to. I've been wanting to open it and check it out for two days." He turned to Bart. "Are you coming?"

The linguist hesitated. "Well, I . . ." He really needed a break.

"Please? I'd like for you to come and see too."

His presence wasn't really required, but Bart found himself wanting to join Jolen, even if he was a bit annoyed with him. He was sifting through a few confusing feelings of discomfort at Jolen's presence. He knew inside it was still the cryptographer. Jolen had the same easygoing attitude as Jewlan, and the same smile and dimple. There was even a similar cadence to his speech pattern.

Jolen also gave him the same pixieish smile Jewlan had on several occasions. Only it looked different on Jolen.

On Jolen it looked nice, much like the coy look Anthony gave him when he wanted to do something Bart didn't want to.

"I need a break." Bart grabbed the outer jacket of his uniform and slipped it on. "Let's go."

Bart caught the furtive glance Carol gave him and hung back for a moment as Corsi followed Jolen out of the Fourth Chamber. "What?"

"You okay? You're awfully pale—and you've got dark circles under your eyes."

"I'm fine," Bart snapped, unable to control his abrupt irritableness. His head *had* started to pound again behind his eyes.

Carol narrowed her eyes. "I'm not sure I've seen you this tense in a while—not since the wedding. You thinking of Anthony or is it Jolen?"

Bart glared at her. "What kind of question is that? Why would my thinking of either them make me tense?"

"Bart—I'm not blind. Neither is Corsi. It's obvious Jewlan has a crush on you, and I think in a fashion you like her. And when she's in Alpha State, female, you're safe. You can't tell me you didn't feel that inside." Carol frowned, the smooth skin between her eyebrows pinched. "Those safeties are off now, Bart. Jolen is quite an attractive man. And you're here, on a planet far away from Anthony, from whom you feel estranged."

"Anthony and I are not estranged." Fury churned in the pit of Bart's stomach. He was shaking. "I'm just not—" He licked his lips. "This isn't really the time to discuss this, Carol."

She narrowed her eyes at him. "Are you angry at me, Bart? You have to be careful here—just for your own personal conduct. Jewlan and Jolen are the same person, understand?"

"Why are you harping at me about this? I told her about myself and Anthony. She—uhm, he—knows I love Anthony. I'm a bit insulted that you think that little of me, Carol. That I would sacrifice what I have with Anthony for a pretty face?"

"Jolen's not just a pretty face, Bart. It's still Jewlan on the inside. It's just become more complicated now that she's a he, hasn't it?"

"Complicated?"

"Jolen would still carry the same feelings as Jewlan. Only Jolen isn't asking something from you—like marriage."

Bart marched around her, heading through the passage.

"Bart, please," Carol called out. "I wouldn't blame you. And I'm not judging you."

He stopped where he was but didn't turn to face her.

"I'm just worried, that's all. You don't seem yourself since your blackout with that drink, and in a close situation like this things can get pretty . . . intense. Just watch what you're doing."

Bart opened his mouth to speak but this time the words crowded in on the tip of his tongue, so many that he closed his mouth instead and continued down the path to the chamber door.

What bothered him more was that she was right.

The panel was located behind a tapestry in the Second Chamber, closest to the door to the Third Chamber, just on the other side of the running water. After pressure-releasing the door, Jolen studied the internal switches for a few seconds before pulling his palm-pad from his back pocket.

"Do you know how to operate it?" Corsi stood just to his left, peering in at the glowing mechanism inside.

Jolen shook his head. "Not at the moment. Just give me five seconds. Most electrical technology works the same, only the engineering of it is sometimes different. Ah . . . there it is."

"Are you sure?" Corsi said. "You know, last time you pressed buttons, there was a worldwide blackout. Maybe we should wait for Gomez to get here."

Jolen leaned out and gave the tall blonde a scathing look. She was right, but he didn't want to admit that just yet.

And this time, he was certain he knew what he was doing.

Jolen moved back behind the panel's door and gave up a silent prayer. He hoped he knew what he was doing and pressed a simultaneous pattern of buttons.

Nothing happened. But then—nothing had happened before.

One of the Starfleet combadges beeped. *"Gold to Corsi."*

Corsi tapped her badge as Jolen moved from behind the panel. He looked for Bart and saw the linguist standing a few feet away.

"Corsi here, Captain. Any change?"

"I'll say. The dampening field's gone. Did Gomez arrive?"

"Not yet. It was Jolen who shut it down."

Carol smiled at Jolen. "Sir, this is Abramowitz. Did you have Haznedl run those tests?"

"Yes, and she just finished with the results. I'll have her download them to your tricorder. I think you'll find her results pretty enlightening. Tev is heading up a detail to help L'Olan get things back in order. I'll divert Gomez back to the city."

Bart spoke up. "Captain, we still haven't opened up the final chamber."

"Go ahead and get it open. It might shed some light on who built that defense system and why. Just don't cause another blackout, please. Gold out."

Jolen moved from behind the panel and stood beside Carol. He watched the data as it rolled across her screen. His first suspicions since triggering the dampening field were right. Things he'd known he was right about but hadn't been able to discuss.

It was a suspicion he'd had ever since finding the Fourth Chamber.

"This is a ship, isn't it?" Jolen looked at Carol as she looked up at him.

She nodded. "Yes. And it's deep into the ground. Though I'm unsure how these chambers fit in." The cultural specialist shook her head. "According to the readings I had Haznedl take, the area around the ship doesn't show any geological stress."

"Any what?" Jolen said.

Bart took a step forward. "She means this ship didn't crash-land in this spot, damaging the platelets around the area."

Corsi spoke up. "Were there any signs of geothermal damage? Like molten rock in the case of thrusters as evidence of a landing?"

"Some. But not enough as evidence that a ship this size landed."

Frowning, Corsi then asked, "Was it built here?"

"That's always a possibility." Bart rubbed at his beard. "The Asarions don't really know much about the previous civilization, save for a few sites such as this one. It would be quite a find if all of them turned out to be downed ships of some kind."

"Or maybe the previous inhabitants built them for a mass exodus?"

Jolen shook his head, though he kept his attention

focused on Bart. *Is he avoiding me? He hasn't looked at me at all.* "Why would a race build such a weapon as this?" He gestured to the panel with a nod. "For an evacuation of this world? I'm more inclined to believe this ship was part of an invasion. Only something went wrong."

"Why do you say that?" Corsi said.

"Well, most of the sites we've excavated are little more than rubble, save for a few temples that all resemble this one. One of our leading archaeologists discovered a set of scrolls forty kilometers from the first temple site whose writing doesn't match anything we've ever found. So we have to ask ourselves; Is that the only evidence we have of the previous inhabitants? And this . . ." He held his hands up to indicate the chamber. "This is all that is left of the invading force?"

"I think we'll know more once we get the Fifth Chamber open." Bart started to turn and leave. He paused and looked back at Jolen. "Is there anything else you haven't mentioned? Any other panels or secret passages that didn't fall into your gender-specific role?"

"Bart!" Carol called out, lowering her padd. "That was uncalled for."

"No, it wasn't." The linguist took a tense step forward and pointed at Jolen. "You've known all this time, maybe even before we arrived, how to turn off that dampening field, and you didn't. Why? Because your gender-specific role was wrong for the task? Do you realize how many sick and injured could have died because of the lack of power? Do you realize how many of those injured were injured *because* of the blackout?"

"That's enough, Bart." Corsi moved to stand in front of him. "You're exhausted. I can see it in your eyes. Not to mention you're shaking. We still don't know what that drink did to you. Get some rest—now that the field's off we have time."

"Do we?" Bart ran a hand through his hair.

Jolen saw that Bart was indeed shaking. He was coming down off that damned stimulant. He needed food. When Jewlan had gone through her Beta-shift, she and the females had shared some fruit and water, but Bart had been hard at work on the door's symbols.

Bart waved Corsi away and turned to leave. He stumbled.

He's going to fall. Jolen moved past Carol and even beat Corsi to the linguist as the slight man stumbled forward. Jolen caught him under his shoulders, amazed at how light he was, and lifted him in both arms.

"Get him to the shuttle," Corsi said as she and Carol followed Jolen out of the Second Chamber.

Jolen glanced down at Bart. His skin was pale against his beard and his eyes were closed. He knew the stimulant had finally worn off. *And I was so blinded by my brilliant discovery that I hadn't been watching him. If anything bad happens to him, I'll never forgive myself.*

CHAPTER

8

Bart felt bad, but he wasn't sure why. And it wasn't an emotional feel-bad as much as a physical one. His stomach felt tight, as if it had crunched up like a fist.

And he was cold.

"Bart, you're going to have to open your eyes and sit up. Otherwise I'm going to pour this down your throat by force."

What? Who was that? It wasn't Carol, or even Corsi, though it had the brute force of Domenica.

He opened one eye, then the other. The light from a lamp behind someone's head was a bit blinding. "Oh . . . déjà vu here. I've had this dream before." He stared up into the smiling face of Dr. Elizabeth Lense. Behind her was Carol, and to the side was Corsi. "Uhm . . . and you were there, and you were there," he smiled at the security chief. "And even you as the cowardly lion."

"Oh, he's fine," Carol said and moved away.

"What was that I heard about pouring something down my throat?" Bart gave Elizabeth a weak smile. "I assure you I'm not so old as to not drink without dribbling."

"Here," she handed him a cup of something warm and he managed to sit up.

They were back inside the shuttle and he was again prone on the same couch he'd passed out on before. *Why is it this trip I seem to be spending more time on my back than upright?* He sniffed the drink. "Smells like chicken soup."

"It is." Lense picked up her small scanner and ran it along Bart's body before checking her tricorder. "Your system's recovering from some sort of shock."

"Poplin," Bart said and sipped the soup. It tasted good and salty in his mouth and he felt his stomach unclench and rumble.

"Actually it was the stimulant Riz gave you. It wore off." Lense closed her tricorder. "I think you'll be okay, but I'd like to run a full set of tests on you in sickbay. I think you should return to the *da Vinci* with me and convalesce there."

He smiled at her, and for a brief second, he believed she understood his need to remain on the planet. "I have a door to open."

"Jolen's already working on the mechanics of it. He hopes to open it without the need to decipher the combination." Carol put her hand over her mouth to stifle a yawn of her own. "You've been asleep for nearly four hours, you know."

Bart gulped down more of the broth, ignoring the burn on his tongue as he moved himself into a sitting position. "Has Jolen been at it long?"

"Not really," Carol said, a slight smile on the edge of her lips. "He stayed in here with you until Elizabeth said you were going to be all right. He was really scared."

Lense's right eyebrow arched. "I noticed that too. You have an admirer, Bart. And a handsome one at that."

Bart bit back a reply and stood. This time he didn't sit down again as he had before, though he came close to it. He grabbed a nearby handrail and steadied himself. "I need to get back to work. With the way that Asarion's luck runs, he'll trigger another blackout by monkeying about with the internal systems. Better if we go through language and symbols."

"Bart." Carol put a hand on his shoulder as Lense moved away. "Don't be angry with Jolen. As Jewlan, she had no choice but to steer away from the knowledge that Jolen afforded her. Her society's norms are very different than our own."

"They're stupid, Carol. I've been with you on countless worlds and I've seen things that would normally curl my beard, but this . . ." He shook his head. "This edges on plain stupidity. Aren't lives more important than societal norms?"

"Not always," Carol said and her voice was sad. "And you know that. Just don't be too harsh on him, okay? He was worried sick until Elizabeth pronounced you healthy. I'd say you were more grumpy."

"I am not grumpy."

"Bart, you've been a grump ever since the wedding. And don't think I don't know why, because you told me.

And now you're even grumpier because there's another man in the situation, a man in that cave who likes you and admires you, same as Anthony."

"Wait, what have I missed here?" Lense paused while repacking her medical bag. "Bart, are you and Anthony having problems?"

"Yes." Bart closed his eyes. "No. Look, I don't know. I'm just not . . . ahhhh . . ." He set the cup of broth on a side counter and rubbed at the back of his neck. "Look, it's just complicated, all right?"

"What, that Jolen was a woman first?" Carol said.

Lense frowned. "Wait—that was a woman?"

Bart leaned forward. He was half fascinated with Carol's outburst as much as angered by it. "No, and yes. Complicated meaning me, my life, my past. I just can't . . ." He straightened and closed his eyes. Two deep breaths. "I can't risk that kind of commitment—not again."

"And with Jolen, there is no commitment." Carol took a step forward. "You like him, Bart. And that's eating at you. With Anthony you were safe. He's slotted into his time, his place in your life. Neat and orderly. But Jolen is here. And he's not neat, and he's not orderly. And he won't stay. Jolen is not in the Alpha State. And for the first time someone else has turned your head."

Lense's eyes widened and Bart noticed the shadows had vanished, for a moment. "Bart, what about Anthony? Do you care about that young man? The one that was just in here?"

"He cares for Jewlan, which means he cares for Jolen."

"Stop it." Bart put up his hands. "I do not care for Jewlan, or Jolen, in any romantic or physical way. I'm going back to work." He moved to the shuttle's doorway.

"Do too," came Carol's soft reply.

Bart held his tongue as he walked out into the brisk night toward the cave's entrance. The stars were bright and twinkling—a spattering of diamonds over a black velvet surface.

He passed through each chamber, ignoring the first one, his attention drawn by the second one and then halted by the Third Chamber. Since they'd walked through the chambers the first time, something nagged at him about them. He was no culturalist, but he'd been around Carol enough to know that each ascending period in this ship did not match the one before.

Cultures moved along specific patterns, with similarities in pottery, art, and sometimes design. There was no such progression in each of the chambers. If these chambers were meant to be displays of these people's history, then it was a mishmash of styles and culture.

But what if each chamber worked in a ranking order? What if the former inhabitants of this ship kept their people in specific roles. From primitive, perhaps the laborers, and then on up to artisans, and then leaders?

Bart came around the corner of the Fourth Chamber's slight pathway to the door. Jolen sat at the table, a piece of parchment spread out before him. He was drawing something with a tipped pen.

"Are you sure that's such a good idea?"

The tall Asarion popped up from the chair like a buoy submerged in a sea. His face paled before a smile cracked the surface and warmth flooded his cheeks. "Bart . . . you're okay?"

"I'm fine. Just a slight bad reaction to that stimulant. But I'll live." He looked up at Jolen, again caught by the intense blue within his bright eyes. They were Jewlan's eyes, of that he had no doubt. "Look, about what I said. I was angry—and I spoke out of turn."

"No, no." Jolen set his tools on the table, carefully avoiding touching the scrolls. "You were right. For you, that is. For me, speaking such suspicions to my own people—though they were the right course and saved lives—well, I was already in enough trouble."

"But did you know about the field and the panel all along?"

"Not in so many words." Jolen took a step closer to Bart. "I didn't put things together until I watched and listened to you and Carol. Then it all made sense and I was free to do what needed to be done."

Bart rubbed at his beard as he moved away from Jolen to the table. "Still . . . from now on, when you have any thoughts on something, feel free to tell me, okay?"

"Sure. I can do that." He ducked his head and smiled. "I'm glad you're okay, Bart."

"Yeah, yeah, I'm fine." He nodded to the drawing. "That's very good. What is it?"

"It's a schematic of the panel I found." Jolen nodded toward the door.

Bart turned and saw an exposed area of wires and glowing circuits. "Nice. Made any progress?"

"Not yet." Jolen sat back down. "I'm still working on the mechanism."

"Well." Bart picked up one of the parchments he'd been working on before Jolen's Beta-shift and then spread it out beside Jolen's drawing. "I found the reference for the fifth symbol here, in the fifth scroll from the temple. Now, I can cross-reference the meanings back to my own people's histories when they too believed that the four basic elements needed the fifth element for creation. That fifth element is spirit. Or, taking a lead from your own palm-pad, love."

When he looked up from his sketches he was surprised at the wide-eyed look of horror on Jolen's face. His mouth was pulled tight in a thin line and his hands, resting atop the table, balled into fists.

Bart frowned. "What is it? Are you ill?"

"No, I can't—" Jolen stood, the chair scraping against the tile floor. "I can't look at this. It's not my work, Bart. I can't help you with the language anymore. I must work on opening the door a different way."

Something snapped somewhere inside of Bart. He'd been patient through all of this nonsense, and the Prime Directive be damned. He slammed his fist down as hard as he could on the table, rattling the inkwells and sending the scrolls tumbling to the floor.

Jolen immediately lunged to retrieve them but Bart reached out and took his arm, pulling him back. "Oh, no you don't. This is bullshit. Don't you dare tell me in one breath that you can't work with me on language anymore, that you no longer care about symbols and meanings and then you try and protect those scrolls."

The Asarion paused and then stood, looking at Bart. The two were close in height, with Jolen only a centimeter higher. "I—they should be protected."

"Why? They're not a part of your mechanic's profession. They're scrolls with words on them, Jolen. Just words. Why would you try and protect them?"

The dark-haired man blinked several times. "I—I have to protect them."

372   Phaedra M. Weldon

"Because it's your job? No, because you love them,
Jolen. Because you still have the same love of words and
paper and meaning and symbols that Jewlan has. Because it's a part of you, and no shift in gender is going to
change that. It never will."

Jolen looked down at the scrolls. "Please, let me pick
them up."

Bart realized he still had a firm hold on Jolen's arm
and released it. The tall Asarion immediately bent down
and started gathering up scrolls.

Well, that went well, you arrogant nit. With a sigh, Bart
moved to the other side of the table and knelt down facing Jolen. He picked up a scroll and heard Jolen sniff.
"Jolen, I'm sorry. I'm just—this is frustrating for me. I
don't come from a society that has gender-based rules—
well not anymore. It did once. But we got past that. And I
still have this headache from the stimulant."

"You miss him, and yet you are angry with him."

Jolen's words cut through the awkward situation and
brought his attention up sharply. He stared at Jolen, who
had fixed him with a piercing blue stare. "What? Who?
What do you mean?"

"Anthony. You are angry with him. Is it because you
are not married?"

*Oh, man, not this again. How did we go from gender-
based stupidity to being married?* Bart lowered his shoulders. "Jolen, there are just some things I'm not comfortable with. And talking about marriage, or even the
thought of it, is one of them."

"Why?"

How many times had he asked himself that question?
And how many times had he avoided the answer? Was

it because he was afraid of commitment? Could be. Or was it because he felt he'd limit his options by being tied down to one person?

"I don't think you're going to resolve your conflicts with Anthony until you resolve them within yourself." Jolen shifted from his knees and sat down beneath the table. "For my people, marriage means a lifelong commitment. This is because when one of us decides to have children, the very act of childbirth ends all shifting for the rest of our lives."

Bart nodded. "Carol had said as much."

"But did you know only female Alpha States can do this? And only a male Alpha State can seed a female Alpha State? The great escape from the Borg drastically cut our population to nearly an eighth of what it was, Bart. Before their invasion of our world, we had only a few conclaves that practiced gender-specific roles. What is the first priority when settling a new world?"

This was easy. "Procreation. To continue the species."

"Yes. We were female-Alpha-State heavy in those early decades, because so many of them gave birth, locking themselves into female-only roles, until the balance between states tipped the other way, and our male Alphas became too few. We decided then to limit ourselves and the gender-specific roles came into play again. We've kept a precarious balance between science and defense in this manner. The only midpoint is medicine. It is shared by both genders."

"I see." Bart shook his head. "No I don't see. Why must roles in life be gender-specific at all?"

"When the Borg came, our men *and* women fought bravely. And they died. The lucky ones did. Those that were assimilated—we have no idea what their lives became afterward. But it depleted our birth-giving females. Many of our surviving leaders believed this was because we'd allowed them to fight." He looked away, his eyes unfocused as he remembered another time, another world. "We weren't perfect, Bart. Far from it. Men had taken the role of leadership because of their aggressive natures. Especially Alpha States. We had wars, fought on our own soil. And some of those battles were over our way of life." He refocused on Bart. "There had always been those that believed in freedom of choice, and those that believed in roles."

Bart searched the man's face. What he saw was sadness, and some regret. "Those that believed in roles had a greater argument, didn't they? They had the leverage of survival with them."

"Yes."

"Maybe I can see that point. A little."

Jolen leaned his head to his right shoulder. "Do you, Bart? To give birth is a miracle in our society. And to do so, both parties must proclaim a lifetime of love, because both states make the commitment, on both sides. Family is very important to us." He swallowed. "My own mother died before I had my first shift. I was two years overdue, and she was worried about my acceptance in society. They tried to have another child, but she died in childbirth, and my sibling died with her."

Something hung in Bart's throat at Jolen's mention of having a sibling. He was swept back along the chain of his own memories, to a moment in his childhood. There had been a door at the end of the hall. The smells of coppery death filled the house as the doctors worked on the destroyed cells.

And beyond that door there had been screams.

Terrible, pain-riddled screams.

His father had stepped from that door, his face a mask of torment. He had looked down at his frail son, a boy born so sickly they hadn't predicted him to live more than a month at best.

Little Bartholomew had proven them all wrong. He *had* lived.

But from the look on his father's face, his sister had not.

"Bart?"

The linguist blinked. He was back again beneath the table in the Fourth Chamber of a mystery ship. There were no longer smells of death in the air, but the musty scents of old ghosts. He took in a breath, his body shuddering. "I—I was remembering the day my sister died. My father was an archaeologist. My mother was a cultural specialist like Carol. We were on a Federation world, checking out some ruins. I had been fascinated by the writing I'd found in one of the caves. And I . . ."

Bart paused. The memories of that afternoon came crashing back. How long had he hidden them away? How long had he shoved them to the back of his life?

He felt a strong hand cover his own. Bart looked at Jolen. Really looked at him. He saw a man. Not a species. But a caring, feeling individual. "What happened?" Jolen's voice was soft. Easy to listen to.

Bart swallowed. "I found the warnings—too late. The cave wasn't a temple as we'd thought. It was a place of punishment, where the wicked were sent to die."

He could see it all again. *Oh God, no . . .*

She'd been standing by the monster's head, the carved,

stone image of what Bart had thought was a lion, but later learned was the representation of law.

Of punishment.

And of death.

Their father had been near the side, examining a panel discovered the day before.

Bart had just translated the basic consonants and vowels of the language and was in the ship, applying what he'd learned to the writings on the temple's walls. He'd believed the site was a temple. It was safe for them to go inside.

"Bart, you're shaking." Jolen reached out and took the linguist by the arm. "Bart?"

He'd heard the screams then, and learned what had happened to her.

"Acid," Bart stammered, his voice low. "Corrosive to anything and everything. It covered her. Ignited her skin. Burned her alive. There was nothing the doctors could do."

Jolen touched Bart's cheek with his hand. His hand was warm and Jolen smelled faintly of jasmine. "Bart— you didn't know. Not even your parents knew."

"But I should have. I translated it wrong!"

The Asarion looked stricken. "You did?"

"I'm the one who told them it was a religious temple. I told them it was safe inside—even when I couldn't go in myself."

"Couldn't go? You weren't allowed inside the temple?"

"No. I—I wasn't a very healthy child. My kidneys started failing early on in childhood and I was bedridden most of the time. The Federation's medicine couldn't even regenerate new organs. I'm allergic to the compounds used in Retlax Five. Nothing could stop my organs' deterioration. I was dying."

Bart felt his own hand squeeze harder. And he wondered if he did this because he wanted Jolen to hurt just as he was hurting. How dare he force these memories back to the surface.

How *dare* he dismiss them.

"Bart, what happened? Why do you push those who care for you away? Is it because she died?"

"No," he looked directly into Jolen's bright eyes. "I live because she died. They transplanted her kidneys, Jolen. And for over forty years I've always suspected I stole her life."

The Asarion gave Bart a furrowed brow. "There's something else you're not telling me."

Bart tried to pull away, but Jolen held his arm and put a warming hand on his shoulder. He didn't want to remember. He didn't want to tell this complete stranger his childhood horrors.

The pain in his heart.

But somehow, it felt right to pour his soul out to Jolen. "I think on a subliminal level, my parents never forgave me—or so I believed. After the operation, I was sent off to Starfleet Academy. My parents disappeared not long afterward—they'd rented another explorer ship and returned to the planet. Supposedly to bury their daughter."

"Bart, I'm sorry."

"I was eighteen when they left. And I dropped out of the Academy. I focused my education solely on cryptography, and languages, on alien symbols and linguistics. I became the best I could be." He smiled. "I even fell in love. I didn't want to . . . but it happened."

"Why didn't you want to?"

Bart ignored the question, not ready to give his answer just yet. "His name was Kyle Levington. He was a Starfleet officer. Fresh out of the Academy and had a year before his first assignment onboard the *U.S.S. Nemits*. He wanted to know where my parents had gone. I'd met his, and he wanted to see mine. I arranged for a ship to take us back to the world my parents had returned to."

He started to shake at the memory. *No, no . . . I don't want to remember this. I can't remember this.*

But he did.

They'd found his parents' ship, but it had been abandoned so long ago. Bart had never told Kyle about what the temple had done to his sister. About what had happened.

"I stayed in the ship, looking at the what they'd left behind. There was no trace of their bodies, and I'd mentioned the temple. I wasn't paying attention to where Kyle had wandered off to."

Jolen's skin paled. He tried to hold on to Bart, but the linguist moved away. He stood and took two hesitant steps to the door, facing the opened panel. "He'd gone into the temple. I heard him call out for me. And then I heard his screams. But it was too late. I saw him . . ."

The memories came fast. Faster.

Too fast.

The room tilted on Bart and he reached out for the wall. He touched a warm body instead and felt himself being folded within Jolen's arms. He heard the Asarion's heart beating.

He heard someone crying.

Bart didn't realize the muffled sobs belonged to Jolen.

"You want to deny yourself happiness." Jolen spoke softly, and gave Bart a soft kiss on his brow.

"I—I didn't want to fall in love, because I had her life. It was all borrowed time. Somehow, I felt I should dedicate my life to a greater good. She would never know love, never find happiness in the arms of another—so why should I?"

"And you believed—and still do—that Kyle's death was a punishment."

And there it was. So simple. A classic textbook case of self-denial by guilt. He nodded. His shoulders shook. No one had ever seen him this way.

No one.

Not even Anthony. These were the things he should be telling Anthony. Those important if not painful moments that shaped who and what he was.

Jolen pulled him close. "Shhhh . . . I am here, Bart. I am here."

CHAPTER

9

Jolen sat on the floor, comforting Bart. It had been a horrible story—and one the linguist had buried deep.

And though it pained him to see Bart in agony, Jolen felt honored that he would share those memories with him.

With me. He stroked the sleeping man's thick, gray and black hair. He wondered again what Bart would look like without the beard. Younger perhaps. Less worried? It didn't matter. A small seed of sadness germinated within his own soul. They would find the key to opening the door. All would be well. And Bart would leave.

And Jolen would be alone, again.

It did not matter. Not really. And he made a promise to himself, and the dozing linguist, that he would be there for him.

Always.

"Oh."

Jolen looked up from Bart's face and saw the doctor. She stood just inside the cleared area, her hand to her mouth, her eyes wide. "Greetings, Dr. Lense. Please, come in."

She gave a tight smile and took a step closer. "I'm sorry—I was checking on Bart."

"He's resting. I do apologize again for Riz giving him that stimulant. I shouldn't have allowed it."

Lense's smile became a chuckle as she knelt down beside the two of them. "Well, after my own brief encounter with her, I'm not sure if you'd have been able to stop her. I'm not even sure Corsi could have." She pulled a small device from her bag, the one Jolen had seen her use earlier, and passed it over Bart. "Endorphins, adrenaline levels all appear to be normal." She frowned as she tilted her head to her right shoulder. "He looks awfully peaceful. I'm not sure I've seen him that relaxed in a while."

"He—" Jolen stopped himself. He'd been about to say that Bart had shared a great burden with him, but thought better of it. No, those memories were between the two of them. If Bart wished them shared, then he would have to do it himself. "He still seemed tired. So I offered him a place to rest."

"Yeah." Lense's right eyebrow arched high. "I noticed."

Jolen smiled and felt the heat rise from his chin to his face. He noticed too the way Lense often put her hand over her abdomen, and remembered hers and Bart's conversation. "I hear you are with child?"

The Asarion wasn't sure how to read the expression

that crossed the doctor's face. It appeared to be a mixture of hesitation and sadness. "Yes . . . I'm pregnant."

"You're not happy about this?" Jolen shook his head.

The doctor absently rubbed her abdomen again. "I—well—I'm not sure yet. And I guess in a way I'm a bit tired of that question, you know?"

"I think I might. Is the father happy?"

This time Elizabeth's face darkened, though not in anger, but in infinite sadness, and he reached out to touch her shoulder. "That—well—that's complicated, Jolen. He's dead, and yet I think if he knew, he would be *very* happy." Lense suddenly got a faraway expression in her eyes.

Again Jolen frowned at her. "Something wrong?"

"Oh, no, no. It's just that after my recent experiences, I've sort of gotten pretty good at seeing a train wreck before it happens." She lowered her hands. "And this one looks like it might be a doozy."

"Train? Like in shuttle? Do you suspect there is something wrong with the shuttle outside?"

"No, no . . . never mind." She looked around the floor and picked up one of Bart's worksheets. "What's this?"

"Bart discovered the fifth symbol as love, or spirit in your culture. But we're still stumped on the sixth. Four known elements and a theory. I was trying to apply the science of building toward the science of communication to come up with the answer. Nothing."

She frowned. "Earth, air, fire, and water, the four basics. And you said love, or life or spirit."

"Yes."

"Well, I'm no linguist, but it seems to me the outcome of all of those things would be death."

Silence hung thick in the air between them as the two stared at each other.

"That's it!" Jolen moved so quickly Bart nearly fell from his lap.

Lense moved at the last minute to stop the linguist's head from hitting the hard floor. Jolen blushed and shook Bart's shoulder. "Bart? Wake up—we have it. We have it!"

"Hmm . . . ?" The bearded linguist stirred and then opened his eyes. He looked up into the face of Elizabeth and was obviously embarrassed. "What happened? Did I have another episode?"

"No, no." Jolen pulled at his shoulder until Bart was in a sitting position. "Your doctor here solved it." He set the paper in Bart's lap. "Six symbols. Earth. Air. Fire. Water. Spirit or love. What comes from the elements of life?"

"Life?" Bart rubbed at his eyes. "I'm not sure I'm following."

Jolen hesitated. "Think of the story you told me, about you." He glared at Bart, not wanting to divulge anything he wasn't supposed to. Bart's eyes widened slightly and he nodded. "What came out of death?"

The linguist blinked. "Life. My life." Bart's expression lit up. "That's it!" He turned to Lense. "You're a genius."

"No, not really. I'm just—mmgrphh!" was the doctor's response as Bart reached out and kissed her.

He pulled away and smiled. "Sorry—I'm just excited."

"Oh, yay." Lense wiped her mouth with the back of her hand. "And sweaty. First Anthony at the wedding, then you. I think I'm gonna stay away from both of you from now on." She rose and moved toward the exit. "I'll tell the others we're going to give this a try, all right?"

Bart set the paper to the side beneath the table. "What can I do to help you?"

"This." Jolen knew it was wrong, and he knew he had no right to intrude on Bart. But he couldn't help his own feelings. He reached out and with a hand behind the linguist's head, pulled him close, and pressed his lips to Bart's.

The beard prickled against his upper lip, and he knew the linguist remained unmoving because he had not expected Jolen's action. For an instant, Jolen felt Bart return the kiss.

Until he felt the man's hands pressing on his arms, pushing him away.

With a sigh, Jolen released Bart and dipped his head, embarrassed. "I'm sorry, Bart. I just—I don't think I've seen you that happy since you arrived. And it's . . ." He shrugged. "I'm sorry. And I promise I won't tell anyone else the things you told me."

He watched carefully as Bart put a hand to his lips and nodded, if not a bit slowly. "Sh-ure. I just . . ." Bart swallowed and stood. He turned and straightened his outer jacket. "Please don't do that again."

Jolen had expected this reaction and accepted it. It was enough that Bart had felt close enough to share his tragic past with him. And if that was all he would ever receive from the linguist, then it would be enough.

After standing, the Asarion shook his head. "I'm afraid I can't promise that."

Working together, the two of them were able to draw up a readable schematic for the workings of the door mechanics. Once Jolen was confident he could open the door by simply triggering the mechanism itself, just in case the symbols didn't work, Bart called Corsi, Carol, and Lense and explained what they were going to do.

"Is there any protocol in place for safety?" Corsi said.

Jolen gave the female a broad grin. "I've mapped out the mechanism and I'm confident I can open it, in case something goes wrong."

"Eh." Carol put up her finger. "Don't say that."

Jolen stepped up to the door, his finger hovering over the keypad. "Everyone ready?"

"Wait." Corsi pulled out her phaser and set it for stun. "Ready."

"I don't think we'll need that."

"Bully for you." She moved in front of Carol and Lense. "Ready."

Jolen looked at Bart, who nodded, and then winked.

That small gesture seemed to smooth things over. A little bit. Maybe Bart would forgive his indiscretion. After taking a deep breath, Jolen pressed the combination. Earth, Air, Fire, Water, Spirit, Death.

At first nothing happened.

Then . . .

A loud *chunk* noise interrupted the silence. The party looked up and around them.

"That didn't sound healthy," Lense said. "Was it?"

Bart held up his right hand. "Wait . . ."

Another *chunk* noise and the door began to move into the door to the right. Stale, warm air rushed out of the opening and the others coughed. Jolen moved back fastest and held on to Lense's outstretched hand.

When the grinding noises ceased, no one moved. The darkness inside resembled a matte, black curtain. No light filtered in or out.

Carol looked at Bart. "Anything happen?"

Bart tapped his combadge. "Faulwell to *da Vinci*."

No response.

He tapped it again and repeated the call.

Still no response.

Something crashed several times in succession outside of the room. Corsi's eyes widened. "Those were the chamber doors." She turned and took off at a dead run.

Jolen looked at Bart. "This isn't sounding very good. You think we made a mistake?"

Bart tried hailing Gomez, Tev, Stevens, and Pattie. There was no response. Corsi came barreling back around the corner of the path's entrance. "The Fourth Chamber door is shut tight. The code doesn't open it."

"And I think we can assume those other crashes were the secondary chamber doors closing as well." Jolen gave a long, frustrated sigh.

"We're trapped," Corsi said.

"I only hope the dampening field isn't back up," Bart said and looked directly at Jolen, though the look wasn't an accusatory one. "Because right now, we can't get back to the Second Chamber panel to shut it off."

CHAPTER

10

Captain Gold was on his way to the bridge when something hit the starboard side of the *da Vinci*. He made it to the bridge doorway before the ship was rocked again.

"Report!" he barked as he nearly fell through the door.

"We're experiencing a bombardment of some kind," Anthony Shabalala said from his position at tactical. "We've got systems shutting down all over the ship!"

"*Captain!*" Lieutenant Nancy Conlon's voice filtered over the bridge's speaker. "*We've got to move the* da Vinci *now!*"

"What's going on?"

"*We're being hit by regular magnetic pulses, sir. They're increasing in strength regularity—as if whoever is tossing them our way is reading damage and then increasing exponentially.*"

Gold's artificial hand gripped the back of the chair and

nearly crushed the hard plastic beneath the upholstered back. He pulled himself into it and turned to face the front viewscreen. "Wong, you heard Conlon. Move us out of the range of that thing."

"Aye, sir."

The captain then turned to operations. "Haznedl—any word from the surface before this happened?"

The operations officer shook her head. "None sir. We've lost all contact with the surface."

"*Gevalt*," Gold muttered and looked back to the front viewscreen. As the ship moved farther away from the planet, the less it tossed and swayed in space.

Once the bombardment stopped, the captain contacted Conlon in engineering. "Damage?"

"*Some major systems are down—warp core isn't, though. Coolant safeties are nominal. Don't order us into warp too soon.*"

"Any chance of a transport?"

"*Negative. Sir, we get anywhere close to that planet again as long as those EMPs are shooting out and we'll be dead in the water.*"

Gold disconnected and looked back to Haznedl. "Get me one of the away teams. I don't care which one. And I don't care how. Just find a link to our people."

"Sir?" Wong said. "I'm picking up some sort of . . . countdown."

"Countdown?" Gold stood and moved to stand behind Wong. "How are *you* receiving a countdown?"

"It's on the same frequency modulation the maxim message was on, transmitted on subspace." He looked up and over his shoulder at the captain. "It's definitely a countdown."

Gold stood and looked at the viewer at the aft view of the planet. "But a countdown to what?"

"I do *not* believe this," Stevens said as Gomez, Tev, Vinx, and Soloman moved into the darkness of the control room of the fusion generator. Gomez focused her light on Stevens. The temperature had remained at a pleasant level, though to Gomez, Stevens appeared to be more than a little hot under the collar. "We just got the damned thing powered up."

"Well, we've also lost all contact with the *da Vinci*," Gomez said as Tev came to stand beside her. "All the power's gone. The city's under full blackout, again."

"What did they do out there this time?" Stevens rubbed his eyes with the base of his palms. "I have never felt so useless."

"None of us have," Gomez said. "This blackout is more powerful than the first one. Nothing is working except low-power-emitting flashlights such as these." She held up the light in her hand. "For right now, we'll have to wait it out and see. Maybe Jolen can shut the dampeners off again."

"Maybe," Stevens said and looked up at the darkened cavern where the fusion reactor sat. Silent. "Maybe."

Ten minutes after the chamber doors shut, the lights came on in the Sixth Chamber.

Bart reached out and touched Jolen's arm for support.

Nothing in his long life had prepared him for the majesty of what the light revealed to them. Not even the pyramids of Regolas IV could rival the extent of the inner cavern.

Carol spoke, her voice echoing throughout the cavern. "Well, this was definitely an attack vessel."

"You think?" Bart couldn't control the sarcasm in his voice. Rows and rows of machines of mass destruction were laid out before them. All of it was coated in a thick layer of dust. The crew of the *da Vinci*, plus the Asarion, were dwarfed by the sheer size of some of the tallest of them. "What—what are half of these?"

Corsi stepped forward, her phaser still drawn. "I'd say the majority are tanks—on leg-stalks. There are gunnery vehicles as well. Shuttles. Over there." She pointed with her free hand to a row of dust-coated spheres. "I'd say those are water vehicles."

"It would take centuries just to pick through this," Jolen said as he took several steps forward.

Bart reached out for him. "Careful—we don't know if there are any more booby traps in here."

"You think we just triggered one?" Lense asked. She sounded small in the chamber.

Bart heard something other than their breathing and held up his hand. "Listen." The sound came from somewhere to their immediate right. He turned to see a door a meter away and moved quickly to it.

Jolen was right on his heels, as was Corsi. A quick study of the door and the inset symbols and Bart recognized the same code that opened the Second Chamber, where the shutoff for the dampening field had been. He relayed this to the others.

With a glance at Jolen, Bart depressed the keys. The

doors opened with an old, grinding noise, as if the mechanism hadn't been used in centuries.

And from the looks of things, it hadn't.

Yet there was still power—and loads of it.

The room's interior lit when Bart stepped through the door. It was a sparse room, not covered in dust as was the larger cavern. He guessed it to be a control room. Waist-high to ceiling screens lit up with snow, one at a time around the room until they were all active. A central console the shape of a boomerang sat in the center. Its controls lit up as Bart neared.

Jolen came to stand beside him. "Do you recognize the symbols?"

Bart nodded. "So do you—so don't even pretend with me that you don't." He examined the console and noticed a line of moving symbols. Frowning, he pointed to it. "I'm no computer expert, Jolen, but does that look like a countdown to you?"

The Asarion moved closer to the console. He rubbed his hands together and started pressing keys. After a few seconds he looked up at one of the center viewscreens.

Bart looked up as well as Carol, Corsi, and Lense entered the room as the moving symbols showed on the screen.

"Is that a countdown?" Corsi asked.

"I'm afraid so." Jolen continued to depress keys.

Bart watched him, amazed at his skill. Jewlan's skill. A skill they could have used when all this began.

"Oh, no," Jolen said softly. "This ship—and it's definitely a ship—this ship's counting down to what I can only compare to a warp core breach."

"A what?" Corsi took several steps toward them. "This ship's warp core is still active?"

"Well, the power to send out that dampening field came from somewhere. It's my guess that we triggered a self-destruct." Bart looked at the console. "So if it's a self-destruct, then there has to be a way to shut it off."

"Where?" Jolen glanced around the panel. "I don't see one."

"How long?" Corsi asked.

"How long?" Bart looked at the counting symbols. "Oh, ten minutes, give or take a second or two."

"The dampening field is also up and running again," Jolen said. He pressed a few keys. "Apparently this command area isn't affected by the field, which I might add, now has a range that could reach your ship."

"Captain would've gotten the *da Vinci* out of range in that case," Corsi said. "What exactly is going to happen once that counter hits zero?"

Jolen looked up at the security chief through a furrowed brow. "Boom?"

"Great." Bart continued studying the console. "Jolen, I can read this stuff but I can't make heads or tails of the mechanics of it. There has to be a command switch—some sort of failsafe."

"Bart, I can't start to—"

"Come off it!" the linguist exploded. "Just help me here. Your social morals be damned. You can read this language as well as read the science. You worked with me to open that damned door in the first place. Now make a choice and stick with it. Be both Jewlan and Jolen. Dammit man, be who you are!"

"Bart," Carol said in a warning tone. "You can't force him to do things that are against his culture."

"Don't tell me *you* of all people are spouting Prime

Directive rhetoric at me when we're about to explode."
Bart rubbed at his chin. "Don't you want to see Vance
again? And what about Elizabeth and her baby?"

She looked injured at that moment and Bart made a
mental note to buy her something nice when this was
all over with. Maybe whatever it was she'd wanted to get
Vance for his birthday.

"Wait," Jolen said. "I'll do it. I will—only I'm not really
sure what the code is."

"Code?" Bart looked back to the engineer.

He punched a few buttons and the flying numbers
were replaced by a set of six dashes. Jolen pointed at
them. "As far as I can tell that is the stop code. The abort
sequence. But I have no idea what it would be."

"You can't shut down the reaction without it?"

"Nope. I'm locked out unless this single barrier is
knocked out of the way. And I don't care how good a
linguist or cryptographer I am, male or female, I don't
know what it would be."

"I might," Bart ran his fingers through his hair. "Let's
try the six symbols. The ones that opened that door."

"Hell, why not? How much worse can it get?"

Bart held up a finger. "Never—*ever*—say that. Now, I
think we triggered something when you opened it manu-
ally. Just from the little we've learned of this ship and the
chambers outside. We have four of them, each representing what looks like a period of time. It's evolution, Jolen.
This culture was a conquering people, but they did so
with the reason of technological dangers." Bart wasn't
sure where this sudden insight came from. Maybe it was
the effect of the Poplin. Maybe he was just so damned
tired. But the pieces seemed to be falling into place.

"Carol, think of it. Classes. This ship was built on the classes of their society. They start out primitive and then become stagnant, unified as having no characteristics. But then there's the chamber filled with so many things. So many accomplishments as pieces of all times. We start in the beginning as earth, which is the first. The second is air, then fire and then water. The fifth is spirit, or love. Which is where they wanted the conquered races to stop in their growth."

Carol took up the analysis. "But like most species, they go beyond. They fall backward."

"Into death," Jolen said finally. "And by using death, they start over again as earth."

"Precisely." Bart pointed to the console. "I'm thinking this isn't a ship that *came* to conquer, I'm thinking this is a ship this world *built* to conquer. Conquer other worlds. Only their own technological advances destroyed them. Notice how we've only seen these ruins. These cultural clues?"

Carol nodded. "They zapped themselves."

"Yes, and it was here they met death. They never went to war, which is why this ship is still full of the weapons. It was buried for all time."

"Until we found it, and activated it." Jolen smiled. "It makes so much more sense now."

"Look, this is great and all, but we have five minutes left," Corsi said. "Would one of you just stop it?"

"Oh. Right." Bart looked at Jolen. "You want to enter the code? Go backward. Start with death. It is technically still an engineering problem."

Jolen nodded. "Just remember the last time I did this—what happened?"

"Stop. Don't think of that." Bart reached out and touched Jolen's shoulder. "Just do it."

After taking a deep breath and holding it, Jolen entered the symbols in order.

Death, love, water, fire, air, and then earth.

This time there was a loud cranking noise and the ground shook beneath them.

"Oh, this isn't good. Did it not work?" Carol yelled over the heaving metal.

"Just the opposite. I think it worked fine," Bart said and reached out to support himself against the console. "But I think the ship isn't going to survive."

"Damn." Corsi yelled, "All of you! Back to the chamber! Let's hope those doors are open now."

Just as Jolen turned to move a heavy vent fell from above and struck his upper torso. He slumped forward against the console and then fell to the ground.

"Jolen!" Bart called out. When the man didn't move, he knelt beside him and checked for a pulse. There was one. He was only unconscious. With a grunt he bent down and moved Jolen around.

Corsi appeared next to him and heaved Jolen over her shoulder in a firefighter's carry. Once he was secured, the two moved together through the control room's door.

Great tanks shook in their moorings and began to collapse onto themselves as the ship shook in its death throes. They ran out of the Sixth Chamber, through the Fifth and to the door of the Fourth. All the doors were open.

Bart ran as fast as he could. He was still weak, and was grateful that Corsi came back to carry Jolen's weight—he could never have handled it. He was barely able to carry his *own* weight. As they made their way into the First Chamber, he stumbled. Something painful jabbed at his left ankle and he yelled out as he fell.

Hands grabbed at Bart's shoulders and pulled him out of the way. As he was dragged out of the First Chamber and into the cool, dark Asarion night, he cried, "Jolen!" before the ancient ship collapsed.

CHAPTER
11

Bart took in a long, deep breath before setting his mostly healed ankle and foot onto the floor of his room in the Asarion hospital. It hurt, but not too terribly. He didn't plan on staying on it too much. His plans were to speak at the Conclave with Captain Gold on Jolen's behalf and then spend a nice quiet rest in his quarters aboard the *da Vinci*.

After walking around the room—reassured he wasn't somehow permanently impaired—Bart returned to the edge of the bed and sat back down.

A knock at the door brought his gaze up from his foot.

Jolen stood just outside, his forehead marred by an ugly set of bruises and several sutures. He was dressed less formal in a pair of soft, beige-colored slacks and a white, button-down shirt with a high collar, the top of which just brushed the edges of his dark hair.

He was beautiful.

"Are you okay?" Jolen's voice was light.

"Yes. I'm fine. Please, come on in." Bart pushed himself back onto his bed and smiled at Jolen as he stepped in. The engineer held a thin box in his hand. "I'm going to call this my accident-prone assignment. Seems I spent a lot of time on my back—and not in the fun way."

Hmm. Oversharing.

But Jolen only smiled. "I'm sorry so much happened to you. Especially the Poplin."

"No, that was the stimulant that disagreed with me, and I'm not sure I'm sorry anything happened to me at all. It's been a growing experience for me." He chuckled. "Even at my age."

"I'm glad."

Bart nodded to the box. "What's that?"

Jolen held it out to Bart. "A thank-you. From me to you. For all you've done. And for being a friend to me."

Bart held the box in his hands. "I'm not sure what to say."

"Say nothing. Just open it. Please." Jolen sat on the bed beside Bart. Their shoulders touched.

He pulled at the twine ribbon and opened the box carefully. Inside was a ream of perhaps two-hundred and fifty sheets of soft, clothlike paper. Bart pressed his hands against it and felt of the texture. So much like silk.

"It's Poplin paper, made from the same tree the drink is made from." He smiled. "It won't have the same effect, so don't worry. But before my world was destroyed, the Poplin was the tree of friendship. And the tree of attraction. As the drink was used to relax inhibitions, the paper was used to write letters of endearment to the one you care most for." He shrugged. "I figured you might want to write Anthony letters on this paper."

Bart wasn't sure what to say. He turned his head and looked deep into Jolen's beautiful, bright eyes. This close, he could see what made them appear so bright. It was the dark pupils that almost retained their full round shape even in the light.

"Thank you."

Jolen smiled. "Have you ever considered shaving your beard?"

"No."

Jolen nodded and continued to stare.

Bart knew what Jolen intended to do.

And this time he allowed himself to enjoy the kiss.

The ship was under way from Asario and on to the nearest starbase for a diagnostic. The coolant system still wasn't working up to "before-blast-from-planet standards" in engineering and Gomez and Conlon both insisted on the side trip.

Bart was given a few days leave for convalescence and he intended on maximizing it to its fullest.

He stared at the round puddle of white cream in his left hand. It had the consistency of whipped cream. He brought it up to his nose and inhaled the pungent, minty aroma. With a look at his reflection in the mirror, Bart carefully smeared the cream over the lower half of his face.

Rinsing his hands, the linguist took up the razor he'd carefully replicated. He placed it firmly but gently against the top of his beard over the right cheek, and with a firm even stroke, pulled it down and under his chin. The crackle of his beard hairs falling like tiny soldiers in battle resounded in his ear. At first, he hesitated, but then plowed on, so to speak.

Once he was finished, Bart rinsed his face in cold water and studied his reflection. He'd never worried about looking older. Not even now was that the catalyst for shaving. He'd intended to take a picture of himself without the beard and send it to Jolen before growing it back again. But as he turned his face to the left, and then the right, Bart considered leaving it bare and smooth for a while.

He could just see the gaping face of Fabian later in the day when his roommate got off shift.

After toweling his face, Bart lightly limped over to his desk and retrieved his finest nibbed pen from the sonic cleaner. As he set the pen in its stand, Bart looked at the stack of eight pages he'd written Anthony that morning. He'd told him everything, from his sister's death, to his life, and then of Kyle's death. He told Anthony exactly why he feared marriage, that in the back of his mind he felt he didn't deserve to be happy, and that he knew it was stupid. Ridiculous. Still, it was how he felt.

They sat in their stack, these pages, unread into the recorder. Flat. Untouched.

Would he send them?

Bart picked them up and limped to the recycler. With a sigh, he held them just over the top. *These pages hold the words to me. And somehow, if I destroy them, will I be destroying a part of myself? Maybe.* With a sigh, he deactivated the recycler and neatly folded the pages in half and then in half again. He slid them into an envelope and sealed it, and then tucked the package away.

Maybe one day he'd send them to Anthony. No preamble. No subspace recording.

One day. But not today.

He then pulled a single sheet of the new Poplin paper from the wooden box and wrote the first words, *My dearest . . .*

The scent of jasmine filled the small cabin and he paused, his thoughts returning to Jewlan. To Jolen. And the kiss.

"My dearest Jolen, just a brief note . . ."

THE CLEANUP

Robert T. Jeschonek

For Wendy, Mom, and Dad,
for all their love and support

CHAPTER

1

Just before the Jem'Hadar booby trap killed Or-Lin, her twin sister, Em-Lin, told her to shut up or she would come down and *make* her shut up.

Em-Lin *thought* the message to her, actually, communicating via the telepathic link that the two Miradorn women shared. The thought was so filled with anger that Em-Lin would have felt guilty about sending it, given the fact that her sister died right after receiving it—if Em-Lin had not been so completely brain-fried by the experience of having her linked twin die, for all intents and purposes, in Em-Lin's head.

It was the most devastating experience of Em-Lin's life. Nothing in her thirty-two years of existence had prepared her for the moment of Or-Lin's death.

When the two of them had returned to the work site

that morning, Em-Lin had not expected any trouble. She had been in a good mood, looking forward to the week's vacation that she and Or-Lin were set to begin the next day. As much as Em-Lin loved her work, restoring the ancient shrine of Ho'nig in the caves of Mirada's moon, Zasharu, she was ready for some relaxation back home on Mirada.

Soon, though, she and Or-Lin were going at it. Though they, like all Miradorn twins, considered themselves two halves of the same self, those halves were sometimes at war with each other.

I'm marrying Sil-Vo, Or-Lin had said in Em-Lin's mind from the opposite end of the huge shrine. *When we go home for vacation, I'm staying there with him*.

Em-Lin was lying on her back atop a scaffolding four stories above the stone floor, cleaning a mural on the vaulted ceiling. After receiving Or-Lin's thoughts, Em-Lin dropped the tool she was working with, and it clattered down the scaffolding on the long trip to the floor.

What? Em-Lin's thoughts were in a whirl. Miradorn twins almost never separated from each other; if Or-Lin planned to stay on Mirada, she planned for Em-Lin to stay there, too. *You can't be serious*.

Sil-Vo's twin, Qua-Vo, will accept you as his wife, said Or-Lin, this latest thought rippling with hopefulness.

I can't believe this, thought Em-Lin. And she truly couldn't. Miradorn twins—in other words, ninety-eight percent of all Miradorn—shared everything. At that very moment, for example, even as Em-Lin stared up at the ceiling mural that she had been cleaning, she saw Or-Lin's work in her mind's eye, watching as Or-Lin polished the bas-relief gold floor plates near the entrance to the shrine.

It was rare for one twin to manage to hide something from the other—not impossible, but rare. Apparently, Or-Lin had done just that, concealing her intentions toward Sil-Vo and masking certain events, like Sil-Vo's proposal of marriage, from Em-Lin's attention.

How did you keep this from me? thought Em-Lin. She felt betrayed, offended, confused—and dizzy, which was not a good thing to feel on top of a scaffolding four stories above a stone floor.

Or-Lin let out the telepathic equivalent of a deep sigh. *I didn't want you to know until it was definite.*

Definite? Em-Lin felt her hurt (and dizziness) dissolving into raw, churning rage. *Since when is this definite?*

In her mind's eye, Em-Lin saw Or-Lin's reflection in the gold floor plate that she was polishing. Her bright white hair swept back from a sharp peak on her forehead, flowing down over her shoulders all the way to her waist. Her face had a roughly triangular shape, with a broad forehead tapering down to a small, rounded chin. Her eyes had softly glowing white irises set against black sclera, the result of a rare genetic condition that the Miradorn people had nicknamed "star eyes."

In other words, she was the spitting image of her twin, Em-Lin.

I love Sil-Vo, said Or-Lin, looking her reflection in the eyes as a way of defiantly meeting her sister's gaze. *Come or don't come. It's all the same to me.*

Again, Em-Lin was stunned. She pulled her mind back a little from Or-Lin's, hoping that she had misunderstood.

You don't mean . . . Division, do you? She floated the thought tentatively, scared to find out the answer to the question but needing to know it more than anything.

Maybe it won't come to that. Or-Lin was trying to be conciliatory. *Like I said, Qua-Vo is interested in you.*

So there it was, laid out between them like giant, fiery letters burning in midair. Or-Lin was on the floor, and Em-Lin was four stories up on her back atop a scaffold . . . but a far greater separation was in store for them if Em-Lin opposed the marriage.

Division. Short of death, it was considered the most awful thing that could happen to Miradorn twins.

When twins were divided, the Priests of Duality put up a psychic wall between them, partitioning the thoughts and senses of one twin from another for the rest of their lives.

To Miradorn twins, Division was like taking one person and cutting her in half. The fact that Or-Lin could even *consider* it boggled Em-Lin's mind.

Not only that, but there were other obligations involved. The thought of abandoning them was equally mind-boggling to Em-Lin.

What about the promise we made? Em-Lin gazed up at the mural on the ceiling but saw only Or-Lin's chilly stare reflected in the gold floor plate. *If we leave here, we break that promise.*

I'm tired of keeping the promise, thought Or-Lin. *I just don't care about it anymore.*

Em-Lin was aghast. *How can you say that?*

Thanks to that stupid promise, we're throwing ourselves away for something that won't even happen in our lifetimes! Or our children's lifetimes, or our children's children's lifetimes, probably!

You didn't feel that way three years ago, thought Em-Lin.

I was naïve. I believed that this was all I could want out of life, but I was wrong. I've changed.

Em-Lin cast her mind back to the time when she and her twin had made the promise. The people to whom they had made the promise had made them feel like heroes.

Coincidentally enough, just as she thought of those people, she saw a trace of them again—the first trace that she had seen in many months.

She saw it through Or-Lin's eyes, though she didn't recognize it at first. It was a symbol drawn in what looked like black ink on a corner of the gold plate that Or-Lin was polishing. The symbol represented a letter from the alphabet of the people to whom Em-Lin and Or-Lin had made their promise.

Em-Lin first noticed it three minutes before Or-Lin exploded. She didn't understand it, however, until thirty seconds before the explosion.

Much later, Em-Lin would blame herself for not paying more attention to that symbol sooner, but the truth was, she overlooked it with good reason. Even as her mind's eye brushed over the symbol (seen through Or-Lin's eyes), Em-Lin was distracted by the argument with her twin sister.

We can't leave here, said Em-Lin, casting her thoughts over the link with renewed strength. After letting Or-Lin surprise her repeatedly, she was determined to regain a dominant posture. *Our work is vital to our people's future.*

Thanks for reminding me! Or-Lin's words were heavy with sarcasm. *You've just changed my mind again! I really do want to stay here with you!*

So you don't care about anyone but yourself, right?
Through the link, Em-Lin watched her twin's hand polishing the gold plate, working the specially treated chamois cloth closer to the symbol inked in the corner.

All I know is, I want a life. Or-Lin moved the chamois closer to the symbol. *If that means breaking a meaningless promise, I'll do it.*

Meaningless? Em-Lin's thoughts were so superheated that they practically smoked on their way across the link. *The Vorta didn't think it was meaningless!*

Or-Lin rubbed the symbol on the plate. She checked her work, saw that the symbol was still there, and rubbed again, harder. *He really brainwashed you, didn't he? I can't even stand listening to you anymore. I think I want Division whether you want to go with me or not.*

You're lucky I'm not down there right now. Em-Lin was furious. *You're lucky I can't slap you right across the face for that.*

You just can't stand it that I'm right. Or-Lin was still rubbing the symbol.

Shut up! Shut up, or I swear, I'll come down there and make you shut up!

Just then, she made the connection. At that moment, she realized the significance of the symbol that she was seeing on the gold plate through Or-Lin's eyes.

Get away from there! Em-Lin shot out the screaming thought like a spear on fire, volume all the way up, punching straight into Or-Lin's mind. At the same time, she tried with all her might to will Or-Lin's hand to pull back from the symbol on the plate.

But that was one of the things that a Miradorn twin

could never do. She could see through her twin's eyes, feel what her twin was feeling, send and receive thoughts to and from her twin . . .

But she could never control her twin. Not even to save her life.

What? Or-Lin stopped rubbing but did not move her hand from the symbol. *Get away why?*

Booby trap! Em-Lin rolled off her back and climbed down the scaffolding as fast as she could.

Through her sister's eyes, Em-Lin watched as Or-Lin lifted the chamois away from the symbol, which was glowing with rapidly increasing intensity.

Get away!

But even as Em-Lin flashed warning after urgent warning into her sister's head, she knew that it was too late.

The symbol flared with blinding brilliance. Em-Lin had an impression of Or-Lin's arms swinging up in front of her face to block the light.

Then, because one twin could feel what the other was feeling, especially in times of great stress, Em-Lin felt the explosion hit Or-Lin. A burst of force erupted up and out from the gold plate in the floor, ripping through Or-Lin's body in a single, blazing instant.

Em-Lin's scream echoed through the vast central chamber of the shrine. In shock, she released her grip on the scaffolding and fell.

Instead of dropping the full four stories, Em-Lin landed on a platform one story down. She lay there on her back for what seemed like hours, her starry eyes staring blindly upward, one arm hanging over the edge of the platform.

Much later, she would be surprised to learn that her sister, not Em-Lin herself, had been the one blown to pieces. This, Em-Lin only accepted as truth after extensive convincing by hospital personnel and the injection of several large doses of sedatives.

Even then, when Em-Lin realized that she was still alive, she knew that she would never be right again.

CHAPTER 2

Commander Sonya Gomez was having a hell of a time paying attention to her tricorder as she scanned the breathtaking interior of the shrine of Ho'nig.

The shrine had been built in an enormous natural cavern. The walls, ceiling, and floor were cut from native stone, a kind of gold-veined ruby marble that had been polished to a smooth finish.

The place was vast and filled with treasures, so many that every time Gomez thought she'd seen them all, she spotted another one. Statues carved from massive gemstones of many colors perched on marble pedestals, gleaming in the light of worklamps positioned throughout the chamber. Altars, pillars, pulpits, and alcoves were adorned with multitudes of gold, silver, and crystal relics.

It was a huge and beautiful place. The fact that it was dedicated to Ho'nig, a religious figure with whom Gomez had some familiarity, served to increase her interest in it even more.

That was why she had to force herself to focus on the tricorder scans and doing her job.

Reviewing some results that she had missed while gawking, Gomez nodded for the benefit of those who were watching her. "There are even more booby traps in here than your people detected, and those are just the ones that aren't cloaked."

Pika Ven-Sa, the old high priest who was showing Gomez's team around the shrine, snorted and shook his head. "Thanks a lot, Dominion!" he said to the ceiling. "So glad we gave that whole *alliance* thing a whirl!"

Fabian Stevens, who was working alongside Gomez, elbowed her in the side. "I like this guy," he said with a grin. "He's got *spunk*."

Gomez kept scanning with the tricorder. "You did the right thing, not trying to defuse them yourselves," she said, glancing at Ven-Sa. "Let's just say there're some nasty surprises around here."

"We only regret that one life was lost before the traps were discovered," said Ven-Sa's grimmer twin, Chi-Sa. Chi-Sa wore the same gray Pika priest robes as Ven-Sa, but he wore them with stark gravity instead of sardonic attitude. "We are grateful for Starfleet's assistance in this matter."

"Now *that* was an easy call to make," said Ven-Sa. " 'Hello, Starfleet? Sorry about that whole teaming-up-with-your-worst-enemies-in-the-big-war thing. Any chance you might stop over and knock out a couple Jem'Hadar booby traps in the holy shrine in the caves under the surface of our moon?'"

"Don't forget the part about the big pilgrimage to the shrine in two days," Stevens said with a smirk.

"Just to make it more interesting," said Ven-Sa, "the *Chala Ho'nig*, a pilgrimage of beings from a host of spacefaring species in the Alpha Quadrant, is converging on the very same moon."

"Remember our many converts in the Gamma Quadrant, as well," Chi-Sa said solemnly. "The word of Ho'nig has spread like lightning beyond the wormhole."

"Like I said, that was a tough call to make," said Ven-Sa. "Good thing you Federationists don't hold grudges."

Gomez flashed Ven-Sa a smile, but she knew that relations between the Federation and the Miradorn were not all sweetness and light. The pain of the Dominion War was still pretty fresh in the Federation's little corner of the Alpha Quadrant. The Miradorn had aided the Dominion in noncombat roles, serving chiefly in logistics support, but the fact remained: help of whatever kind from anyone, including the Miradorn, had fueled the war machine that had taken so many lives and nearly brought down the entire Federation.

Gomez personally held no grudge, though. Her only concern was the success of the mission. "It's in our mutual best interest to clear out these booby traps," she said. "And I think we'd all like some answers about why they're here."

"Good question," said Stevens. "There's some major ordnance planted around this shrine. What are the traps protecting?"

Ven-Sa snorted. "Or are they just a farewell gift from our former allies? They're not really known for leaving showers of candy and flowers when they pull out, are they?"

"Just look what they did to Cardassia," said Chi-Sa.

"I think I have an answer for you." The high-pitched, tinkling voice of P8 Blue, the insectoid Nasat structural systems specialist, drew everyone's attention to the rim of the blast crater in the middle of the entryway floor. "Is there supposed to be a massive chamber underneath the shrine of Ho'nig?"

Ven-Sa and Chi-Sa looked at each other and answered simultaneously. "No."

"Well, there is now," said P8 Blue, known affectionately as Pattie to her teammates. "The explosion opened a pinprick hole in its shielding." Pattie returned her attention to the screen of her tricorder, adjusting several controls with her pincerlike digits.

Gomez walked over to stand alongside Pattie and directed her own tricorder into the heart of the crater. "How big is the chamber?" she said.

"If I had to guess," said Pattie. "I'd say it's bigger than the shrine itself."

For a moment, Gomez watched data flickering across the screen of her tricorder. Familiar energy signatures and trace elements told the story. "It's a Dominion facility," she said, "and it's functioning."

"Functioning?" said Ven-Sa. "Functioning how?"

"I can't tell yet," said Gomez. "We need to get down there."

"And to do that, we have to clean up the booby traps."

Stevens blew out his breath and looked around the shrine. "Booby traps set by the Jem'Hadar, no less."

"Without damaging the shrine of Ho'nig," said Ven-Sa, "if at all possible."

"Don't worry," said Gomez. "We came prepared." She waved in the direction of two of the four security personnel who had accompanied the team to the shrine. "Hawkins and Soan have more than a little experience with demolitions."

Deputy Chief of Security Vance Hawkins coolly met Gomez's gaze. For reasons unknown to Gomez, he did not seem to be in a particularly good mood today. "We'll do our best," he said.

Beside Hawkins, the diminutive Bajoran Lauoc Soan simply nodded in agreement.

"What can we do to help?" said Ven-Sa.

"We could use a guide," said Gomez. "Someone who knows this shrine and the surrounding caves inside and out."

"Done," said Ven-Sa. "No one knows this place better than Em-Lin. She and her sister were spearheading restoration efforts here at the shrine."

"Em-Lin's sister died in the explosion," said Chi-Sa.

Gomez frowned. "Will Em-Lin still be fit to work here then?"

Ven-Sa shrugged. "If it means saving the shrine. This place is her passion, that's for sure."

"All right then," said Gomez. "We'd better get busy. We only have two days until the pilgrims get here."

"If we're lucky," said Chi-Sa. "They seem to show up earlier every year."

"'It is better to be one year early than one minute late,'" said Gomez.

Ven-Sa brightened. "You are familiar with the teachings of Ho'nig?"

Gomez pinched her thumb and index finger close together. "Just a little." She had met a Bolian follower of Ho'nig during her mission to Sarindar. The Bolian, whose name was Zilder, had left her a copy of the *Se'rbeg*, the holy book of Ho'nig, when he was killed by the murderous *shii*.

Ven-Sa bowed. "Perhaps you and I can speak further of his teachings," he said.

Gomez shrugged. The truth was, she thought she might enjoy talking about Ho'nig with the priest. For reasons that she could not quite put her finger on, she had found parts of the *Se'rbeg* inspirational. She almost hated to admit it, because Zilder had gotten on her nerves while trying to convert her, but she sometimes felt drawn to the teachings of Ho'nig.

"Maybe later," Gomez said to Ven-Sa. "First things first. Could you find our guide while we bring down some equipment from the *da Vinci*?"

"Consider it done," said Ven-Sa. "Please be patient with Em-Lin, however. Losing her sister was very traumatic for her, and she's not really been herself lately."

"I can only imagine," said Gomez. "Each set of twins functions as a single being, right?"

"That's something of an oversimplification," said Chi-Sa, "but that's more or less it."

Ven-Sa cleared his throat. "Let's just say that when a Miradorn loses her twin, the . . . attachment . . . doesn't end overnight."

"Especially when the loss is traumatic," said Chi-Sa. "There can be a . . . continuation."

"What your people might call a haunting," said Ven-Sa. "This is what Em-Lin is going through."

"Thanks for the heads-up," said Gomez, trying to imagine what a Miradorn haunting might be like. "I'll keep that in mind."

CHAPTER

3

"Vance," said Commander Gomez. "Will you work with the local security personnel to establish a perimeter around the shrine?"

Four men—two sets of Miradorn twins in blue-and-silver-uniforms—stepped forward, and Vance Hawkins nodded. "I'm on it," he said without hesitation.

Inside, though, as he looked at the four Miradorn with their familiar widow's peaks and pasty skin, Vance thought of Jomej VII and felt a chill.

"Shall we?" he said, waving toward a spot to one side of the plaza in the cave outside the shrine. As the four Miradorn walked toward the place that he had indicated, Vance summoned the rest of the security team from the *da Vinci* with a bob of his head.

Everyone gathered in the plaza. Vance introduced Soan,

Tomozuka Kim, and T'Mandra. The Miradorn introduced themselves as Boz-Nu, Yet-Nu, Saf-Lig, and Gre-Lig. It was all very businesslike but perfectly friendly.

Vance shook hands with all four of the Miradorn, and he was no less professional than always—but underneath it all, deep underneath, he was crackling with tension.

One instance of abusive behavior by a handful of people did not mean that an entire species was no good. Vance knew that. In time of war, people often did things that they normally would never do. Vance knew that, too.

Still, he was not comfortable around the Miradorn.

"We have twelve men on shrine detail," said Boz-Nu. "We have another thirty-six from surrounding precincts on call for the pilgrimage. How about if we bring them all in early?"

"Sounds good," said Vance. "I'd like to see a map of these caves."

Saf-Lig drew a disc-shaped holoprojector from a pouch at his hip. As he raised the projector, his hand brushed past a holster slung at his side. The black grip of a handheld weapon stuck out of the holster, curved and padded for comfort.

Vance had seen weapons like that on Jomej VII.

At the touch of a button, a glowing blue map leaped out of the holoprojector, rippling in midair in the middle of the group. "This is the shrine of Ho'nig," said Saf-Lig, stirring his finger in a large block of space in the center of the three-dimensional map. "I suggest we set our perimeter in a dome configuration, securing the caverns above the shrine as well as the ring of caverns fanning out on the same level as the shrine."

Vance nodded, staring intently at the map—though, actually, he was looking right through it at the holstered device strapped to Saf-Lig's side.

It was a Miradorn "puppet gun," the ultimate in personnel control devices. Why bind a prisoner or opponent with physical restraints when the puppet gun can inhibit his actions by manipulating nerve clusters in his brain?

The puppet gun enabled its user to take complete control of a target's body. A user could make an attacker freeze in his tracks, make a one-hundred-eighty-degree turn, and waltz right into a waiting cell.

A user could make a target do other things, too. Things like turn against his own allies or sabotage his own handiwork.

Or degrade himself in humiliating ways in front of other people. That was how Vance had seen the puppet gun used by the Miradorn at Jomej VII.

"The real challenge comes when the pilgrims start pouring in," said Saf-Lig. "It will be difficult keeping them away from the shrine."

"I'm hoping the *da Vinci* can solve that problem by holding off any landings or beam-downs until we're done," said Vance.

"That will be a challenge," said Yet-Nu. "There are multiple landing sites and access points in this region of Zasharu. If I may illustrate." Yet-Nu adjusted a control on the holoprojector in Saf-Lig's hand, causing the view to zoom out to include a bigger wedge of the moon.

As Yet-Nu said his piece, Vance listened and nodded, but his mind still swam with dark memories.

He remembered Miradorn guards with puppet guns in the prison camp on Jomej VII during the Dominion War. Federation and Klingon prisoners forced to perform in degrading ways for an audience of interrogators. Vance, part of the team sent to liberate the camp, was himself taken over and manipulated until reinforcements arrived and freed him.

Until that day, Vance had not known what it felt like to have control of his own body taken away from him. Afterward, back aboard the *Prometheus*-class *U.S.S. Shiva*, he found that he could not get that terrible feeling out of his mind.

And he never did. He never really got over it.

That was why he was having trouble relating to the Miradorn in a buddy-buddy way. That was why his heart just wasn't in it as he listened to the Miradorn talking about local security opportunities.

The Miradorn might have worked only in noncombat roles for the enemy, they might have had a reputation as the least malevolent of Dominion allies, and they might now be bending over backward to get in good with the Federation, even to the extent of renaming their homeworld "New Mirada" . . . but Vance would never forget that day on Jomej VII. He would never forget the red-haired Miradorn man who directed the puppet gun at him, and how the Miradorn's twin giggled as Vance was made to crawl on all fours like an animal.

And how he was made to do other things before it

was all over. Screaming screaming *screaming* inside the whole time.

"Do you find these arrangements acceptable?" said Boz-Nu, snapping off the holoprojector image of the shrine's surroundings.

"Absolutely," Vance said with a sharp nod.

But he did not return Boz-Nu's smile. And when Gre-Lig reached out in his direction, Vance did not shake his hand.

CHAPTER

4

The huge, hairy Miradorn threw his arms around S.C.E. cultural specialist Carol Abramowitz and hugged her tightly against him. His name was Brag-Ret, and his jolliness was rather overwhelming.

"*Welcome* to New Mirada!" His voice was deep and resonant as the notes from a tuba. "*Already* your presence has made this a *brighter* and more *beautiful* world!"

"Thanks," said Carol as Brag-Ret rolled her from side to side over his great, spongy gut. She winced at his cologne and the wiry bloom of blue-green hair tickling her face and neck; the hair seemed to be part beard and part chest hair bursting from the wide open collar of his purple and pink striped shirt.

Brag-Ret held on to Carol for one moment more than she thought was absolutely necessary, then unclamped his beefy arms from around her. "And as if *fate* had not *blessed* us enough already," he said, turning toward *da Vinci* Chief of Security Domenica Corsi, "*another* extraordinary beauty walks among us this *glorious* day!"

As Brag-Ret opened his arms wide for another embrace and took a step toward Corsi, she fired a warning glare in his direction. Brag-Ret hesitated, cocking his head appraisingly to one side.

Fortunately, Carol was able to catch Corsi's eye before an interplanetary incident ensued. Carol gave Corsi her best "please-just-let-the-big-smelly-man-hug-you" look, raising her eyebrows and nodding emphatically.

It was enough, though Corsi shot Carol a dark "I'll-get-you-for-this" look over Brag-Ret's shoulder as he hugged her.

Carol shrugged in reply. She had beamed to the surface of New Mirada with Corsi and Betazoid security officer Rennan Konya to take the temperature of pro-Federation efforts among the Miradorn. Starfleet was intensely interested in how the onetime Dominion allies were shaping up, especially given their world's strategic importance. Why alienate the big, hairy welcome wagon in the first five minutes of the visit? Brag-Ret could yet provide valuable insight into recent developments on New Mirada, in which case the hugs from hell were a small price to pay.

Still, when Brag-Ret's female twin, Sog-Ret, lumbered into the room and headed straight for Carol with arms spread wide, Carol had second thoughts. She suddenly decided that she would rather be on New Mirada's moon, Zasharu, helping Gomez defuse deadly Jem'Hadar booby traps.

"*Welcome*, travelers!" said Sog-Ret, her voice shrill and sharp like the caw of a crow. "We *delight* in your *magnificent* presence!"

As she wrapped her thick arms around Carol and hugged the breath right out of her, Carol noticed two things about Sog-Ret.

One, her perfume was even stronger and more sickening than Brag-Ret's cologne.

Two, her beard and chest hair were thicker than Brag-Ret's.

Interesting choices for the welcome wagon, thought Carol, turning her head away from Sog-Ret to try to catch a breath.

It was then, as Sog-Ret bounced her up and down over her monstrous breasts and stomach, that it occurred to Carol that perhaps Brag-Ret and Sog-Ret did not represent the welcome wagon after all.

CHAPTER

5

Just as Em-Lin walked through the arched doorway leading into the shrine, her feet left the floor. A startled gasp escaped her as she floated upward, drifting toward the distant, vaulted ceiling.

Instinctively, she twisted and fumbled for a hand-hold or foothold, finally hooking the toe of her work-boot under a sconce alongside the doorway. Swinging around, she clamped both hands onto a statue of Yolo, the Phylosian disciple of Ho'nig, which was mounted on the wall.

It was only then, as she hugged Yolo tightly and had a look around, that Em-Lin realized that she was not the only person floating in the shrine. Several beings in Starfleet uniforms and two Miradorn priests had also left the floor. Like Em-Lin, the Starfleeters stayed in one place by hanging on to something, but the priests drifted upward with no sign of stopping.

"Little help, anyone?" said Pika Ven-Sa, who was one of the ones not holding on to anything. His gray robes billowed around him as he slowly ascended, revealing the bright yellow garment underneath. "Why don't we just beam out of here?"

Near Ven-Sa, a Starfleet male with dark skin crouched on a stone railing, holding on with both hands. "The Dominion shielding is disrupting our transporters," he said, watching the rising priest.

"Yet another wonderful booby trap," said another man in a Starfleet uniform. This man had lighter skin than the other man and dark hair. He clung to one of the sixteen pillars ringing the altar in the center of the shrine, pillars representing the sixteen Hearts and Holy Worlds of Ho'nig. "Nothing like an antigravity field to give you a lift."

"And a drop when it runs out of juice," said a black-haired Starfleet woman who was clinging to another of the pillars.

Em-Lin tightened her grip on the statue of Yolo. The thought of gravity suddenly returning and dragging her down hard made her acutely uncomfortable.

So did the sight of so many Starfleet uniforms, actually. Em-Lin knew it was politically incorrect, but her time in the service of the Dominion had left her with lingering dislike and distrust of Starfleet and the Federation. They had been the enemy during the war, after all, and she and her world had been poisoned against them. In addition, Em-Lin knew people who had suffered because of Starfleet actions during the war—and she herself, though strictly a noncombatant, had seen firsthand what Starfleet personnel could be capable of, at least in time of war. She knew that she would never forget her experience at the Rasha Nom depot, a Starfleet attack that had left her and Or-Lin as two of only three survivors out of twenty-four Miradorn.

Em-Lin would have to work with these Starfleeters, and she would find a way to act professional at all times when dealing with them, but she knew in her heart that she could not truly embrace them. In that way, she was on the same wavelength as the rest of her people, contrary to the overblown displays of Federation love designed to bring much needed aid to the depressed economy of New Mirada and Zasharu.

"How long will the effect last?" said the black-haired Starfleet woman on the pillar, directing the question to the two figures working in the altar space below her.

A diminutive, pale-skinned Starfleeter with a high, bald head worked in a rectangle of blinking circuitry set into the silver altar. "Two-and-a-half more minutes," said the little man, his hands flying over the flickering circuits. "The effect will steadily intensify, then cut out completely at the end of that time."

"Not good!" said Ven-Sa, still drifting upward. "Not exactly what I wanted to hear!"

"Any chance of a more gradual letdown?" said the black-haired woman.

"Working on it," said the little man. He shifted to one side, and Em-Lin saw a blue, multilegged shape beneath him. At first, she thought that it was his lower body, but as she continued to watch, she realized that the shape was not part of him at all. In fact, the little man was actually sitting on top of what looked like some kind of device or creature. It was hard to tell from a distance. His legs were wrapped around it, and it seemed to be keeping him from floating away.

A flutter of movement caught Em-Lin's eye, and she turned her head to see Pika Chi-Sa falling up against the ceiling of a side chamber not far from her. The ceiling was about five meters above the floor, and Chi-Sa ended up stuck flat against it.

"Just for the record," said Chi-Sa, his voice echoing through the shrine, "I never wanted to join the Dominion to begin with."

"Not what you said at the time," Ven-Sa said curtly. Em-Lin noticed an edge of panic in his voice as he continued to climb toward the peak of the main chamber's ceiling.

Suddenly, then, Ven-Sa gasped as he dropped ten meters and stopped. In the side chamber across the shrine, Chi-Sa also fell the same distance and froze in midair.

"What's up, Soloman?" said the black-haired woman on the pillar.

"Or down, as the case may be," said the Starfleeter with the light skin and dark hair.

"A . . . 'hiccup' in the system," said the little bald man at the altar panel. Apparently, his name was "Soloman." "I'm trying to reprogram the device to let everyone down gently, but it's not being very cooperative."

"Why should this one be any easier to deal with than the first five?" said the dark-haired man. "My favorite so far was number three, the heat-seeking, flying buzzsaw."

"We're just lucky no one's been killed yet," said the black-haired woman. "That buzzsaw came pretty close to lopping your head off, Fabian."

"For such a one-track-minded bunch of sourpusses, the Dominion sure get creative with their booby traps," said Fabian, the dark-haired man.

"I'll try to warn you next time the . . . hiccup!" said Soloman.

Suddenly, Ven-Sa and Chi-Sa dropped three more meters, then shot straight up again. Chi-Sa's climb stopped when he slammed into the ceiling of the side chamber. Em-Lin heard a loud crack, and Chi-Sa howled in pain.

Ven-Sa stopped when he hit the ceiling, too, but his ceiling was four stories up, at the highest point of the shrine. He was pinned there, looking straight down, his back stuck against the very mural that Em-Lin had been in the process of restoring when all this began.

In other words, when Or-Lin died.

As if the mere thought of Or-Lin had been enough to conjure her from the dead, Em-Lin heard her voice in her right ear at that moment. It sounded as clear as day, as clear as it had every time her dead twin sister had spoken to her since the explosion.

Let go, said Or-Lin's voice. *I love you and I will protect you.*

Em-Lin shivered and held on more tightly to the statue of Yolo. She knew that her dead twin's advice was no good. She knew further that the Or-Lin who kept appearing to her, speaking to her, and touching her—but never two of those at the same time—was a *dugo tenya*, or trauma-induced hallucination.

Still, the voice unhinged her. As much as she knew

intellectually that it belonged to a phantom, she could not quell her emotional response of intense, unreasoning fear.

And longing. Longing to reunite with the one whom she had lost.

More accurately, the half of herself that she had lost.

Please let go, said Or-Lin. *I love you and I miss you.*

"I miss you, too," whispered Em-Lin, but she did not release her hold on the statue.

Fortunately, then, she was distracted by the voices of the others in the shrine. The *living* others.

"How much time till the device deactivates?" said the black-haired woman clinging to the pillar.

"Thirty seconds," said Soloman. Em-Lin noticed that in spite of the stress that he must be under, his voice remained calm and matter-of-fact. "But I have an idea. I'm going to try a different approach."

"Please make it a quick one!" Ven-Sa shouted from the distant ceiling of the chamber.

"This circuitry is morphic," said Soloman, "and so is the programming. It continually changes to circumvent attempted disruptions." His fingers danced so fast across the flickering panel that Em-Lin could not follow their movements. "I need to insert my own changeling applet and fool the system into thinking the new program is from the same parent as itself."

"You can do that?" said Chi-Sa.

"Either I can," said Soloman, "or I can't."

"He can," said Fabian. "You better believe he can."

Soloman's fingers continued to fly. "Wait!" he said, leaning closer to the open panel. "I was in a sandbox the whole time!"

"Sandbox?" said Chi-Sa.

"A subsystem partitioned from the main program," said Soloman. "Firewalled all around and completely nonfunctional . . . but I'm tunneling through to the real system, and . . . everybody hold on tight!"

"Hold on to *what*?" said Ven-Sa, his voice high and wild with panic.

Em-Lin felt herself grow slightly heavier. Far above, Ven-Sa slowly fell away from the ceiling and drifted downward as if he barely weighed more than the air around him.

"It's working!" said Chi-Sa, also floating down from his high perch.

"I told you he could do it," said Fabian.

"Great job, Soloman," said the black-haired woman.

"Actually, Commander Gomez," said Soloman, "I have some bad news."

"What is it?" said Gomez.

"I seem to have triggered some kind of failsafe," said Soloman. He turned, and Em-Lin realized for the first time that the blue, multilegged shape underneath him had a face. "Once this applet has run its course, I believe that all the remaining booby traps in and around the shrine of Ho'nig will activate at the same time."

"This ought to make life interesting," said Fabian.

"To say the least," said the blue creature under Soloman. Its voice was high and bright and echoed through the shrine like tinkling bells rung by Pika priests during a holy ceremony.

"Vance," said Gomez. "Call in Soan. In fact, bring in your whole team. Miradorn security will have to maintain the perimeter."

"Yes, sir," said Vance, the dark-skinned man on the stone railing.

"Everybody stay sharp," said Gomez. "All hell is about to break loose."

"Again," said Fabian.

"I hope you won't mind if I excuse myself," said Ven-Sa, who was midway to the floor by now. "I just remembered, I have an important appointment in a few minutes."

"Coincidentally," said Chi-Sa, "so do I."

CHAPTER
6

"Here we are," Brag-Ret said calmly, though he had just raced the hovercar at top speed in a heart-stopping slalom through the city and slammed it into a parking dock so hard that Carol just *knew* she had thrown her back out. "Let's see how the children at *this* school celebrate Federation Day!"

Carol looked at Corsi, who rolled her eyes. They both knew that it was no accident that their visit to New Mirada happened to coincide with the first annual Federation Day. In fact, Carol would not have been surprised to learn that it was Federation Day every time a Federation official dropped by New Mirada.

Sog-Ret burst from the hovercar and dragged Rennan out after her by the elbow. "Let's go, guys!" she said. "We only have fifteen *riglis* till we have to be back across town again!"

Carol slumped in her seat and watched miserably as Brag-Ret hustled Corsi out onto the moving walkway. She felt like a child herself, being hurried between tourist attractions on vacation by overzealous parents.

Truly, Brag-Ret and Sog-Ret brought new meaning to the term "overscheduling." In the two hours since beaming to the surface, Carol, Corsi, and Rennan had been propelled on a nonstop tour of the capital city of New Mirada, a capital that the Miradorn had renamed "Federation City" since the end of the Dominion War.

Already, in just two hours, the away team had visited three grade schools, two retirement homes, two hospitals, and a shopping complex, never spending more than fifteen minutes at each one. Though no one but Brag-Ret and Sog-Ret had access to the actual schedule, Carol got the impression, from hints that her guides had dropped, that the rest of the day would be at least as jam-packed as the first half had been.

And about as helpful, no doubt. Carol had seen quite enough staged imaging opportunities for one planet, thank you very much. The only thing she learned from all the pep rallies and key-to-the-city/student artwork/home-baked pastry presentations was that the New Mirada chamber of commerce was trying *way* too hard to make an impression.

Plus which, all the high-speed hoopla made her wonder what exactly the Miradorn *didn't* want her to see. The thicker they laid it on, the more suspicious she became.

Case in point. "Oh my!" said Brag-Ret, gasping as he

helped her from the hovercar. "The sunlight serves to enhance your beauty even *more*. I would not have thought it *possible*, but your loveliness grows with each passing *moment*."

Carol thanked him dutifully as the moving walkway carried her into the building. Yes, she realized, it *was* possible to hear how beautiful she was too many times in a single day. She resolved never to share this intelligence with Vance Hawkins.

As the ruckus of excited Miradorn children reached her from the open double doors up ahead, Carol made a decision. The way things were going would have been absolutely fine if she were on a simple goodwill tour, but her assignment was to dig in and assess the true state of mind of the Miradorn people vis-à-vis the Federation. She wouldn't be doing that if she kept glad-handing and small-talking for the rest of her visit.

Clearly, it was time to revise the itinerary.

When the walkway had deposited her in the noisy auditorium, Carol strolled past Sog-Ret to stand alongside Corsi.

"Hey, Domenica," said Carol, whispering in Corsi's ear. "I've got an idea."

"Me, too," said Corsi, glaring at the mob of young Miradorn children fidgeting and jabbering in the rows of seats before them. "Does yours involve settling these kids down with a wide beam phaser set on stun?"

"My idea is more along the lines of making a run for it," said Carol.

"That works, too," said Corsi.

Rennan, who was standing on the other side of Corsi, leaned in with a grin. "Count me in."

Carol sighed. "Why do we bother whispering with a Betazoid around?"

"Who said we were going to invite you?" Corsi said sternly.

"You need my superior fighting skills," said Rennan.

Corsi snorted. "I dare you to read my mind right this minute."

Rennan stared at her for a moment, then grimaced. "Now *that's* harassment, Lieutenant Commander."

"I don't know what you're talking about," said Corsi, and then she turned back to Carol. "So when do you want to run for it?"

"Good question." Carol looked around the auditorium. She saw Brag-Ret and Sog-Ret standing near the door, talking to a woman in a businesslike navy blue outfit who looked like she might be a school official. "I say there's no time like the present."

"So how do we make this happen?" said Rennan.

"Leave that to me," Corsi said with a nod. "Stay here until you get the signal. Then make a run for the hover-car."

With that, Corsi walked over to the school official and asked a question. Smiling, the official answered, after which Corsi nodded and marched out the door.

"I wonder what she said?" said Carol.

"She asked for directions to the ladies' room," Rennan said with a smirk.

Three minutes later, just as the school official had introduced Carol and Rennan, and the children were stomping their feet in applause, a piercing whine blasted through the auditorium.

All at once, every child in the room got up and

marched in an orderly fashion for the exits positioned
in the middle of each of the four walls. The adults, including the school official, observed the evacuation and
shouted occasional instructions to the children.

Rennan elbowed Carol's arm. "I'd say this must be our
signal."

"Good guess," said Carol, and then the two of them
darted out the nearest door. They made it out just ahead
of a double-file formation of Miradorn children.

Brag-Ret and Sog-Ret were not so lucky. Though not
far behind Carol and Rennan, the bombastic, bearded
twins were stuck in the auditorium, hemmed in by columns of children.

Once out in the hallway, Carol and Rennan broke into
a run. When they got to the dock, they found Corsi behind the wheel of the hovercar, revving the engine.

"Nice work," said Carol as she jumped in beside Corsi.
"You really know how to stage a diversion."

"Nothing like a good, old-fashioned fire drill," said
Corsi, whipping the hovercar away from the dock the
second Rennan's posterior hit the backseat. "Provided
you can find the right switch to pull."

CHAPTER

7

Just as Soloman leaped away from the altar in the shrine of Ho'nig, sixteen beams of destructive white energy punched down from the circle of sixteen columns and pulverized the altar into a swirling cloud of dust.

Vance raced toward Soloman, dodging a flying grenade and a shower of sparks along the way, only to be stopped in midstep by an arm that broke off a bejeweled statue and slammed into his chest. Vance went over backward, collapsing to the stone floor with a jarring impact. It was just as well, as it turned out. As he lay there, looking up, a sheet of bright green energy slid across the space above him, crackling as it lopped off the backs of pews and the top half of a statue of a pious-looking Brikar.

Just before the statue's head and shoulders dropped, Vance threw off the stone arm that had knocked him down and hastily rolled out of the way. A heartbeat later, the top of the Brikar crashed onto the spot that Vance's lower body had just occupied, breaking into chunks of rubble and sending up a puff of dust.

It was his ninth or tenth superclose call in the five minutes since the Dominion failsafe had triggered every remaining booby trap in the shrine at once. At the rate he was going, Vance thought it was pretty unlikely that he would walk out of the shrine alive, especially given the fact that he had used up all of his nine lives on S.C.E. missions long ago.

Somewhere in the middle of the mayhem, Commander Gomez was shouting orders, trying to coordinate the team's efforts to deflect and deactivate the multiple threats. So far, Vance had been having enough trouble just dodging deathtraps to be much help disabling them.

"Soloman?" said Gomez. "Are you all right?"

"Yes, Commander," Soloman said from not far away, "but the altar access terminal has been destroyed."

"Then go help Pattie at the west wall terminal," said Gomez. "See if you can implement a flash-purge from there."

"On my way, Commander," said Soloman.

"And be careful!" said Gomez.

"Understood," said Soloman. Watching from the floor, Vance could see the dim outline of the Bynar hurrying past through the drifting clouds of smoke.

Vance sat up and smacked the combadge on his chest. "Lauoc!" he said. "Report!"

"So far, so bad," Lauoc said over the combadge, shouting over the deafening whines of nearby weapons fire. "Kim and T'Mandra are pinned down. I made it to an *access panel, but this morph tech is giving me the grand-daddy of all headaches. Every time I think I've disabled something, the morphic system reconfigures to work around what I did."*

"What's your location?" said Vance, cautiously getting to his feet.

"I'm at an access point in the back wall," said Lauoc, *"trying to shut down a heat-seeking missile launcher . . . no, wait. It's reconfiguring again."* As noisy as the place was, Lauoc's disgusted curse came in loud and clear over the combadge. *"Now it's a quantum bomb set to go off in . . . three minutes. It's big enough to bring down the shrine and the entire city sector around it."*

Vance was moving before Lauoc's last word, charging toward the back wall of the shrine. As he ran, he heard projectiles whistling and the beams of energy weapons wailing around him, but he did not slow down or look around. Out of the corner of his eye, he spotted something big swinging toward him, and he kicked up his pace enough to get out of the way just in time.

A second later, he heard a woman scream behind him, and he whipped around. By the light of an overhead explosion, Vance saw a white-haired woman pinned to the wall between the prongs of what looked like the head of a giant pitchfork. From a distance, Vance could not tell if the prongs had pierced the woman's body.

Even as the countdown in his head ticked away the seconds until the quantum bomb would go off, Vance ran toward the woman instead of Lauoc. As he got closer, the first thing he noticed was that one of the prongs had indeed drawn blood from the woman's side.

The second thing he noticed was that the woman was

a Miradorn. The pearlescent skin and sharp peak of hair drawn all the way down to a spot between her eyebrows were dead giveaways.

Vance charged up to the woman and immediately grabbed hold of the fork. He pulled back on it with all his strength, but it would not budge.

The woman gasped in pain, and her eyes shot wide open. For the first time, Vance got a clear look at them.

Even in the midst of the crisis, he was struck by how strange and beautiful they were. Except for the irises, the eyes were black, flecked with gold glitter; the irises themselves were glowing white rings suspended in the darkness.

"Please hurry," said the woman, clamping her eyes shut against the pain.

"Done and done," said Vance, bracing a foot against the wall and giving the fork another yank. This time, it came free, and he tossed it aside.

"Gotta go," he said, his mental countdown swiftly approaching zero.

Gasping, the woman followed him. "My name is Em-Lin," she said. "I think I can help."

CHAPTER

8

"*Please* let me take a look," Em-Lin said a second time, louder and more firmly than the first. "Unless either of you has a *better* idea right now." Ever since she had followed Vance to the access panel for the quantum bomb system, he and Lauoc had blocked her view of the controls.

Now that Em-Lin had gotten their attention, Vance and Lauoc looked at her, then at each other, then back at her. Em-Lin saw naked and abundant skepticism in their eyes, but that was okay. She did not much care what the Starfleeters' opinions of her might be, as long as she was confident that she could do the job.

Lauoc was the first to step aside. "We have less than a minute before the quantum bomb goes off," he said, raising his voice over the latest round of weapons fire.

"It's a morphic system," said Vance. When he jabbed

a finger into the circuitry, glowing wires slithered away from his touch and reformed a connection several centimeters beyond his fingertip. "Shape-shifting technology."

Em-Lin nodded and pushed forward to the open access panel in the wall. By her reckoning, the bomb would detonate in thirty-five seconds.

There was no time for explanations, and they were unnecessary anyway. Em-Lin knew all about morphic circuitry.

The Dominion had taught her well.

Gritting her teeth against the latest surge of pain from the wound in her side, Em-Lin thrust her hand into the hip pocket of her burgundy coveralls and found the tool that she needed. It felt like a metal rod at first, but came to life when she touched it. As her fingers wrapped around it, the tool wrapped around her fingers, twisting and twining like a fast-growing vine.

She drew the device from her pocket and focused her thoughts on it, reaching out with her mind just as she had always done with Or-Lin. She felt the tool waiting, its tiny, fuzzy brain vibrating softly with the simple question that was the sum total of its desires:

What do you want me to do?

Em-Lin sent back the answer: *Turn off the bomb.*

As soon as she thought it, Em-Lin felt the tool reshaping itself for the task ahead, growing dozens of tiny, silver tentacles around its tip. When she raised it toward the open access panel, the tentacles fluttered excitedly, reaching straight out for the maze of flashing circuitry inside the opening. The tool itself grabbed hold and pulled itself the rest of the way into the gap.

"What *is* that thing?" said Vance.

Em-Lin silenced him with a wave and continued to focus her mind on the tool. At this point, the slightest distraction could mean complete disaster.

Inside the access point, the tool's tentacles grew and branched and flowed along circuitry pathways like liquid. Em-Lin felt the circuitry reacting, realigning itself to escape the intruder and preserve functionality . . . but the tool sensed every change and shifted the shape and qualities of its extrusions to compensate.

In the end, the tool was smarter and more agile than the bomb system. The bomb's control program tried one last surprise maneuver, attempting to use the tool itself to trigger detonation, but the tool caught on fast and shuffled the corrupted code into final deactivation commands.

With fewer than ten seconds left until the scheduled explosion, the quantum bomb system went permanently offline.

"All clear," said Em-Lin.

Vance kept looking from her to the tool and back. "What I want to know, is where can I get one of those?"

"Me, too," Lauoc said.

"Pretty sure we're going to want to buy 'em in bulk," said Vance.

Em-Lin's smile turned into a grimace as the pain in her side flared up. She sagged, releasing her grip on the tool, and Vance automatically wrapped an arm around her shoulders.

"You need to see our doctor," said Vance.

Em-Lin shook her head and reached for the shape-shifting tool. *Deactivate all booby traps*, she told it with her mind as soon as her hand made contact and the gelatinous substance of the device wrapped around it.

The answer flashed right back to her: *Cannot.* The tool showed her why with a series of images flickering over the link.

Disengage, Em-Lin told the tool, and then, though she didn't think it would understand, she sent it this, too: *Thank you.* Always be nice to your tools, her father had taught her.

"We can't shut down the other booby traps from here," said Em-Lin. "After activation, each trap operates independent of the overarching system. We'll have to work on one device at a time."

"If by working on the devices, you mean getting medical treatment for your injury," said Vance, "then great."

Em-Lin tried not to let Vance or Lauoc see her wince at the pain in her side, but she did not think that she hid it very well. "Do we have to get across the shrine anyway?" she said. "To get to the medical care, I mean."

"We do," said Lauoc.

"Then if we're already going in that direction," said Em-Lin, "it won't matter if we make some stops along the way, will it?"

Something exploded nearby, and Vance shook his head. "All right," he said. "But we're running you right out of here if you start getting worse."

"Fair enough," said Em-Lin. "Where's the next terminal?"

It was then, just as she slowly started forward, supported on either side by Vance and Lauoc, that Em-Lin heard Or-Lin's giggling voice in her ear once more.

I have an idea, said Or-Lin. *Why not set off the next bomb? Why not come join me, and bring the Starfleeties with you?*

Em-Lin did not dignify Or-Lin's questions with an answer. She was not about to get into an argument with a *dugo tenya*, and she certainly had no intention of doing its bidding.

Even though it wasn't like she didn't have any Starfleet blood on her hands already.

CHAPTER
9

"You can buy us as many drinks as you want," said the surly, scrawny Miradorn man. "It won't change the fact that *we don't like the Federation*!"

"Fair enough, fair enough," said Carol, raising her hands in a gesture of surrender. "I can accept that, Ti-Lat. All I want to know is, what do you like the *least* about the Federation?"

With a wide grin plastered across his face, Ti-Lat looked around at the mob of Miradorn drunks crowding Carol, Corsi, and Rennan at the bar. "Where to *begin*?" said Ti-Lat, and everyone in the room roared with laughter.

Finally, thought Carol. *Some honest answers. The kind you don't get at a grade-school assembly.*

"Excuse me," said another male Miradorn bar patron, tapping Carol on the shoulder. "I seem to have run dry."

The man's female twin tapped Carol's other shoulder, raised an empty glass, and turned it over. Only a single drop ran out. "This mysterious dry spell seems to have affected me as well."

Smiling, Carol waved at the bartender. "Another round for everyone," she said, "and it's on Starfleet!"

Every Miradorn in the barroom groaned and groused at once. Corsi looked alarmed, scanning the discontented crowd for signs of impending violence, but Carol wasn't worried. As long as Rennan, with his Betazoid sensitivities, looked relaxed—which he did—Carol knew that the danger was minimal.

Meanwhile, the information that she was getting was worth every Miradorn credit that she spent in Pash-Ta's Place. Where better to find out what people *really* thought than at a bar? Carol was growing happier with each passing minute that she had insisted on finding a place like this immediately after she and her team had escaped from Brag-Ret and Sog-Ret at the grade school.

With a fresh round in the offing, Ti-Lat downed his remaining half glass of lavender-colored liquid and slammed the glass down on the bar for a refill. "So what do I like *least* about the Federation, huh?" he said gruffly, which was how he said everything. "I've got one word for ya: *synthehol!*"

The crowd in the bar erupted in laughter and shouts of agreement. "How do you people *drink* that swill?" hollered someone. "You can't even get an honest *hangover!*" said someone else.

Corsi looked alarmed again, but Rennan stayed cool. "I can't argue with you on *that* one," Carol said with a rueful nod. "So what else don't you like?"

A disheveled Miradorn woman who had a crazy look in her eye and smelled like she hadn't bathed in a long time stumbled in front of Ti-Lat. "Tellarites!" she said, her toxic breath blasting Carol square in the face.

"What an obnoxious bunch!" someone said from the crowd. "It doesn't say much for your Federation, having them as members!"

"I say cut 'em loose!" said the crazy-eyed woman, giving Carol another blast of rancid breath.

Carol smiled as she thought of Tev. "I'll pass it along," she said. "What else don't you like?"

"The Prime Directive!" someone shouted.

Everyone roared in agreement. "Ooo, look at me," Ti-Lat said in a high-pitched voice. "I'm too *good* to interfere in the affairs of *primitive* species, even though they're the ones who *need* my help the most!"

"Too good?" hollered a man from the back of the room. "How about too *greedy*? They don't want to *share* what they've got!"

"And the Miradorn made a name for themselves *without* them!" said Ti-Lat. "When the Federation turned us down a hundred years ago, we managed to find *other* friends to help us!"

Rennan leaned past Corsi to catch Carol's eye. "The Prime Directive was applied here?" he said to her.

Carol nodded. "Long story," she said, hoping Rennan would read her mind or at least her expression and catch on that now was not the best time to go into it.

As always, Rennan got the message. He closed his mouth and leaned back without further comment.

"Primitive?" said Ti-Lat. "They called the *Miradorn* primitive?"

"We're *superior!*" said the crazy-eyed woman.

"Why, the Federation's nothing but a bunch of *pugla yort*," said Ti-Lat.

"'Half-mades,'" Carol said quietly in answer to Corsi's questioning look.

Ti-Lat caught the exchange and nosed in close to Corsi. "You're incomplete," he said, wobbling a bit from the intoxicants he'd been drinking. "Well, except for the relatively small percentage of twins you put out."

"Small compared to us!" said the crazy-eyed woman. "We're practically *all* twins!"

"You're only half there!" said a huge, bald Miradorn man with glittering tattoos on his scalp and arms. "How can you expect us to respect you if you're only half as good as we are?"

Carol nodded solemnly, taking in what was going around. Ti-Lat and the others were giving her valuable insights; though she had been aware of Miradorn prejudice toward nontwin Miradorn, she had not known that it extended to other species, and she had not known that it was as deep-seated as it seemed to be among the bar patrons. It was a fascinating contrast to the rah-rah attitudes that Carol's handlers had treated her to in the string of staged pro-Federation events.

The big question now was, were these resentments typical of the general population of New Mirada? And if they were, how might they manifest themselves in future dealings with the Federation?

Carol had a feeling that Brag-Ret and Sog-Ret would have simultaneous strokes if they knew what the Federation visitors were hearing right now.

"Anyway," said Ti-Lat, slapping Carol on the back. "No

hard feelings, right? I mean, this is all between friends, of course."

"Of course," Carol said with a smile. "We're all friends here."

"Make no mistake," said Ti-Lat. "We might not be crazy about the Federation, but we sure need you ever since the Dominion left us high and dry."

Corsi raised an eyebrow. "You need us for what?"

Ti-Lat drained the last drops of lavender liquid from his glass and turned it upside down. "We're broke," he said with a cockeyed grin. "We liked the Dominion, we really did, but they cleaned us out."

"We don't wanna marry you," said a man in the back, "but we sure could use a little Federation aid right now."

"So what you're saying is, you don't like the Federation," said Carol.

"That's exactly right!" shouted someone.

"Not a bit!" said someone else.

"You don't like our synthehol or our Prime Directive," said Carol, "and you think we're inferior *pugla yort*."

Ti-Lat nodded thoughtfully. "I'd say that about sums it up."

"But you want assistance from the Federation," said Carol, "because the Dominion, whom you *did* like, plundered Mirada's treasury."

"Yes," said Ti-Lat. "That's right."

"Don't forget how we need another round of drinks," said the crazy-eyed woman, waving a glass in Corsi's face.

"Gee," said Corsi. "You people sure make it hard to say no."

Carol just grinned. Strangely enough, she was glad to hear that the Miradorn didn't like the Federation.

More accurately, she was glad to hear the truth, because she had sensed it all along.

"Another round it is," she said. "And we'll start it with a toast. To the United Federation of Planets!"

As Carol raised her glass high, every Miradorn in the room jeered and groaned . . . which just made her smile widen.

CHAPTER
10

In addition to her skills as a restorationist, and apparently a changeling technology whiz, Em-Lin had a special talent that was becoming increasingly evident: she was great at rubbing Sonya Gomez the wrong way.

This talent began to show up shortly after the booby traps in the shrine of Ho'nig were shut down. Em-Lin had deactivated most of them with her handy changeling multitool, and Soloman had cleaned up the rest with a morphic computer virus that he'd whipped up on the fly.

As the dust settled, Dr. Elizabeth Lense treated Em-Lin's side, patching the wound left behind by the flying pitchfork. Lense had been outside the shrine during the booby trap barrage, which Gomez knew was a good thing; Lense was pregnant, the result of a relationship she'd had while shipwrecked on a dangerous planet in an alternate universe. *We really need to get her an assistant*, Gomez thought, not for the first time. However, when she brought it up with Elizabeth, the doctor brushed the notion off.

Pressed for time because of the approaching pilgrimage, Gomez debriefed Em-Lin while Lense ran the dermal regenerator over the wound site. It was the first time Gomez had had a chance to talk to Em-Lin. It only took nine words for Em-Lin to get on Gomez's bad side.

"I thought you were supposed to *preserve* the shrine." Those were the nine magic words with which Em-Lin managed to get off on the wrong foot with Gomez.

Though Gomez had been predisposed to think well of Em-Lin after the way she'd helped end the booby trap crisis, Em-Lin had pretty much thrown all her goodwill out the window in one heave. "That was never our primary objective," said Gomez, "but we certainly did our best to achieve it."

"Right." Em-Lin took a long, meaningful look around the shrine. "This is your best."

If a big cartoon thermometer were measuring Gomez's rising temper at that moment, the tip of the thermometer would have been throbbing red, radiating rippling heat lines, just about ready to explode.

"No one died," Gomez said tightly. "Given the level of difficulty involved, I'd say that's best enough for me."

Em-Lin shook her head and kept looking around at the damage, of which there was plenty. Gomez followed her gaze, further annoyed because she could understand why Em-Lin was so unhappy with what she saw.

The massive chamber was scarred and charred from one end to the other. The altar had been obliterated, and eight of the sixteen columns around it had been toppled. The floor was littered with debris from shattered statues and smashed reliquaries. The wildly colorful and intricate mural spanning the vaulted ceiling had been smudged by clouds of smoke and dust.

"Two years," said Em-Lin. "My sister and I worked two years to restore this place. She *died* restoring this place. Now all that work is gone."

Because of the Dominion, thought Gomez. *Because your people joined the Dominion and gave the Dominion the run of the place. Don't forget that part.*

At the same time she thought it, though, Gomez felt sorry for Em-Lin. It wasn't like she personally had forged the alliance with the Dominion. However Em-Lin looked at it, she was the victim of circumstances beyond her control.

Gomez shifted gears to focus Em-Lin away from what had been lost. "Thanks to you, the damage wasn't as bad as it could have been," she said. "That changeling device of yours was extremely effective in interacting with the morphic systems."

Em-Lin patted the hip pocket of her burgundy coveralls, as if to reassure herself that the device was still there. Suddenly, then, she cocked her head to one side, as if she were listening to something that Gomez could not hear.

"What is it?" said Gomez.

Em-Lin shook her head. "Nothing."

Gomez cleared her throat. "You saved some lives here today. If that quantum bomb had gone off, we'd all be dead right now."

Em-Lin had a distracted look on her face. She looked

away, then back, then away from Gomez again. "I was trying to save the shrine," she said. "That's all."

In other words, our lives don't matter to you. Gomez sighed. *I get it.*

Lense, who was medicating Em-Lin's side via hypospray, looked up from her work and rolled her eyes for Gomez's benefit.

All right then, thought Gomez. *No more niceties. You want strictly business, you've got it.*

"The changeling device," she said. "It's a leftover from the Dominion?"

"No," said Em-Lin. "Our scientists based it on Dominion morphic tech, but it's strictly Miradorn design."

That piece of information gave Gomez new respect for the Miradorn scientists. "Our team's setting up to break through into the lower chamber. We've detected signs of functioning Dominion equipment there. Any ideas what we might find?"

Em-Lin shrugged. "I didn't even know the chamber existed until today." Her eyes drifted away from Gomez, and she resumed staring into space.

"Given the knowledge you seem to have of Dominion technology, we can use your help," said Gomez. "Whatever's down there could be a hazard to the pilgrims."

"I'm sure the pilgrims will have the best *Chala Ho'nig* yet," said Em-Lin, "what with the shrine in ruins and all."

"Not exactly ruins," said Gomez.

"Not yet, maybe," said Em-Lin.

The cartoon thermometer was now straining to burst. "Let's just see if we can prevent anyone else from dying. How does that grab you?"

Em-Lin did not answer. She was too busy staring into space. Her eyes slid from side to side as if she were following the movements of something invisible to Gomez and Lense.

Pika Ven-Sa had mentioned earlier that Em-Lin was haunted after the death of her twin. Was that what Em-Lin kept staring at—the ghost of her sister?

Gomez could not quite suppress a shiver as Em-Lin's eyes slid closer and closer, as if whatever they were following was moving over to stand right next to Gomez herself.

Whatever or whoever.

Clapping her hands together, Gomez said, "Okay then. What's the good word, Elizabeth?" When Lense didn't respond, Gomez repeated her name.

"Hm? Oh, sorry, Commander." Lense closed her med-kit and nodded. "She's good to go."

I am definitely having that conversation about an assistant with Elizabeth again—maybe this time with the captain in the room. "Follow me, Em-Lin," said Gomez, taking a quick step away from the spot where she had been standing. "Let's find out what's down below."

On her way past the space that Em-Lin had been watching, Gomez felt another shiver, though she knew that she had much more to fear from a functioning Dominion facility than any supposed ghost.

CHAPTER
11

"And *fire*!" said Pattie, watching as the blinding golden beam of the phaser drill punched straight down into the crater in the floor of the shrine. The beam stabbed at the tiny hole in the obsidian-like shielding, sending up showers of sparks.

This was the same spot where Em-Lin's sister had been killed by an exploding booby trap; even after all the other explosions and weapons fire in the shrine, this was still the only site where the Dominion shielding under the floor had been breached.

The job now was to turn a pinhole into a hatchway through which people and equipment could pass. The good news was, according to Pattie's analysis, the shielding was practically impenetrable, a smart changeling tech product that could reshape itself to prevent penetration, but the section of shielding around the pinhole had been effectively "killed" by the explosion. The shielding's reformative capabilities had been negated.

Now, it was just a matter of applying the proper force to the right points around the pinhole. Done correctly, the procedure could cut a good-size hole in the shielding without sending the ceiling crashing down on whatever was in the chamber below it.

Pattie, of course, knew no way to do the job other than correctly.

She had ordered the phaser drill from the *da Vinci* and retrieved it from a beam-down site outside the zone of interference around the shrine. With help from Fabian, she had set it up on a tripod over the crater.

So long as she wasn't about to set off some undetected last-ditch booby trap, everything would work out fine.

As Pattie continued to steer the drill and watch the readouts on her tricorder, she heard someone walk up behind her. "What's our status?" said Commander Gomez, raising her voice over the loud whine of the drill.

Turning, Pattie saw that Gomez was accompanied by the Miradorn woman, Em-Lin. Pattie could see that Em-Lin was in a terrible mood—not that she could blame her, after what had happened to her sister and the shrine.

"We've punched through several points in the weakened section of the shield," said Pattie. "Time to connect the dots."

Pattie tweaked the drill's control panel, and the phaser beam slowly traced a wide arc around the circle of pinholes that she had cut. Sparks and smoke leaped out of the crater as the beam sliced through the obsidian shielding, leaving a fiery red track in the black material.

"Even without its changeling properties, this is still tough stuff," said Pattie. "Its tolerances are unbelievably high. I'd say it's a good thing the Dominion didn't deploy it during the war."

"We didn't see *any* of this changeling tech during the war," said Gomez. "I wonder if the Dominion was holding back, or if it was just a late development?"

Gomez had directed her question at Em-Lin but got no response. In fact, Em-Lin was turned away from Gomez, gazing at something that Pattie could not see.

Pattie had been around enough to know that just because she couldn't see it, that didn't mean that something wasn't there. Grabbing her tricorder, she quickly recalibrated it and aimed it in the general direction of the space at which Em-Lin was staring.

But according to the tricorder, there was nothing more in the empty space than met Pattie's eyes. If, as the priest had suggested, Em-Lin was being haunted, the ghost was undetectable by conventional sensors.

"Too bad there's no one here who used to work for the Dominion," Gomez said loudly, staring hard at Em-Lin. "Maybe they could answer our questions about changeling tech."

In addition to ignoring Gomez's comments, Em-Lin walked away without explanation.

Gomez shook her head and blew out her breath in frustration. She hiked a thumb in the direction of Em-Lin, who was still walking away. "This is the same woman who shut down half the Jem'Hadar booby traps and saved all our lives an hour ago."

"I get the impression her tolerances aren't quite as high as the Dominion shielding's," said Pattie, wiggling her antennae for emphasis.

Gomez sighed. "Let me know when you're done here," she said, starting after Em-Lin.

"Commander," said Pattie. "Something just occurred to me."

Gomez stopped. "What's that?"

"What if the Dominion wasn't holding back the changeling tech because it could help them win the war?" said Pattie. "What if they abandoned it because it's somehow too dangerous to use?"

"And we might be about to encounter great peril because of it?" said Gomez.

"Exactly," said Pattie.

"Then I'd say that would be pretty much par for the course, wouldn't you?" said Gomez, shooting Pattie a wink before scooting off after Em-Lin.

Pattie made the tinkling sound that was her equivalent of human laughter and turned back to the controls of the phaser drill.

CHAPTER
12

So maybe the truth isn't always such a great thing,
thought Carol Abramowitz as the burly, curly-haired
Miradorn male tied her to a chair. *Maybe I was better
off not knowing just how much the Miradorn dislike the
Federation.*

While Carol was being strapped to the chair, she
watched the Miradorn's twin shackle the unconscious
Corsi to an overhead metal beam in the dungeonlike
basement. Rennan already hung alongside her, also out
cold, his face bruised and swollen and his uniform torn.

As outcomes went, this was the opposite of optimal.
Thanks to the magic of twenty-twenty hindsight, Carol
realized that it had also been highly avoidable.

If only she had not bought that one last round of
drinks back at Pash-Ta's. She should have known, as

476 Robert T. Jeschonek

rowdy as the crowd had gotten, that she was pushing her luck. Sure enough, one drink too many per discontented Miradorn, and the gang had turned ugly. Rennan had sensed it coming, but by then, the first glass was already flying across the room toward Corsi's head.

Sadly, the turn for the worse had not ended with a beating at the hands of a bunch of drunken Miradorn. It just so happened that a pair of lowlife opportunists had been lurking among the crowd, and they had quickly seized the chance to capture the away team for their own purposes—which only now were becoming clear to Carol.

There was just one problem.

"There's no *money* in the Federation!" she said when one of the burly Miradorn finally removed the gag from her mouth.

The man, whose name was Zhik-Wu, sneered at Carol. "Everybody knows the Federation's *rich*," he said. "They'll pay to get you back!"

"You don't understand," said Carol, fighting to keep the exasperation she felt from slipping into her voice. "We have a *cashless society*. No *money* to pay *ransoms* with."

"You can't bluff us," said Zhik-Wu's twin brother, Pre-Wu, from across the room. The only visible difference between the twins was that Pre-Wu's blond hair was long and straight, while Zhik-Wu's was curly. "The cash'll turn up when they see we have a couple of Starfleeties for sale."

Carol watched with morbid interest as Pre-Wu set up a video camera on a tripod in front of Corsi and Rennan. As Carol realized what the consequences of her little miscalculation in Pash-Ta's would be, her heart not only sank, it plunged right through one side of the planet and out the other.

The Wu brothers were going to transmit images of the away team to Starfleet to support their ransom demands.

It would be a long time before any of the captured teammates lived down this embarrassment . . . especially Corsi, whose reputation as "Core-Breach" was fueled by legends of her prowess in battle. Her hardcore rep would not exactly get a boost from shots of her shackled in a basement, not to mention stories of how she had ended up there after a mere barroom brawl.

And it was all because Carol had wanted to find out what the Miradorn *really* thought about the Federation.

"So," she said. "Are you going to shoot some holos for your diary?"

"Just showing off the merchandise," said Pre-Wu, tapping commands into a handheld computing device. "We're going to broadcast direct to Starfleetie Command."

Carol rolled her eyes and let her head slump, chin touching her chest. *Please, not Starfleet Command,* she thought. *We will never live this down.*

"What do you think?" Zhik-Wu said to his brother. "A million bars of gold-pressed latinum per hostage?"

"We can do better," said Pre-Wu. "How about a million and a half?"

Carol raised her head from her chest. "Did I mention that the Federation's a cashless society?" she said.

"Why not ask for two million apiece?" said Zhik-Wu. "It can't hurt to ask, can it?"

"Then I say three," Pre-Wu said with a greedy grin that exposed the worst dental care that Carol had yet seen on New Mirada. "I think that's good."

"I think that's our magic number," said Zhik-Wu, reaching out to shake Pre-Wu's hand.

"For the last time," said Carol, "the Federation has no *currency*. When you make your ransom demand, that is *exactly* what they will tell you."

Zhik-Wu stared at Carol with a bemused expression on his face, then looked up at the ceiling. "Hey!" he hollered, directing his voice upward. "They're trying to tell us the Federation has no money!"

"Lies!" said a voice from upstairs, what sounded like the voice of an old woman. "The Federation is *loaded*!"

"There." Zhik-Wu smirked smugly at Carol. "You see?"

"Who was that?" said Carol, looking up at the ceiling.

"Mother," said Pre-Wu. "She knows everything."

Carol felt like she was trapped in a truly bizarre nightmare. "That's good," she said, "because in that case, I've got a few questions for her."

"You're lucky you were lying," said Zhik-Wu, adjusting some controls on his handheld computer.

"Why is that?" said Carol.

Suddenly, the old woman's voice again shouted down from above. "Because if we aren't paid by the deadline," she said, "we'll have to start killing hostages."

"That's our ultimatum," said Pre-Wu.

"So it's a good thing the Federation's loaded," said Zhik-Wu.

Carol looked up, wondering just how good the old bat's hearing was. Then, she looked down, wondering if a day that had started out so harmlessly could possibly end with her or one of her teammates stone-cold dead at the hands of a couple of Miradorn morons.

CHAPTER
13

Thank you for coming down here, sister, said Or-Lin's voice in Em-Lin's head. *This place will be your tomb, and we will be together forever in death.*

Em-Lin stood frozen as the others continued ahead of her, fanning out in the dark Dominion chamber under the shrine of Ho'nig. Or-Lin's voice had become stronger and clearer than ever, as if Or-Lin herself were becoming more real.

Do not be afraid. I will be with you every step of the way as you die.

Em-Lin took a deep breath and tried to steady herself. The beam from the wrist beacon on her right arm shook in time with the shivers rippling through her body.

It was getting harder for her to hold herself together, which she knew was not a good thing right now. She had accompanied the Starfleet team and their Miradorn security escort in descending through the hatchway that Pattie had cut into the secret Dominion chamber, and who knew what fresh dangers lurked around her.

Em-Lin turned slowly in a half circle, casting the light from her wrist beacon at the banks of dormant equipment lining the walls. She wondered where Or-Lin would appear next and what the *dugo tenya* would say when next she whispered in Em-Lin's ear.

She wondered also how Or-Lin could possibly be growing stronger and more real. Typically, a *dugo tenya* faded away as time passed, completely disappearing after days, weeks, or months, depending on the nature of the traumatic death and the force of the twins' original bond.

To Em-Lin's mind, the strengthening of Or-Lin's *dugo tenya* could mean one of three things: Em-Lin was losing her mind; Or-Lin was not a figment of Em-Lin's mind at all, but a genuine ghost (though Em-Lin had never believed in such things before); or . . .

Or Or-Lin was not the dead one, and Em-Lin was the one who was fading away.

Suddenly, someone touched Em-Lin's shoulder. With a cry of surprise, she leaped away from the contact, heart thundering as if it had enlarged to fill her entire chest.

Whipping the wrist beacon around, Em-Lin caught a face in the bright circle of light. It was a familiar face, but not the one that she had expected to see, not Or-Lin's.

It was Vance Hawkins of Starfleet.

"Sorry if I spooked you," he said. "You probably shouldn't separate from the group down here."

"Oh . . . no, that's . . ." Em-Lin's breathing was fast, and her pulse raced. She pressed her hand to her chest, trying to regain control of herself. "No problem."

Em-Lin saw an unmistakable glint of concern in Vance's eyes. "Are you sure you're all right?" he said, squinting against the beam of the beacon. "I can send you back up to the shrine with Kim or T'Mandra until we get the lights on down here."

"No . . . thank you. I'm fine." Em-Lin swung the beacon away from him. Just as she did so, she thought she saw something behind him. Something or someone.

A shape at the edge of the light. Something or someone in the darkness, less than a meter away.

Em-Lin swung the beacon back around to Vance, but the shape was no longer behind him. Instead of relief, however, Em-Lin felt more anxious than before, wondering where exactly the shape had gone and what it had been.

Vance threw up an arm to shield his eyes from the light. "How about if we catch up with the others?"

"Sure," said Em-Lin, her voice shaking as she peered into the darkness around her. She heard a rustling noise then, and she spun, cutting the shadows with her wristbeacon. The light caught just the tail end of something moving fast, flickering past.

"Em-Lin?" said Vance, taking hold of her right arm.

You will not leave this place alive, said Or-Lin's voice, whispering in Em-Lin's left ear, after which Or-Lin giggled softly.

Em-Lin's skin crawled, and she threw herself at Vance, anchoring herself to the one living person she could find in the darkness.

It was just then that the chamber filled with light.

Immediately, Em-Lin looked all around for a sign of the *dugo tenya*. She found nothing.

"Excuse me," said Vance, gently freeing himself from her grip. "All clear, ma'am."

Em-Lin pulled away and straightened her burgundy coveralls. She felt embarrassed, but just a little. Her fear of the lurking *dugo tenya*, be it a figment of her traumatized mind or an actual haunting spirit, was still her foremost emotion.

"Shall we?" said Vance, gesturing toward the rest of his teammates, who were gathered around a huge, glowing tank filled with liquid in the middle of the massive chamber. "I don't want to miss anything."

Em-Lin nodded. She even managed a small, quick smile. As little as she cared for Starfleeters after her experience at the Rasha Nom depot during the war, there was something about Vance that she liked, something that impressed her even in the thick of her conflict with the *dugo tenya*.

"Me either," she said, starting forward, listening as she walked for a set of following footsteps that did not belong to Vance: the footsteps of her dead twin sister.

CHAPTER

14

"It looks like a lava lamp," said Fabian, gazing appreciatively into the transparent, red-tinted tank in the heart of the vast chamber under the shrine. "Only a lot bigger."

The tank was several meters in diameter and extended high overhead, almost to the ceiling. It fattened as it descended toward a bulge at the base, resembling a laboratory flask.

A ring of instrumentation encircled the base, complete with control panels, monitors, and sensor prods extending into the tank itself. Clumps of some kind of protoplasmic substance were suspended in the liquid inside the tank, constantly oozing together and flowing apart to form new configurations.

"What's a lava lamp?" said Gomez.

"A late-twentieth-century tabletop lighting device,"

said Fabian, "as you would know if you ever accepted the invitation to join me in my *Disco Kung Fu Superstar '76* holo-program."

"What's disco?" said Pattie.

"Never mind," Fabian said with an exasperated wave. Something told him that instead of trying to explain disco to a Nasat, he should quit while he was ahead. "So what's it supposed to do?"

Soloman sat at one of the control terminals mounted at the base of the giant tank. "Unknown at this time," he said, a trace of annoyance in his voice. "The morphic systems down here are incredibly robust. They are resisting my efforts to crack the programming or database."

"Guesses, anyone?" said Gomez, slowly walking around the base of the tank.

"No guess yet, but I have information," said Pattie, standing up on her hind legs and aiming her tricorder at the tank. "The clumps in the tank are similar in composition to Em-Lin's changeling multitool, which in turn bears a strong resemblance to Founder physiology."

"Could it be a Founder nursery, maybe?" said Fabian, reaching out to touch the surface of the tank. A jot of static electricity snapped the tip of his finger as he made contact. The tank's surface felt warm and surprisingly rough to the touch, like gritty sandpaper.

"There's biochemical activity," said Lense, scanning the tank with a tricorder on the opposite side from Pattie. "I'm reading neuroelectric activity as well, but no cellular mitosis. No cell division. The organic clusters could be fetal life-forms in some sort of cryogenic suspension, but they're not growing and developing right now."

"Maybe it's some kind of supercomputer," said Fabian, "utilizing cultured changeling material to process information the way we use bioneural gel-packs."

"Whatever it is," said Gomez, "I think it might be a prototype. An experimental construct. I've never seen or read about anything quite like it being used by the Dominion."

"There we go." Soloman lifted his hands away from the keyboard that they had been battering. "I think I just about have it. I should be inside the secure shell in a matter of minutes."

"Great," said Gomez, and then she turned to Em-Lin, who was standing off to one side with Vance. As usual, Em-Lin looked thoroughly distracted, staring off into space with a troubled frown knotting her features. "Em-Lin." Gomez raised her voice to cut through whatever vision was holding the Miradorn's attention. "Em-Lin. You've had experience with changeling technology. Any thoughts on this device?"

When Em-Lin did not respond, Vance gently elbowed her in the side. Em-Lin's focus swung back to everyone else's shared reality instead of whatever was going on in her head, though she was confused enough that Gomez had to repeat her question.

Back on track, Em-Lin stepped closer to the giant tank. She gazed up at it, the glow from within suffusing her pearly skin with a red tint.

"I don't have a clue," she said, "but I'm not really qualified to judge. I was basically a menial laborer."

Fabian shot Gomez a look, frowning at what he considered to be an obvious lie. Shutting down all those

Jem'Hadar booby traps had not been the work of a menial laborer.

Gomez nodded in agreement. "A menial laborer who can manipulate sophisticated Dominion technology with ease. What exactly was the nature of this 'menial labor,' anyway?"

Fabian watched Em-Lin for a reaction, but he was disappointed. Her attention had already drifted to whatever invisible distraction lay on the floor at her feet.

"Em-Lin?" said Gomez. "Hello?"

"Good timing on the zone-out," said Fabian. "I'm starting to wonder if she really sees anything there after all."

"Coincidentally, I was just wondering the same thing," said Gomez, glowering at Em-Lin.

It was just then, after Gomez spoke, that four things happened in a row. They happened so close together that Fabian immediately decided they were connected.

The first thing that happened was that Soloman got up from his chair at the control panel and said, "I'm in. I'm through the shell."

The second thing that happened was that the giant red tank suddenly changed color, shifting to bright yellow, and started to rotate. Inside the tank, the protoplasmic clumps began to spin, swirling in circles and accelerating the speed at which they merged and split apart.

The third thing that happened was that the Miradorn security personnel, Yet-Nu and Boz-Nu, started screaming hysterically. Yet-Nu dropped to the floor, and Boz-Nu bounced his head repeatedly against the side of the tank.

The fourth thing that happened was this: Em-Lin also screamed and fell to the floor. "Get away from me!" she said, throwing her hands protectively over her head and looking up in terror as if someone were standing over her. *"Leave me alone!"*

As Vance rushed to Em-Lin's side and Soloman leaped back into his chair and resumed attacking the keyboard, Fabian shrugged. "I'm pretty sure we're about to find out what this thing is supposed to do. What do you want to bet it's extremely dangerous and nearly unstoppable?"

CHAPTER

15

"Since you have failed to meet our ransom demands," said Zhik-Wu, "we must kill our first hostage. Which one will it be?"

Slowly, Zhik-Wu turned in a circle, pointing the tip of the long, jagged blade at Corsi, then continuing on to Rennan.

He stopped at Carol. "I choose this one," he said, shaking the knife in Carol's direction. "No one can save her! She dies now, and her death will be on your head, Federation!"

As Zhik-Wu took a step toward her, Carol shook her head. "Too over the top. And since you insist on going with the line about the Federation's head, I'd at least make it 'heads,' okay?"

"She's right!" said Mother Wu from upstairs. "Make it 'heads'!"

"All right, all right." Zhik-Wu looked sick and tired of being told what to do. He ruffled the heap of curly blond hair atop his head and shuffled over to Pre-Wu, who stood behind the camera.

"You know what I think? I think you're ready to go live." Pre-Wu grinned and slapped Zhik-Wu on the back. "You're gonna make us rich, brother!"

Carol's heart beat faster as she realized that Zhik-Wu was done rehearsing his part. At her urging, he had practiced for the last hour or so, running through what he would say during each broadcast—from the initial demands to the killing of the hostages. She had done her best to drag things out, making as many suggestions as she dared and delaying the first broadcast to Starfleet—until now.

Any minute now, the Wu brothers would shoot images of their prisoners to Starfleet Command. Everyone would know that Carol had made a dumb mistake, and that Corsi and Rennan had been caught flat-footed in a bar fight.

At least it wouldn't matter for long, once the Wu brothers killed their hostages, which, inevitably, they would do when the cashless society of the Federation failed to pay the ransom.

So there was a silver lining to this whole mess after all, Carol supposed.

"Do I look okay?" Zhik-Wu asked his brother.

Pre-Wu brushed a stray curl back from Zhik-Wu's forehead and nodded proudly. "Just relax. Reach across the link to me if you get nervous."

"What are you waiting for down there?" shouted Mother Wu. "Do you want me to call Starfleet myself?"

"No, Mother," Zhik-Wu and Pre-Wu said at the same time.

"Then let's go!" said Mother Wu. "I'm getting bored!"

The brothers looked up at the ceiling and shook their heads, then smiled at each other.

"I've got a good feeling about this," said Zhik-Wu, walking over to stand in front of the camera.

"You're going to knock 'em dead," said Pre-Wu, giving his brother a big thumbs-up sign.

It was just then, at that exact moment, that the Wu brothers started screaming.

They fell to the floor at the same time, writhing and clutching at their heads. Zhik-Wu knocked over the camera, which crashed down on Pre-Wu, but Pre-Wu was so completely caught up in his own agony that he didn't seem to notice.

Whatever affected the brothers, however, did not seem to have touched Mother Wu. "What's going on down there? Boys? Are you all right?"

Carol watched the twins thrashing on the floor in front of her. Just moments ago, they had been talking about killing her and her teammates, but she still felt compelled to try to help them.

"They're in pain," she said, shouting over the twins' screaming to reach Mother Wu. "It seemed to hit them both at the same time."

"I'll be right down!" Mother Wu sounded intensely annoyed instead of deeply worried about her sons. "And I will warn you right now—I'm ready for you, Starfleetie!"

"What does she think you're going to do?" said Corsi. "Talk her into hurting herself?"

Surprised, Carol looked in the direction of her shackled teammates. Sure enough, Corsi's eyes were wide open and staring back at her.

"Domenica!" said Carol, glad that her friend was awake, if not especially mobile. "If you're about done hanging around over there, we could use a foolproof escape plan right about now."

"Looks like we've already got a distraction," said Corsi, nodding toward the screaming Miradorn twins on the floor. "Just throw me a phaser rifle, and I'll get us out of here in nothing flat."

"It's a deal," said Carol, "just as soon as you cut through my bonds and set me free."

Corsi smirked. "I'll take care of that in a minute, just as soon as I figure out what story I'm going to write up in my mission report instead of the actual truth."

At that moment, a shrill voice cut through the commotion. "What did you do to my boys?" Following the harsh sound of that voice, Carol looked over and up, spotting the voice's possessor as she cautiously descended a spiral stairway in a corner of the basement.

Carol immediately recognized the voice as belonging to Mother Wu. She did not, however, connect the real Mother Wu with the image of the ancient, wrinkled, hunchbacked hag that she had built up in her mind to go with that sharp voice. Mother Wu, as it turned out, was pretty, petite, and much younger than Carol had imagined. Her hair was long and black and glossy, without a trace of gray, and her skin was smooth as a peach. She looked too young, in fact, to have two grown sons like Zhik-Wu and Pre-Wu.

She did not look out of place, however, handling the double-barreled Jem'Hadar disruptor rifle that she was keeping trained on Carol.

"Do I *look* like I could do anything to your boys?" said Carol, straining against her bonds for emphasis. "I was hoping that *you* could tell *me* what happened. They both started screaming and dropped to the floor at the same time."

As Mother Wu crossed the room, she narrowed her eyes at Carol, sizing her up. Without shifting the rifle's aim away from Carol, she swung her attention to Zhik-Wu and Pre-Wu on the floor.

As Zhik-Wu screamed and twisted at her feet, Mother Wu stared down at him. "What's wrong with you?" she said, loud enough to be heard over his cries. "Tell me what's wrong!"

Zhik-Wu kept screaming hysterically with eyes clamped shut and fingers clawing at his skull.

"Do these look like the symptoms of any Miradorn illness you know of?" Carol said to Mother Wu.

"Brain fever, maybe," said Mother Wu, "but their skin hasn't turned orange yet."

"Maybe you should get a doctor," said Carol.

"I don't trust doctors," said Mother Wu.

"Then maybe you should untie me and let me help," said Carol.

"I'll call a doctor," said Mother Wu, and then she went back upstairs.

Five minutes later, she returned to the basement. The expression on her face was equal parts mystified and highly irritated.

"What?" said Carol. "What is it?"

"I can't find a doctor," said Mother Wu. "I can't find anyone to help."

"Why?" said Carol.

"Everyone in the city has come down with the same thing that Zhik and Pre have," said Mother Wu. "According to the news broadcasts, the whole world seems to be coming down with it."

CHAPTER

16

Now, now, said Or-Lin as she bent down over Em-Lin. *Try to calm down, sister. It isn't the end of the world, is it?*

Em-Lin shivered, staring up wide-eyed from the floor of the Dominion chamber. Somehow, Or-Lin had become more real, manifesting for the first time since her death so that Em-Lin could perceive her with multiple senses at once. Em-Lin could hear her, see her, and feel her touch all at the same time, as if she were still alive right there in the room with her.

This, to Em-Lin, was not a welcome change. Her resurrected sister had the same twisted edge that she had been flaunting since the explosion that had killed her.

Death isn't what it used to be, apparently. Especially down here. Or-Lin smiled as she looked around the chamber, her gaze lingering on the giant tank at its heart.

Ironic, isn't it? If that bomb hadn't blown me up, no one would have found this place and come down here. You wouldn't have brought me here, and I wouldn't have gotten such a big post-life recharge.

"Em-Lin?" Another voice broke through then, a voice that Em-Lin recognized as Vance's. "Can you hear me?" She tried to focus on that voice and block out Or-Lin's, but she felt sluggish and had trouble tuning out her sister.

"Go away!" said Em-Lin, but Or-Lin continued to smile down at her. For his part, Vance looked uncertain as to whether or not he was the one Em-Lin was telling to leave.

Slowly, Or-Lin shook her head. *I'm not going anywhere, big sister. Thanks to the Vorta's device and the little Bynar, I'll be with you all the time now.*

"What?" Em-Lin's heart raced at the thought of the *dugo tenya* becoming a permanent part of her life. She had loved her sister when she was alive—except at the end, when Or-Lin had threatened her with Division—and she did not wish her ill now that she was dead, but she knew that going through life with a *dugo tenya* would be enough to drive her out of her mind.

The little Bynar hasn't mastered changeling programming yet, said Or-Lin. *He accidentally ramped up the system's output far ahead of schedule. The good news is, the power boost made me more real than ever. The bad news is, the system is out of control and will pretty much wipe out the Miradorn species.*

"Em-Lin?" said Vance, his voice sounding very far away. "Tell me what's wrong."

I want us to get off on the right foot for our new

arrangement, said Or-Lin. *That's why I'm going to help you fix the Founder's device and save the day.*

"I don't want to fix it," said Em-Lin.

Why not? After all, you helped build it in the first place.

"I've given them a mild sedative," said Lense, withdrawing the hypo from Boz-Nu's arm. "It's limiting the expression of the seizures but not stopping them."

"What's causing them?" said Gomez, staring down at Boz-Nu and Yet-Nu on the floor. The two men squirmed and groaned fitfully, grimacing in agony as they clawed at their skulls.

"I'm still working it out," said Lense. "The seizures originate in the overlobe, the part of the Miradorn cerebral cortex that governs the extrasensory linkage between twins. In both men, neural activity in the overlobe has exceeded all normal levels and become highly erratic. Em-Lin's different, though."

Gomez looked across the chamber to where Em-Lin sat back against a wall, talking to thin air while Vance tried to press a bottle of water into her hand.

"In what way?" said Gomez.

"A different region of her brain has been hyperstimulated," said Lense. "A lobe associated primarily with functions related to REM sleep and dreaming."

"What's the prognosis?" said Gomez.

"With Em-Lin, I have no idea," said Lense. "The men, I believe, will eventually suffer permanent damage from the seizures. Perhaps fatal damage." Lense let out a long breath.

"Are you okay, Elizabeth?" Gomez asked. The doctor looked a bit ashen and very fatigued.

"I'm fine. Just need to sit down for a second."

Gomez didn't buy that in the least, but there were more pressing issues. While Lense found a chair, Gomez walked to the control panels at the base of the tank and asked Soloman and Fabian, "Any idea how widespread the effect might be?"

"We're still trying to figure out what the effect *is*," Fabian said without turning from his work.

Better safe than sorry, thought Gomez. She touched the combadge on her chest. "Saf-Lig?" she said, calling the Miradorn security officer whose team was protecting the shrine above. She planned to instruct him to evacuate the entire local quadrant of the surrounding city in case the effect spread outward from the Dominion facility.

That was what she would have told him to do if he had answered her call, at least. She tried to reach him a total of five times before she gave up on him; she tried his twin brother, Gre-Lig, but got the same result.

It was then that she knew, even before she contacted the *da Vinci*, that the Miradorn seizure effect had done more damage than had been immediately apparent from the isolation of the Dominion facility.

CHAPTER
17

The street outside Mother Wu's house was filled with screaming Miradorn of all ages. Flames and smoke billowed out of the windows of nearby homes. In the distance, Carol saw a hovercar shoot from the sky at a steep angle and plunge toward the ground, its crash landing marked by an explosion.

"It's usually a quieter neighborhood than this," said Mother Wu. "I've never seen it like this before."

Carol nodded. She had a feeling of terrible awe at the chaos around her, amplified by the awareness that the same scene was taking place all over the planet of New Mirada at the same moment.

It was overwhelming. Carol was filled with the primal urge to run, to get away before whatever was destroying these people turned on her, too. At the same time, she felt torn in a thousand different directions because there were too many suffering people just in that one small area and she could never hope to help them all.

When the familiar shimmer of the transporter effect appeared in front of her, Carol immediately felt relieved. Four of her shipmates materialized, bringing with them the hope that even this apocalyptic disaster could somehow be averted.

Without waiting for introductions, Mother Wu pushed in front of Carol and eyed the new arrivals. "Which one's the doctor?" she said. "You?" She pointed the barrel of the disruptor rifle at the chest of Ellec Krotine, one of the two security guards who accompanied the medical team.

"Uh, no," the Boslic woman said quickly.

"Our doctor's on Zasharu," said Carol. Stepping forward, she gestured at the human woman standing beside Krotine. "Nurse Wetzel will do what she can for your boys."

Mother Wu looked disgusted, but she lowered the rifle. Carol had lived up to her end of the deal, summoning medical assistance from the *da Vinci* in return for being freed from her bonds in the basement.

Now it was time for Mother Wu to complete the bargain. "Why don't you show Nurse Wetzel where your sons are?" said Carol. "And while you're at it, unshackle my friends."

"All right, all right," said Mother Wu, heading back into the house. "Follow me." Sandy Wetzel fell into step behind her.

"How about that gun?" Carol shouted after them.

Mother Wu blew out her breath and stomped back to

Carol. "I expect it back," she said, tossing the rifle into Carol's arms.

It was the last provision of the deal between them. "Thanks," said Carol. "And good luck with your boys." Carol thought that was a pretty generous thing to say, considering the "boys" had kidnapped her and her team and threatened to kill them, but Mother Wu seemed unimpressed and marched away without another word.

"Such a sweet woman," said Krotine dryly. "Why isn't she screaming her lungs out and rolling around on the ground like all the other Miradorn out here?"

"I don't know," said Carol. "Maybe because she doesn't have a twin? I haven't seen one, anyway. It's just a guess. Have the engineers been able to figure out what's causing this?" She spread her arms wide to encompass the screaming madness all around them.

The other security guard, Madeleine Robins, said, "Whatever's happening, it's hit Zasharu, too. Apparently there's some tech device in the old Dominion facility there. Tev's taking a team down there to try to figure it out."

Just then, a little girl with short brown hair hurled herself to the street in front of Carol, screaming and twitching. Not far away, her twin lay silent and still on the pavement, eyes and mouth gaping at the sky.

Dantas Falcão, the medical technician who had beamed down with the team at Carol's request, ran to aid the twin. Carol was right behind her.

CHAPTER
18

"You want to know what's causing the seizures?" said Fabian. "Everything."

"Everything?" said Gomez.

"Everything," said Fabian. "In a manner of speaking."

"But not all at once," said Soloman.

Gomez stood behind the two, watching as they worked at the control panels around the base of the tank. "Consider my curiosity aroused," she said. "Tell me more."

"This device is a transmitter," said Fabian, thumping the transparent tank with his fist. "It's broadcasting the signal that's affecting the Miradorn's overlobes and triggering the seizures."

"We experienced difficulty isolating the signal," said Soloman, "because it is a morphic signal. A *changeling* signal."

"The *type* of transmission is constantly changing," said Fabian. "It might start out as a subspace radio wave, then switch to an X-ray or ultraviolet light or electromagnetic radiation or a stream of tachyons or chronitons. While in transit, the signal cycles randomly through a multitude of types and frequencies of transmittable waves or particles."

"Wow," said Gomez. "How is that even possible?"

Fabian shrugged. "We haven't figured that out yet."

"But we know what happens when the signal is received by a Miradorn brain," Lense said from the floor, where she was treating Yet-Nu and Boz-Nu. "The signal turns the Miradorn's own linking abilities against them. The overlobe, which is already capable of sending and receiving neuroelectric signals, opens the floodgates. The overlobe goes into overdrive. It fires off bursts of neuroelectric energy in all directions like a porcupine firing quills, only continuously. It blasts other Miradorn minds and opens itself up to identical blasts from those other minds in turn."

Gomez thought for a moment. "But Miradorn should only be able to link with their twins, right?"

"Yes," said Lense. "This device effectively links much larger groups, though it does so in a destructive fashion."

"Larger," said Gomez. "How large? Do we know the range yet?"

Pattie spoke up from a control board on the opposite side of the tank. She was standing on her hind legs, manipulating controls with the pincers on her forelegs. "The entire moon," she said. "The signal strength from this transmitter is enough to reach all Miradorn on Zasharu."

"But not beyond?" said Gomez.

"Not beyond," said Pattie.

"But the same phenomenon is blanketing New Mirada," said Gomez. "Therefore . . ." She touched her combadge. "Gomez to Tev."

"Tev here." The huge, hysterical crowd in the background sounded even more hysterical than before.

"There's a second transmitter," said Gomez. "It must be on the surface of New Mirada."

"I suspected as much," said Tev.

Of course you did, thought Gomez. "Contact the *da Vinci* and initiate a search from orbit," she said.

"Leave it to those crazy Founders," said Fabian. "They set up *twin* transmitters to fry the minds of the Miradorn people, who are predominantly *twins*."

"For those who like a little irony with the suffering they inflict," said Gomez.

"You just described the Founders, all right," said Fabian.

"We'll continue to work with the Zasharu device," Gomez told Tev, "and we'll notify you of our progress."

"We will do the same," said Tev, his voice nearly drowned out by the commotion surrounding him. *"In the meantime, Corsi, Abramowitz, Wetzel, and Falcão are mounting a triage effort."*

"Is a security detail with them beyond Domenica?" Gomez asked.

"Affirmative. Robins, Konya, and Krotine are there as well. Bartholomew and I will attempt to do something useful."

"What's that supposed to mean?" Gomez snapped.

"Simply that medical efforts are fruitless as long as we are unable to halt the established progression of the attacks."

"Then we'd best stop talking and start—"

"Commander!" said Dr. Lense.

Gomez spun toward Lense. The first thing Gomez noticed was that Boz-Nu was convulsing and wailing on the floor, but Yet-Nu was not.

"Yet-Nu is dead," said Lense. "I don't think his brother will be far behind."

CHAPTER
19

"I wish you would die again," said Em-Lin, talking to the empty space to the right of Vance Hawkins's head. "I wish you would die and stay dead this time."

Vance got up from crouching in front of Em-Lin and rubbed the back of his neck. No matter what he said or did, he could not seem to get through to her. She was lost in the depths of the haunting vision that had completely superimposed itself over reality since the Dominion transmitter had kicked into high gear.

It figured. The only Miradorn he could stomach, a Miradorn who had earned his respect by single-handedly defusing a quantum bomb booby trap and saving many lives, and she was locked up tight in a world of her own with the ghost of her dead twin sister. He had listened to her talking to her sister, Or-Lin, long enough to know that it was not a pleasant world to inhabit.

Maybe it was time for him to stop trying to bring her out of it. If she had been any other Miradorn, in fact, he would not have tried as long as he had already. It wasn't his job, anyway; Lense, not the deputy chief of security, was responsible for treating nonresponsive victims of trauma.

So why was he even now trying to think of a way to break through to Em-Lin?

She had proven herself to him by saving lives, but the truth was, she had worked for the Dominion. For all he knew, she could have contributed, directly or indirectly, to the prison camp operation on Jomej VII.

Still, he had a gut feeling that she deserved to be rescued from the private hell in which she was suffering. In addition, Vance hoped that her expertise with changeling technology might help to deactivate the Dominion transmitter and save the Miradorn on Zasharu.

He crouched down in front of her again. Maybe, he thought, it was time to try something more creative. If this didn't work, he could always summon T'Mandra from patrolling the shrine above and ask her to try a Vulcan mind-meld as a last-ditch effort.

Vance activated his wrist beacon and aimed its beam directly into Em-Lin's eyes. At first, Em-Lin continued to look off to one side, watching her invisible tormentor. Then, Vance moved the beacon into the space that she was watching, fixing it right on her eyes, and when he slid it away, her gaze followed it.

Before Em-Lin's eyes could drift back to the empty space into which they had been staring, Vance spoke.

This time, however, was different from all the other times when he had tried to reach her by talking.

For one thing, he was shouting in her face. For another thing, his words were not actually directed at Em-Lin.

"Or-Lin," he said, holding the light from his beacon steady in Em-Lin's eyes. "I need to talk to your sister. *Please*, let her talk to me."

Em-Lin's eyes flicked to one side, then back, then away again. She did not say a word.

"It's an emergency," said Vance. "Dominion devices are killing the people of New Mirada and Zasharu. I believe Em-Lin can help deactivate them."

Em-Lin's eyes returned to focus on the light from Vance's beacon . . . then slid back to the empty space again. Her mouth opened, but still she said nothing.

"Please, Or-Lin," said Vance. "Let her talk to me. I only want to save your people."

"She's here all the time now," Em-Lin said suddenly, her eyes returning to the light. "Before, it was only some of the time."

Vance switched off his wrist beacon.

"To me, she's like a living, breathing person," said Em-Lin. "I can see her, hear her, and touch her all at once. Not that that's a good thing. We weren't exactly getting along before she died, and our relationship hasn't improved since then."

"Thank you for letting your sister talk to me, Or-Lin," said Vance.

"You both want the same thing," said Em-Lin. "You want me to help repair the Dominion transmitter."

"Can you do it?" said Vance. "You know your way around changeling technology better than any of us."

"I can do some of it," said Em-Lin, "but I'm not familiar with all the components. You'll need someone else to do the rest."

"Do you have someone in mind?" said Vance.

"Or-Lin," said Em-Lin. "My dead twin sister says to tell you she'll be happy to help."

CHAPTER
20

Carol threw back her head and screamed as loud as she could. Even then, she was drowned out by the sea of screaming Miradorn all around her.

But it helped her to keep going, and that in itself was pretty amazing.

Falcão was so overwhelmed by the ongoing chaos that she didn't seem to notice Carol's outburst. Of the rest of the triage team, only Corsi looked in her direction, and then only briefly. As for Rennan, it was impossible to tell if he had dismissed the scream with his telepathic abilities as not signaling danger, or if he was just too distracted by the mob of shrieking children who were clawing at him, too distracted to pay any attention.

Every last one of them was in hell—the triage team and the Miradorn children and grown-ups and old-timers—so why *not* scream? Those who weren't screaming on the surface of New Mirada were in a tiny minority today.

The same for those who were trying, in the face of utter hopelessness, to lessen the suffering. Carol's triage team of four was outnumbered by the thousands out there in the street in front of Mother Wu's house.

And every single victim of Overlobe Syndrome whom they tried to assist ended up comatose and dead. So far, Carol had not met a single survivor.

Just now, in fact, right before Carol's own screaming fit, twin infants had died in her arms. Two tears ran down her face, one for each of the babies, as she caught Corsi's eye.

Without a word, Corsi pushed her way through the crowd and took the babies from Carol. She disappeared in the screaming horde, taking the tiny bodies to the same place where she had been delivering all the dead. Carol did not know where that place was, and she had absolutely no desire to see it.

Moments after she gave up the infants, Carol found two more children, no more than toddlers, screaming in the middle of the street. One of them, a boy, had a bloody head wound that clearly required immediate treatment.

Carol turned to call for Falcão—and caught her breath. The barrel of a very large gun was aimed right at her, less than a meter from her face.

A tall Miradorn man with patchy silver hair held the gun with one hand. The other hand clawed at his head, and his features were contorted in an agonized grimace.

He was shaking, and he looked unsteady on his feet. "Make it stop," he said, his voice breaking. "Make it stop make it stop make it stop!"

"I'll do what I can," said Carol, extending a hand. "Please give me the gun."

Suddenly, the man released a shuddering howl. His eyes clamped shut, and his finger squeezed the trigger.

Before Carol could react, she felt something slam into her and knock her to one side. She heard the piercing, oscillating whine of a disruptor beam blast by as she toppled onto the writhing bodies of afflicted Miradorn on the pavement.

Looking up, Carol saw someone trying to wrestle the gun away from the man. It was a Miradorn woman, and Carol instantly recognized her as soon as she caught the briefest glimpse of her face.

The woman was petite and pretty, with glossy black hair and smooth skin. Though she was older than she looked, she overpowered the gunman in a flash, wrenching away his weapon and knocking him unconscious with a single chop to the side of his throat.

Carol knew her as Mother Wu.

"I'm back," said Mother Wu, stuffing the gun in a pants pocket and reaching out to help Carol to her feet.

"Thank you," said Carol. "Thank you for the rescue."

"I'm here to help," said Mother Wu. "What do you need me to do?"

Carol hesitated before asking the question on her mind, but then she asked it anyway. "What about your boys?" she said.

"Nurse Wetzel couldn't do anything for them," said Mother Wu. Her voice was matter-of-fact. "They're both dead."

Carol looked at her, strangely filled with pity for Mother Wu and her "boys." They had kidnapped her, but she felt only sympathy and sadness for them now.

It was the same way she felt about the whole planet, she realized. The Miradorn had helped the Dominion bring death and destruction to the Federation, and hard feelings remained on both sides, but now that the Miradorn were suffering and dying, nothing that had happened before seemed to matter.

All that was left was the sympathy of one creature of flesh and blood for another. In the end, that was what all life boiled down to.

A single tear traced its way down Carol's cheek. As the world continued to scream around her, she lunged forward and wrapped her arms around Mother Wu, hugging her tightly.

Mother Wu was stiff against her and never relaxed. Eventually, though, she reached around and patted Carol's back as if to comfort her.

As if Carol were the one who needed comforting.

CHAPTER
21

The King of Half the Known Universe exhaled his last, rattling breath in the arms of Lieutenant Commander Mor glasch Tev.

The king, whose name was Ag-Liv, had thrown himself on Tev as soon as Tev had opened the door to the throne room. Screaming in pain, Ag-Liv had begged Tev to do something to make it stop, but Tev had not been able to help him.

Jo-Liv, the King of the Other Half of the Known Universe, lay nearby, shrieking and tearing his hair out and rolling around on the floor.

Even the Kings of the Known Universe were helpless in the face of Overlobe Syndrome. True, they were largely figureheads in a constitutional monarchy, their titles symbolic holdovers from the days before contact with other species, when the Miradorn had fancied themselves the center of the universe. Still, it said a lot about the state of affairs on New Mirada that two of the most powerful, well-protected men on the planet were as defenseless against Overlobe Syndrome as the lowliest Miradorn living in a gutter.

"Here, boss," said Makk Vinx, the Iotian security guard who had beamed to the royal palace with Tev and Bartholomew Faulwell. Vinx reached out and took the weight of King Ag-Liv from Tev. "Lemme get this for you."

As Vinx carried the king across the room and lowered him onto a throne, Tev snorted, trying to clear the scent of death from his sensitive Tellarite nostrils. Between the mayhem in the streets and the overabundance of dead in the halls of the palace itself, Tev had inhaled far too much of that terrible scent for one day.

Scanning the room with his tricorder, he found the changeling signal that he had been following. From orbit, Ensign Haznedl at ops had located three possible sources of the signal. After beaming to the other two sites, Tev had finally found the location of the Dominion transmitter on New Mirada, the ironic "twin" of the device on the moon of Zasharu.

Now that he had found it, Tev thought that he should have guessed the correct site in the first place. As on Zasharu, the transmitter had been hidden under a long-standing locus of power—political this time instead of spiritual. As the shrine and the royal palace were not likely to be disturbed by demolition or new construction, both sites were quite safe for secret underground installations. Tev really should have known.

Not that he would ever admit that to anyone for as long as he lived.

"The Dominion transmitter is directly beneath this room," said Tev, continuing to watch the readouts on his tricorder. "I am literally standing on top of it."

"'Scuse me," said Vinx. "This other bigwig over here's about to kick the bucket."

"The only way we can help him is by rendering the transmitter inoperative," said Tev. "Assuming we can get to it, of course."

"There's a problem?" said Bart Faulwell, who was examining an intricate, sculpted emblem like a coat of arms on the wall behind the thrones.

"As on Zasharu, the underground transmitter chamber is heavily shielded," said Tev. "It is also protected by a plethora of Jem'Hadar booby traps."

"And here we are without a changeling multitool or an expert on Dominion technology," said Faulwell. "And more Miradorn are dying every minute."

Tev paced the floor of the throne room and thought for a moment. One solution came to mind, but it relied on the use of experimental technology. Given more time, he would prefer a traditional approach to the situation, one involving tested and more predictable techniques, but time was in short supply. The Miradorn crisis was quickly becoming an extinction-level event.

Tev needed to do what was necessary to end this disaster as fast as possible. He needed to take a chance on his unproven creation and hope for the best.

He touched his combadge. "Tev to *da Vinci*," he said. "There's an equipment case labeled UNCERTAINTY on a rack in my quarters. Please retrieve that case and beam it down to me immediately."

CHAPTER

22

"So what Em-Lin's saying is," said Fabian, "we don't stand a ghost of a chance of stopping the changeling transmitter without her dead sister's help."

Vance winced at the pun. "Not in so many words, but yeah." He looked around at his teammates, who had gathered to discuss the offer of help that Em-Lin—and Or-Lin—had made to him.

"The question is, can she deliver the goods?" said Fabian.

"The part about her sister," said Gomez, looking directly at Lense. "Could there be any truth to it?"

Lense glanced over her shoulder to be sure that Em-Lin was still out of earshot, resting against a wall on the far side of the chamber. "It's possible," she said when she turned back to the group. "Em-Lin herself might possess the full knowledge, and she prolongs the fantasy that

Or-Lin has survived by claiming to channel the knowledge from her."

Vance shook his head. "I've spent time with Em-Lin,"
he said. "If the dead sister is nothing but a fantasy, she
must be one *hell* of a fantasy."

"I tend to agree," said Lense. "There might be something at work here that isn't under Em-Lin's control."

"Then whose control is it under?" said Fabian.

"Its own, maybe," said Lense. "Instead of a vivid fantasy or memory construct, it could be similar to the Vulcan *katra* passed on before death—a copy of a person's
consciousness imprinted on a host's brain. Em-Lin might
be dealing with a lingering remnant of Or-Lin's mind,
one with access to all of Or-Lin's specialized knowledge
and skills."

"In which case, Em-Lin's making her offer in good
faith," said Gomez. "The dead sister's consciousness
really would be helping her work on the transmitter."

"How wonderful," said Soloman. "To have a departed
companion continue to guide you after death."

Although Vance knew that Soloman would have loved to
still hear the thoughts of his deceased bondmate 111—he
had gone to extreme lengths just to talk to an alternate-
universe version of her not too long ago—he knew there
was no joy in this. "I bet Em-Lin wouldn't agree, and that
worries me. As badly shaken up as Em-Lin has been, I don't
think Or-Lin's been treating her very well lately."

"That suggests another possibility to explain Or-Lin's
influence," said Lense. "What if Or-Lin is a *katra* or a
fantasy or some other kind of echo of consciousness, and
she's been twisted by the effects of the Dominion transmitter? Who knows what her real intentions might be?"

"Sounds like just the kind of ghost we don't want any-where *near* that transmitter," said Fabian.

"Or-Lin's presence has definitely gotten stronger since we came down here." Vance looked up at the huge yellow-tinted tank as it continued to turn, the protoplasmic clumps melding and dividing and spinning in the fluid inside it. "Em-Lin went from zoning out periodically to zoning out all the time. After a while, I had a hell of a time just getting through to her. Even then, I had to talk to Or-Lin first."

"She didn't answer you, did she?" said Fabian.

"Not directly," said Vance.

"That you know of," said Soloman. "What if Or-Lin has taken over?"

Vance looked across the chamber at Em-Lin, and he felt uneasy. "I hadn't thought of that."

"All right," said Gomez, raising her voice just enough to command her teammates' full attention. "We could speculate all day about this, but people are dying every minute we stand here and talk. The bottom line is, do we need Em-Lin's help?"

"As I said earlier, this system is far more robust than the Dominion systems we encountered in the shrine." A flicker of annoyance crossed Soloman's features. "I have attempted to apply a variation of the morphic virus that I used on the booby traps, but without success."

"This is some kind of hyper-changeling tech down here," said Fabian. "It's so good at staying a step ahead of us, I've been wondering if it can see the future."

"I'll take that as a 'yes,'" said Gomez. "We need her. Let's take her up on her offer."

"And hope the dead sister isn't thinking some dead

Starfleeters might be fun to hang around with," said Fabian.

"We'll watch her carefully," said Gomez.

"I do not know if we could tell if she does anything wrong," said Soloman.

"My invisible friend isn't sure he can keep the invisible ghost in line, either," said Fabian.

"We'll just have to do our best," said Gomez. "Vance, please tell Em-Lin that we accept her and her sister's offer. We'd like them to start working on the transmitter immediately."

Vance turned in Em-Lin's direction. "Yes, sir," he said, feeling sorry for Em-Lin and at the same time worried that she might destroy him and his shipmates when she got her hands on the Dominion device.

And at the same time as all of that, he felt something that he had never expected to feel for a Miradorn after that terrible day on Jomej VII.

The concern of one friend for another.

CHAPTER

23

"Just keep that thing away from me," said Bart, taking a step back from the polished, milky-white sphere in Tev's hands. "I can't *believe* you built something based on a device that actually *killed* me once!"

Tev scrolled a fingertip over the surface of the bowling-ball-sized sphere, adjusting the fluidic controls sandwiched between the layers of the device's smooth skin. "You have nothing to worry about, Bartholomew," he said, though he wasn't entirely sure that was true. "The Luck Pulse generates a limited and precisely calibrated probability effect."

"Which has never been tested in the field," said Bart.

Tev shrugged. "A technicality."

"And it's never been tested in the lab, either," said Bart.

"But the holosimulations have had impressive results,"

said Tev. That much, at least, was true, though holosimulations were of course a completely different animal
from real-world builds.

"So *help* me, Tev," said Bart, pacing nervously back
and forth. "If that thing kills me like the other one did, I
will haunt you for all eternity."

Tev nodded and continued adjusting the sphere's controls. He understood Bart's reaction, given the source of
the tech that had gone into the new device.

Tev had based the Luck Pulse on elements of the Uncertainty Drive, a probability-warping propulsion system found onboard an ancient derelict starship called
the *Minstrel's Whisper*. The malfunctioning Uncertainty
Drive had deluged the crew of the *da Vinci* with distorted
luck, one aspect of which was the death of Bart Faulwell.
Bart had been returned to life after Soloman convinced
the drive to deactivate, but it was natural that he would
be apprehensive about a device with similar properties.

"Seriously, Tev," said Bart. "Remember how unpredict-
able the Uncertainty Drive was."

"Because its systems had degraded over millions of
years," said Tev. "And keep in mind, the drive was a lot
more complicated than the Luck Pulse. The simpler the
system, the less prone it is to breakdown."

"Yeah, but remember the part about how it *killed* me?"
Bart shook his head. "I mean, the drive did. The drive
killed me."

Tev got along well with Bartholomew and took no
pleasure in making him uncomfortable, but it was time
to take action. "If this works, we could knock out the
booby traps all at once." Tev made a final adjustment to
the sphere's fluidic controls and cradled it in his hands.

"Frankly, if I did not think it would work, I would not waste my valuable time trying it. Similarly, if I thought it was likely to do you harm, I would not have this device anywhere near you."

Bart did not seem to be convinced of the Luck Pulse's harmlessness. Halfheartedly, he smiled and raised a shaky thumbs-up gesture. "All right then," he said, backing away from Tev and the device. "Good luck with that."

Tev pressed the red activation whorl on the skin of the sphere. In ten seconds, the device was set to emit a pulse lasting thirty seconds, after which it would automatically deactivate.

If, of course, the device's probability-altering field did not create a malfunction in its own timing mechanism. That was one of the factors that Tev still wasn't a hundred percent sure about yet.

He drew the sphere back and up with one hand. Then he took three steps, swinging the sphere forward, and released it to roll across the floor of the palace throne room.

Tev hurried out of the huge chamber, from which everyone else had already been evacuated. Just as he turned to watch from the other side of the doorway, the Luck Pulse sphere flared with blinding white light.

Within seconds, deadly-looking Jem'Hadar booby traps began falling from hiding places in the walls and ceiling, clattering to the floor without firing a single projectile or energy beam or explosive. The thrones themselves fell to pieces, both at the same time, revealing hidden gun emplacements that sparked and smoked and burst apart with loud pops.

Tev felt a surge of satisfaction as he looked back and

forth between the readouts on his tricorder and the visible effects in the throne room. "It's working," he said. "The booby traps are spontaneously self-destructing."

"Now that's the way to do a job," said Vinx. "You never gotta get your hands dirty."

Just then, with ten seconds remaining on the duration of the Luck Pulse, an unexpected movement in the throne room caught Tev's eye. Peering into the dim far corners of the room, he glimpsed a dark figure ducking behind a fat pillar. He continued to watch closely.

The next thing he knew, he was stumbling backward, heart racing, as a fierce-looking creature leaped out from behind the pillar. Tev saw black fur, a long snout, and a foaming muzzle packed with jagged, gleaming fangs.

The creature was bipedal and stood at least twice as tall as Tev. As it scanned the chamber with bulging, bloodshot eyes, Tev recognized its similarity to certain canine species native to Earth. Its features were exaggerated and unnatural, but it resembled a Terran animal that Tev had seen images of in the past.

Specifically, it looked like a wolf.

When the creature caught sight of Tev, it charged straight for him. Terrified, Tev tripped over his own feet as he tried to run and fell to the floor. The creature continued to charge.

That was when the entire royal palace collapsed. As debris blasted down from above, crushing the creature in mid-lunge, the Luck Pulse sphere stopped glowing, its thirty seconds of operation finally expiring.

CHAPTER
24

"*I'm pleased to report that thanks to my admittedly unorthodox solution, all booby traps installed in the royal palace have been eliminated,*" Tev said over Gomez's combadge. "*Also, a hole has spontaneously opened into the underground transmitter chamber, so we do not have to cut through the shielding.*"

Gomez frowned. Since contacting Tev a moment ago for a status report, she had been getting a suspicious vibe. Though his report was glowing, she wondered about the actual state of affairs on his end of the call. "What's that I hear in the background? Some kind of crumbling sound?"

"*It's just dust settling,*" said Tev. "*Some . . . shifting . . . occurred during the deactivation process.*"

"Shifting." Gomez no longer had any doubt that Tev was glossing over the truth. She did not, however, have

528   Robert T. Jeschonek

time to explore the subject further. "I'm glad your 'unorthodox solution,' whatever it was, proved to be so effective."

"*Thank you,*" said Tev. "*However, I cannot, at this time, recommend using the Luck Pulse on the changeling transmitter.*"

"The *what* pulse?" said Gomez. Conveniently, Tev had left out the minor detail that he had used something called a Luck Pulse to deactivate the booby traps.

"*The unpredictability factor associated with the Pulse's effects is much higher than I had originally anticipated,*" said Tev. "*There is simply too much uncertainty involved.*"

The mention of the word "uncertainty" got Gomez's attention, reminding her of another device that dispensed its own brand of luck, but she received another call over her combadge and could not pursue the questioning further.

"I'll get back to you," she told Tev, and then she touched the combadge to switch to the second call. "Go ahead."

"*Whatever you're planning to do, Gomez, do it now,*" said Captain David Gold over the combadge link. "*The situation is deteriorating fast.*"

"How could it get any worse?" said Fabian, listening in as he and Vance led Em-Lin to the transmitter's control console.

"*The progress of the syndrome has accelerated,*" said Gold, "*both on New Mirada and Zasharu. The death rate is skyrocketing.*"

"How long do we have?" said Gomez.

"*If the death toll continues to climb at its current rate,*" said Gold, "*the Miradorn species will be nearly extinct within two hours.*"

Gomez watched Em-Lin settle into a chair at the console. Em-Lin's lips were moving, but she clearly wasn't speaking to Vance or Fabian. Her eyes were fixed on the empty space to her right.

Gomez was not exactly overflowing with confidence that the fate of an entire species rested in the hands of a woman who did most of her talking to someone who existed only in her head.

"We're taking steps, sir," said Gomez. "Our Miradorn guide claims to have specific and detailed knowledge of this particular device."

"Then I won't keep you any longer," said Gold. His voice was tight. *"Good luck, Gomez."*

"Thank you, sir. Gomez out." As the connection severed, Gomez closed her eyes for a moment and cradled her face in her hands.

A sentient species was on the verge of depopulation so sweeping that it might as well be called extinction. The Miradorn who were left when it was all over, a relative handful of nontwins who did not contract Overlobe Syndrome, would be so few that the task of repopulating their species would take ages.

And everything was riding on one woman with an attitude problem and her personal ghost.

At the touch of a hand on her shoulder, Gomez looked up and to the left. Lense looked back at her, a grim expression etched onto her features.

More bad news, thought Gomez, and she was right . . . not that it was much of a deductive leap given the way things were going.

"Boz-Nu just died," said Lense.

Gomez sighed. "They're going fast," she said. "Pretty harsh treatment if you ask me, especially since the Miradorn never crossed the Dominion."

"Scorched earth, maybe?" said Lense. "Leave nothing and no one that could benefit your enemies?"

Gomez shrugged. "Maybe it's just another case of revenge against the Solids."

"Complete with poetic justice," said Lense. "Twin devices use the Miradorn twins' own linking abilities against them."

"To kill them," said Gomez.

"No." Em-Lin spoke up suddenly from her seat at the control panel several meters away. Gomez and Lense both looked in her direction. "That's not what this device was meant to do."

Neither Gomez nor Lense had been speaking loudly. Gomez was surprised that Em-Lin had overheard any of their conversation from so far away. *Maybe the ghost was closer to us than Em-Lin*, she thought.

"How do you know?" said Gomez.

Em-Lin ran her fingers lovingly over the rows of glowing, multicolored controls. With practiced precision, she pressed a sequence of buttons in rapid succession.

When she finished, the giant tank changed instantly from a reddish glow to a bright blue one. The tank's rotation slowed, and the clumps suspended inside it reversed the direction of their spin.

"I know," said Em-Lin, "because my sister and I helped build it."

CHAPTER
25

Em-Lin had a very special medal. It was permanently attached to her body, on a spot just below her left clavicle. It shifted shapes, camouflaging itself against her skin when anyone but Em-Lin set eyes on it.

It was a changeling medal, affixed to her chest by one of the Vorta. Or-Lin had received one, too.

Em-Lin remembered the ceremony well. It had been the proudest day of her life.

"Em-Lin," the Vorta had said solemnly, holding out the crystalline medal before him. "In recognition of your extraordinary service to the Dominion, I bestow upon you the Order of the Gods."

Em-Lin's heart had pounded like a giant drum. A tear had descended her face as the Vorta tugged her top down just enough to expose the skin below her clavicle.

"Your efforts and those of your sister have helped to ensure the future glory of the Miradorn people." Slowly, the Vorta had pressed the medal against Em-Lin's bare skin. "The Fuser that the two of you have built will bless your people with a unity and divine fulfillment that few species have ever experienced."

As the medal melted into her flesh, Em-Lin had felt a sharp, burning pain. She had clenched her teeth to keep from crying out.

She felt a similar pain today as she pushed her hands through the smooth, shape-shifting casing of the huge tank, immersing them in the hot, thick liquid inside.

"You helped *build* this thing?" said Gomez.

Shut up, lady! said Or-Lin, who was standing close to Em-Lin at the base of the tank. *Can't you see she's trying to* concentrate?

Em-Lin caught one of the floating clumps inside the tank. She kneaded the clump with her bare hands, feeling the fizzing of a static electric charge in the gritty, claylike mass.

"My sister and I were psycho-engineers," said Em-Lin. "The Dominion put us to work in a weapons lab at Rasha Nom."

"Starfleet knocked out Rasha Nom early in the war," said Stevens. Like Gomez, he stood nearby and watched Em-Lin's every move as she worked on the Fuser.

Em-Lin nodded. "Twenty-three Miradorn died in that attack," she said. "All of them noncombatants."

"Noncombatants building a cannon that fired killer nightmares," said Stevens.

Em-Lin ignored his remark. "After the attack on Rasha Nom, my sister and I were glad to be transferred home to Mirada to work on the Fuser."

"Is that what this is?" said Gomez. "A 'fuser'?"

Or-Lin slammed her hand down on the control panel. As always, Em-Lin was the only one who heard her do it. *Tell these people to* shut up! *Tell them to leave us alone if they want us to fix this thing!*

"It's a gift from the Vorta to the Miradorn," said Em-Lin, "and yes, it's called a Fuser."

"Some gift," said Stevens. "It's wiping out your entire species."

"Shut up," said Em-Lin. "Just shut up."

Sometimes, Em-Lin still thought about the day when they had added the final ingredient to the Fuser.

It had happened on the last day of the war. According to the Jem'Hadar, a Starfleet strike force was on its way to liberate Mirada. Never mind that the Miradorn hadn't *wanted* to be liberated.

The Vorta who had supervised the construction of the Fuser had stared up at the device alongside Em-Lin and Or-Lin. All that was left to do was to add the morphic plasma in which the processor meat would be suspended.

"Time to make history," the Vorta had said. "We have to switch it on and seal it in before Starfleet gets here."

"The Fuser on Mirada has already been activated and sealed off," Or-Lin had said. "The process has begun."

The Vorta had nodded. "Low power transmissions will lay the groundwork. Then, the system will gradually boost its output. The self-determining AI will monitor conditions and take appropriate action. Someday, when the AI decides that the time is right, the system will connect every Miradorn mind in a new Great Link."

"I only wish that we could live to see it," Em-Lin had said.

"We will see to it that you are remembered for your role in this great leap forward," the Vorta had said. "When the day of final joining arrives, your story will be fed to all minds in the Miradorn Great Link. All will know that you built this device and that you watched over it by tending the shrine above after the Dominion's departure."

"I still wish that we could see it," said Em-Lin, "but I guess it's enough to know that we're helping to make our world a better place."

"As their reward for loyalty to the Dominion," the Vorta had said, "your people will know the ecstatic, never-ending joy of complete unity."

"What a time that will be," Em-Lin had said, "and the Miradorn will have you to thank for it."

"Your people always had it within them," the Vorta had said. "The telepathic links between Miradorn twins would have eventually evolved into a species-wide network without our help. We're just accelerating the process."

Or-Lin had sighed. "I guess we'd better add the morphic plasma and get the Fuser online."

"No," the Vorta said. "No plasma."

"I don't understand," Em-Lin had said. "The Fuser won't work without the plasma."

"I have a substitute," the Vorta had said. "Something even better."

"This is the first you've mentioned it," Or-Lin had said. "What is this substitute exactly?"

With that, the Vorta had simply smiled.

I miss him, too, said Or-Lin, resting a hand on Em-Lin's shoulder. *These Starfleeties will never understand.*

Em-Lin nodded and kept working.

But still . . .

Or-Lin cleared her throat. *You missed a node*, she said. *X-7 on the dark side.*

Em-Lin realized that her sister was right. "Thanks," she said, mashing a nub on the bottom of the clump that she was handling, then pressing it through to the top and folding the clump around it. "I got it."

Just then, after several moments of silence, Gomez spoke up. "Any idea how much longer you'll be? We still have to deal with the device on New Mirada."

Em-Lin did not answer her. She was not feeling particularly charitable toward Starfleet personnel at that moment.

Do you wonder if the Vorta can still feel us? said Or-Lin, resting a hand against the tank. *Do you wonder if he knows we're working with the enemy?*

"I hope not," said Em-Lin, releasing one claylike clump inside the tank and grabbing another. "He was like a father to us."

"Father to who?" said Gomez. "All I asked was how much longer you'll be."

Or-Lin went on talking as if she couldn't hear Gomez, as if Gomez were the silent and unseen *dugo tenya*. *I know what the Vorta would want us to do here*, she said.

"No you don't," said Em-Lin. "Times have changed."

Yes, I do, said Or-Lin. *One of the advantages of being dead is that I get to talk to other dead people.*

Em-Lin turned, but the only dead person she saw was Or-Lin. "He's here?" she said.

"Who's here?" said Gomez.

You can't see him, but yes, said Or-Lin. *He's here. He wants you to save our people . . . and turn the Starfleeties into carriers.*

"Carriers of what?" said Em-Lin.

Or-Lin crouched alongside her and tugged her hands free of the tank. *A killer psycho-virus*, said Or-Lin, beaming with beatific delight and wrapping Em-Lin's hands in her own. *A virus that will obliterate every sentient mind in the Federation of Planets.*

CHAPTER
26

Em-Lin stared silently at her sister for a long moment. "The Fuser can do that?" she said.

Or-Lin nodded. *It's one of the functions I worked on. One last booby trap for an occasion like this.*

Em-Lin frowned. Apparently, Or-Lin had been even better at hiding things from the link between them than Em-Lin had known.

And the Vorta, their beloved Vorta, had not been solely motivated by altruistic impulses. Even if his *dugo tenya* were not speaking through Or-Lin right now—and Em-Lin tended to think that it was not—he must have approved the addition of the viral option to the Fuser's systems.

Either that, or Or-Lin had devised the viral option herself—but Em-Lin had a hard time believing that Or-Lin, alive or dead, would want anything to do with massacring the Federation. Or-Lin had been difficult from time to time, and at the end of her life, she had threatened to seek Division from her sister, but Em-Lin could not believe that she was a mass murderer.

Suddenly, another possibility occurred to Em-Lin. She realized that she should have thought of it before, but she had been so traumatized by recent events that she had readily accepted certain things at face value.

Things like the *dugo tenya*.

Well? said Or-Lin, still beaming and clasping her twin's hands. *Shall we follow the Vorta once more, my beloved sister?*

It could not have been more obvious, now that Em-Lin had finally managed to see through her own veil of shock. Why had Or-Lin gone from, *I think I want Division whether you want to go with me or not* to calling Em-Lin her *beloved sister?*

"Let's do it," said Em-Lin. It would be better to play along until the time was right. For now, it was enough that Em-Lin had regained a measure of awareness and self-control.

Or-Lin released Em-Lin's hands and leaped up to give her a quick hug. *Oh, sister, I just knew you'd do the right thing!*

Em-Lin nodded. In the distance, she heard Gomez's voice calling to her, and she tuned it out. The only voice that mattered now was Or-Lin's—but not because Or-Lin was a *dugo tenya*.

It was because she was something else altogether—yet another application of changeling technology.

All right then, said Or-Lin, swiping a tear from her eye. *You need to reconnect with the plasma matrix.*

Em-Lin pushed her hands through the morphic skin of the tank and back into the hot, fizzing plasma.

Let's reconfigure the Fuser to reduce the transmission levels, said Or-Lin. *Go to Polyp L3.*

"Wait," said Em-Lin. "First, tell me which polyp controls the viral option. I don't want to risk activating it by accident."

Or-Lin leaned close and pointed a finger at a crescent-shaped clump floating upward in the convex tank. *"Right there. Polyp Q90. We'll engage it when we've finished resetting the transmitter and eliminated the threat to our people."*

"Thanks," said Em-Lin, and then she grabbed hold of the Q90 polyp with both hands.

Em-Lin, let go of that for now. I just told you, it controls the viral option.

"I know what you told me," said Em-Lin. She plunged her thumbs into the claylike meat of the polyp. Immediately, its resident intelligence pinged her mind with fuzzy-feeling thoughts like those of the changeling multi-tool that she had used to deactivate the quantum bomb.

What do you want me to do? said the polyp.

Em-Lin! Or-Lin's voice became loud and angry. *I said leave that alone and reset the transmitter!*

Hello, Em-Lin said to the polyp, remembering her father's advice.

What do you want me to do? said the polyp.

Stop it, Em-Lin! shouted Or-Lin, her voice boiling with rage. *Do what I tell you!*

The louder her sister got, the more Em-Lin knew that her theory was right—and the more she knew exactly what she wanted the polyp to do.

Please deactivate the Fuser, she thought.

The Fuser on Zasharu or the Fuser on Mirada? thought Polyp Q90.

Em-Lin had not expected to be given a choice, but she was grateful for it. The sooner the two devices went offline, the greater the number of Miradorn lives she would save.

Both, thought Em-Lin.

No! said Or-Lin, shaking Em-Lin by the shoulders. *Stop it or I'll kill you!*

"Shut up," said Em-Lin. "Just shut up."

She smiled to herself as she felt Polyp Q90 shut down the system. She had been right about Or-Lin.

Or-Lin was not a true *dugo tenya*. She was not a remnant of Em-Lin's dead twin, and she was not a trauma-induced hallucination or dream.

She was the Fuser's last defense. She was a booby trap.

"The self-determining AI will monitor conditions and take appropriate action." That was what the Vorta had said.

Em-Lin now knew that that was exactly what the Fuser's AI had done. Created with adaptive changeling technology, sophisticated enough to manage an accelerated planetary psychic evolutionary process, the Fuser's AI had been equipped to defend itself against any threat.

Even the threat of Em-Lin herself.

It had conjured the image of her dead sister to distract, confuse, and mislead her. How else to stop someone who had helped build the device from shutting it down? Em-Lin's guilt at not soon enough recognizing the trap that had killed her sister had given the image more than enough power to twist her.

And in the end, to prevent her from finding the "off" switch, the AI had lied to her, telling her that it was the one thing that it thought she would never touch: the controls of a psychic virus that would murder trillions.

But Em-Lin had seen through the deception.

The Fuser on Zasharu and the Fuser on Mirada have been deactivated, said Polyp Q90.

Thank you, Em-Lin said with her mind. It wasn't easy to concentrate with Or-Lin shaking her by the shoulders and then beating on her back with her fists, but Em-Lin managed to send another message to the polyp.

Are you capable of permanently deactivating the Or-Lin simulacrum? she said.

Yes, said Polyp Q90.

Stand by, said Em-Lin, and then she yanked her hands out of the plasma matrix. Whirling around, she grabbed Or-Lin's hands, stopping the pounding on her back.

Or-Lin shivered and sobbed in her grip, her face twisted in an expression of mixed fury and agony. She looked like someone who had lost everything, someone who was completely and irreversibly shattered.

Em-Lin knew that she was not her sister, that she was not anyone at all and never had been. But she looked like Or-Lin, and she sounded like Or-Lin, and she felt like Or-Lin. It was enough for now.

Em-Lin released one of Or-Lin's hands and reached up to stroke the side of her face. "I'm sorry that I didn't always do the right thing," she said. "I'm sorry that I didn't notice the trap that killed you sooner."

Or-Lin choked on a sob and shook her head wildly. *Don't do it*, she said. *Don't do it don't do it don't do it.*

"I forgive you for hurting me," said Em-Lin. "I will miss you and love you forever."

No, please, whimpered Or-Lin. *Don't do it.*

Then, though the woman before her was nothing but an illusion, Em-Lin leaned forward and pulled Or-Lin into her arms. As she hugged her, Em-Lin shut her eyes tight and began to cry, too.

"Good-bye, my sister," said Em-Lin.

Then, she cast her thoughts to Polyp Q90: *Please permanently deactivate the Or-Lin simulacrum.*

Done, said Polyp Q90.

"Done," said Em-Lin, opening her eyes to see Gomez and the other Starfleeters staring back at her. "I'm all done."

CHAPTER
27

Tev welcomed ten pilgrims to the shrine of Ho'nig before the first near-fistfight broke out over his bad manners, which was a lot better than Vance had expected. Vance was impressed that the Tellarite had exercised such admirable restraint in honor of the official start of the *Chala Ho'nig* festival.

Nevertheless, Vance tipped off Gomez, and Gomez substituted Lense for Tev. No use starting an interstellar holy war if it could be avoided.

Especially after the ordeal of the last two days. Everyone on the Starfleet team was thoroughly exhausted after dealing with the toys that the Dominion had left behind after the war—and their hands were still so full dealing with the aftermath that Vance thought they would be hard-pressed to handle any more surprises. Indeed, it seemed like that—even though the war had ended over a year ago—that they kept having to clean up after it. Kharzh'ulla, Luaran, Coroticus, Sachem II, and now this . . .

Right now, in fact, even as pilgrims arrived for the *Chala Ho'nig*, S.C.E. teammates and *da Vinci* crew members worked alongside Miradorn volunteers to repair damage to the shrine. Even Captain Gold was among the cleanup crew, sleeves rolled up and sweat beading his forehead as he helped to clear debris from the altar area.

Vance and Lauoc pitched in here and there as they patrolled the crowd, looking for lapses in civility among the diverse and pious pilgrims. So far, as disruptive to prayer and meditation as the cleanup crew must have been, not one pilgrim complained or caused a problem.

Not a single pilgrim failed to pitch in and help, either. Miradorn, Brikar, Damiani, Phylosians, Benzites, Xindi, and members of many other species worked side by side to restore the place they revered to its original state.

And as they worked, the pilgrims sang a beautiful and complex hymn they created on the spot. Vance had never heard anything like it in his life.

He was actually slightly irritated when someone interrupted his enjoyment of the singing by tapping on his shoulder.

"Excuse me." Vance turned to see Pika Ven-Sa looking back at him. The Miradorn priest, once so snarky and vigorous, looked downcast and defeated—with good reason. His twin brother, Chi-Sa, had died during the Overlobe Syndrome outbreak less than a day ago, just minutes before Em-Lin had deactivated the Fusers.

"I'm looking for Commander Gomez," said Ven-Sa. He looked about ten years older than he had a day ago.

Vance nodded. He felt sorry for Ven-Sa. "Right this way, sir," he said, and then he led Ven-Sa across the shrine to Gomez.

Gomez was removing the smudges of smoke damage from a statue at the subatomic level with a quantum distiller. When Vance and Ven-Sa approached, she switched off the pulsing, bright blue beam and raised the yellow-tinted goggles to her forehead.

"Pika Ven-Sa," she said, her voice and expression somber. "I was sorry to hear about your brother."

Ven-Sa sighed and nodded. "This has been a most difficult day," he said.

Gomez put the distiller in a tray on her tool cart. "I was glad we didn't lose you, as well," she said, removing her goggles.

"I cannot say that I feel the same right now," said Ven-Sa. "I am only half here, you see. Half of me—Chi-Sa—is dead."

"It must be terrible," said Gomez.

"I console myself by remembering that the universe often conceives joy from pain," said Ven-Sa. "Chi-Sa is dead, but I believe that the disaster that took his life has begun a change in the attitudes of the Miradorn toward Starfleet and the Federation. Seeing your people struggle to help ours, both here and on New Mirada, seems to have changed some minds."

Gomez nodded. When she glanced at her tool cart, she seemed to get an idea. "Are you in a hurry?" she said to Ven-Sa.

Ven-Sa shrugged. "Why do you ask?"

"I could use a hand here, actually." Gomez picked up the quantum distiller and pointed it at the statue on which she'd been working.

"I'm afraid I don't know much about restoration work," said Ven-Sa.

Gomez grinned. "Well, you will soon," she said. "And maybe we can talk a little about the *Se'rbeg* while we're at it."

Ven-Sa rubbed the back of his neck and looked at the floor . . . then looked up at Gomez and nodded. "All right," he said. "I can spare a few minutes, I suppose."

Gomez flashed Vance a quick wink, and he smiled and turned away. It was then that he noticed that a crowd of pilgrims had gathered at the far side of the shrine.

Immediately, Vance rushed over to find out what had drawn the pilgrims' attention. He pushed his way through to the middle of the crowd, which was where he saw what all the fuss was about.

The center attraction was Em-Lin.

As soon as she saw Vance push through the crowd, her face lit up. "Chief Hawkins! Is it already time for our meeting?"

Vance caught on fast. "You're late, actually. Please come with me."

"Wait a minute," said a towering, snake-headed Selay in yellow pilgrim's robes. "We have a few more questions. We hope to determine if the Savior of the Temple has interacted with Ho'nig while speaking to the dead."

Em-Lin sighed with exasperation. "I already told you. I never spoke to the dead. The ghost of my dead sister was an illusion created by the Fuser's defense systems."

"That's what *you* think," said an orange-furred,

fierce-looking Chalnoth. "Ho'nig's message might be *hidden* in your memories."

"Yes," said a Tamarian, a member of a species that spoke only in cultural metaphors. "Haglis eating an *uvod*! Tyro and Bumpas climbing a *revlok* in the Prelva desert before Creshlippa! Yaffa cheating the Vrellig!"

When the Tamarian had finished, everyone stared at him for a moment. Then, a human asked, "What the hell are you *talking* about?"

"Theon breaking the Numoprax?" said the Tamarian, shrugging apologetically.

"All right, all right," said Vance, taking Em-Lin by the hand. "Excuse us, please. We have an important meeting to attend."

For an instant, the Selay and Chalnoth blocked Vance's path. He met their vaguely hostile gazes with a doubly dark glare of his own, and they stepped aside.

Once clear of the crowd, Vance led Em-Lin to a secluded alcove off the far end of the shrine.

"How are you doing?" said Vance as he let go of her hand.

"Fine," said Em-Lin. Relief was evident in her voice and expression. "I wish they wouldn't be so persistent." She gestured in the direction of the pilgrims. "I mean, I have nothing to offer them."

Vance grinned. "Maybe you should make something up," he said. "Like, 'Ho'nig promises eternal ecstasy in the next life to anyone who provides constant comfort in this life to his servant, Em-Lin.'"

Em-Lin smiled. "Don't tempt me. How about if I point them in your direction and tell them *you're* the chosen one? What would you ask for?"

Vance thought for a moment. "A few days ago, I

would've asked for the addresses of the Miradorn who tortured me during the war. Now, I think I'll settle for the address of the Miradorn who saved my life, in case I'm ever in the neighborhood."

Em-Lin's smile disappeared, and she stared at the floor. "If my sister and I hadn't built the Fuser, your life wouldn't have been at risk to begin with. And three million Miradorn would still be alive."

"If you hadn't built it, the Vorta would have gotten someone else to do the work," said Vance. "And anyway, the Fuser wasn't meant to harm anyone."

"I wonder if the tribunal at my trial will agree with you," said Em-Lin.

"They're going to *try* you?" said Vance.

Em-Lin nodded. "For being an accomplice to mass murder. They'll try the Vorta and my sister in absentia."

Vance was stunned. "But you didn't activate the Fuser," he said. "You *stopped* it. You saved *billions* of lives on Za-sharu and New Mirada. Hell, they're erecting a *statue* in honor of you for saving the shrine of Ho'nig!"

Em-Lin shrugged. "Someone has to take the blame."

"Why aren't you in custody now?" said Vance.

"There's a waiting period before a trial," said Em-Lin. "It's called the *hastanoj*. During the *hastanoj*, enough time is allowed to pass that the facts of a case blur, and public opinion shifts. Also, the defendant has time to exercise other options and . . . *remove* the burden of punishment from the courts. *Hastanoj* literally means 'do it yourself.'"

Vance stared at her, absorbing what she had told him. Not long ago, he would not have worried much about her plight or that of any Miradorn. Even a "Starfleeter" raised to respect and appreciate diversity in all its forms could still sometimes find his heart hardened by bitter experience.

But today was a different story. Memories of the puppet-gun-wielding Miradorn of Jomej VII had been dimmed by memories of a Miradorn woman who had saved the lives of Vance, his teammates, and billions of others.

Reaching out, he folded her hands between his own. Her pearlescent skin shimmered in bright contrast to his rich, dark brown.

"When the *hastanoj* ends, contact me," he said. "I'll testify on your behalf."

Em-Lin blinked, white irises glowing against the space-black sclera of her "star eyes." "You'd do that for me?" she said.

Vance shrugged and grinned. "Sure—if I don't have anything better to do that day, anyway."

A look of intense vulnerability and gratitude flowed onto Em-Lin's face. She blinked quickly, as if tears were on the way, and took a step toward Vance. He thought that she was going to hug him.

Then, she caught herself. She rubbed her eyes hard with the heels of her hands, and the vulnerable look was gone. Em-Lin was back to her normal self (normal when she wasn't seeing ghosts, anyway), complete with sharp edges.

"I guess maybe you Starfleeties aren't all bad after all," she said gruffly.

"Not half as bad as some people say," said Vance.

ABOUT THE AUTHORS

WILLIAM LEISNER is the author of the acclaimed novels *Star Trek: The Next Generation: Losing the Peace* and *A Less Perfect Union* (from the *Myriad Universes* collection *Infinity's Prism*). He is a three-time winner of the late, lamented *Star Trek: Strange New Worlds* competition and has contributed tales to the official celebration of *Star Trek*'s fortieth anniversary in 2006 and *TNG*'s twentieth anniversary in 2007. A native of Rochester, New York, he currently lives in Minneapolis.

KEVIN KILLIANY has been the husband of Valerie for nearly a third of a century and the father of Alethea, Anson, and Daya for various shorter periods of time. In addition to his *Star Trek* fiction (*S.C.E. Orphans* and *Honor* as well as three short stories in *Strange New Worlds*), Kevin has written for *Doctor Who* and several game universes, most notably *BattleTech*, *Shadowrun*, and *Mechwarrior*. His two science fiction novels, *Wolf Hunters* and *To Ride the Chimera*, were published by Roc. When not writing, Kevin has been an exceptional children's teacher, drill rig operator, high-risk intervention counselor, warehouse grunt, ESL teacher, photographer, mental-health case manager, college instructor, and paperboy. Currently Kevin works in family preservation services, is an associate pastor of the Soul Saving Station, and manages to keep writing short stories while working on his first mystery novel. Kevin and Valerie live in Wilmington, North Carolina.

PHAEDRA M. WELDON has loved *Star Trek* since watching *The Original Series* reruns with her dad, and regrets he didn't live long enough to see the new *Star Trek* movie. The thrill of writing in the *Star Trek* universe was a lifelong dream, realized when she met Dean Wesley Smith in 1997 and learned of the *Star Trek: Strange New Worlds* anthology. Since then, she has published two *Starfleet Corps of Engineers* ebooks, as well as *The Oppressor's Wrong*, Book II in *The Next Generation* series *Slings and Arrows*. She has had numerous short stories published with Daw Anthologies, and writes regularly for Catalyst Game Labs in their *BattleTech* and *Shadowrun* universes.

Currently she is writing for Berkley in her urban fantasy original series, *The Zoë Martinique Investigations*. She was recently tapped to write a novel for the show *Eureka!* and is working on several other original projects. Presently she lives in Atlanta, Georgia, but will be moving to Maryland to be with her geneticist husband and precocious daughter. She can be found online most mornings at seven o'clock, writing her daily pages in original work, and at night pounding the keyboards for original universes. If there is one thing she's learned, it's that there are three constants in the universe: Death, Taxes, and *Star Trek*.

ROBERT T. JESCHONEK is an award-winning science fiction and fantasy writer whose fiction, essays, articles, comics, and podcasts have been published around the world. His stories appeared in three volumes of *Star Trek: Strange New Worlds*, winning the Grand Prize in Volume VI. He is one of a select few writers invited to write stories in Peter David's *New Frontier* universe—"Oil and Water," starring Burgoyne, in *Star Trek: New Frontier—No Limits*. Robert's young adult urban fantasy novel, *My Favorite Band Does Not Exist*, is coming soon from Clarion Books/ Houghton Mifflin Harcourt. He wrote a collection of science fiction and fantasy stories, *Mad Scientist Meets Cannibal*, for PS Publishing in England. His work has also been featured in *Space and Time, Postcripts, Abyss & Apex*, several DAW anthologies, and numerous other publications. His wife, Wendy, helps make his writing possible by supplying inspiration, encouragement, and editing support. Visit his website at www.thefictioneer .com and follow him on Twitter at @TheFictioneer.